Winning It All

Winning It All

VICTORIA DENAULT

FOREVER
YOURS

New York Boston

Cover photography by George Kerrigan. Cover design by Elizabeth Turner. Cover copyright © 2016 by Hachette Book Group, Inc.

Forever Yours
Hachette Book Group
1290 Avenue of the Americas, New York, NY 10104
forever-romance.com
twitter.com/foreverromance

First published as an ebook and as a print on demand: September 2016

Forever Yours is an imprint of Grand Central Publishing. The Forever Yours name and logo are trademarks of Hachette Book Group, Inc.

The publisher is not responsible for websites (or their content) that are not owned by the publisher.

The Hachette Speakers Bureau provides a wide range of authors for speaking events. To find out more, go to www.hachettespeakersbureau.com or call (866) 376-6591.

ISBNs: 978-1-4555-4125-6 (print on demand edition), 978-1-4555-4124-9 (ebook)

For my brother Ken. I admire you more than you know.

Acknowledgments

I couldn't have begun to write this book without the incredible support of my husband, Jack. Thank you for believing in me and pushing me to believe in myself. You have a unique way of making me believe the impossible is possible and I love you more than words can say.

To my amazing agent, Kimberly Brower—I can't tell you how much I appreciate your career guidance, sage editing advice, and incredible enthusiasm for not just my work but for the literary world in general. You are the best agent ever!

Thank you to my editor, Leah Hultenschmidt, for your amazing insights and suggestions. Sebastian and Shayne are snarkier and sexier because of you. To everyone at Forever Yours that touched this book, be it through PR, cover design, copyedits, or any other way, thank you so much. Knowing I have such an amazing, talented team working with me helps me sleep at night and keeps me sane (well, saner than I would be without you. LOL).

To the friends who take it upon themselves to be my unpaid PR team and personal cheerleaders—Sarah Jillain, Crystal Richard, Shelda Kirkland (lil' B), Crystal Shepeard, Sandra C, Mike Hiron, Bev Tyler, Peter Milligan, DeAnna Zankich, my family, and so many more—I adored you all before I started this journey (yes, even you, Peter) and I'm so blown away by your enthusiastic support.

Thanks to UCLA Extension, particularly the Writers' Program—Linda, Carla, Cindy, Katy, Jeff, Sarah, Phoebe, Chae, Nutschell, and Amanda. You all work/worked tirelessly to create and run a program that helps make dreams come true. Also, as a former employee I have to say, you all made work feel like play and coworkers feel like family, so thank you.

Despite having a background in marketing, I am not at all skilled at marketing myself. Because of that I am so incredibly thankful for all the bloggers and fellow authors who take the time to promote, review, and recommend my books. I don't know what I would do without you all. The romance community is an amazing place to work thanks to all of you.

Last but never least, thank you to all the readers who have given the Hometown Players a chance. As Sebastian would say, *Je t'aime.*

Prologue

Sebastian

There's no way we can lose now. With only sixty seconds left in the game, the San Diego Saints need three goals just to tie it. Not going to happen. Their captain, Beau Echolls, gives me a hard shove when no one is looking.

"Stop touching me. No matter how hard you try, my greatness won't rub off on you," I taunt and give him my most annoying, cocky grin.

He scowls at me. His eyes narrow and his lip snarls. "Fuck off, Deveau. You fucking suck."

"More goals than any other defenseman in the league this year," I brag, leaning forward and tightening my grip on my stick as the ref holds the puck over the face-off circle. "You've scored how many goals this year? I've lost count. Is it one or two?"

The ref drops the puck, but I don't have a chance to get into the play before Echolls cross-checks me, hard. Beau is a big boy—six foot four and probably over two hundred pounds. The slam of his stick across my back sends me face-first into the ice.

The pain through my shoulders is blinding for a second, but rage soon takes over, and it's all I see as I jump up. My gloves are off before I'm fully upright, and as I skate toward him he's flinging his own gloves across the ice. I'm expecting the linesmen and the ref to grab both of us, but the game has been getting more and more aggressive with every period, and they're done putting out fires. I hear the ref call out, "Let 'em go!" and it's on.

The fight is brief. We're yanking on each other's jerseys and spinning around, and then Echolls swings twice and misses both times. I swing three times and land two—an uppercut and a haymaker that knocks the asshat flat on his back. The crowd, because we're in San Diego, is mostly booing the crap out of me, and I could not care less.

As the ref peels me off Echolls and skates me toward the penalty box, I lift my arms and grin at the crowd. I fucking love that. It's why I chose to play defense and why I also choose to be an enforcer on the ice. I live to get under the skin of the other team and their fans. It's a rush like nothing else.

We pass Jordan, who's laughing in delight at me. "Gordie Howe hat trick. Nice job, Deveau."

I grin as I realize he's right. Tonight I scored a goal, got an assist, and now a fight, all in one game. The ref gives me a little shove toward the tunnel. "Only ten seconds left, just go to the room."

"Yes, sir." I grin, and he shakes his head and skates away.

I get a few pats on the back from my teammates as I pass the bench, exit the ice and head to the locker room. Feeling much better now. That fight drained the frustration I was feeling over the uncomfortable conversation I'd had with my ex-girlfriend earlier today. We'd broken up the day before I left on this road trip after dating for about two months.

In the last couple of weeks things had changed with us. Andie started getting too possessive. She wanted to hang out every single free minute I had and would get angry when I wanted to stay home alone or go out with just the guys. She insisted I call her three times a day from road trips. Three times. When we were in Montreal and Toronto last week I called her only once one day, and she woke me up at four in the freaking morning and started ranting at me, telling me I was selfish and that if we were going to be serious about this relationship I needed to respect her needs. As soon as I got home I explained to her that my needs weren't the same as hers and that we'd be better off going our separate ways.

Another one bites the dust.

I walk into the empty locker room and start to peel out of my equipment. My left wrist is throbbing a little bit from the punches I landed, but I try to ignore it and bend to untie my skates. As I tie a towel around my waist the rest of the team filters in.

Alex Larue tosses a glove at me. "Wanna grab a celebratory drink?"

"Pas ce soir." I shake my head and tell him no in French before explaining in English. "It's been a long week, and we have an early flight tomorrow."

Alex looks around the locker room. "Jordy? Chooch? Avery?"

They all shake their heads no. Alex looks like we just ran over his cat. "You guys and your monogamy are killing me!"

"Actually," I say and adjust my towel, "Andie and I broke up."

That gets everyone's attention. They all turn to me with varying looks of sympathy.

"Sorry, buddy," Jordan tells me quietly. He *should* feel sorry for me; he's the reason I started looking for something serious. Last year Jordan got back together with his high school love, Jessie. They have this crazy kind of attraction and admiration for each other that made me start wanting more than my usual fun but superficial one-night stands.

"You wanna go out after a home game, I'm there," I tell Alex. "But there's no point to hookups after away games. It won't lead to anything."

"Come on," Alex moans as we walk to the showers. "You have to admit the free and easy hookups are fun. And *easy*."

I hang my towel on a hook and turn on the water. "There is more to life than easy pussy, Alex."

"You know that's your problem, right?" Avery interrupts, his eyes are serious. "You want a serious relationship with someone you meet in a meaningless hookup."

"What are you talking about?"

"How did you meet Andie again?" Avery asks.

"She found him on the dance floor at a bar after a game and dry-humped him until he took her home," Alex explains for me, because he was right next to me when it happened.

"Exactly." Avery nods like he's just enlightened me, but he hasn't. So then he sighs and adds, "When was the last time you heard of an epic romance starting with dry-humping and nudity before phone numbers are exchanged?"

I think about that. Jessie and Jordan, the couple who put this whole committed, meaningful relationship notion in my head, definitely didn't meet like that. They'd been high school best friends.

"Doesn't mean it can't happen," I argue, because it's the truth.

Avery chuckles as he turns off his shower and reaches for his towel. "Leave it to your abstinent French ass to do things the hard way."

"At least I'm doing it at all," I counter back. The guy hasn't had a girlfriend in all the years I've known him. He's never taken a girl home that I've ever seen, or even kissed one. There are rumors it's happened once or twice but Westwood's sex life is like Sasquatch. No one knows for sure if it's real.

I'm still thinking about Avery's words when I crawl under the sheets of my hotel bed an hour later. He's not wrong. The simple, standard way of finding a girlfriend would be to ask friends to set me up or go on dating sites and find people who have been prematched to my wants and needs. But the fact is, with my job, I don't feel comfortable going on a dating site. I make millions a year and have a face that is fairly recognizable. It isn't an option. And as for asking friends…well, that just seems so…forced.

I've always been a believer in fate. I want the right person to wander into my life organically and unexpectedly. Avery is right. I am looking for that sexy, spontaneous encounter—the kind the best one-night stands are made of—and then I want it to be more. That's who I am and who I will always be. Someone who likes a challenge, who never takes the easy route and will take passionate and wild over comfortable and calm any day. If that means I crash and burn—a lot—so be it.

Chapter 1

Sebastian

W ho is *that*?"

When Avery asked me and a couple of other Winterhawks to attend the grand opening of Elevate Fitness, a gym one of his college buddies owns, I wasn't super thrilled with the idea. Now as I stare across the crowded, two-story foyer, I'm happy I agreed to come.

Avery shrugs. "No idea. Judging by the fact she's holding a wine bottle, I'd say either part of the catering team or works here at the gym."

"Or she's a hardcore alcoholic who is owning it," Jordan Garrison adds. I laugh. Avery chuckles. His fiancée, Jessie, smacks him in the chest but she's smiling.

"She's gorgeous," I mutter as I sip my martini. It's more an observation to myself, but I can't help but say it aloud as I watch the girl in the clingy emerald dress refill someone's wineglass.

"You have a girlfriend, Seb," Jessie reminds me quietly but sternly.

"Not anymore," I reply as I glance at her. She doesn't look as surprised as I would expect.

"What happened to Dawn?"

Jordan wraps an arm around his future wife and speaks for me. "Same thing that happened to Andie four months ago and Melissa two months ago. And the same thing that will happen to the woman over there if he has his way."

"Whoa now," I say, and I'm a little offended. "I wanted it to work. I *always* want it to work."

"Uh-huh," Jordan says, but it's dripping in sarcasm.

"Not all of us find true love at eighteen," I remind him. "But you can bet when I do, I won't screw it up."

"Ouch." Jordan clutches his chest like he's wounded, but he knows I'm right. He and Jessie spent years not speaking before they finally reconciled last year. I glance back at the beauty in the emerald dress. She's talking with the owner, Trey Beckford. It's quite the fancy event for a gym. Open bar, the best caterer in Seattle and everyone is dressed up.

"You should ask Trey who she is," I advise Avery, the reason we're all at this event. Trey and Avery played in college together but Trey dropped out—of school and hockey—his junior year while Avery left for the NHL.

"What do I look like to you? eHarmony?" he replies and rolls his eyes. Avery has always been a little on the intense side, but lately he's been even more uptight than normal.

"You owe me for making me put on a suit for this thing," I counter and adjust the knot on my tie, as if to prove my point.

"You wear suits to games all the time," he argues and rolls his eyes.

"Yeah, and that's enough time in them. I should be at home in sweats right now." I sigh, which is dramatic, even for me. "I wish we hadn't traded Alex. He was such a great wingman."

Avery looks over at Emerald Dress. "Why don't you try introducing yourself and asking for her number. I know that's not usually your way, but it works for the rest of mankind."

"What's Seb's way?" Jessie asks.

"Get naked and ask questions later." Jordan laughs at his own joke—loudly. Emerald Dress is close enough to hear him now and glances up at us. My eyes catch hers for just a heartbeat, long enough to see that they're a smoky blue, maybe gray? Without the slightest reaction at all, she continues her conversation with a brunette about the same age in a white dress, turning her back to us. No one seems to even notice the moment but me.

My sister wanders over. She's my date for the night, like she always is when I have an event and I'm single. Stephanie smiles brightly at me. "This place is really awesome! Even the bathrooms are state of the art. And the changing rooms look more like a fancy spa than a gym locker room. You have to check it out."

I nod. "I will."

Stephanie sighs. "I'd kill for another glass of champagne."

I glance at my now empty martini glass. "I'll find you some."

"*Merci*." Steph smiles. and I give her a wink.

I walk over to the bar, which will serve as a juice bar when this place opens, but right now it is covered in bottles of liquor. There's a pretty redhead behind the counter smiling at me as I approach. "You're Sebastian Deveau."

I smile and respond in French, because women love that shit. "*Oui*."

Her smile deepens and her eyes get wide with excitement. "I love you. I'm a huge Winterhawks fan and you're my favorite. I was at the game where you got that scar."

She points to my chin, and I lift my hand and trace the small white line that runs along my jaw where the end of a stick from a Los Angeles Sinners player caught me last season. It wasn't that big a deal, but I remember there was a ton of blood all over the ice, and it looked fucking gross.

"I was so scared for you. But you came right back out after they stitched you up and finished the game." She tilts her head and sighs, her eyelashes fluttering like a Southern belle admiring her Prince Charming. I chuckle.

"Yeah, it looked worse than it was. And hey"—I grin cockily—"clearly chicks love scars."

She looks confused by that and blinks her big blue eyes. "But it was horrible to see you hurt. You don't need a scar to look good."

I nod and realize that she's so not my type. "That's very sweet. My sister is dying for more of that champagne they were pouring earlier. Do you happen to have some?"

"I'll grab a fresh bottle from the back," she says with a smile and scurries off.

I'm about to turn and scan the hefty crowd for Emerald Dress again, but suddenly she's standing in front of me. She's holding a bottle of the champagne I've been looking for. Her eyes lock on mine, and her posture straightens. Her eyes are a deep, smoky gray color just like I'd thought but this close I can see the flecks of blue and green peppered around her irises. Her brown hair is messy in that way that's on purpose, and her skin is this amazing ivory color with freckles across the bridge of her nose she's trying to diminish with subtle makeup. Her body is even more perfect up close than it appeared across the room. She's lithe but tight and toned.

I smile my special reserve smile. The one I only break out for special occasions that involve special people I am not just trying to impress but trying to undress. She takes it in, starts to turn pink and lowers her eyes. For a second I'm disappointed. Is she a delicate flower type? Damn, I hope not.

"Just what I was looking for," I murmur and wait before adding, "Veuve Cliquot."

"We might be out," she says, the pink tinge to her cheeks receding as she tips the bottle in her hand to show it's empty. "But if you flashed that smile at Sara she's probably off wrestling the last glass out of someone's hand just to give it to you."

I fight a laugh. "You like my smile?"

"I didn't say that," she answers quickly, and a sexy little smirk covers her own pink lips. "And I'll never say that, because women like Sara will say it enough for the rest of us."

So much snark. I think I'm in love. I *know* I'm in lust.

"Great party," I say to her as a compliment because she might be the caterer if she knows the staff's first names. "And this place is incredible. I don't think Seattle has ever had such a high-tech gym."

"Fitness center," she murmurs back and her voice is soft and sexy. "Elevate Fitness is for the marathoners, the Iron men and women, the professional athletes looking to take it to the next level or for the housewife, businessman and average Joe looking to change their lifestyle."

"You've got their slogan memorized?"

She points to my empty martini glass. I nod and watch every move as she slowly turns and bends, her hips twisting and her ass jutting out toward me as she leans over to pick up the bottle of Grey Goose. *Mon Dieu,* the things I will do to her when she lets me…

"I should. I wrote it." She gives me another sexy little smile. So she's not the caterer. She works here. Instructor or business manager or…Avery had mentioned the owner, Trey, was "married to a great girl"…fuck. Is she Trey's wife?

"I teach classes here," she clarifies before I have time to panic.

"Let me guess…" I let my eyes wander slowly over her, leaning on the counter to get a gratuitous look at her long, shapely legs. "Spin class instructor?"

She shakes her head and slides my drink over to me. I make sure my fingers graze hers as I take the glass off the counter. The feel of her skin sends a ripple down my spine right into my groin. Fuck, she is already under my skin. I've never experienced something so intense so quickly before, and it makes me move away first. She likes that. It makes her blush again.

"Wanna have another go?"

I smirk. I can't help it. I know she means another guess, but…"I haven't had a first go…yet."

She blinks those big, sexy gray eyes and then she smiles. It's wide, it's deep and it's full of suggestion. She starts to speak, but before anything comes out Sara is back holding a bottle of pink champagne. "Found it! Last bottle."

She starts to uncork it, smiling so brightly at me I want to squint. I turn my attention back to Emerald Dress. She looks at the champagne and realizes I must be getting a drink for someone else. I can see the thought skitter across her expression. She doesn't like it. I like that she doesn't like it. But before I can explain it's for my sister, she announces, "I should go. Excuse me."

I watch her tight little ass swing back and forth under the silky material as she saunters off down a hall to the left of the main room where everyone is gathered.

Chapter 2

Shayne

I can convince myself that whole thing with the tall, dark stranger in the perfectly fitted midnight blue suit was no big deal for about fifteen minutes. I act like it didn't happen while I check to make sure the saunas are pristine. I pretend it was just a casual conversation while making sure the women's changing room is immaculate and the showers are sparkling. I blame the bottle of wine Audrey made me split with her at her apartment while we got ready for my overreacting to the mild flirtation. But by the time I get to the men's changing room I can't ignore the dampness in my thong or the way my heart is still beating furiously.

Apparently I'm not the only one who was moved by the encounter, because the door flies open and my best friend, Audrey, is standing there with her hands on her slim hips and her big brown eyes blinking at me furiously. "That guy you were talking to is sex personified."

I smile. "Tell me about it."

"I heard him talking to someone earlier, and he's French, which is sexy as fuck. He's got that whole smoldering thing going on with those intense blue eyes—which, by the way, have been glued to your fine ass all night. And I do mean your ass. Your actual butt. He's checking you out, in case you were wondering. And don't even get me started on—"

I raise my hand to silence her. "I didn't mean you should actually tell me about it. Trust me, I know," I tell her as I glance into the showers to make sure they're pristine, and that no one is in there eavesdropping. Trey will be giving informal tours of the facilities as the evening progresses, and I want everything perfect. "Between you and me, he was hitting buttons inside me I didn't even know existed."

"Who the hell is he, anyway?" Audrey asks, walking over to the mirror and fluffing her long perfectly coiffed dirty blond hair. "I saw him talking with a bunch of other suits before the bar encounter, but I didn't recognize any of them. Except they're all hot."

"Trey was inviting the local businesses in the area, which include law firms, an accounting firm and a couple investment bankers and the staff at the fancy restaurant in the building next door. He must be one of them," I say absently and try not to think of that jolt of electricity that I felt when his fingers slid over mine as I passed him his drink. "If he's a lawyer I needed to get myself in legal trouble ASAP."

"Yeah, you do." Audrey winks at me. "Shayne, you have to go back out there and talk to him."

"Easy now, slugger." I laugh but…I'm shocked at how much I actually want to. It was embarrassing, really. I'd never had such an instant and overwhelming reaction to a guy before.

My friend Audrey had. More than once. When we were in college she could go from zero to hot-and-heavy make-out session with a guy she had met fifteen minutes earlier. Shortly after we moved to Seattle, Audrey met her current boyfriend, Josh, and her wild days were over.

Josh is a great guy and I've never seen Audrey happier, but now she is hellbent on living vicariously through me. My unfortunate sex drought seems to upset her way more than it does me. Every time we go out for a girl's night she tries to convince me to flirt with some random guy. It is hysterical and annoying. One-night stands are so not my thing. But then again I don't exactly want celibacy to be my thing either.

Audrey said I liked to keep one foot on firm ground and that I'd never taken risks or leaps. Audrey's middle name was leap. From the moment we met in the dorm bathrooms in freshman year at Syracuse University, I both envied her and judged her. I'd never met anyone with a messier life. Not even my brother, Trey, who has battled addiction issues, had as crazy a life as Audrey. Of course, if she wasn't impulsive, she wouldn't be here in Seattle with me. When I graduated college we'd gotten an apartment together in Syracuse and both started working. A year later I decided to move back here to help my brother start his business, and she agreed to come with me. It was nowhere near her home or family—they were in New Hampshire—and it was nowhere near anywhere she'd ever lived before, but she didn't even blink. She just loaded her shit into my Kia Soul and hopped into the passenger seat with a smile.

"I bet your vagina has cobwebs," Audrey announces with a sad expression, and I roll my eyes. "Do you even remember how to have sex?"

"I'm sure it's like riding a bike," I snark back.

"Test your theory." Audrey is the only person I know who can trump my snarkiness with her own. "Ride *him*."

I shake my head at her like she's an incorrigible puppy, but as I think about how this night has gone…I have to admit I want to. Watching him watch me from across the room and then swapping innuendos felt like foreplay. It made my skin tingle and my heart race and the long-dormant space between my thighs comes to life. I might actually even masturbate tonight. I haven't bothered to do that in…months. I blush at the thought.

"What're the red cheeks for?" Audrey inquires and then claps excitedly. "Oh! You want to do it! You want to sleep with him!"

"Of course I do. He's delicious," I confess, and it makes her clap again. "But I won't."

Audrey sighs dramatically. "Come on, Shayne! Live a little!"

"I live just fine."

"Nuns get more action than you," she retorts, and I laugh. Then she digs into her purse and pulls out a tiny, square foil packet. She shoves it at me, and I take a step back like she's trying to hand me a tarantula.

"Take it. In case you change your mind," she urges, and I look at the condom, horrified. She rolls her big brown eyes and presses it into my palm.

I open the door to leave the changing room, planning to throw the condom into the closest trash can I find, and come to face-to-face with my future masturbation material. He stops, but not as quickly as he could, or should. I know he sees me as soon as I see him, which is about two feet away in the narrow hallway, but he keeps walking toward me. He doesn't stop until he's basically towering above me, his wall of a chest almost touching me. I can't help taking a step back, but his hand goes to my elbow like he's holding me in place so my step falters and I stay wedged up against him. I cover the silver packet in my hand with my fingers to hide it from him.

"Were you…" Why is my heart racing? I suddenly feel serious and giddy at the exact same time. This is intense, and that makes it feel ridiculous because I don't even know his name. That and the wine, which I rarely drink, is making me loopy. I swallow and push out the rest of my sentence. "Looking for the restroom?"

"No. I was looking for you."

He glances past me briefly, to notice Audrey. He gives her a quick nod of hello. I turn to face her, away from him, and with no other option, subtly shove the condom under the front of my dress and into my padded bra. Audrey steps up beside me grinning like a crazy person. "I'm Audrey. I'm her best friend. And I'm going to disappear now."

Her heels click in quick succession as she darts down the hall, pausing only for a second to glance over her shoulder and mouth the words "Do him" at me.

"I never got your name," he explains, pulling my gaze away from my crazy friend and back to his stunning face. "And I never gave you mine."

"Shayne," I reply, barely above a whisper for some reason.

"What?"

"My name is Shayne."

"That's a boy's name."

"My father wanted a boy," I explain for the millionth time in my twenty-four years. "He got one later, but I was born first so…"

"I'm calling you Shay," he announces, and I'm a little stunned that he has just arbitrarily renamed me. "It's more feminine and soft, like you."

I want to explain to him that I'm hardly feminine or soft. I'm a tomboy. I prefer sweats and ponytails to makeup and heels. And soft? Sure, he fills out a fancy suit well, but I'm the daughter of a professional athlete, and my job is fitness. I bet I could kick his ass. I don't *want* to kick his ass…but I wouldn't mind grabbing it. That's why I don't get too flippant with him even though I should. Desire trumps all, apparently.

His lips spread slowly into a hot little smile, and his hand slides from my elbow down to my wrist. He could circle it twice with his fingers if he wanted to, I can tell. Big hands. Much rougher than I would expect from a businessman.

"Sebastian," he says, his voice deep and his smile growing broader. His name is like velvet coming off his tongue with a French twist to it. I have a feeling he could recite a grocery list and I would want to touch myself. Jesus.

I swallow again and smile back. "Sebastian is the crab in *Little Mermaid*."

"What?"

"I'd rather have a boy's name than a crustacean's."

His smile gets boyish and he chuckles, and it rumbles up from his chest right through me. It's infectious, and I start to giggle. His hand at my wrist slips to my hand. We are holding hands. I am holding hands with this French lawyer-or-accountant-maybe-even-waiter stranger.

"You've got one smart mouth," he tells me as I stare up at him. He tilts his jaw and dips his head a little. "I like smart mouths, Shay."

"Good, because I don't intend to change, Frenchie."

"Frenchie?"

I give him a little shrug. "If you're changing my name I'm changing yours. And it's either Frenchie or Crabby."

"Frenchie because of my accent?"

I nod. "Sure. Although I'm sure there are other French things you're good at besides the accent."

He likes that. I can tell by the way those bright eyes narrow in that smoldering way Audrey mentioned and fall to my lips. I wonder if that stupid ruby red gloss I put on is still there. Audrey said it would last all night but since I usually never wear lip gloss, or anything other than Chapstick, I have no idea if that's the truth.

"I'd like to show you exactly what I'm good at."

Holy shit. Is he for real? Did he just outright proposition me?

He lets go of my hand and reaches between us, cupping the side of my cheek gently but also with this unreal sense of power...dominance. And I like it. It's making me quiver.

His thumb moves over my lips and his head dips even lower and his sexy face blurs because he's so close. I can feel his breath as he exhales and then—nothing. No breath. No movement. His eyes are focused on my lips and his mouth is slightly open, a fraction of an inch from mine. My insides are a riptide of anticipation and fear and lust. I can't just stand here. I have to either pull away or do the unthinkable. I can't stop looking at his face. Besides the fact that it's gorgeous with his dark eyebrows and his pale eyes and his plump, symmetrical lips, it's covered in the most...sinful expression. Deliciously sinful, like he's already doing incredibly hot, dirty things to me in his mind. And that's why I decide to do what I would normally consider unthinkable. Because I've never seen someone look at me like that before, and I want to be the person he's already undressed in his head.

I rock up ever so slightly on my strappy black heels and close the distance between our mouths. He responds instantly—with a smile. I can feel it against my lips and I want to freak out. He thinks this is funny? OMG, he better not think this is funny! His hand at my neck pulls me a little closer and his lips fall from the smile and press harder into mine and his head tilts and…he thinks he's won.

I pull back slowly but with conviction, even though my body feels like it's being gravitationally pulled back toward him and my brain is screaming DON'T STOP. I break the kiss. I am nothing if not competitive, and I will not let this man—this delectable stranger—feel like he's won some kind of flirt-off. No. Absolutely not, no.

I don't pull back far, just enough to break our contact. My eyes flutter open at the same time his do, and any hint of that smile on his lips is gone. I see the debate flickering behind those unreal crystal blue eyes and dark, heavy eyebrows. I feel the hesitation. His hand on my jaw gets looser. His thumb lifts up like it's going to sweep my lips again, but it doesn't. He stops because I pulled back, and it's made him uncertain. Good. I don't want to be the only one off-balance here. But he doesn't want to stop—I can sense that, feel his desire radiating off of him. I can see the debate in his head dancing behind those light eyes. Does he play it cool and wait for me to make another move, or does he just go for what he wants, admitting to himself, and to me, that he can't resist just as much as I can't?

He tightens his grip on me, and I smile for the briefest second before it's forced from my face when he leans in and captures my lips again. This time he's the one who gave in. Now we're even.

He takes a step toward me, and I think he's going to push me up against the wall, but he doesn't. He takes his other hand and presses it flat against my lower back and pulls me into him so tightly that the air is pushed from my lungs. It's fine. I wasn't really breathing anyway. When his tongue slides into my mouth I swear to God it causes actual sparks as soon as it touches mine. I feel heat rush from the contact down through the rest of my body. It causes me to make some weird noise—a soft, gentle moan—and I wrap my arms around his neck, my fingertips skimming the back of his hair where it meets the collar of his jacket.

"I need to see you. Somewhere other than here," he whispers into the kiss.

"I can't leave." It's all I can manage because I don't want to stop kissing him.

"Neither can I…" he whispers back into the kiss.

"You're here with your coworkers?" I question, remembering the glass of champagne he had Sara get him and finally pulling my lips from his. "Or someone else?"

"Coworkers," he says after a pause.

"Are you with the accounting firm or the law office?"

Before he can answer, footsteps echo on the concrete and we step away from each other. Sara appears at the end of the hall. "Hey!" She pauses to give Sebastian an extra-long, extra-flirty smile before turning back to me. "Trey is looking for you. He's in the weight room with Avery Westwood."

I make a face at that name, but she's too busy batting her eyelashes at Seb to notice.

"Tell him I'll be right there," I reply and she nods, waves flirtatiously at Sebastian and then retreats, leaving us alone again. I frown. "Trey owns the place. He invited his stupid hockey friend Avery Westwood. He's trying to woo him into doing an ad for us."

He smirks at that; it's deep, dark and delicious. "Sounds like you're not a Westwood fan."

"I hate all hockey players." He looks taken aback and I realize "hate" is a really strong word, even if I mean it. "It's a long story, but trust me, I have my reasons."

He pauses for a second but then he reaches up and cups the side of my face again. My whole body tingles. He's going to kiss me again and I want him to, but any second my brother or Sara or someone is going to come looking for me, and this moment will be gone—maybe forever. Suddenly, my urge to prevent that from happening is all-consuming, and I grab his hand and cross the hallway to the door to the laundry room.

Without thinking, I push it open and pull him in after me.

Chapter 3

Sebastian

I'm about to kiss her again and internally debating how to tell her I'm a hockey player—someone she just professed to hate—when she suddenly pulls me across the hall, opens a door that has a small silver plaque on the front marked *Private* and pulls me inside.

She flips on a light. It's a long, narrow room painted an ocean blue. Along one wall are three industrial-size front-loading washing machines. Across from that are four industrial-size front-loading dryers. On the wall opposite the door is floor-to-ceiling open shelving filled with bright blue-and-orange towels monogrammed with the gym logo. Next to the door is a metal folding table.

I look over my shoulder and, sure enough, there's a perfect silver deadbolt just above the handle. I smile. When I look back at her she's smiling too. "Out there I was just going to kiss you," I explain to her in a quiet but confident tone. "If that door gets locked, I am going to do a lot more than kiss you."

She walks toward me, her cheeks turning a delicious pink, and just when I think she's going to kiss me, she slides to my left, her hand reaching behind me. As her lips ghost the edge of my jaw, I hear the undeniable scrape of the lock twisting. I reach up and grab her face in both my hands and our eyes lock. She looks slightly nervous but very excited. "I am going to make you come so hard, baby."

Before she can react to my promise, I cover her mouth with my own and part her lips with my tongue. She kisses me back, matching my passion. Her mouth is warm and soft and it's like taking a small lick from a delicious ice cream cone on a hot summer day. It's perfect but not nearly enough. I move a hand from her face to her waist and pull her against me as I move my hips, pressing my hard-on into her stomach.

She responds by reaching down and grabbing my ass.

Oh fuck, this girl is perfect.

Chapter 4

Shayne

Am I doing this? I've never done this. I said I would never do this. But...oh, my God...I think as he pulls my earlobe between his teeth. Holy crap, I want to do this. With him. Here. Now. I can usually pretend like my sex hiatus is no big deal, but it's been two years and four months and suddenly, that is a big freaking deal.

"No regrets," I whisper as I let him push me back into the room until my ass hits one of the dryers. I was saying it to myself, not him, but he heard, and his ice-blue eyes find mine.

"I promise you'll have none," he whispers and devours my mouth again as I shove his suit jacket off his shoulders.

This boy can kiss. He's dominant and forceful and it's hot as hell. He owns my mouth. He knows it too, I can tell, and the competitive nature that has always driven me doesn't even seem to care that it's being owned. Because every kiss, every pass of his tongue over mine, every nip of his teeth on my bottom lip leaves a hint that giving in will be worth it.

He's made some big promises. And it's been so long that if he doesn't fulfill them, I might actually cry. His sexy smirk and snarky mouth and mind-blowing kisses are the only reasons I suddenly want to be satisfied by something other than my own hand so please, *please* may he deliver.

His hands slide over the silky green fabric of my dress, slipping over my sides and my hips until they reach the hem, and then he starts to slide back up, under the dress, and I don't even feel the slightest inclination to stop him. In fact, when he reaches edges of my thong I whisper, "Take it off."

I don't even know who I am anymore, but it doesn't feel as wrong as I thought it would. Somehow it feels like this version of Shayne Beckford has always existed, locked away somewhere inside of me, but no one ever had the key—not even me. This stranger, Sebastian—hell, I don't even know his last name—he has the key. I know that revelation will scare me later, when I'm home alone and overanalyzing the crap out of this. And I know that will happen because the Shayne Beckford that exists normally is still alive somewhere inside of me. She's just been hog-tied and locked in a closet.

His fingers feel oddly rough for an accountant or lawyer or whatever hell he is as they trace the hem of my thong, scraping the inside of my thigh and making me shiver. He smiles into the kiss we're sharing, and so I slip my hand in between us and cup his hardness through his pants. Just as I was hoping, it makes him shiver back. Good. Now we're even.

Except we're not even. Nothing about this feels like fair game. The way my body is responding to him, he's definitely got the advantage. And as I rub my hand up his length—*way* up—I realize he's got the advantage on a lot of men too. In fact, if you took both men I've been with and put them together, they're probably the size of what Sebastian has in his pants. Oh man, I am really going to do this.

His fingers move out from under my dress, and he suddenly grabs my hips and lifts me, dropping my ass on the edge of the dryer. Then as he attacks my neck, sucking on the sensitive flesh, he pushes my dress up over my hips and hooks his fingers into my thong. He drops my underwear onto the floor without glancing at them, thankfully, because they're soaking wet and not very sexy, just plain cotton, heather gray—the kind I wear under my yoga pants. I reach for his belt.

Panic starts to seep into the edges of my lust. I still want him, I do, but I don't know what the hell I'm doing. I don't know the etiquette for this. Should we set rules here? Are there rules? Do I ask if he has a condom, or just give him the one I shoved in my bra earlier? Is that hot? Pulling a condom out of my bra? Or is it slutty? Oh God, I'm clueless.

I get his pants undone and start to shove them off his hips but it's hard because he has such a tight, hard ass. Seriously. It's like a rock. A big, round, hot, sexy rock. His hands slide up my thighs, and once his pants are at his ankles I start to slide my own hands under his dress shirt. His stomach and chest are just as hard as his ass. Seriously, he must spend all his free time working out. That either means he's already a member at another gym and I'll never see him again or that he's a workout-aholic and he's going to be so impressed by this place he joins. I don't know which scenario makes me more nervous—never seeing him again or seeing him every day after this.

"Shay…baby…" His voice is soft but chastising, his accent heavy. "I'm about to touch you for the first time, *really* touch you, and you're frowning."

I realize I've been stuck inside my head and I didn't even realize his fingers are pressing against my inner thigh, inches from...And then two are inside me and my mouth opens in a wordless gasp. He covers it with his own mouth and his tongue starts to move in rhythm with his fingers and I start to tingle—down *there*. Oh my God, I can't come. It's too soon. He'll think I'm like some weirdo who never has sex. It's too needy and desperate...isn't it? Besides, if I'm coming, I'm not doing it without him. Oh God. I am going to...

I push him back. He looks startled for a second and then he smiles—it's victorious and I blush. "You don't want to come?"

"Yes, I do. I just..." I scramble in my head for a way to make this hot. But I've never been the sexy, sultry type of girl. So I just pull the condom out of my bra and lean forward and press it into his rock-hard chest. "I want you to earn it the old-fashioned way."

He looks at the condom against his chest and smiles, his blue eyes flickering with something that looks like excitement and desire. Thank God I didn't turn him off. "Challenge accepted."

I'm really going to do this, I realize as I watch him drop his boxer briefs without any hesitation or modesty. He's got a pretty dick. I can't believe that's even a thought rolling through my head, but it is. I've never thought that about any dick before, but his is long and thick without being too thick, and it looks like a work of fucking art. I think I've lost my fucking mind.

He rips open the condom package and slides it on with one hand as he reaches out with his other hand and grabs me by the back of the neck and pulls me into another kiss. "Slow or fast? Light or hard?"

"Surprise me."

I spread my legs, making room for him between them, and his hand slides down my neck to my back and then to my ass. He holds me on the very edge of the dryer and slides into me in one steady movement. I drop backward onto my elbows, arching my back, and he makes this sound in the back of his throat. Yeah. This is insane and I fucking love it.

The next several minutes are a blur of sensations—no thoughts, just tingles and friction and groans and moans. Somehow we end up with my legs over his shoulders as my whole back is pressed to the dryer and wall behind it. The bottom of my dress is up to my rib cage now, my lower half completely on display to his roaming eyes, and I don't even care—in fact, it gets me hotter. He's moving hard and fast and then he leans over me, pinning my legs between us, and pushes in deeper than I think I've ever experienced in my life and—he hits the on button and the dryer spins to life, shaking my whole body, and then I explode. I swear I see fireworks and God, and I bite my lip to keep from screaming as my orgasm destroys me.

A second later he arches his back and grunts and then drops onto me. His skin feels warm and damp through his dress shirt, and he sucks gently on the skin just below my right ear and whispers, "You are the sexiest woman I have ever—"

The doorknob twists. It's as loud as a car bomb for some reason, and we both jump. I suddenly crash back to reality. I'm at the opening of my brother's gym—the place where I teach yoga and nutrition—and I just fucked a stranger in our laundry room. Oh my God, what the hell is wrong with me? I push him away, jump off the dryer and grab my underwear off the floor.

"He has a key!" I whisper furiously. "If that's Trey, he has a key!"

Sebastian's face morphs into panic as well, and he burst into motion, shoving his underwear up over his condom-covered dick and reaching for his pants at his ankles. I try to smooth my hair and reach for the door just as the handle starts to turn again. And it opens.

Thankfully, it's not my brother. It's my coworker Sara, who will teach Pilates when this place officially opens on Monday. I smile at her like a drunk cheerleader after a pep rally. "Hey! I was just giving Sebastian a tour."

Sara's eyes are about to bulge out of her head. I'm too scared to look back. Is he dressed? Please let him have his pants on. She doesn't say anything for a moment, and all I can hear is the empty dryer rumbling as it spins. Oh God, this is so awkward.

"Someone spilled some beer in the lobby. I need towels," Sara says in a weird tone. "The door was locked."

"Oh. Oops." I shrug and push past her. Once in the hall, I turn back and see that Sebastian did get his pants up. But his dress shirt is rumpled and untucked and his chestnut hair is completely askew. I am so busted.

"Trey is still looking for you," she says pointedly.

"Right. Okay." I glance from Sara to Sebastian and then, in a high-pitched voice with an awkward wave, I say, "Bye!"

I turn on my heel and scurry down the hall. Oh my God, what a crazy night. I'm still flustered and feeling a little wild when I find Trey in the cardio room—talking to my parents. And just like that, the universe has thrown a bucket of cold water on my amazing and crazy night.

My father looks up and smiles as he sees me. "There you are, Shaynie! Trey says you're running this event, but we've been here an hour and haven't seen you anywhere."

He leans in and wraps his arms around me, hugging me tightly. I pat his back and wiggle free. My mom then leans in and air kisses both my cheeks before scrutinizing me with her perfectly made-up blue eyes. "Your hair is…Did you style it yourself? I could have gotten you an appointment with my girl Monique, you know."

I try to smooth the flyaways. I'm sure it looked acceptable pre-Sebastian. Images of our little spin cycle sexcapade fills my head and I feel my face flush. Trey notices and gives me a confused look. "You all right? You're all red."

"I was demonstrating the equipment for some potential clients," I lie and shrug when his face twists into an even more confused expression, because he knows I'm not nutty enough to demonstrate fitness equipment in a cocktail dress and heels.

"Good for you, Shaynie." My father squeezes my shoulder. "We have to do what we can to help my boy. That's why I'm here. My celebrity should earn him a few members."

I fight the urge to roll my eyes. Dear old Dad is a retired hockey player and former Seattle Winterhawk. But it's been years since he's done anything really active and it shows. I doubt his presence is going to sell gym memberships for Trey. That's why my brother invited the current Winterhawks captain and his former college teammate, Avery Westwood.

"Speaking of hockey celebrities, where is that douchebag from the Winterhawks?" I ask Trey, which gets me a scowl.

"Avery is…" Trey's eyes scan the room. "He's here somewhere. I was talking to him a few minutes ago."

"Westwood is here?" My father perks up. "That'll make a great photo opportunity. Two Winterhawk legends. I'm going to track him down and get the girl from the paper to take a photo."

My father turns and walks into the crowd. I finally roll my eyes. My mother sighs because she catches me, and that almost makes me want to roll them again. But Trey intervenes. "Shayne, why don't you go get Mom some of the champagne?"

"Sure thing," I mutter, and ignore her comment asking if it's Veuve Cliquot or Ruinart because she prefers Ruinart. Of course she does. It costs more and she prefers anything that spends more of my dad's money. I can't blame her for that, though. She earned that money through pain and suffering—and denial.

As I make my way back over to the bar, my eyes scan the room for Sebastian, but I don't see him anywhere. Sara eyes me suspiciously as she pours the champagne. "Were you fooling around with Sebastian? In the laundry room? During the party?"

"I was giving him a tour of the facilities."

"*Your* facilities?" Sara asks and adds, "I don't think that's allowed. Trey would be pissed."

"Sara, are you a Pilates instructor or the HR department?" I snap as I grab the champagne and storm back into the crowd. As I make my way over toward my mom, who is chatting with Trey's wife, Sasha, I catch my father making his way down the hallway toward the changing rooms. He's got his hand on the small of someone's back. Someone in a red dress.

The hair on the back of my neck stands up and my gut twists uncomfortably. And then my feet start to follow him. I make it to the hallway just as he places a big palm on the men's changing room door and the hand on the small of this lady's back slips to her ass.

"Dad!" I holler sharply.

He spins, his hand falling to his side, and a placating smile fills his face. "Shayne, honey, I was just showing our old friend Elsa the state-of-the-art facilities. Do you remember Elsa? She used to do PR for the Winterhawks when I played."

Elsa smiles, but it's forced and tinged with panic. "Shayne? Oh my gosh, I haven't seen you since you were this high."

I glance at her hand hovering around her waist to indicate how tall I used to be. I tighten my grip on the champagne and debate throwing it at both of them. But then, as I've learned from catching my dad being a cheating bastard more than once, that only makes *me* look bad. So instead I smile and say, "Well, other than my height, not much has changed. I still love gummy bears, hate hockey, and my parents are still married."

She turns the color of her dress and then, with nothing more than a nod, she excuses herself and walks past me back into the main room. My father glares at me. "What the hell was that about?"

"We both know what that was about," I reply tersely and turn to leave, but he puts his hand on my shoulder and walks with me.

"Shayne, Elsa is now a writer with *Seattle Living* and I was trying to charm her into a feature on this place. That's why I had Trey invite her," he informs me, his voice low.

"Your hand was on her ass, Dad."

"We're old friends."

I stop and glare up at him. Did he really just say that? Does he really think that's a reasonable excuse? I open my mouth to say something, but I have no idea what a child should say to a parent in this situation. I shouldn't have to know!

My mother walks up to us and reaches for the glass in my hand. "It may only be Veuve but I'm parched, so it'll have to do."

"I need to track down Elsa," my father mutters before he walks away.

"Elsa?" my mother repeats, but he's already gone.

"Elsa who used to work for the Winterhawks," I explain and try not to frown.

My mother's eyes get dark and her lips drop from the artificial half smile she usually has plastered on her face like a mask. "I know who she is."

The way she says it, the tone that drips with disappointment, tells me she knows exactly who she is and that this isn't the first time my father has had his hand on Elsa's ass. Fuck. I swallow hard. "Mom, I…"

"I hear she writes for the lifestyle magazine. I hope she writes a nice piece on this place," my mother says, the fake half smile firmly back in place. "Trey deserves some success."

And before I can say another word, she turns to chat with someone else.

I need some air. My parents and their screwed-up marriage is, as usual, suffocating me. I make my way for the back door, just off the cardio room.

On my way I notice Trey talking to Avery Westwood. He's the face of the NHL, so I recognize him even though I haven't watched a hockey game in years. I wonder if he cheats on his girlfriend too. Lifestyle over love, I once heard a goalie's wife say with a simple shrug. It was probably one of the sickest things I've heard, but it's how my mother lived her life. And I promised myself that would never be my motto or my life. I push open the exit door and step out into the parking lot. I take a deep breath and try to regain the sense of euphoria I had in the laundry room with Sebastian.

Wait a minute…I just had sex with a guy I barely know and that's bringing me peace? Who am I? I wonder if the sex with random women brings my father peace. The idea that it might, and we would have something like that in common, horrifies me. So does the idea of going back into that room and being around my parents, and now I'm embarrassed to see Sebastian again too. So when the caterer comes out, slightly panicked that we might run out of booze, I happily volunteer to pick up more. I need to get out of here.

Chapter 5

Shayne

By nine a.m. I already knew it was the worst morning ever. The gym opened the day after the party, which was almost two weeks ago. You'd think I'd be used to my schedule by now. But my alarm didn't go off and I woke up twenty-five minutes late, instantly startled, then immediately panicked. As I ran through the apartment in a rush to get ready, I stepped in cat vomit that Roy had left as a present some time during the night. Once I finally sprinted out of my house and got into my car, it wouldn't start. I hissed every swear word I could think of in English, and for good measure I added the few I knew in Spanish. Then I called Audrey and listened to her swear before agreeing to come and get me and take me to work.

Audrey works as a bartender at Liberty, a super-trendy bar in Capital Hill. She probably hadn't even gotten home until a few hours ago, so I did not stop thanking her profusely the whole drive to the gym. I could have called my brother, which Audrey pointed out more than once, but Trey lives on the other side of the city, close to the gym but far from my apartment. Plus he was probably already at the gym by the time I woke up. I thought about calling his wife, Sasha, but she is seven months pregnant so I didn't want to be bothering her if I could help it.

"Seriously, Audrey, thank you so much," I coo as she turns onto South Weller Street, where Elevate is located.

"Yeah, yeah. But I am not picking you up for the barbeque tonight," she mutters. Her chocolate eyes narrow, as if to prove she's serious.

"Really? Not even if I pay you gas money?" I ask desperately. I really don't want to take public transit there; it'll take forever. And a cab or Uber will cost too much.

Audrey smirks at me as she pulls to a stop in the gym parking lot. "I have a feeling you'll find someone to drive you. Out!"

She orders me out of the car. I'm too late to spend any more time pleading with her. I open the door and close it behind me as Audrey yells out, "Feel free to call me later and tell me how your day is going."

She winks at me, which is totally weird, and waves as she pulls away. I realize I'm about to miss the beginning of class—the class *I'm* teaching—so I don't have time to figure out why she was smiling deviously with that last comment. I push it from my mind and run into the building. I barely look up as I storm into the gym. I toss my bag at Sara behind the front counter, no time to put it in my locker, and rush into the yoga room. Trey is in there checking the temperature. He sees me and crosses his arms over his broad chest, but I ignore my brother and just start talking to the crowded room as I make my way to the front.

"Okay, everyone, welcome to hot yoga!" I clap my hands and

reach the front where someone, probably Trey, has already laid out a mat for me, thankfully.

The room is full, which is exciting. We've been open a little less than two weeks and business has been slowly but steadily picking up. This is my first full class. Although I know he's irked I barely made it on time, Trey gives me a quick smile, happy about the attendance.

I see several faces who have started to become familiar. There's Mrs. Waters, who signed up the first week for our Senior Strength program; three sorority girls from the nearby university, who are also taking beginner CrossFit classes; Tom Orsen, an accountant from the building across the street, who took my Paleo seminar last Monday, and…

Frenchie.

Just like that. Out of nowhere. Completely unexpected. He's here in my yoga class twisting on his mat, his eyes focused on me. I must have gasped because two people in the front row freeze midway through the first pose and stare at me.

I smile and force myself to calmly coo out the next move. The class is very basic introductory hot yoga class and an hour long. It feels like twenty hours and two minutes at the exact same time. The entire time my mind is racing and my heart flipping inside my chest like a dolphin putting on a show at SeaWorld. My eyes keep landing on him like he's the center of gravity in the room. I can't stop myself.

He's in the center of the back row. I must have pushed right by him and not even noticed when I scurried into the room. He's trying valiantly to do all the poses, but struggles more than I would have expected with most of it. Such a long, thick, chiseled body…but he's as graceful as an inebriated stallion. When he attempts the Noose Pose, even though I purposely gave an easier option, he tumbles back onto his ass with a thud. The sorority girls are all staring at him, have been the entire class, and he gives them all a giant grin. They giggle, and he chuckles back. It's been twelve days since I last saw him—technically since the only time I've ever seen him—and damn if he isn't even better looking than I remembered.

That admission, and the fact that he's in front of me at all, has me in a tailspin. I never had a one-night stand before, and I always assumed that when you did have one, it meant you only had to see the guy once. But clearly Frenchie didn't read the fine print. For some absurd reason, I'm really glad he didn't. Some part of me, under the layers of panic and fear and awkward confusion, is really excited to see him again.

By the time class ends, his heather-gray Winterhawks T-shirt is dark with sweat and sticking to his broad chest and sculpted shoulders. I glance at the logo on his chest, the giant, dumb bird, and realize I've found his first flaw: he's a hockey fan. He takes off his baseball cap, also with the Winterhawks logo, and his golden brown hair flies everywhere. He wipes sweat from his face with his towel before dropping the hat back on his head backward. I might have sighed, unintentionally, but if I did, it blended in with the three sorority girls who were doing the same thing.

Mrs. Waters comes over and asks me a question about one of the poses, and I happily give her a long explanation, grateful for the distraction. When she leaves, though, there's only one person left in the yoga room. And his bright blue eyes are on me.

He doesn't move closer. He just stands there, water bottle in one hand, towel over his shoulder, smiling at me. It's just a small smile. His full lips turned up in the corners and his eyes twinkling. I can't help but smile back. His grins are more contagious than the plague.

"Hi, Shay," he says softly.

"Hello, Sebastian." I should be using his nickname to keep it light, but I'm rattled and off my game. What the hell is he doing here?

"Miss me?" he asks. White teeth flash and he tilts his head just a little bit. He's a goddamn world-class flirt. I roll my eyes even though my grin grows too.

"I don't know you, so I can't miss you, Frenchie," I reply flatly and carry my mat over to the pile in the corner.

He just stands there staring at me and smirking. And then he changes the subject. "So yoga, huh?" he says.

"Certified instructor since college. I taught a few classes to help pay my way through school, and when I graduated I realized I'd rather keep doing it than find a job that applied my English lit degree," I tell him and pull my hair from my ponytail, giving it a quick shake, trying to get the sweat in it to dry. Of course, it's not going to dry, because we're still standing in a stifling hot room. "Then I got an online degree in nutrition."

Sebastian nods. "I'll have to take one of your seminars."

Something hits me. "How did you know I was teaching this morning?"

"I was at Liberty last night with some...buddies," Sebastian explains, his accent sounding as hot as I remember as he says the name of my best friend's workplace with a sexy French twist. "Your friend Audrey recognized me and brought us a free round of drinks. She told me you were teaching this morning."

I smile ruefully. Now I know why she agreed to get me here on time and why she wanted me to call her and tell her how my day went. That bitch. God love her.

"Hey! You two looking to melt into puddles?" Trey calls out as he walks into the room and right over to the thermostat, cranking it down quickly. Just as quickly as he walks in, Trey walks out, but not before calling over his shoulder at me. "Shayne, we need to talk before you work the juice bar."

"Sure thing!" I call back. My eyes land on Sebastian again as I start to walk out of the room. "I have to get going. I need to shower and talk to Trey and grovel for almost being late thanks to my stupid car not starting."

He nods, following me. "Need help showering? I'm really good at scrubbing backs."

I roll my eyes and point to the sixty-seven-year-old Mrs. Waters standing by the juice bar. "I don't think Mrs. Waters would appreciate it. Unless of course you promise to scrub her back too."

Sebastian's smile drops. I turn and walk toward the women's changing room, and a part of me wants nothing more than for him to follow me right in there anyway. It doesn't surprise me that I'm still so incredibly attracted to him. He was cocky and charming and I haven't been able to stop thinking about the sex for the entire twelve days. So I hesitate before disappearing into the changing room and turn back to look at him. He's just standing there, smirking and completely checking out my ass. I flush. Again. Our eyes meet, and I find my mouth moving and words coming out. Thoughts I shouldn't voice but for some reason I am. "Are you...heading out?"

He shakes his head slowly: no. "I'll be at the juice bar. Waiting for you."

I don't know what to say to that, so I say nothing and disappear into the changing room, making sure to wiggle my ass as I go, since it's probably still being ogled.

And I can't help but think about the sex again now as I shower and change. By the time I've changed into clean yoga pants and one of our tangerine Lycra staff shirts, I'm tingling from the memories. It's hard not to dwell on that night and all its naked, panting, sweaty glory—because it was so out of character for me and it had felt like the best decision I ever made in my entire life. Until the euphoria wore off, anyway.

It was what it was—one night of sex, my first orgasm by another human in ages, but nothing more. Because if it wasn't a one-night stand to him, why did he wait twelve days to pop back up in my life? I shouldn't get my hopes up just because he's here now. He probably just needs a place to work out before his next triathlon or Iron Man or whatever extracurricular activity gives him that body. I need to keep my irrational hope in check.

He's exactly where he said he'd be when I emerge from the women's changing room. Just sitting on a stool, leaning on the counter, sipping one of our Green Giant smoothies and looking like sex on a stick. Damn him. I walk right by him with no acknowledgment and head into Trey's office. Trey frowns at my entrance, and I know exactly what he's annoyed about.

"I'm sorry. My car wouldn't start," I say honestly and give him a little shrug.

"When was the last time you had it serviced?" he asks gruffly.

"Two, maybe three years ago?"

"Years?! Christ, Shayne." He frowns and runs a hand over his buzz cut. Trey is and always has been big, burly, loud and gruff. He's a born-and-bred hockey jock. Really, my father never gave him any other choice. But deep down he's more than a bulky body and a loud mouth. He has a sensitive side, a vulnerable one, which is why when he suffered a career-ending injury in college, he couldn't handle it. But after rehab it became clear Trey was a smart businessman, and he worked hard to save money and create a business plan investors would get behind. On top of all that, despite our constant bickering, I know he's got my back, and I think I've proven I will always have his.

"I don't have anyone else who can cover for you, Shayne. You're our only yoga instructor right now," he reminds me with a stern look in his dark blue eyes.

"I know. And it won't happen again, cross my heart." I use my finger to trace an X over my heart.

"Will *that* happen again?" His gaze shifts to the wall of his office that faces the juice bar. I follow his gaze.

I flush and drop my gaze to the polished concrete under my feet. I inwardly curse Sara, who told him that she caught me and Sebastian in the laundry room. "Definitely not. No."

"Definitely?" he repeats, and when I look up at him his eyebrows are raised skeptically.

"Yeah. I told you before; it was just a one-time thing."

"How do you know?"

"Because it only happened once," I reply smartly and cross my arms. "Listen, Trey, my personal life is personal. And your rule about not banging customers wasn't broken. He wasn't a customer. In fact, I could have banged everyone at that event because no one had signed a membership agreement yet."

"Stop! Please do not talk about banging anyone, let alone *everyone*." He closes his eyes and tries to shake some clearly uncomfortable image out of his head. After taking a deep breath he looks at me again. "Well, the 'no sexual contact with members' rule applies now. He just bought a yearlong membership."

"What?!"

He nods. "Yep. And clearly he intends to use it. He's a nice guy too. If he hadn't boinked my sister, I'd probably like him."

"Yeah, he's a charmer. He'll charm the pants right off you."

"Apparently."

Our eyes meet and embarrassment washes over me. I know I'm the color of a fire truck right now, but I ignore it and act inappropriately indignant anyway. Because that's my go-to when I've got no leg to stand on. "Whatever. If you're going to fire me for something that happened with him *before* he was a client, then I'll sue your ass, bro. And I would hate for my future niece or nephew to have to live in a cardboard box while I own your empire."

He cracks a smile. "You have such a smart mouth, you know that?"

"Maybe we'll get lucky and your child will inherit it," I say and wink before turning and exiting his office.

Sebastian is still sipping that damn smoothie. I slip behind the bar because I'm covering it while Sara teaches a Pilates class, and I start to clean up the area. It's pretty immaculate but the alternative is to turn around and just stare at him, and possibly drool, so cleaning it is.

"Come on…" he says to me cajolingly. "Tell me you thought about me. You know you did."

I pull my eyes from the sink where I'm scrubbing a nonexistent stain. "What are you even doing here? You must be a member at a gym somewhere already."

"What makes you say that?"

"The fact that I could bounce a quarter off your ass," I blurt out. "Or your pecs. Or your biceps."

"Ah, so you have been thinking about me." He winks. I fight another hot flush.

"Why are you working out here suddenly?"

"I'm not working out." He shrugs. "I'm doing yoga."

I give him a glare. He chuckles. "At least now I know how you were so flexible that night."

I blush instantly. It surprises him. "You're shy? Now?"

Yes, now. Because you've seen me half-naked and twisted up like a pretzel. And you're referring to it!

"I'm hardly shy." I look up, trying to give him a hard stare. He is sucking gently on his straw, his eyes twinkling. When he pulls away, a tiny dollop of the smoothie drips onto his bottom lip, and that tongue of his—the one I am intimately acquainted with—slips out to lick it up.

"You're purple," he whispers and grins triumphantly.

"I'm still hot from my workout," I lie and turn my back to him as I organize the trays of fresh fruit behind me.

"I have to get going. Gotta get to work," he says, and I nod without turning around. I wait but I don't hear him leave. Finally, I can't help but turn around. He's still sitting there, eyes glued to me. He shakes his empty smoothie cup and I reach out with just my arm to take it, keeping my body as far away as possible. Our fingers brush and he takes his other hand and wraps it around mine on the plastic cup. He tugs until I take a few steps forward. Now the only thing separating us is the granite bar top. He smiles. It makes me smile, but my knees are shaking.

"I thought about you, Shay," he says softly and then he lets go, jumps off the bar stool and walks toward the exit. I stand there watching his cute little butt leave, my hand suspended in midair holding his empty cup. I fight the insane urge to wrap my lips around the straw he'd been sucking on.

Chapter 6

Sebastian

Six hours later I'm leaning against the light post directly outside the front doors to the gym, waiting. The weather's unseasonably warm. Winter broke early in Seattle this year and it's already flip-flops and T-shirt weather in April. I've never been a fan of the rain here, but Seattle has brought me a lot of joy.

My mom met her new husband here, I have deep bonds with my teammates, the fans are great, Stephanie got clean here, I won a Cup here. I've actually started to think of Seattle more as my home than my hometown in New Brunswick or where I grew up in Quebec.

I play aimlessly with my phone as I wait and try not to stress. I don't usually do this, chase a girl. But she looked incredible this morning in yoga. And Audrey was so excited last night when she suggested I surprise Shay at work this morning. I was full of confidence, and a little whiskey, when I agreed. When I walked into the bar with Chooch I had no idea Audrey worked there. To be honest, I forgot I'd even met her at the gym opening.

We'd just gotten home from our road trip and I was wiped, but

Chooch was dealing with some relationships issues. He and his fiancée were not doing well and he didn't want to go home right away. He asked me to meet him near his house for a drink. Audrey recognized me and reintroduced herself. She was friendly and welcoming, even bought Chooch and me a round of drinks. I'd managed to bring the small talk around to Shayne without being pathetically obvious. Long after Chooch left, I was still there chatting to Audrey. And then her boyfriend, Josh, showed up and he recognized me. I had just hired Sutter Brothers Financial Group about four months ago and Josh works with Paul, my financial advisor. He'd seen me in the office and he knew I was a Winterhawk. He and Audrey both invited me to the barbeque.

How could I say no? Shay was all I had thought about on our road trip. I'd had more than my fair share of hookups in places a lot weirder than a gym laundry room. But there was something about doing that with Shay that made it somehow dirtier, sexier, hotter than I'd ever experienced. I think it was the conflict I could see on her face. She wanted me as much as I wanted her, but there was a glimmer of nervousness in her eyes that intrigued me. She was all smart mouth and tough words, but something soft and innocent was underneath. I really wanted to discover it.

Then this morning Shay mentioned her car was dead and I decided to be bold and just show up here and drive her to the party. I hadn't thought twice about it until I got here. Now I have nothing to do but wait and overthink this bold move. Will she be grateful for the lift? Will she think it's sweet? Stalkerish? Nah...she'll like the confidence, even if she won't admit it.

Still, when she saunters out of the building at 5:15 p.m., I'm actually nervous. She's changed out of the yoga pants and staff shirt and into a soft, black, strapless dress that reaches the sidewalk. She's got on a turquoise necklace and matching earrings and her long, wavy brown hair is loose. She makes my dick hard.

Shayne is digging in her bag, not watching where she's going, so I step right out in front of her, and she slams into me. I grab her by the waist to keep her from falling over as she bounces off my chest. The impact causes her sunglasses to tumble back off the top of her head, and I reach out with one hand and catch them behind her back before they shatter on the pavement.

"Good reflexes," she says in a stunned voice. I take the sunglasses and slide them gently on top of her head again. My other arm is still around her back, holding her to me. She doesn't attempt to step away.

"You should watch where you're going," I say is a hushed whisper as I stare down at her intently. My head is dipped, and hers is tilted up, so our foreheads are almost touching.

She blinks, regaining her composure. "You should watch where *you're* going."

"I knew exactly where I was going," I say and wink at her.

She frowns, slips her sunglasses over her eyes and speaks with an aloof tone. "I've got to go."

"Date?" I can't help but ask, even though I know the answer and that's not it.

"Plans," she replies evasively, and shrugs her tiny, tanned shoulders. I wish those sunglasses weren't covering her pretty gray eyes. They're the most expressive part of her, and right now I'd love to know what she's thinking.

"So how are you getting to those plans?" I ask as I lean back against the light pole again. "Someone picking you up?"

She laughs breathlessly and shakes her head. "Seattle has a very good public transit system, Frenchie."

She starts to walk down the sidewalk past me but I reach out and grab her wrist, spinning her back to face me. "You know what's better than city transit? My Aston Martin."

"If you're into pretentious vehicles that scream 'I have a small penis,' then yes, I guess it is better," she retorts, but she's letting me pull her toward the small parking lot where my car is.

I click the remote to unlock the doors, and then I pull open the passenger door and wink at her. "You didn't seem to have a problem with my size."

Her lips twitch at that, and she says simply, "The details are blurry. I don't remember much about it at all, really."

Ouch.

I motion toward the open car door, but she stands perfectly still and just stares at me. Is she really going to get on a bus instead of spending time with me? Really?! "I'll take you to your barbeque."

Her eyes grow wide. "How do you know where I'm going?"

"I called the psychic hotline," I quip back. When the only motion she makes is to cross her arms I add, "Get in the car and I'll explain on the way there. Promise."

She sighs heavily and takes a step toward the open passenger door. As she slips by me I whisper in her ear, "I remember every single second of that night."

"It was a long time ago," she mutters quietly but with a tone in her voice that says that bothers her. Good. That means she missed me, even though she won't admit it.

"I know. I'll explain that too. Eventually." I slip into the driver's seat and start the car and glance over at her. I swiftly veer out into traffic and hit the gas pedal. She glares at me through her sunglasses. "How do you know about the barbeque?"

"We have mutual friends," I reply.

"Who?"

"Relax, Shay, honey."

"My name is Shayne," she huffs.

"Whatever, Shay."

Chapter 7

Shayne

His middle name has got to be Arrogant Bastard because that's what he is. He's driving with this sexy little smirk on his lips and his eyes are sparkling and he's winked at me more than once and my God, when did arrogance start making me hot? I could bail on him—jump out of the car at the next stoplight...but I won't. I sat my ass in this delicious little sports car all by myself because I want to be here. But why does *he* want me here?

By getting in the car did I just give him the impression it's totally cool that we had sex, that I still don't know his last name, and that he just disappeared for twelve days afterward? Is he interested in me? If he is, then why did he disappear? Is this his attempt at another random hookup? If it is, will I give it to him? Is that what I do now?

No. It's not. I just hate public transit and I'm lazy after a long day of work and maybe, just maybe, if I spend more time around him, maybe this will be something...more. Is that possible? Am I being naïve? Would veteran one-night-standers scoff at my stupidity? "Seriously. Who told you about the barbeque?"

He drives like an Indy 500 champion—fast but in control. His eyes don't leave the road. And the smirk on his pretty little lips doesn't leave either. I sit staring at the cocky excuse for a smile, trying to decide if it angers me or creates that damn tingle.

"And how did you know I was going? I need to know which friend shares my personal business with strangers," I tell him in a clipped tone as I cross my arms like an angry teenager.

"The hosts of the party invited me. You know, your college roommate and her boyfriend," Sebastian replies flippantly. "They're great, by the way. It'll be your loss if you disown them."

"What?!" I'm beyond shocked. "Audrey invited you?"

He smirks at my reaction, glancing quickly over at me before taking a turn fairly fast. "Josh did. He was at the bar last night too, and I know him. From Sutter Brothers. I just didn't know he was dating Audrey. Small world, *n'est pas*?"

"I don't speak French," I mutter back. He knows Josh from Sutter Brothers? Josh works at one of the biggest wealth management companies in the Pacific Northwest. Does that mean Sebastian is also a financial advisor? Or is he one of their millionaire clients? I stare at the luxurious car I'm sitting in. Holy shit, I think he's a client.

"Does he manage your portfolio?" I ask, trying to sound casual. I don't care about money. I honestly don't. None of my boyfriends have had a ton of money…Mind you the last time I had a serious boyfriend was college. And I repeatedly turn down my parents' money. I could be living in a much nicer apartment, with a car that works, if I wanted to take their handouts. Seriously, money doesn't matter, but…did I just bang a millionaire?

Frenchie shakes his head. "No. His coworker Paul does. Do you know Paul? Oberman?"

I shake my head and swallow, but my throat is unexpectedly dry, and I cough. He slows the car to an acceptable residential speed as we pull off a main street and start through the more residential area that leads to the park.

"You're a millionaire?" I manage to choke out and instantly regret it. I probably sound like a gold digger or something.

He reaches over and pats my hand on my thigh. His smirk slips a little, but then he shrugs his broad shoulders. "Yeah."

"I thought you were an accountant or a lawyer or waiter or something." Seriously, why won't my mouth stop spitting out words? At least I managed to stop coughing.

"You sound disappointed." He is still smirking. I amuse him. Nifty.

"I don't care what you do for a living," I say airily, finally gaining control of my words and actions again. "It was a one-night stand."

"We'll see about that," he replies in a deep whisper filled with promise.

I bite my lip and turn and stare out the window. He slows as two kids run through a crosswalk holding dripping ice cream cones, and I smile. When I glance at him, he's smiling too, and it's not cocky, it's just pretty.

Just past a newly renovated apartment building he takes a left down a road that looks like a dead end. There are only a few homes on it, and then the road narrows to essentially a one-way—even though it's not—and the houses disappear. It's nothing but overgrown grass and weeds. The property technically belongs to the city, but no one maintains it like they do the other park areas. It's a popular place for locals because it's less touristy than the other areas around the lake.

Sebastian pulls over behind Josh's red SUV at the top of the hill. Other cars line the rest of the narrow roadway. He turns the car off and hurries around to help me out. I ignore his outstretched hand, haul myself out of the smooth, deep leather seat, and storm ahead to the picnic tables by the water.

I glance down the small rolling hill to the party. There are about a dozen people already here. They've set up chairs and towels on the long, slim strip where the grass gives way to sand by the edge of the lake. Josh and some other guy in a trucker hat whom I recognize as one of Josh's friends are placing rocks in a circle to enclose what will become a fire pit. I march toward Audrey, who's setting up camping chairs around the fire pit the boys are building. She's grinning at me like a fool.

"So, how was your day?" She winks at me.

"Fuck you, you traitorous whore," I say flatly and flop down in a chair.

"I see you found a ride." She wipes the condensation off the can of beer in her hand and flicks the water from her fingers at my face. It splatters all over my sunglasses.

As I remove them to clean them, I glance over my shoulder. Josh has jogged up to help Sebastian with the two coolers he's pulled from his trunk. I didn't realize he brought stuff. So now I'm the jerk who grabs a ride and abandons him. Perfect. I stand to go back up there, but with Josh's help he doesn't need me, so I allow myself to unabashedly admire the sight of Frenchie. He looks sexy as hell in his casual clothes. Just as sexy as he does in a suit. And in sweaty workout wear. His hair is an intricate, tousled mess, curling slightly at the ends. My fingertips tingle with the need to touch it. His hair was so soft and deceivingly thick when I held on to it that night while I came…

I give my head a shake to fight the heat rising in my body. "You should have warned me." I pull my gaze back to my best friend and give her a pointed stare.

"You said you didn't care if you ever saw him again," Audrey reminds me, shaking the water out of her dirty blond hair. "You said it was no big deal and you were over it."

I swallow. I did say that. A few nights ago when she came over for wine and *Scandal*. And clearly I was rather convincing. Or maybe not, judging by the devious glimmer in Audrey's brown eyes. I frown at her. "A heads-up would have been cool," I repeat firmly.

"So have you fucked him again yet?" she asks in a voice that is way too loud for my liking.

I shush her and frown. "Of course not! We just drove here."

"I'd fuck in that car," she replies with a shrug of her tiny shoulders, and I flip her the bird.

Suddenly there's a beer dangling in front of my face. I tip my head back and see Sebastian smiling down at me from behind my chair. "Something to cool off that hot little temper of yours, *ma belle*," Seb says softly as he gives the can a little tilt from side to side.

Butterflies take off from my belly and bounce off my rib cage. My hormones are clearly ignoring the memo my brain sent regarding this matter. I stand, turn to face him, and take the beer from him. He's cracked it already. I tilt my head skeptically and switch the cans, giving him the one he offered me and taking the one he just sipped from.

"You could have roofied this one," I explain. "You can never be too safe."

With that I leave him standing there, his mouth hanging open. Audrey laughs and I hear Josh say, "Yeah, 'cause Sebastian has so much trouble finding a chick that he has to drug them."

I ignore them all and stomp over to where a few friends are playing volleyball.

Chapter 8

Sebastian

Two can play at this game, I remind myself as I watch Shayne. She's sitting on the top of the picnic table, legs crossed under her dress, while some dude in a trucker hat talks her ear off as she eats carrot sticks with ranch dip off her plate.

She's been talking to him, and only him, for the last hour. The sun is quickly setting and the whole lake is reflecting golden light from the pink-and-gold sunset and it's making her look even hotter. And naturally that's making me nuts. Josh started a fire. Audrey is pulling out marshmallows and hunting down sticks. The air is still muggy and warm, and my mood is making me even hotter under the collar.

It's one thing for her to brush me off. I mean, I guess I kind of deserve it since I haven't explained why I've been MIA for almost two weeks. I really want to, but I can't tell her I'm a hockey player just yet, and I haven't figured out how to lie without really lying. I could say I was on a business trip, which is technically true, but what if she asks me what I do? I've already admitted I have money, which is also not a lie, so she's probably curious how I earn it.

I have to tell her what I do, but I want to get back to what we were that first night. And I'm not just talking about the sex part. I'm talking about the way she smiled at me, the way she flirted. The excitement in her eyes. I want to bring that out again. I want her to feel that again so she's willing to make an exception to her silly hockey hate thing.

The douche in the trucker hat leans down and whispers something in her ear. Shayne tips her head back to laugh, but when she rights herself, her eyes find mine. And I am suddenly very certain she wants me to see this. I stand up from the camping chair I'm sitting on by the fire and walk right up to a blonde I met earlier named Carly. She made it clear that she was interested in me earlier with the way she flipped her short blond hair and begged me to be her volleyball partner.

"So how'd you do out there?" I ask, and nod my head toward the sandy makeshift volleyball court.

"We lost." She frowns and then puts her hand on my chest. "But I would have won if you'd been my partner!"

I glance over to where my new friend Josh, who was her partner, is standing staring at us. He heard everything. I give him a quick "sorry, bud" look and he shrugs. I look down at her and give her my best puppy dog face.

"I wanted to play," I say, making sure my voice is soft and deep, the way I talk to sports reporters after a tough loss, because chicks have told me they love that. "But I'll let you in on a little secret..."

I let my sentence trail off and hold my breath as I glance around as if to make sure no one is paying attention, when in fact I'm making sure I have Shayne's full attention. My eyes catch hers briefly, and she quickly looks away, which means she's riveted to my little scene. I bend so my head is right next to the blonde's ear, and I use my hand not holding a beer to push her chin-length hair back so I'm right against her ear. "I'm kind of injured."

As I pull back her big blue eyes flare and her hand moves from my chest to my elbow. She squeezes it sympathetically. "Oh my God, really?"

Her voice got louder so I shush her, and I notice Shayne isn't even pretending not to pay attention anymore. "Nothing serious, just a strained tendon in my wrist, but we start playoffs soon so I need to be careful," I say quietly, because I haven't told anyone—except the trainers and my coach.

"What happened? Did you fall on it on the ice or did someone hit you with a stick or something? What do they call that? Slashing, I think?" I nod, and she smiles like she thinks she's a genius for figuring it out.

I smile and try not to think about the fact that the team doctor looked a little more concerned yesterday than I would have liked. "No big deal, I shouldn't miss any games. I landed a punch wrong in a fight. Just bad luck."

She nods and lifts her red Solo cup to her lips, taking a sip before smiling at me and batting her eyes. "Maybe your luck will change tonight?"

I watch her walk away, back over to her gaggle of girlfriends by the shore. Wow. That's too easy. But I want Shayne. Only Shayne.

I glance over at her, and she's staring right back at me. She says something to Trucker Hat, jumps off the table and makes her way over to the fire—right where I'm standing. She stops half a foot from me, her eyes set on the crackling fire in front of us.

"Hope you brought a condom, Frenchie," she murmurs, still looking at the fire.

"You don't have one in your bra this time?"

Even in the low light I can see the red flush on her cheeks that that comment is causing. God, I fucking love making this girl blush. As always, she recovers much more quickly than I'd like.

She steals a glance at me and subtly points to Carly with the index finger wrapped around her beer. "She looks like she's got more STDs than IQ points."

"At least she's not in a trucker hat," I retort and snort a little in disgust. "Make sure he double bags it."

She can't keep a straight face at that comment. She cracks a grin and I grin back. She's got one hell of a smile. It's like it starts in her toes and pulls up her entire body. It's honestly contagious. I lean toward her. "Oh, and by the way, next time you stock up on condoms, make sure to buy Magnum. That one the other night was a little tight."

"Wet Hide and Go Seek!" Audrey yells from the water's edge.

A roar erupts and people start peeling out of their clothes. I look to Shay for some indication of what the hell that means. She turns her back to me and yanks her dress down, leaving it in a pile on the grass. She's in nothing now but a coral strapless bikini, and the sight makes my jaw drop so low I'm surprised it's not hitting the sand. I watch her step out of her flip-flops and take a few steps toward Trucker Hat, who is beckoning me from the shore.

Then Shay and everyone else on the beach except for Josh, who is counting down loudly from fifty with his back to the shore, is running into the water.

I don't want to be left behind so I yank my shirt over my head, drop my keys and my cell, kick out of my shoes and run for the water. It's fucking cold! But I would follow Shay and her coral bikini into the Arctic if I had to, so I clench my teeth and keep wading in.

Shay's stopped to pull her hair up. Trucker Hat hasn't bothered to wait for her, thankfully. I run toward her, water splashing up around me, and I give her ass a tiny smack as I blow by her and dive under. When I pop back up I turn toward her. She's a shadow now, but when I hear her say, "Fucking Frenchie!" I know she's smiling and I smile back

She's slowly sinking deeper and deeper into the water and I can see her wincing at the cold as she does it. I swim over and reach out and grab her hand and yank her forward until the water is up to her shoulders. She squeals, but it sounds like a delighted squeal. The kind of squeal my dick wanted to make as soon as she dropped that dress and revealed that tiny bikini. I keep hold of her arm and pull her as I swim deeper into the lake, away from Trucker Hat.

"So what the fuck are we doing?" I ask her, because I don't know what Wet Hide and Seek is. When everyone ran to the lake I just followed along.

"We've been playing this for years. Started in college. We used to get drunk and hop the fence at the outdoor pool on campus. The lights are always off at night and it's pitch-black, like this," she explains, and she keeps swimming with me even though I've let go of her arm. "The goal is for everyone to 'hide' in the water. Because it's so dark, you can't see a thing. The person counting has to swim out and, by feel and sound only, try and find people. You can swim around or stay put. It's ridiculously juvenile but somehow also incredibly fun."

I can barely touch the bottom of the lake now, so I'm sure she can't. Something brushes by my foot, probably some lake plant or maybe a fish, but when it brushes by her she squeals again and splashes backward into the water. I'm on her instantly, pressing a wet hand to her mouth as she finds her footing.

"Shh! Josh's almost done counting," I warn her.

She bites down on my palm. I swallow a yelp and yank my hand away. "Since when do you like it rough?"

"One lightning-fast quickie and you think you know anything about what I like?" she says and turns and starts to swim away from me, toward the long dock that juts out into the water from the left side of the half-moon beach.

I easily swim along behind her. She reaches the dock and raises her arms, bobbing up in the water so her hands can grab onto the wooden planks above her. She steadies herself just as Josh yells out, "Ready or not here I come, bitches!"

I tread water directly in front of where she's hanging from the dock. My eyes are level with her stomach, I think, but there's not enough light to be sure. I want to reach out and touch her, but I want to do it with my tongue, so I refrain completely.

"You know your attitude is making this lake even colder," I whisper to her quietly. I can't see her but I can hear her breathing. "If you aren't careful, it's going to freeze over."

She doesn't say anything for a minute, and then another blast of cold air. "I'm sorry if you're used to more fawning or stalking or something after a fling."

The water ripples around me so I know she moved, and I hear the wood creek from the dock. Did she let go or just adjust her position? Is she swimming away? But then she speaks, and her voice is still coming from in front of me. "Would you like me to create an I Slept with Frenchie Facebook page?"

There's more attitude inside her than there is blood or oxygen. And I fucking couldn't be more turned on right now. "I was out of town," I say, because even though the snark is hot, I need to clear the air.

"What?"

"I left the morning after we met," I explain quietly into the darkness. "And I got back last night."

"Oh."

"And since you disappeared as soon as you climaxed, I had no way of contacting you until this morning." I go on swimming a little closer to where I think she is. "Until I took your little stretching class."

"Yoga, not stretching. And you should take a few more. You've got the flexibility of a rock," she mutters.

She stops talking as we watch a shadow, most likely Josh, swim in the other direction and someone else flail and scream as he catches them. It sounds like Audrey.

"Now she'll join Josh and hunt the rest of us down," Shay whispers.

When we're sure that their splashes are getting farther away, we resume our conversation.

"Do you have a boyfriend?" I ask bluntly.

"You think I slept with you when I had a boyfriend?"

"I think you're a sexy, smart, beautiful woman who bends in yoga pants in front of men all day," I reply calmly. "So it's possible in the last twelve days you found someone else to lock in the laundry room."

She laughs at that. It's soft but I can hear it and it makes me smile. "You were my last fluff-and-fold."

"So you're single?" I move closer—very slowly so as to not disturb the water and draw attention.

"Yes."

"Because you had the most amazing sexual experience of your life in a laundry room a few week ago and now everyone else would be a disappointment." I say it like it's a statement of fact and not a guess.

"Frenchie, your ego is out of control," she whispers, but she's almost breathless.

"I have to believe it was amazing for you," I tell her, the anonymity of the pitch-black making it easy. "Because it was amazing for me."

She says nothing. Not a word. I reach out and find her bare stomach hanging in front of me. I touch her hips, feeling the edge of her bikini bottoms. Her breath hitches. I hear it. I'm about to pull her down and into a kiss when she hisses. "Someone is swimming this way!"

I slip under the dock with her. I reach up and grab the boards above me, right next to her, and inch a little deeper under the dock. She moves with me. We're hanging side by side almost midway under the dock when suddenly there's a small splash and a hand swings out inches from us. Someone giggles. It's Audrey. She pauses in front of us. Her arm reaches out again, barely missing my stomach, and then she gives up and turns and swims away.

When I know she won't hear the movement in the water, I move forward with my hands, then let go of the dock with my left and swing around so I'm hanging directly in front of Shay, facing her. I can make out the outline of her face and body at this close proximity. My injured wrist is starting to ache but I don't give a fuck.

"You know all the right lines," she says, and she sounds annoyed.

"With you there are no lines," I tell her honestly.

"Shut the fuck up," she hisses, but I can feel the smile in her voice.

"Make me."

It happens so fast I don't really know what's going on. She swings her body forward and lets go of the dock. Her arms hit my shoulders and her legs wrap around my waist. She's not trying to kiss me; she's trying to drown me! She's not heavy, but with my gimp wrist, I can't hold us up, and we plunge under the water.

Submerged in the cold lake, I cup her ass briefly and pull her into me, knowing damn well she can feel my mostly hard dick pressed against the space between her legs, and then I bite her shoulder lightly before letting go, pushing away and breaking the water's surface. I feel Josh's big hand slam down on me as soon as I'm up.

"Gotcha!" he bellows.

I lunge forward and my hand makes contact with the back of Shayne's head as she breaks the surface of the water. "Gotcha!"

"Damn it!" she bellows, and Josh and I laugh.

Chapter 9

Shayne

It's late and everyone is finally packing up and going home. I should too. I have to work tomorrow *and* I need to wake up extra early so that I can take the bus, since I never did get my car to a mechanic. My eyes find Sebastian sitting across the campfire. That blonde is talking to him and he's nodding every now and then, but his eyes are looking straight forward, over the dying flames and right at me. He winks at me. I roll my eyes at him and act annoyed, but oh my God, I want him so badly it's making me squirm. I stand up and instantly rub my arms. It's cold away from the warmth of the dying embers. I glance over at Audrey, who is packing up her cooler with Josh.

"Can I grab a lift home?" I ask her.

She glances up at me and smiles, her eyes sliding from me to Sebastian. "Hey, Seb! Shay needs a lift home. Can you help her out?"

"Audrey! I meant—"

"Of course!" Sebastian says easily, and he starts to stand. "That's what friends are for!"

"Naked friends," Audrey adds so only I can hear, and I slap the air in her general direction.

Sebastian walks over and casually drops an arm over my shoulders. "Hey, buddy! Ready to go?"

I heave a giant, agitated sigh and try to shrug out of him, but I fail as his hand grips my shoulder tightly to hold me in place. "Oh, and Sebastian," Audrey says as she starts to walk toward Josh's SUV. "She'll probably need a lift to work tomorrow morning, so maybe you should just spend the night."

"Audrey!" I snap, my face flushing instantly. I throw my empty beer can at her.

She dodges it and laughs. "Call me tomorrow, Shaynie!"

I raise my middle finger at her even though she can't see it in the dark. Refusing to acknowledge the cocky smirk I *know* must be on Sebastian's face, I finally peel out of his arm and retrieve my empty beer can and throw it in the garbage. Sebastian pours the rest of his on the fire, extinguishing it completely. I glance around subtly and am relieved to find Carly, his blond admirer, seems to be gone. I was worried he would drive her home too. At least now I know he's going to take me home and not fuck her in his car immediately afterward.

Unless he heads to her place after he drops you off, my brain reminds me. It's not unimaginable to me because it's happened to me. My first college boyfriend, Dustin, used to drop me off early after dates claiming he was tired from hockey practice and then spend all night at sorority parties picking up girls. I push down the uncomfortable thought and turn to where Sebastian is dumping the ice from one of his coolers onto the now-dead fire. He looks up as I grab my bag off the picnic table and pick up his other cooler. He smiles. It's not the cocky, smartass smile I'm used to. It's softer, gentler, more humble. I like it just as much as his cocky one.

"You going to tell me where you live or should I just drive aimlessly around the city?" he asks me softly as he loads the coolers into the trunk.

"Head west. I'll talk you through it," I reply and walk to the passenger door.

He opens my door and then walks around and gets in the car. Wow, his game is on point. He can play the flirt, the cocky egomaniac and the gentleman. I'm sure he figures one of these personas will work on me, but I'm not like other girls. I try to ignore the pointed little voice in the back of my head that says I've already given in to him, just like other girls, and that I want to give in to him again. Because damn it, he's hot. And he wasn't blowing me off. He was out of town. He could be lying to me, but my life is generally a series of badly timed events so I can totally believe I met the hottest man on the planet the day before he got on a plane.

He starts the car and begins down the narrow, dark street. I keep stealing glances at him while he drives, when the occasional streetlight illuminates his profile. His hair is wavy from the lake water, and he's got significant five o'clock shadow happening on his strong jaw.

"So how are you a millionaire?" I can't help but ask.

"Guess."

"Dot-com? You invented a popular website? An annoying app that the kids are obsessed with?" I say partly joking.

He chuckles and it's so deep and sexy I feel it between my legs. "'The kids'? What are you, eighty years old? In your day did you walk to school uphill in a snowstorm in bare feet?"

Now it's my turn to laugh. When we're both quiet, he shakes his head. "Not a dot-com."

I stare at the dark road ahead. "Trust fund? You're parents are rich, so you don't have to do anything but gym, tan, laundry all day every day."

He makes a face like he ate something rotten. "No trust fund. I earned my money."

He has a proud tone to his voice, and it makes me even hornier for him. I may not care about money, but I do care that whomever I date is a self-made man. I mean, not that I'm dating him. Because I'm not. He hasn't even asked me on a date. He might not...

"So what then?" I demand.

"Nah. I like this game. You're going to have to earn it," he says firmly. "Keep guessing."

Chapter 10

Sebastian

Right on Frey," she murmurs as I drive, taking a break from our little guessing game. So far she's guessed internet mogul, trust fund baby, international spy, French winery owner and porn star. That one I took as a compliment.

I nod and turn the car as directed. It's risky letting her guess, in case she says professional athlete, but I also like the way she's getting flustered and slightly annoyed. There is something about keeping her off balance that I find ridiculously addictive. I'm totally shocked that she agreed to let me drive her home, because she's been nothing short of an ice queen all night. Except for about a second in the lake, but that came and went so quickly I'm not even sure it was real.

"So how come you didn't ask Trucker Hat for a lift home?" I can't help but ask.

"Not interested," she replies lightly with a shrug. "And before you say something snarky, remember, I didn't ask you to drive me home either."

"But you didn't object," I remind her. She frowns, points left and I turn.

She sighs like she's disappointed and points to my right. "The tall one on the left at the end."

"This is…an interesting area," I tell her and gently do a U-turn so I can park against the sidewalk next to her building.

"It's not as sketchy as it looks," she murmurs as we watch a guy with a shopping cart full of cans go by across the street and turn into an alley.

I raise an eyebrow at her. She shrugs. "It's affordable and clean. And I'm hardly ever out at night anyway. Sorry we can't all live in Capital Hill."

"I don't live in Capital Hill," I correct her with a smile. "I almost bought over there, but they wouldn't let me merge three units into one. Had to move into a place closer to the water."

She laughs softly next to me. "The tragedies of being a billionaire are endless, aren't they?"

"I'm not a billionaire," I argue and feel a little weird, like I always do, when my paycheck comes up. It's mind-blowing that I make the money I do, but I work my ass off for it. Inside, though, I'm still that goofy kid who grew up in a three-bedroom, hundred-year-old house with a leaky roof in rural Quebec. The kid who had to mow neighbors' lawns in the summer and shovel their driveways in the winter to afford new hockey equipment. "My place here, though, is pretty sweet. Just finished renovations a couple months ago. You should come see it. But you have to take off your shoes at the door. And, you know, the rest of your clothes."

I see her eyes flare, and she covers her face with her hands. I laugh. "Again with the shy thing!" I reach over and gently pull her hands from her face.

"How come you didn't drive Blondie home?" she asks me out of nowhere.

"Same reason you didn't ask Trucker Hat for a lift. Not interested," I tell her and then drop my eyes and look at her hand in my lap. I squeeze it lightly, willing her to get the connection—that I chose to drive her because I *am* interested.

"I should go," she says quietly, with the slightest tremble in her voice that tells me she really doesn't want to go. "I have to work in the morning."

"And I have to work out in the morning," I reply and turn my head to meet her eyes. In the weak light from the street they look pale gray. Her hand pushes the door open but she doesn't move to leave. I stare at her and lick my lips before taking the final shot.

"So do you want me to drive you to work tomorrow?" I ask, trying to keep my voice flat and nonchalant. "Since your car is still out of commission."

"That would be…convenient." She swallows and her eyelashes flutter ever so slightly. "But you would have to get up extra early to get here. I need to be there by eight thirty."

"Yeah…" Here goes nothing…or something…"Well, if I stayed here, instead of going home, that would save me some time."

She smirks, but I don't smirk back because I'm not just trying to flirt here. I am full-on propositioning her. Her smirk slips into something softer and sexier. "That's probably the sensible option."

If my dick had arms, it would be high-fiving me right now.

Chapter 11

Shayne

I feel like I'm in a dream as I open the door of my building and usher him inside. Sebastian, my mysterious French one-night stand, is here. With me. In my apartment. I've wanted this to happen again for the last twelve days. I've dreamt about it—not figuratively like daydreaming but actual hot, unconscious sex dreams about us having another incredible night.

But does this mean something? Is this just another random hookup and he'll disappear for another two weeks? Does he want this to be more, or is he looking for a bed buddy? Am I ready to be a bed buddy? Do I have what it takes to fuck without emotion? Because I did feel something more than an orgasm last time. He's all I've thought about since. If he does simply want a bed buddy, will I do it? Are the orgasms worth it? Should I turn around right now and tell him to just go home? Or throw some blankets on the couch and lock my bedroom door?

"Something is wrong," he says softly as we climb the stairs to the top of the four-story building. "You're too quiet."

"I'm just trying to figure out why I've invited a stranger to spend the night in my house," I confess, because why the hell not. "And what we're doing."

I steal a glance at him. He's smiling playfully as he says cheekily, "Stranger, huh? Don't worry, I'm not a serial killer and I'll only tie you up if you ask me to."

Okay, so he didn't exactly answer me, but damn, now I'm thinking about being tied up by him. That might be hot…

We hit the fourth-floor landing and walk down the hall to my front door. I open it and hold it for him to enter. He walks in and waits in the hall, kicking off his shoes, as I lock the door behind us and walk into the living room. I flip on a tall floor lamp in the corner. The room illuminates, and Sebastian blinks and shoves his hands in his pockets, glancing around.

"Nice place," he admits sheepishly.

"Thanks." I give him a quick smile and as we stand there staring at each other, I decide to turn on the snark before it gets awkward. "So do you want to sleep on the couch? It's a pull-out and it's got a new mattress."

He tilts his head just a little and cocks an eyebrow as if to say *are you kidding me?* "No. I don't want to sleep on the couch."

"The floor? I have a camping mattress I can dig out of storage." I bite my lip to keep from smiling.

"No."

"Do you hang by your toes from the ceiling like a bat?"

He lets out a whoosh of air, a smile playing on those lips I am lusting after. "I sleep in beds. Only beds. Do you have a spare bedroom?"

I shake my head. He steps forward and grabs my hand and shrugs. "Then it looks like we're sharing."

He's pulling me toward my bedroom. Roy, my cat, stares at us with judgment as we pass him where he's sprawled on the back of the couch. I give him a glare right back. Maybe if I hadn't gotten him fixed, he wouldn't be so judgey.

Once in the bedroom, Sebastian flips on the lamp on my night table and promptly pulls his shirt over his head. I openly gape at him. His chest is beautiful. That soft, sexy smattering of chest hair and smooth skin spread tight over his rippled stomach and wide, muscled shoulders and back. Flawless except for a scar on his right shoulder. He must have had surgery for an injury. Even though he was shirtless in the river earlier, I couldn't see him clearly. And in the laundry room when we were half clothed everything happened so quickly it was a blur. Tonight I intend to blatantly drink in every ounce of him so I can remember it in case it doesn't happen again.

"What?" he asks innocently as I try to avoid drooling. "I don't sleep in a shirt."

He playfully tosses it at me. It hits me in the chest and I catch it. An idea comes to life in my evil little head. I yank down my dress and let it pool at my feet. I've still got my bathing suit on but it doesn't stop him from raking his eyes very slowly and heavily over my body. I pretend not to notice, but I feel a tingle that sweeps my body with the path of his cobalt blue eyes. I pull his shirt over my head and slip my arms through the sleeves.

"I *do* sleep in a shirt," I say and smile triumphantly.

He's amused. I can tell by his smirk, but he cocks an eyebrow. "And a bathing suit?"

I reach under the shirt, twist my hands behind my back and undo my bandeau top. It falls to the floor. Then, carefully, making sure the shirt covers all the parts facing him, I wiggle out of the bottoms.

He's watching me intently and undoing his shorts at the same time. I gaze at him a moment longer than I should, drinking in how fantastically sculpted his upper body is and that sexy inverted triangle of muscles that leads below his navel and around his hips. My mouth actually waters.

He drops his shorts and doesn't even begin to hide the bulge I can clearly see in his black boxer briefs. I act like I don't see it—I should win a fucking Academy Award—and then I turn to my dresser and pull out a pair of my undies to slip on. I pick a pretty pale pink lace pair that are for going out, not sleeping. But in this case, I will make an exception.

I turn back to him, placing my butt against the dresser so when I bend to slip the panties on he doesn't get an eyeful. But when I glance up, it's me who gets an eyeful. Sebastian is now completely naked. My mouth hangs open and I stand up, panties hanging, forgotten, from my hand.

"I sleep naked." He shrugs, smiling, completely immodest.

"Frenchie…" I whisper his nickname so softly I don't know if he hears it. I swallow and say in a louder, steadier voice, "You're not going to be sleeping tonight."

And there it is. I chose instant gratification—and the consequences be damned. I drop my panties on the ground and start toward him, climbing on top of my platform bed on my knees. He does the same and meets me in the middle of the mattress. His hands reach for the bottom of his shirt I'm wearing and slowly, gently, he pulls it up over my head.

"Then you won't be needing this," he whispers before dipping his head, cupping my jaw and connecting our lips.

Suddenly it's like we're in a race and someone shot the starting gun. We attack each other. My hands fly up into that glorious hair—it's as soft and thick as I remember. Sebastian's arms wrap around my back, and he grabs two big fistfuls of my bare ass. Our tongues are battling too, our lips fused together.

Our bodies are pressed flat against each other from the knees up and Sebastian's hard cock is pressing firmly into my abdomen; I fight the urge to whimper. I take one hand from his hair, move it between us, and wrap my fingers around his cock. His body tightens and relaxes in a nanosecond, as he pushes his hips into me, moving his erection in my grip.

"Shay...I want you so fucking bad." There's no snark or attitude, just lust deepening his voice. "Last time blew my fucking mind. I get hard every time I think about it. And I think about it a lot. You do too. Admit it."

I make a noise. It's supposed to be a *yes,* but it's more of a moan because his hands have left my ass and are cupping my breasts. His strong fingers are tugging and rolling my nipples and it's creating ripples of pleasure that are rolling down my spine and pooling between my legs. I work my hand around his cock. It's just as long and thick as I remember. And I can't wait to feel overwhelmed and almost split in half like I did in the laundry room. My pressure is firm but gentle, and I rub my thumb over his leaking tip on every pass, which causes him to push into me harder each time. One of his hands moves up to the base of my neck and the other one moves south, over my pubic bone and down. His index finger travels right down the middle of the cleft between my legs.

He smiles into the kiss. "You missed me too."

"Maybe." I nip his collarbone.

He moves his hand from the wetness he discovered and wraps it around my back, pressing me right up against him and forcing my hand to abandon its work. With a quickness I don't anticipate and his strength, which I always underestimate, he flips me down onto the mattress. I'm midsqueal when his tongue takes up residence in my mouth again.

He's got one thigh between my legs, his hands pressed into the bed on either side of my head. I wrap my hands back into that gorgeous fucking hair of his as he uses his arms to drag his body upward, his muscular thigh grinding against my sex on its way up.

I will not groan. Not first. No way.

My hands slip down his back, nails grazing lightly over his flesh, until they reach his ass and then I grab on—hard. His mouth covers mine again and I pull him upward, causing his thigh to rub my aching pussy once again. He smiles into the kiss so I bite his bottom lip.

"Admit it…you want a repeat of that night as badly as I do," he says and dips his head, using his tongue to make a trail up my neck and toward my ear.

"Please say you have one of those Magnums you bragged about."

He lifts his head and then his body again. That rock-hard, beautiful thigh makes glorious contact against my clit again and this time I buck my hips to keep the friction going as long and hard as I can. I move my hand back down to his cock and wrap my fingers around it again. This time I use my other hand to cup his balls, and when I pump his dick I squeeze "the boys." His sky blue eyes actually roll back in his head. I grin triumphantly and do it again. And again.

Chapter 12

Sebastian

I will not be the first to moan. No fucking way. She is the type of girl who will never let me live it down.

I push up on my arms and away from her. She lets go of my cock and balls because she has to, but as soon as her fingers are gone I really want to moan—my discontent. I gaze down at her. She's grinning and her face is flushed, and her eyes are like charcoal pools. Her dark hair is fanned out above her head in waves. She's beautiful. I want to take it slow suddenly. I want to savor her and whisper confessions in her ear, like how much I thought about her on my road trip. But I know this isn't the time. Tonight, her impatience and her grin and her attitude are telling me she wants to cut to the chase.

I lean over the side of the bed and dig in my wallet for the condom I had the good sense to bring. I tear the package open with my teeth and quickly roll the condom on. I can't remember the last time I was this turned on. Oh, right, in the laundry room at Elevate Fitness.

Before I can lie back down on top of her, she's up on her knees in front of me again. Her delicate hand snakes its way around the back of my head and into my hair, and as she kisses me I grab her waist and yank her up into my lap. She's up high on her knees, her face tilted down toward me as I sit back on my heels. She moves her knees so she's straddling me. Holding tight to her narrow hips, I start to push her down on my cock.

My mouth falls open and my head tilts back a bit and a moan—loud, clear and wanting—rumbles out of me. I think she's moaning too, but I don't even fucking care anymore if I'm breaking first. She's so fucking tight and warm and wet, and I want her to know how much I adore it.

When her butt reaches my lap and I'm fully sheathed in her perfect, sweet pussy I find my words. She's breathing heavily, her pretty tits heaving in front of me. She opens her eyes and we stare at each other. Her expression changes. It's not guarded or wary or wry like it usually is. She looks soft and vulnerable and even more gorgeous than ever before.

"You feel even better than I remember," I confess, and I splay my hands across her naked back, pulling her to me in almost a hug. Her face curls toward my neck, and I feel her tongue trace a path up to my ear. She lifts her hips; I slide out of her just a little bit.

Before she can slide back down onto me I jerk my hips up—hard—and push up into her. She gasps. With my arms crossed around her back, I reach up and hold her shoulders as I move, pushing up and down, up and down. She may be on top, but I'm riding her instead of her riding me. And then there it is—a moan. Soft and low and filled with desire and need. Hearing her break feels as good as an overtime goal.

"Sebastian..." she gasps and holds tighter to me, wrapping her arms around my neck. It's so soft and needy and *oh my God, I'm going to come.*

I pinch my eyes closed and stop. Freeze completely still and force images of my grandmother into my mind. Shayne either doesn't know what I'm doing or knows exactly what I'm doing and wants me to fail because she keeps moving her hips.

Grandma! Grandma! Grandma!

I bite her shoulder. "No, you don't."

I flip her so she's flat on her back, managing to keep my dick inside her. She's smiling at me.

"Didn't like that position, Frenchie?" she asks in mock innocence.

"Liked it too much," I admit and reach for her leg. My hand cups the back of her toned calf and I haul her right leg up over my shoulder before dipping down to hover over her. "Mmm," I say, appreciating her flexibility before giving her a little thrust. "Yoga is good for something."

She giggles at that and wraps her free leg around the backs of my thighs. I thrust into her again. And again. I find a rhythm quickly. She likes it and I feel her back arch just the slightest. I drop down onto my elbows so my body is even closer to her. When I thrust this time, I roll my hips up, arching my own back a little to make sure my pubic bone rolls right over her clit.

Shay whimpers and her back curls this time, bringing her clit in closer contact on the next pass. She loved this position last time and nothing has changed. As my balls start to tingle and my stomach clenches, I realize I fucking love it too.

"Come, baby," I beg softly.

"Ah!" She grabs my head and kisses me as she orgasms. With her pussy clenching hard around me and her soft velvety tongue in my mouth I come. Hard.

Chapter 13

Shayne

When I wake up, the sun is softly filtering in through my gauzy white curtains. I'm on my back. Sebastian is on his side, facing me, his left arm and leg draped over me. I feel both elated and panicked at the same time. Or actually in succession. I'm elated because, damn, last night was satisfying and fun, but also panicked because I have no idea what comes next.

I turn my head to look at him while he sleeps. His brown hair is curling and sticking up everywhere. His long, thick, dark golden brown lashes flutter ever so slightly with every deep breath and I swear to God he's smiling just the slightest. I may never see this sight again so I drink it in and try to sear it into my memory. My hand gently grazes over his cheek, the stubble tickling my fingertips.

Here in the early morning quiet, without his smug smile or cocky stare taunting me, I can admit he is the most beautiful man I've ever known. It makes my heart clench and desire pool between my legs at the exact same time. As my fingers slip toward his pretty mouth, he kisses my fingertips, letting me know he's awake.

"Morning," I whisper.

"*Good* morning," he emphasizes.

"Great night."

"Hell yes." He laughs and uses his arm draped over my stomach to pull me so I'm on my side facing him. His eyes finally open. They're a little less pale and icy this morning, the gray circle around the outside darker than usual.

"You have to go to work soon, don't you?" he asks.

"Not too soon," I reply and move closer to him.

His hand slips down my back to my bare ass, and his lips graze mine. The graze turns into a light kiss, which turns into a deep kiss. He rolls onto his back, taking me with him so I'm lying on top of him. Instantly I feel his hard length pressed in between us. We keep kissing. Long, deep invasions of each other's mouths. The heat of both our bodies increases and my core starts to ache. I want him this morning as much as I did last night.

"I suck," he groans suddenly into the kiss. I pull back a little and look down at him. He looks guilty and almost shameful. "I only brought one condom."

I blink. Is he fucking serious? "When have you ever just slept with someone once in one night?"

He looks a little shocked. "Lots of times, actually. You're the exception, Shay, not the rule."

My heart does a backflip. Sebastian runs a hand through my hair, tucking it behind me ear. "Do you have any?"

I shake my head. He looks devastated, and I take it as a supreme compliment. It makes me feel incredibly confident. I smile deviously at him.

"You do suck," I agree and start to move down his body, under the duvet. "Lucky for you I suck too."

"Shayyyyyyyyy." He holds the *y* until my mouth on his hard shaft strangles his voice.

I lick him from balls to tip and then cover the entire tip with my lips. I suck and pull off him and then do it again, moving a little lower, taking more of him into my mouth. And then a little lower again. With every tight, wet pull off of his beautiful dick, he groans. One of his hands finds my hair and the other pushes the duvet down so he can watch me work. I decide to stop teasing and the next time my lips cover him, I slide all the way down his shaft, enveloping him in the warm wet that is my mouth.

"Fuck, yes," he hisses and pushes up into me.

I have to fight the urge to gag. He's so damn big! "Sorry, baby," he whispers sensing my slight discomfort.

I start to move in a rhythm, sucking hard and making sure my tongue swirls all around him and my hand around his base works him at the same pace and pressure. I'm proud at how quickly he goes off, like a bomb, in my mouth. I swallow every ounce and slowly pull my mouth away. I look up and his head is pushed back into the pillow. His cheeks are pink and he's got one hand against his forehead as he struggles to find air. I grin and flop down beside him.

"Damn," he whispers with a self-conscious chuckle. "You make me a quick shooter."

"If you'd brought another condom, we could have worked on building up your stamina."

"Next time I'll bring two or three," he says with a grin. "Boxes."

I laugh. The fact that he said "next time" makes me want to do a victory lap around the bedroom. My alarm beeps from the night table.

"Ugh. Work." I turn it off and pull myself out of bed, tugging the sheet so it comes with me.

"Need someone to scrub your back?" he asks, pushing himself up on his elbows and giving me an unobstructed view of his defined chest all the way down to his hips where the duvet is pooled around him.

"I would take you up on that, but I'm fairly certain it would lead to other activities that will make me late for work," I tell him. "Trey will fire me."

"I'll find you another job." He winks.

Unfortunately, I've got to get in that shower because if I'm late again, Trey will lose his ever-loving mind. I leave Sebastian alone in my bed.

Chapter 14

Sebastian

Her hair is still damp, and she's twisted it up into one of those half-bun, half-ponytail things girls do that look messy and perfect at the same time. She's in black capri yoga pants with a band of teal blue fabric around her tiny waist and a teal Lycra tank top. She's carrying her workout bag and a bright pink hoodie.

I stand by her front door and try not to get a hard-on as I check out her ass in those pants. Jordan was right: whoever created yoga pants is a genius. He should know, since his wife is a physical therapist and lives in them. Shayne heads to the small, round glass dining room table and pulls a banana and two shiny red apples out of the fruit bowl. I smirk. "Don't eat that banana in the car. It'll distract the fuck out of me."

She suppresses a giggle and smiles, tossing me one of the apples. "This banana is a piece of cake. I've had much bigger things in my mouth just this morning."

I fight a flush, and a wave of blood flies to my groin on that comment. She starts toward me. Just as she's about to pass me and reach for the front door, I push her up against the wall and kiss her. She tastes like toothpaste and cherry lip gloss.

She pulls back, tasting the toothpaste in my mouth too. "You used my toothbrush?"

I nod and kiss her again. When I pull back, her pretty nose is scrunched up in mock disgust. "Gross, Frenchie! Get your own."

"I have my own." I shrug and take her overstuffed bag off her shoulder before exiting the apartment. "Next time we'll have to stay at my place so I can use it."

My eyes subtly dart toward her to judge her reaction to that. I see her pretty mouth start to move upward in a smile, but she pulls her lips into her mouth to stop it. I've dropped the "next time" bomb a couple times since last night, hoping she'll take the hint. This isn't a one-time—I mean two-time—thing. This is something I want more of—a lot more of. She hasn't acknowledged the same, verbally, but her half smiles give me hope.

She's quiet on the car ride over, flipping stations on my Sirius XM satellite radio until she comes across some AC/DC and then she cranks it. I smile. "Back in Black" isn't my idea of morning music, but she's smiling and singing along, and that I like. I make a quick left into the Dunkin Donuts parking lot and get into the drive-thru line. She turns down the radio and looks at me. I ignore her and order two large coffees and a toasted blueberry bagel with strawberry cream cheese.

"You need a coffee," I tell her. "You barely got any sleep last night."

She rolls her eyes. "Are you my dad or my bed buddy?"

Bed buddy?

"Neither," I say pointedly. "I want to be much more to you."

The amusement on her face disappears, and I want to say more, but the guy in front of me has moved on and it's our turn at the window. The girl working is about eighteen or nineteen with long blond hair in a big ponytail sticking out the back of her hat and too much makeup. She glances up at us and starts to repeat the order, but stops.

"Sebastian Deveau. Oh. My. God. You're Sebastian Deveau!"

"Hi." I smile and give her a little awkward wave. She turns scarlet and smiles.

"Oh my God. Seriously?!" She's almost squealing. I laugh and glance at Shayne, who is watching the scene from behind her sunglasses, and even with half her face covered I can tell she's confused. But she won't be for long. Fuck. This is probably the worst way for her to find out what I do for a living, but I'm trapped. I can't stop this from happening. So I take a deep breath and look back at the girl. She's completely flustered.

"Sorry! It's just you're my favorite player," she gushes. "My brother wants to play for the Winterhawks one day. He's at University of Washington on a hockey scholarship right now. We love watching you play."

"Thanks. You're very sweet. Tell your brother I wish him luck. Umm…how much was my order again?"

She shakes her head, further embarrassed. "Nothing. It's on me."

She hands me a bag with the bagel and then the two coffees and for the first time she realizes there's someone else in the car. Her eyes move up and down Shay and it's easy to see she's judging her. She might as well hold up a scorecard with a number out of ten on it. If it was me, Shayne would get a perfect ten, but something tells me this girl doesn't see it that way.

"I can't let you pay," I say with an easy grin.

"No. I want to! You can get me back one day," she suggests happily and lowers her eyes, batting her big mascara-covered lashes in an attempt to be flirty. I glance at Shayne, who is now staring at me openmouthed.

"You're a hockey player." She whispers this so only I can hear, and it's filled with confusion—and contempt? Yeah, this is going to go as badly as I thought it would. Fuck.

"You can buy me a drink at the bar or something," the cashier girl suggests excitedly. "My girlfriends and I have fake IDs and we like to go bar hopping. Do you ever go to Liberty or The Sunset? I heard you do."

Hell no, my brain screams. I glance at Shay, who is still staring at me; her hand holding the coffee I gave her is just hanging there, frozen, in midair. Her free hand rests on the console between us. I cover it with my own hand, immediately lacing our fingers together.

"That's so sweet of her, isn't it, baby?" I ask Shay, and then reach up and pull her hand to my mouth and kiss her knuckles. I turn back to the Dunkin girl. "Thanks. Do you want me to sign anything or something?"

"Ahhh…" She's been thrown off by the show of affection I just gave Shayne. Thrown off and probably heartbroken. Whatever. She'll get over it. She leans over and gives me a pen and asks me to sign the receipt from my order. I ask her name and sign it. *To Amy. Thanks for my morning coffee. Sebastian Deveau #8.* Shay watches me sign and I swear I hear her whisper, "Oh God, no."

I hand it back to Amy and give her a big smile before covering Shayne's hand with my own and driving away. As soon as we're back on the street, Shay yanks her hand away.

"What the hell, Frenchie!" she bellows. "Why didn't you tell me you're a hockey player?"

She's mad, but worse than that, she looks betrayed. Damn. I start to scramble for a way to fix this or, at the very least, minimize the damage. "I was going to mention it at some point, I swear."

"Really? When?"

"Soon," I promise and then I can't help but add, "I'm honestly surprised you didn't know."

"How would I know?"

"Because everyone knows," I say with a shrug.

"No. Not everyone knows," she argues back. "Does Audrey know? Audrey can't know."

"Audrey probably knows," I counter and slow to a stop at a red light. "I mean Josh knows. He's a huge fan and he works with my financial advisor. Also your boss, Trey, he probably knows. My team's captain is his 'stupid hockey player friend,' as you put it the other night."

"I have to go," she states flatly and starts to open the door to the car. The light has turned green and I'm letting the car roll forward, about to hit the gas. But when I realize she's going to get out even if I'm moving, I quickly yank the car to a spot at the curb in front of a fire hydrant.

"Shay, is it really that big of a deal?"

"I can never come back to that Dunkin Donuts again! She's going to spit in my coffee every time!"

I laugh. "Not if you're with me. I'll just have to come with you every morning."

She has both feet out of the car now and she's just reaching for her bag, about to jump out. I reach over and grab her arm. She flinches. "I'm not going to get coffee with you again because we aren't going to be together again."

I blink. "Why?"

Her face contorts with something dark. Something I really do not understand but that makes my stomach grow cold despite the hot coffee in it. "Well, for one thing, you lied to me, which I would have expected if you'd told me you were a hockey player. And I will not date a hockey player. I won't. Ever. So bye."

"You've got to be kidding," I blurt out as she yanks her arm free and slips out of the car.

"Nope. Not kidding," she says firmly and shoves her sunglasses back into her hair. "So thanks for the memories…I guess…but forget my name, okay?"

"Shayne!" I call out as she starts down the street.

She ignores me completely and turns the corner up ahead, disappearing into the bustle of morning pedestrians. What the hell just happened?!?

Chapter 15

Shayne

It's amazing I've made it through most of the day. This morning I had two nutrition classes to lead and then I covered a shift at the juice bar. I was like a zombie throughout all of it. My brain was all Frenchie, all the time, and the bomb a horny drive-thru girl dropped on me this morning. He is a fucking hockey player. One who hides it so he can get in my pants. And he got in my pants. How the hell did I not know? The Winterhawks players are treated like celebrities around Seattle. He's probably on the news and in newspapers all the time. How did I not recognize him?

I bet Trey knows he's a hockey player. And if Josh knows that, then Audrey probably knows it and didn't tell me. And if that's true, then a potential boyfriend isn't all I've lost. Because Audrey knows exactly why I feel the way I feel about hockey players. She is supposed to understand and support me and my decisions. Instead she stood there and let me hook up with him. Twice. Oh my God, I slept with a hockey player, not once but twice. I had four hockey-related orgasms. I hate myself.

There's more than one reason I promised myself from a young age I would stay away from professional athletes, and hockey players in particular. Even now, in my twenties, I still feel they're valid reasons. That sport alone has ruined my life and the lives of people I love. And it, like most professional sports, breeds a self-entitled, arrogant, insensitive type of man who is incapable of loving anyone but himself and his equally dickish teammates. I know how unreasonable that sounds to people who don't know me—and haven't lived my life. When I first explained my all-encompassing hate to Audrey, she didn't understand it either. But then, our first year of college, she came home with me for a weekend and came to one of Trey's hockey games with me and met my parents. She's understood ever since. Or so I thought.

Maybe none of this matters anyway. I mean, he *is* a hockey player. And despite his little hints that he wanted to see me again, he's already had me—twice—so he's bound to be at least halfway over it—over us. My firsthand experience tells me hockey players don't have long attention spans when it comes to females.

On my break I head to the garage where I had the car towed. They tell me they still don't know what's wrong with it. Just the news I need to put the crappy icing on a craptastic day. The whole seven-block walk there and back I do nothing but think of Sebastian. Why did the sex have to be so good? Why did he have to make me come? Why did he have to be so perfectly flirty? Why does he have to wear skates for a living? When I get back to work, I head to the large staff lounge. There's a wall with a sink, cupboards, fridge and microwave to the left. In the center of the room there's a table with chairs. At the back of the room on the left is a couch and a chair facing a flat screen on the wall. Next to that are two small workstations with laptops. I head there to do some research on green power foods to bulk up my next presentation. Somehow, though, I start googling Sebastian Deveau.

He's been with the Winterhawks his entire career. He was drafted in the first round. He was a superstar in juniors. He had the most penalty minutes and the most short-handed goals in the league his first year. A defenseman. If there are levels of hockey hate in my heart, the deepest one I have is for defensemen, so *of course* that's what he plays. Just like my father. Of fucking course. He went through a contract negotiation last year and now makes three and a half million dollars a year. There's the fuel that sparks the fire of greed, belligerence and insensitivity: the money. Hockey players make so damn much that they don't have to be accountable for anything. They can just buy their way out of—or into—anything they want. I know because my father made the highest salary of any NHL defenseman when he was playing ten years ago.

I read a few new articles with playoff predictions, since the season ends next week and apparently the Winterhawks have already secured a playoff spot. Sebastian is mentioned a lot. One article is about how he fought too much in the conference final last year and spent too much time in the penalty box. I frown. Another says Sebastian leads the league in points by a defenseman this year and is poised to set a new Winterhawks record. Beating the old one set by…Glenn Beckford. There is some sick joy in knowing my dad's record, which he still boasts about, will be erased, but it's matched by the horror I feel knowing that it'll be broken by a man I've seen naked.

I find a blog that talks about how he used to live with Jordan Garrison when Jordan first joined the team and how it was like a frat house. I can't imagine the women that have traipsed through there. Then again, I can. I wonder if I should get tested. I mean, yes, we were safe, but...

My eyes wander to the menu at the top and my hand, as if acting on behalf of my hormones, clicks the images button. Hundreds of photos of him on and off the ice fill the screen. Man, he's pretty.

"Whatchya doing?"

I jump and quickly close the laptop, spinning in the chair to face Audrey, who is standing by the door.

"You know I thought you were dead or something," she tells me, stepping into the room. "He's athletic. When you didn't call me this morning I thought maybe he had accidentally fucked you to death."

"Classy, Audrey." I roll my eyes. "Remember this wasn't my first naked Sebastian rodeo."

She laughs and flops down on the couch. "Oh, I remember. You walked around for a week with that goofy smile on your face."

"Like you said, he's athletic, which makes him fun to be naked with. But do you know why he's so muscly?" She averts her eyes. She knows! "Audrey! How could you let me do that?"

She leans toward me from her position on the couch, her eyes pleading. "I didn't always know, I promise! I found out the other night. But the first time I had no idea. I thought he was a weight-lifting accountant, just like you did."

"But when you knew, you didn't tell me!" I'm honestly upset.

My best friend gets off the couch and walks over to me, pulling me up from the chair I'm sitting in and hugging me. "I'm sorry. I should have. It's just...you already liked him."

"I don't even know him," I argue, but I'm hugging her back.

"Well, biblically you know him," she counters, and I know she's smiling over my shoulder. "And you liked him. He made you come, Shayne, and no man has ever—"

"I know, but that's not reason to risk repeating my mistakes," I reply. "You of all people should know the risk is high."

She pulls back, putting her hands on my shoulders and staring at me like a mom would to a daughter whom she's lecturing. "I know. I still regret dating Tyler and setting you up with his teammate. God, they were both such dirtbags, but they hid it so well at first. Fuckers."

I think back to how charming Tyler, the captain of the Syracuse hockey team, was when he and Audrey started dating. He brought her flowers and took her on romantic dates. He was funny and sweet and went out of his way to be nice to her friends. He was so captivating, and Audrey was so happy, he had me willing to go on a date with his teammate Dustin, who was interested in me, apparently.

Dustin was equally charming—and so I decided to waive my "no hockey players" rule, which I implemented thanks to dear old Dad. And for about a year I thought it was the best decision I'd ever made. Even after Audrey found out Tyler had "accidentally" slept with someone else and they broke up, I stayed with Dustin. He was different—even Audrey, with her broken heart, thought so. And then one day there was a knock on my dorm room door, and a girl I'd never met before told me she'd gotten chlamydia from my boyfriend last week, and I should get tested.

He swore she was some kind of crazy puck bunny stalker and was lying. But when the test results came back positive—and he accused me of giving it to him even though I'd been a virgin when we hooked up—I never spoke to him, or any hockey player, ever again.

"But Sebastian isn't Dustin or Tyler," Audrey declares.

"He's not? Let's see…They were hockey players, they were charming, they were handsome…" I give her a hard stare. "Sounds pretty similar to me. Oh, and he's a Winterhawk, just like the biggest cheating hockey player out there, my dad."

"But you like him," she argues firmly.

"I liked him when I thought he was an accountant or a stockbroker or…a trust fund baby." I sigh, pulling my hair out of its ponytail and giving it a shake. "I can't like him now. Liking him now would mean…"

"Being like your mother?" she finishes for me, and I nod slightly. She frowns but pulls me into a hug. "He's not your father. And despite what Tyler and Dustin did, I still say not all hockey players are cheating bags of dick."

I huff out an awkward laugh at that. "Haven't met one that isn't."

"Maybe that's about to change," she replies firmly, but I shake my head.

"Look, it's not just that. It's the lifestyle. It's hard—on them and the people they date," I explain, and I mean it. "They're gone for weeks at a time. And their careers can end at any minute with a precarious body check. There's torn ligaments, broken bones and concussion syndrome. He could end up addicted to painkillers, like Trey did before he could even have a career."

Audrey thinks about that seriously. I can tell by the way her smile slips off her face and her perfectly sculpted eyebrows meld together. "Yeah. It's a risk. But shouldn't you at least spend a little more time with him before you write him off? Maybe go for coffee and get to know him?"

"No. He'll just tell me what I want to hear to get what he wants, which is more nakedness," I reply. "He proved that by not telling me about hockey in the first place."

She sighs, disappointed, and drops back down on the couch. "Well, at least you got some great sex out of it—finally. You've been in a drought for years. How you can give up sex now that you've had it again is beyond me. I mean, seriously, you should be like a man on a hunger strike who just tasted bacon."

"Bacon?" I question, and I smile despite the seriousness of my feelings. "Did you just call Sebastian bacon?"

She nods enthusiastically. "Bacon is delicious and so is he. It's also bad for you, like you think he is bad for you. Of course he's also delectable…and rich…and orgasmic—like chocolate." She giggles. "He's chocolate bacon."

I don't want to giggle with her but as usual when Audrey amuses herself she amuses me too. Even if it's at my own expense. This is why she's my best friend and why I'll let her little betrayal slide—this once. "You're ridiculous."

"So are you, but in a way that's a lot less satisfying," she explains and winks at me. "Look, you don't have to commit the rest of your life to this guy, but why not let the chemistry run its course? Work it out of your system a few more times."

"Keep sleeping with him?!"

"Yep."

"Nope." She frowns. I frown. I cross my arms over my chest. "I'm not the bed buddy type even if I'm fairly certain he is, because, you know, hockey player."

My best friend suddenly looks serious. "Says who? You guys have hooked up. No flowers. No romance. Just carnal bliss. If that's not a bed buddy, what is?"

"I was experimenting because you told me to. It was just a one-night stand," I rationalize to both her and myself.

"A one-time thing you did twice?" Audrey still sounds skeptical. She shakes her head, blond hair skimming her shoulders. "I'll be very surprised if you two don't end up naked together again."

I don't say anything. Because I know Audrey, and when she gets something in her head it's hard to change her mind, and I don't even have the energy to try. Besides, time will show her how wrong she is. I glance at the wall clock and stand up.

"You here for my class?" I ask, and she nods. "Let's go. And I expect a thank you from Josh for making you extra bendy."

She rolls her eyes and follows me out of the staff lounge.

An hour and ten minutes later we're both sweaty as we roll up our mats. Well, I roll up my mat. Audrey is still in child's pose. I walk over and shove her hip with my bare foot. "Don't fall asleep, Audrey. I need you to drive me home."

"That piece of shit car still isn't working?"

"Yep. And please do not talk about Connie that way. She's sensitive," I say because Audrey knows I named my car. I've had her since freshman year of college.

"How is it that Trey drives a BMW X3 and you drive a hunk of garbage?" Audrey asks, even though I know she knows the answer.

I roll my eyes as we walk out of the yoga room and into the foyer. "I stopped accepting guilt gifts from dear old Dad a long time ago."

It's the last class of the night. We close in less than forty minutes so the place is relatively empty. I see movement from behind the frosted glass wall the separates Trey's office from the rest of the gym. I tell Audrey I will meet her in the shower and head to his office. The door is open and I waltz right in, intent on finding out if he knew Sebastian was a hockey player, but I freeze because he's got someone with him: a willowy auburn-haired girl I've never seen before.

Trey notices me and waves me in as I'm about to turn around and leave. "Hey Shayne! I want you to meet someone."

She turns to face me and smiles. "Hi. I'm Jessie Caplan."

I step farther into the office and shake her hand. She's got a nice firm grip and a warm smile. And she's stunningly pretty. "Hi. I'm Shayne, Trey's sister, but I also teach here."

"Jessie is my newest hire," Trey announces with a satisfied grin. "She's a physical therapist with a background in sports injuries."

"Cool. Nice to meet you, Jessie, and welcome!"

"Shayne, can you show her around quickly, now that everything is empty?" Trey asks me, and I nod. "Thanks. I've got some paperwork to deal with."

I nod again and head back into the lobby with Jessie behind me. As I show her around I also ask her questions, which she answers freely and openly. She's originally from Maine, went to school in Arizona, and came to Seattle for an internship to finish her school program. They hired her and she stayed. She has nothing but good things to say about her former employer, so I can't help but ask why she left.

She smiles and looks a little sheepish. "I wanted to work a little less than they needed. I'm planning my wedding and my fiancé is away a lot, so it's a lot of work on my end. It's happening back in Maine this summer so it's a lot of phone calls and managing things from afar."

My eyes fall to her hands and I see the giant sparkling ring on her hand. How did I miss that before—it's gorgeous! "Beautiful ring!"

"Thank you." Her already bright smile gets brighter and her green eyes sparkle. "He went overboard. But Jordan isn't a subtle guy in general."

"How'd you two meet?" I ask because whatever she did, I'm doing. I would kill for a wonderful guy that makes me sparkle brighter than a diamond ring, which is what Jessie is doing right now.

"We were childhood friends who reconnected here in Seattle," she explains as we walk back into the foyer.

"What are the chances that you would both end up in same city on the other side of the country?" I can't help but ask, and she laughs.

"Yeah. Fate is funny that way." She laughs. "Trust me, I wasn't pleased about it at first. When we both left Silver Bay, our hometown, we weren't on the best of terms."

I want to ask her more questions because it sounds like a very interesting story, but as we head into the women's changing room, Audrey is heading out. She's showered and changed into a pair of dark skinny jeans and a strapless white top. "Hey! You haven't even showered yet? If you want me to drive you, get your ass in gear. I have to be at work in forty minutes."

"I'll bus it," I say begrudgingly. "Audrey, this is Jessie. She's going to be a therapist here."

"Hey! Nice to meet you. I'm Shayne's friend and the only reason she has more than yoga in her life." Audrey and Jessie shake hands as Audrey laughs at her own joke, and I roll my eyes. "You guys should come by my bar for a drink when you're done!"

The rest of the tour takes longer than it should because Jessie and I are talking a lot. I like her. Not just as an employee—and it's clear she'll be great—but as a person. She's funny and smart and I haven't clicked with someone this easily since Audrey. When we're back in the lobby, she hesitates before leaving.

"Do you want to take Audrey up on her drink idea?" Jessie

asks me shyly. "My fiancé is working, so I'm free for a few more hours."

She's so sweet and she's smiling expectantly and I really could use a drink after what happened this morning. Besides, if I go home I'll just think about Sebastian. I smile back. "Give me ten minutes to run through the shower."

Chapter 16

Sebastian

We lost—badly—and it was mostly Chooch's fault. Of course no one would ever say that out loud—not the coach or the players—but it *was* his fault. He had a horrific game. Sure, one of the goals was a defensive meltdown, which I hold myself accountable for because I took a shitty hooking penalty and that was the reason for the power play that led to the goal. But the other five—yeah, *five*—Chooch simply shit the bed. Coach pulled him halfway through the second, when the Thunder led 6–0. Our backup goalie, Owensen, didn't let in another one, thankfully. And even though Garrison scored one and I managed to deflect one of Westwood's slap shots into the back of the net, we were slaughtered.

I hated losing to the Thunder more than to any other team. They knocked us out of the playoffs last year in a seven-game battle that turned dirty fast. Their assistant captain, Jude Braddock, was the kind of player I hated. He dove and embellished and he would constantly cross-check and hook me, and once he even punched me in the kidney when the refs weren't looking. But the one time I dropped my gloves to fight him, he skated away like a bitch. On top of ending our playoff run, the Thunder went on to win the Cup last year and are in contention this year to do it again. So yeah, I hate them and I hated losing to them.

"How's the eye?" Avery asks me as he pulls off the Under Armor shirt he wears beneath his jersey. He stares down at me, concerned.

I shrug like it's no big deal but as my fingers reach up and trace the two-inch cut slicing through my eyebrow, it's hard to hide my wince. I fought Duncan Darby near the end of the third when it was clear we weren't going to come back from this. Duncan is actually a pretty nice guy. I've met him at league events over the years. But I was frustrated and he was battling with me in the corner for the puck and the guy is a fucking giant and it was like a massive red-headed meat blanket hanging all over me, and I just snapped. When he managed to get the puck I cross-checked him in the back—hard. He turned around, called me a fucktard and shoved me and I immediately dropped the gloves. Unlike his douche teammate Braddock, Duncan Darby dropped his right back.

I'm an enforcer. There's no two ways about it. I have been since I played in juniors back home in Quebec. But what makes me valuable is I also score. A lot. I was the highest scoring defenseman in the league my rookie year. Still, I won't give up the fighting. It's as much a part of my game as anything else. I'm usually smart about it, though. I fight when I have to and I pick my partners carefully—other enforcers, not the stars, and guys who ask for it. But Darby didn't really ask for it and he's not an enforcer. He's also not in my weight class. I'm six feet and two hundred pounds of muscle, which is nothing to laugh at. But Duncan Darby is six four and probably has about twenty-five more pounds on him.

I got him twice with a decent left hook. He got me once, a solid punch just above my left eye, and my skin split instantly. The refs broke us up, and I spent the end of the period in the medical room. Stitches are a real bitch when they don't use the freezing.

"It's starting to swell," Avery comments. "Better get some ice. It'll help."

"What's going to help Chooch?" I mutter under my breath.

"He's having a rough end to the season," Avery replies. It's the same answer he would give the media. Always politically correct and diplomatic. Drives me fucking nuts. "But he'll bounce back. Playoffs are a fresh start. A different energy."

I give him a hard stare. I would love to raise my eyebrows to show how much I think that's horseshit, but it would hurt too much. Avery's dark eyes glance around the locker room. The media has cleared out. It's just the players now, half of whom are in the shower room. Chooch is sitting—and sulking—across the large oval room by his locker.

"This is about what's happening off the ice," I explain quietly. "And if he doesn't figure out that shit fast, we're going to be knocked out in four games in the first round."

Avery grimaces, grunts in begrudging agreement. "So fix this."

"Me?" I question.

"I don't do this relationship crap. It's all you do. So fix it," Avery commands and heads to the showers.

"*Merde*," I whisper and sigh. Jordan walks back in, hair dripping wet and a towel around his waist, and starts to dress beside me.

"You up for a drink?" I ask him as he shakes out his hair like a wet dog. Drops of water smack me in the face.

"Sure. Why the fuck not."

I stand up and walk to the showers. As I pass Chooch I tell him, "We're going for drinks. Don't even try to argue. We're going."

Chooch doesn't speak at all except to suggest Liberty. I don't argue, even though that means I'll have to see Audrey, which will remind me of Shay. I need to figure out what the hell went wrong between us. Why does she despise hockey players so much that she's willing to deny our connection? If Chooch wasn't in such a dark place, I would ditch him and Jordan and drive over to her work and demand answers, but there'll be time for that later. Mike Choochinsky's love life derailing our entire team is more urgent, unfortunately.

Twenty minutes later Jordan parks half a block from the bar, and we walk in silence down the dark, stormy street. It seems Seattle is about to have its first spring storm. The wind is strong, blowing trash and leaves around our ankles in angry little tornados. Luckily the rain is holding off because I didn't bring a jacket other than my suit jacket. Jordan pulls open the door to the bar, and Chooch and I push our way inside. It's busy and loud. I would have picked somewhere quieter, but this is what Chooch wanted.

Jordan, being the tallest of all of us by an inch or two, surveys the room and then points to a table near the back. We weave our way through the crowd and as we pass the bar Audrey looks up, her red lips parting in a surprised smile. I give her a smile and a wave but keep heading to the table. This is about Chooch. Damn it.

"Name your poison, Choochie," Jordan says, slipping out of his heather gray suit jacket and dropping it on his chair as he begins to roll up his sleeves.

"Bourbon. Double. Short glass. No ice."

Chooch doesn't drink hard stuff, so I start to raise my eyebrow at that and then wince. Fucking Darby. Jordan glances over at me. "And you, Rocky?"

"Ha-ha," I reply dryly and shrug out of my own jacket. "Just a Stella."

He nods and starts to weave his way to the bar. I turn back to Chooch. His bushy eyebrows are knitted together and there are heavy lines through his freckled forehead. Chooch looks like the kid on the old *Mad* comic books, if he'd grown up and become a hockey goalie. I push my glasses up on my nose—I had to take out my contacts as soon as I was hit in case my eye swelled up—and I place both arms on the table and lean toward him.

"Talk to me, Michael," I say softly but firmly. I only use players' real names when I'm dead serious. Otherwise it's Jordy or Chooch or Westwood. Or Shithead or Fucknuts, depending on my mood.

"I shit the bed." He gives me a little shrug. "Bad game. It won't happen again. If it does I'll bench myself and give the job to Owensen."

"But why did you have a shit game?" I push and watch him trace the wood grain pattern on the table with his finger.

"Off night."

"But why?" I am not going to give this up, so he better just tell me the truth.

He sighs and finally lifts his eyes to meet mine. "I'm not going to say why. You guys already fucking hate her enough."

And there it is. Exactly what I suspected. I exhale loudly and give him a short nod. I search for a tactful way to respond. "It's not like we want to hate Ainsley. We'd love to love her, Chooch. We would. All of us. The wives, the girlfriends, the players, the fucking staff. We *want* to like her."

He laughs bitterly at that and gives me a hard smirk. It's odd on his youthful, goofy face. It makes him look older than his twenty-seven years. "But she gives you no reason to like her," he admits. "And lately she's been giving me no reason to like her either."

Jordan appears next to me, two bottles of beer in one hand and Chooch's glass of bourbon in the other. He hands me a beer; Chooch grabs the bourbon and finishes half of it in one gulp before Jordan can even lift his beer to his lips.

"So…" Jordan says tentatively, and he glances at me as he sits down. "Are we at the part where he admits his girlfriend is ruining his game, or are we still in denial?"

I try not to smile. I fucking love Jordan Garrison. He has this ridiculous way of being charming and a trainwreck at the same time. Before he settled down, it used to get him an outlandish amount of tail. Of course back then he was more trainwreck than charming, but still. It worked for him. That's never been my goal, hooking up with girls whose names I don't know, but it was still oddly impressive.

What's more impressive, though, is what he has with Jessie. I first met Jordan when he was drafted to the Hawks. I'd already been on the team a year, after spending my first year after my draft in the minors, and this tall blond kid with the crooked smile just walks right on and takes a starting forward position. I'd heard of him, of course; any kid coming up in amateur hockey knew about the legendary Garrison family. Every kid was a better player than the next. I hated him before I met him because I'd busted my ass to be good at hockey. It had never come easy. And I didn't have his perfect siblings. I had one sister who was a high school dropout with drug problems and I had divorced parents. But after about a week I realized you couldn't hate Jordan Garrison. He was a hardworking, solid teammate and just generally a nice guy. And I saw what others might miss: a dark, sad look that came over him when he thought no one was paying attention. That's been gone since Jessie came back into his life.

"As usual, Jordy, you're a soft shoulder to cry on," Chooch mutters and takes another swig of bourbon.

"Choochie, I love you like a brother," Jordan begins and pauses to sip his beer again. "But you and Ainsley are...worse than ever. And I don't even know how that's possible, because it always seemed pretty shitty to me."

Chooch cringes. I can't help but cringe too, even though it's the truth.

"We used to be good together," he explains, the frustration evident in his voice. "I don't know why the hell things changed."

Jordan reaches over and squeezes Chooch's shoulder. "I don't like seeing you miserable, man."

"I don't like being miserable," he admits and swirls the drops of brown liquid left in his glass. "It's got to pass. It's always passed before."

I put my beer down on the table and say quietly, "Has it really ever passed? I mean...if this isn't the first time she's made you miserable, then...it's not going to be the last, Mikey. I think the only way it's going to be the last is if you make it the last time."

His eyes meet mine, and I watch a flurry of emotions tumble through them—anger, frustration, denial and a glimmer of recognition. That glimmer means, deep down, Chooch knows I speak the truth. But still he shakes his head. "I've been with her since I was fifteen, Seb. You don't know what that's like."

"No. I don't," I admit freely. "But if the spark is gone—"

"You always say that," he cuts me off, with an edge to his tone I can't ignore. "I love you, Seb, but you're not the person to give me relationship advice. You haven't had a real one yet."

Wow. He's being a fucking dick. I take another swig of my beer. "I know real love isn't torture, Chooch. Tell him, Jordy."

Jordan glances between us with an awkward expression. "You really want my opinion? On love?"

"You're in it, right?" I reply as I reach up and loosen my tie.

"Yeah." He smiles and I know he's thinking of Jessie. "But that doesn't mean I know shit."

"Just regale us with your take, okay?" I demand.

"True love shouldn't torture," Jordan says and scratches at the blond stubble peppering his face. "But it should have the potential to be. Like, the thought of living without her is torture. Not the thought of living with her."

We both look at Chooch. His dark expression gets darker. Like midnight dark. "I need another bourbon."

"Allow me." I stand up, grab his empty glass as I swallow the last of my beer, and turn to push my way through the crowd to the bar.

I reach the bar, which is crowded, and wait until two guys at the end get their drinks from Audrey and clear a space. She doesn't see me yet. She's spun around to the other side of the bar to serve some other customers. I glance at them while I wait. Long brown hair, big kitten gray eyes. A vibrant smile that sends a jolt of desire into my pants. She's here. I smile. What fucking luck.

Chapter 17

Shayne

I'm so glad you came!" Audrey grins at us. "It's packed tonight, but you guys will get special treatment, I promise. So Shayne will have the regular, I'm sure. What about you, Jessie?"

"What's your usual?" Jessie asks me.

"Mojito," I tell her and tuck my damp hair behind my ear. I wish I'd had time to dry it properly—and style it. Luckily I had a pair of jeans, flats and a semi-cute, although sort of sporty shirt, in my work locker. Luckily Jessie isn't too dressed up either, in a pair of jeans, ankle boots and a sweater, so I don't feel too out of place.

"I'll take one of those too," Jessie tells Audrey, who immediately starts to make our drinks.

"Did you order a Seb-tini?" someone says behind us, and then I feel a hand on my lower back. It's large, firm and warm, and it makes my stomach flutter like a baby dove. I turn and come face-to-face with Sebastian Deveau. He's in a crisp white dress shirt with a loosened silver tie around his neck. His dark hair is tousled and his jaw is dotted with stubble. He's wearing glasses. Simple, dark-framed ones that give him that sexy-as-fuck CEO look. He shouldn't be allowed to own those.

Jessie glances behind me and her whole face bursts into a warm smile. She laughs, delighted. "No Seb-tinis here, unfortunately, so I settled for a mojito."

He steps a little closer so now he's beside me, hand still on my back. With his free hand he wraps Jessie in a hug. I bristle. Oh God, please don't say he's the fiancé. For a brief, irrational but all-consuming second, I believe he is. But then she breaks the hug and says, "Please say the love of my life is with you."

Sebastian knows Jessie's fiancé? He nods, as if answering my question, but he's really answering her. Her grin grows again. "Great! Oh! I forgot introductions. Seb, this is Shayne. She works at the new fitness place I'm going to start at this week."

"Shay, *ma belle*," he purrs. Literally fucking purrs at me. And that hand is still warm, strong and possessive against my spine. "It's an unexpected pleasure to see you again so soon."

Jessie's eyebrows jump toward the ceiling. I start to feel my cheeks heat, but before I can manage to say anything Frenchie leans toward me. "Everything about you seems to be an unexpected pleasure. *C'est fantastique*."

Oh my God, he's speaking French. And it's the hottest thing I have ever heard. I can feel my cheeks evolving from pink to red. He sees it happen, and it makes his smile grow victorious and his tongue slips out and wets his bottom lip. Oh God. I'm dying.

"You two have met?" Jessie is completely confused.

"Shay and I are intimately acquainted," Sebastian tells her, and I want to crawl into a hole and die.

I step away from his touch, and if it wasn't so loud in here I swear you'd be able to hear my ovaries scream in protest. Everything about this man makes my girl parts want to fornicate. It's infuriating and invigorating in equal, overwhelming parts. "Frenchie is a member at the gym. And he was at the open house."

"I know. I was too!" Jessie smiles at me, but the confusion is still visible in her green eyes. And then, suddenly, it's not. Her eyes grow wide and her perfect heart-shaped mouth falls open. "Oh! You wore that green dress to the Elevate opening! You and Seb…oh!"

She starts to giggle. Sebastian looks uncomfortable, and I realize she knows what happened between us that night. Oh my God, I want to die. The only thing easing my embarrassment is that Sebastian looks like he wants to die too, and I'm happy it's thrown his game off. He pulls off his glasses and gives Jessie a pleading look, trying to get her to shut up. Her giggles stop instantly, and she reaches out and touches his face.

"Ouch. Seb!" He winces and I turn to get a full look at his face. The right side, away from me, has a short but deep gash through his eyebrow and forehead. It's red and swollen. The frame of his glasses was obscuring it but now it's on display—and it looks painful.

"Holy crap!" I gasp before I can stop myself.

He likes that. It makes him smile again. "You're worried about me, Shay."

"No," I retort quickly—too quickly. "I just…It looks disgusting."

He frowns a little. Jessie ignores our awkward one-upmanship dance and, as Audrey puts our drinks on the bar and tells us they're on the house, Jessie asks her for some ice and a clean bar cloth. Audrey glances at Seb and her smile turns to a wince. "I hope the other guy looks worse."

"He doesn't," Seb admits, and I try to pretend I'm not concerned.

Because I shouldn't be. This is the kind of stuff that I hate—the hockey fights that these idiots, like my dad and my brother, get into because of some stupid team code, even though they know they'll lose. What profession expects its employees to fuck themselves up on purpose? I hate hockey.

He turns away from me, slips his glasses back on and says to my best friend, "Audrey, can I also get some bourbon and two more beers, please, love?"

Love? He just flirts with everyone, doesn't he?

"Where are you sitting?" Jessie asks him. He points to the far corner of the room, by the back wall. I take my mojito off the bar and hand Jessie hers.

"Let's sit by the window," I suggest brightly. It's the opposite side of the room.

Jessie shakes her head, auburn hair sailing over her shoulders. "Let's sit with the boys. You can meet Jordy!"

She's so excited I don't even have time to dissuade her. She takes my hand in hers and starts toward the back of the bar. She seems to be heading for two guys sitting at a long high-top table by the brick wall near the emergency exit. They're both in suits. There's a freckled brunette who looks like his cat just ran into traffic and a tall blonde with broad shoulders, a chiseled chin and a dimple when he smiles—which he's doing right now as he focuses his blue eyes on Jessie. Her fiancé is smoking hot, I'll give her that. And I know before she even says it that he must play for the Winterhawks too.

When we reach the table he stands up, wraps one arm around her waist and lifts her to his lips. The kiss is subtle, but ridiculously romantic. Man, I want to be kissed hello like that. "This is a very happy surprise," he tells her in a deep voice filled with affection.

"Jordan, this is Shayne. She's Trey's sister and she works at Elevate as a yoga instructor," Jessie says to him, and as we shake hands and he tells me it's nice to meet me, she turns her attention to the sad sack of a hockey player next to him. "Shayne, my fiancé, Jordan Garrison, and his teammate and friend, Mike Choochinsky."

I feel like a child on the verge of a tantrum. I want to drop to the ground screaming and kicking my feet in protest. Why, oh why, does Jessie have to be marrying a hockey player? I liked her! Damn it.

"Hi, guys," I say, and the Mike Choochinsky guy barely raises his head, which is slumped forward with his shoulders, examining the tabletop. Jordan, on the other hand, is the Welcome Wagon.

"Hi! Nice to meet you! I think I saw you at the gym opening, didn't I?" he questions.

I nod and take a big gulp of my mojito before turning to Jessie. "I think I should go."

"What? Why?" She's more confused than ever now.

"I totally spaced. Forgot I have no clean yoga gear for tomorrow. I have to go home and do laundry," I babble, and it's the stupidest lie I've ever told. I take another big gulp of mojito and leave it half finished on the table. "Nice meeting you guys. Have a good night."

Before anyone can protest, I am pushing my way through the crowd. I glance over at Audrey, who is frowning at me over the crowd in front of her. I ignore her and don't stop until I'm on the street. The damp, cool air is refreshing, and I take a deep breath.

I'm really bummed Jessie is with Jordan. I don't want to hang out with someone wrapped up in the hockey world because I don't want to be wrapped up in it. I've spent enough unhappy years involved with it thanks to my father and brother and Dustin. It's confusing because she honestly doesn't fit the mold. I mean, sure, she's pretty—gorgeous, really—but she's smart and she seems independent. The goal of most hockey girlfriends is to land that engagement ring, which is why they're called puck bunnies. They're just hopping from player to player looking for the ring. As soon as they do—sometimes even before, if they're ballsy—they quit their jobs and cruise on his bank account. Jessie is still working. Sure, it's part time, but it's working. And she never mentioned Jordan's profession until she had to. I've been around puck bunnies—a lot of them—like the ones that followed my brother around college and the ones that married my father's teammates. And the ones that tried to destroy my parents' marriage. All of them drop their "famous" boyfriend/husband/fiancé's profession like it's their own personal achievement. Like it earns them respect. Jessie didn't do that. Maybe she's different, but I would have to stick around here to find out and, with Sebastian here, that's too much to handle right now. I'll try and get to know her better at work or something.

I sigh as it starts to drizzle, pull the hood up on my jacket and search for the Uber app on my phone.

"You can't even finish your drink?"

I fight the urge to groan, and I turn around. He's standing under the black-and-white-striped awning that covers the door to the bar. He's still without his suit jacket and he's rolled up the sleeves to his white dress shirt. His tie still hangs loosely around his neck. His glasses still sit perfectly on his chiseled face, ice blue eyes peering out inquisitively from behind them.

"You need to stop wearing those glasses," I tell him flatly. "They make you look like an accountant in a porn movie."

He blinks and then lets out a heavy chuff at that. "If your porn has accounting in it, you're doing it wrong, *ma belle*."

"Stop with the French too," I say, folding my arms over my chest to show my irritation. "Your mother tongue won't work on me."

He looks even more amused than he did by the porn comment. This man is drop-dead sexy when he's amused. I'm getting damp and it's not from the weather. As a couple slips past him into the bar, he takes a step toward me but is still cloaked by the awning. He smirks, crossing his arms over his muscular chest, the white fabric on his biceps pulling snugly. "That's odd, because you enjoyed my tongue last night."

White-hot desire swirls low in my belly and rushes through my veins. Images of him naked and pushing into me, licking and sucking at my skin as he does, spin through my head like I'm scrolling through pictures on my phone. Oh God. Why did it have to be so good?

I try pushing the images of our sexcapades out of my head and try to conjure up different ones. Bitter ones from my past. The reason I have to deny myself the only man I've ever craved. The only man who has yet to satisfy me. I level my gaze at him. "Nothing you do works on me now."

He doesn't respond. He just stares. His gaze is hard. Intense. Confident. I imagine it's the look he gave whoever caused that slice through his eyebrow. He takes another step toward me; this time it brings him out from under the protective cover of the awning. Still, he says nothing. The water starts to dapple his shirt and little droplets coat the lenses in his glasses, but he still says nothing. He takes another step closer.

We're a foot, maybe, apart. Those crystal blue eyes are unwavering, unblinking, narrowed right on mine, and I can't look away. I also can't breathe. He uncrosses his arms. The misty rain is making his shirt see-through. His skin looks so inviting through it. My fingers flex with the need to touch him, so I press my folded arms down tighter on top of them. He can't see out of his glasses now, so he reaches up and pulls them off. My eyes shift to the angry slice on his forehead and the dark sutures holding it together.

"You're not supposed to get stitches wet," I scold and reach up to wipe droplets from his forehead before they reach his cut.

As my fingers brush the skin above his cut, he moves. It's quick and unexpected, so I don't have time to react as he grabs me by the wrist and uses it to yank me closer. As my mouth opens in a surprised gasp, he covers it with his own. I want to protest—I *have* to—but as soon as his tongue sweeps over mine, a switch flips somewhere inside me. My reasoning, my rational thought is turned off, and desire and lust is turned on, filling my body with want. For *him*. And I can't help but kiss him back.

He pushes me back two steps until I'm pressed up against a light post. His hand, still holding my wrist, slides into the narrow space between our bodies, and he presses my hand against the long, thick, hard outline pushing against his suit pants. He breaks this kiss, pulling his lips just enough to speak.

"You still do this to me," he growls and rubs himself into my palm. My hand, controlled by want and not reason, just like the rest of me, wraps my fingers around him. "And I know if I slip my fingers into your jeans right now, they'd come out wet."

I kiss him again. To shut him up. To gain some modicum of control. To keep myself from moaning "yes" and God knows what else. "Come home with me," he whispers into the kiss.

"No," I whimper and manage to find the strength, and common sense, to pull my hand back. I reach behind me and grip the cold, slick metal lamppost to help hold me up, since my legs are shaking. Kissing Seb makes me feel drunker than champagne. "I told you. I had fun. You're good at sex because you're a hockey player and that's what you do, but I'm not into that. I'm not…I didn't mean to be one of your playthings, Frenchie. So no."

I move away from the light post and away from him. "I'm going home. Alone. Good night."

He moves to follow me, and I know that I won't say a damn word to stop him. Oh, God help me…Then three guys bustle by me on the sidewalk chattering away, oblivious to the scene beside them until one of them glances up and sees Sebastian. His eyes widen in recognition. "Holly crap! Sebastian Deveau! Man, that game tonight…that was tough."

Sebastian blinks, and his gaze switches instantly from the feral look he was giving me to an amicable, gregarious smile. "Yeah. Don't worry. Won't happen again."

"I never do this, but any chance we could get a pic with you?"

It's the last thing I hear as I quickly march down the street and away from him. As I hail a cab a block away I can't stop myself from looking back. He's under the awning again, smiling next to one of the guys while another one takes a picture of them on his phone. He did exactly what my dad used to do. Flipped a mental switch and dropped everything that he was supposed to care about for the love and fleeting admiration of strangers. Yeah, I need to stay as far away from this guy as possible. No matter what.

Chapter 18

Sebastian

Four days later I'm standing in my bedroom watching my sister as she laughs at me. Typical Steph. I frown at her and scowl, and she laughs harder so I ignore her and keep unpacking my suitcase. She thinks it's hysterical that this dream girl—Shay—has decided I'm worse than global warming. When her laughter dies down, she says, "Poor nugget. You got wham, bammed and thank you, ma'amed."

"Excuse me?"

She smiles and folds her arms over my Winterhawks T-shirt that she's wearing. Steph lives outside of the city, in Renton, and works as a legal secretary. She often stays at my place when I go on road trips because it's closer to her work in the city. I'd left for a quick road trip to western Canada the day after my rainy altercation with Shay and so Steph squatted. And brought her dirty laundry, as she always does, since her building has communal coin-operated machines and mine are state-of-the-art and free. It's not the first time I've come home and found her in my T-shirt and shorts because everything she owns is in the washer or dryer. Honestly, none of it bothers me.

I'm just so very glad she's in my life because if you'd asked me when I was a kid, I'd have thought she'd be dead by now.

"Wham, bam, thank you, ma'am. What guys do to women. She did it to you."

"I don't do that to women," I reply and throw some dirty clothes from my suitcase into the laundry basket on the floor of my bedroom.

"Seb, your quest for love has left quite the body count."

Is she kidding me right now? "I don't mislead them or lie to them. Every girl I'm attracted to, that I start something with, it's because it has potential. And then, unfortunately, the spark goes away and…it's not like I want it to. What am I supposed to do? Stay with them even when it's just not there anymore?"

"No. But maybe try harder to keep the potential or spark or whatever. Because a relationship is not always going to be unicorns and rainbows, Sebastian." She gives me a small, soft smile. "And just because the flame flickers a little or there's bumps in the road doesn't mean it has to be over. It doesn't mean you'll end up like Mom and Dad or your buddy Chooch and the wicked witch of Seattle, Ainsley."

"Wow. That's a boatload of relationship advice from a woman who has been single since she was eighteen," I say pointedly. Stephanie smiles and raises a perfectly manicured middle finger with a neon orange nail in my direction.

"And trust me, I wouldn't have it any other way."

"Looks like I'm not the only one doing this whole love life thing wrong." She takes a pair of rolled-up dirty socks out of my open suitcase and hurls them at my head.

"Did you even play on this trip?" she asks, changing the subject.

"I played one of the two games," I reply and try not to frown. It's irking the shit out of me that my wrist is acting up. Ever since I punched Beau Echolls it's been sore, and the fight with Darby only aggravated it more. The trainers say it's just a strain, which is good. If I rest it now, I'll be fine for playoffs, which start in less than a week.

"Anyway, this Shay girl is probably just worried you're playing her. Or that you guys moved too fast or something," Stephanie says, and we're back to unsolicited love life advice, apparently. "You're a real Romeo. You make a girl feel special. You get their hopes up, whether you mean to or not. And not all girls feel the fizzle when you do, Seb."

I digest her comments. I know she's right, even if I don't like to hear it. I've had three girlfriends in the last year—Andie, Melissa and Dawn. Dawn and I didn't end amicably. She used to be a paralegal at Stephanie's firm; I met her when I picked Steph up for lunch one day. Dawn was sexy and smart and I asked her out immediately. Our first date was two nights later. There was chemistry and there was good sex, but even though she was book-smart she wasn't very witty and didn't have a good sense of humor.

My life has had some really stressful moments and seriously bad things in it, and levity is all that got me through. I need a woman who can make a quip and not cry when something doesn't go her way. Dawn was a crier. She cried when I was injured in a game and lost my front tooth. Cried like I had just lost a limb or something. Within two days I had a fake tooth implanted, but she cried for a week afterward whenever it was brought up. She cried when she didn't get the promotion she was hoping for. She cried all the time. Within two months the spark between us had turned to ash.

Unfortunately, Dawn didn't seem to see it. When I broke up with her, the day before I met Shay, she was shocked and devastated. And then she was angry. She texted me and called me for weeks insisting we "talk it out" and that we were "worth saving." The morning of this most recent road trip, I got a new phone number. Now she was texting Stephanie about me, which my sister was less than impressed with. I know it made it awkward for her because she worked with Dawn, but I didn't know how to fix it. I certainly wasn't going to date her again.

"If women came with warning labels, I'd have steered clear from Dawn before anything ever started," I tell Stephanie, and she laughs.

"Nah, you wouldn't," she snarks back. "Your dick doesn't know how to read."

"Ha-ha," I deadpan and lean over and give her a tiny shove. She slips off the corner of the bed she's sitting on and hits the floor with a thump. She throws the socks, which were still on the floor, at me again. "Can we get back on track? What am I going to do about Shay?"

"You're going to drive your ass over to her work and confront her. Make her tell you what the problem is. Did she already get her heart broken by one of you lugs, or does she just hate athletes in general, or what? And then, whatever her excuse is, talk her out of it."

She says it so matter-of-factly that it actually sounds simple. But it's not.

"Won't I look like a stalker? And it's late. She might not even be working tonight or the gym might be closed when I get there," I say, and then I realize it's pointless. Steph's right, no matter how illogical it is. I have to see Shay. When playoffs start I won't have time to be running all over town at night looking for her. And I won't be out late at bars where I might stumble into her. And the last thing I need is to be distracted by her—by not having her—while we fight for the Cup.

Stephanie knows me well enough to ignore my argument. Instead she simply points to the master bath. "Go shower. I'll unpack the rest of your junk and head back home. Text me and let me know how it goes!"

She disappears down the hall toward the laundry room with the dirty clothes still left in my suitcase.

Twenty-two minutes later I pull my car into the parking lot for Elevate Fitness. The weather is typical Seattle weather—damp and on the verge of raining. That abnormally warm spring weather front we had when Audrey and Josh hosted the barbeque is long gone and our usual rainy spring is back. I check my watch because I don't even know if the place is still open, but I have to try.

I reach the double glass doors and exhale in relief as it opens in my hand. But is she here? The first person I see as I walk down the empty front entrance toward the lobby with the juice bar is Sara.

"We're just about to close." Her voice is flat and unfriendly. I guess she wasn't impressed by finding me banging an employee that wasn't her in the laundry room.

"That's okay. I'm just looking for Shay. Is she here?"

"Who?"

Right. She must not have been lying when she says no one calls her that. "Shayne."

"Right." She makes a face at that, which almost makes me smirk. I mean, come on, no need to be bitter. "She's around here somewhere. I'm leaving, and I'm supposed to make sure the customers are gone, so…"

She makes a vague hand gesture in the direction toward the front door like she's shooing me. I head that way, unsure how I can try to convince her to let me stay. I pass Trey's office. The door is ajar and I can see him inside. Perfect. I pop my head in and smile. "Hey, Trey! Do you have a minute to chat before you close?"

He looks up from some papers on his desk, and I realize he's scowling. But it's wiped off his face and replaced with a friendly smile when he realizes it's me. "Sebastian! Hey. Yeah, sure. Come in."

I glance back at Sara, who looks annoyed. Trey glances over at her. "You can go, Sara. I'll see Seb out later. I have to wait for Shayne anyway."

She simply nods, gives me one last quick unimpressed stare and continues to the door.

I smile at Trey, but I know it looks weak. I'm not sure what the hell I'm going to say to him. I just wanted an excuse to stick around. "So how's business?"

Trey shrugs. "The start is bound to be slow. It's a brand-new business and, you know, there's a gym almost every couple of blocks in this town so…we're doing almost as well as I expected, so I'm not panicking or anything."

That was not the answer I expected. It's honest, but it makes me a little nervous for him. I've only met him that one time, but he seemed like a great guy, and Avery has mentioned him on and off for years and it's always been positive. I want his business to succeed. He scratches his head and stands up. "I just have to figure out an advertising angle. I put money away for a fairly big campaign and asked Avery to do a celebrity endorsement–type deal, but he's taking forever to get back to me."

He glances past me, probably looking for Shayne. As much as I want to see Shay, that Avery comment has my attention. Avery had been talking about his college teammate Trey and his new gym for months. He was excited for him and happy for him, and I can't believe he wouldn't give the guy an endorsement. My shock must read on my face, because Trey shrugs. "He says he needs to check with his management."

"You mean his dad?" Avery's father is hockey's version of a raging stage mom. Ever since Avery was a kid, he has managed every aspect of the Westwood "brand," as Don Westwood calls it. Who the fuck calls their eight-year-old a brand? He did and still does. "His dad is a bit of a..."

Trey smirks. "Oh, I know."

"He's just stressed with the playoffs coming up. Let me talk to him."

Trey blinks. "Really?"

"Yeah. Sure. No big deal, really."

Trey looks relieved—and excited. I'm happy I could help him, but I also have a feeling this will get me more face-time with Shay. Speaking of... "So you're waiting for Shayne?"

"Yeah. Her piece-of-shit car is still at the mechanic, so I said I'd drive her." He glances up at the clock on the wall of his office. "But she's taking forever, and I have a pregnant wife waiting at home for ice cream I'm supposed to pick up."

"Let me give Shay... Shayne a lift home."

He looks skeptical. "I'm not sure that's a great idea. She expects me to do it."

"I'm sure it'll be fine. We're friends," I reply, trying to make it sound as casual as possible, because as nice as I think Trey is, I'm pretty sure I can't say, *Yeah I've seen her naked a couple of times now.*

"You don't mind?" I can still see he's not convinced it's a good idea. "She lives in kind of a shitty area or else I'd just let her bus it. My parents offered to help her with a down payment on a better place, but she's the most stubborn woman in the world."

"Your parents?"

"Shayne is my sister," Trey says with a look on his face that says he thinks I'm an idiot for not knowing that. But Avery never mentioned Trey's family, and Shay never made that connection clear. Now I definitely can't mention seeing her naked. Although I wonder if the skepticism on his features is because he already knows. Oh God.

I smile through the awkwardness. "Oh! Wow. Well, your sister is in good hands, I promise. I'll get her home safely; just go take care of your pregnant wife. And congrats on the baby."

"Thanks, man." Trey squeezes my shoulder, obviously willing to give in to my idea. "Make sure she locks up. And if she's pissed you're her chauffeur, make it clear it was your decision, okay? I don't wanna deal with her wrath."

I follow him out into the lobby and wave as he walks through the front doors and out into the parking lot.

Chapter 19

Shayne

My last class of the night was a simple Bikram-based yoga class. It was full, and I managed to concentrate on teaching without getting distracted by thoughts of Sebastian. The class flew by, though, and after saying good-bye to everyone as they filtered out and doing a sweep of the other fitness rooms with Sara, I was left with nothing but my thoughts. I wondered what he was doing right now. I hadn't heard from him since the groping and kissing outside Audrey's bar, but that's what I wanted. I wanted him—and our little…whatever it was—to be left in the past. Audrey, on the other hand, didn't. She brought him up every time I saw her this week. "I think he's good for you, Shaynie. He's got you flustered and off balance and you're different with him. You're not so…uptight."

"I am not uptight," I had argued back.

"You're wound tighter than a country singer at the opera."

"That doesn't even make sense."

"Look, you're uptight. All the time, which is insane for a yoga teacher," she told me frankly. "And I swear you're a better yoga instructor since he started giving you orgasms."

I gasped when she said that. "What was wrong with my yoga before?"

"Nothing, but you're more chill out there now. More Zen, less drill sergeant."

Ouch. "Well, maybe I'll find someone else to give me orgasms."

She raised a light brown eyebrow at me. "Yeah? How's that been working out for you the past two and a half years?"

I hate that she was right but she was, and my body knew it. Sex is a glorious thing and because of some sick cosmic joke this hockey player had not only ended my drought, he was supplying earth-shattering ones every damn time. I could go back to supplying myself with orgasms but…just like making a sandwich, it's always better when someone else does it for you.

I've been under the hot shower spray longer than I should be, considering Trey is waiting for me, but it feels glorious. My shower at home is hit-or-miss when it comes to pressure and hot water. This morning there'd been neither, and I didn't want to risk that tonight. I'm feeling tense, despite having just taught a class, and I want the water to relax me. There are four private shower stalls against one of the walls, and normally I use one of those because I'm kind of a prude, to be honest. I don't get the whole public nudity thing, even if it's just in front of other women. But when I'm alone in the gym I always think of *Psycho*'s shower scene, so I just use one of the showers in the large open room.

I'm tipping my head back, rinsing my hair one final time, when the voice echoes in the cavernous tiled room.

"Hey, gorgeous."

I scream and grab my towel off the hook, jumping out of the spray of the water and almost slipping in the soap suds still sliding off me. My heart rate has jumped so quickly and so high that I feel faint. But then my eyes land on Seb.

He's standing in the opening of the shower room, leaning against the wall. He's wearing jeans and a black Henley with charcoal gray sleeves, the two buttons at his neck unbuttoned. His hair is tousled and the scar on his eyebrow is just a pink line now, no stitches.

I'm panting with fear even though there's relief at seeing him and not some serial killer or rapist. His baby blue eyes are running up and down my body greedily so I hug the towel tighter, praying it's covering all my essentials.

"You can't be in here!" I hiss, even though I don't want him to go anywhere.

"Trey's gone," Sebastian explains, trying to soothe me. "He wanted to get home to his wife, so I volunteered to make sure you got home safe and sound."

I'm shivering a little now, because I'm standing soaking wet with only a small towel pressed to my front. "What did you tell him? 'Don't worry, Trey. I'll go watch your sister shower and then take her home'?"

"What's the big deal? I've seen you naked before. I like you naked," he says, his voice dropping an octave. His eyes look like sapphires in the overhead fluorescent lights. "Do you want me to leave?"

"No." The word comes out of my mouth before I can stop it.

"Do you want me to wash your back?" A slow, sexy smile spreads across his face.

"Yes."

Again, it's like I have no control over my mouth. Damn it! If it's just going to verbalize every single thing I think, I'm going to be in trouble. Big trouble.

He smiles at that, and it's like a blowtorch to my feeble willpower. No man has ever looked at me the way Sebastian Deveau does. I can't even explain it—but the desire and genuine pleasure reflected in his eyes as he looks at me, not just now but every time, is exhilarating. He peels off his shirt and unbuttons his jeans, pulling something out of the back pocket before letting them drop to the tile floor. He holds up the foil packet. "Do you want me to do more than wash your back?"

"Yes." *Stupid mouth, could you at least try and play hard to get?!*

He drops his underwear a second later, as he's rolling the condom over his dick, I tell myself that maybe Audrey's right. I do him a couple more times and gradually work him out of my system. Maybe I will stop thinking about him and stop feeling that warm happiness when he looks at me. Maybe I just need to overindulge. Like the time I was eleven and ate all my Halloween candy in one sitting and then got a stomach ache so fierce I didn't want to eat chocolate for months afterward. That's the theory I decide to believe as he kicks off his shoes and steps out of his pants. I drop my towel and walk back to the stream of water. He meets me under it, pushing his strong hands into my wet hair and attacking my mouth. Neither of us is playing the tough guy this time, and we both groan right into the kiss.

My heart is beating wildly again as we make out like crazy under the water. We might both drown, but it would be completely worth it. And hey, if I'm dead I don't have to deal with the fact I'm going back on my own self-imposed rules. He pushes me so my back is up against the tile wall and leans right into me. His skin is wet and warm, and he feels so heavy and good against me. His dick is rock hard and pressed firmly against my belly.

His hands travel down my shoulders, down my sides, over my hips and around to my ass. "I'm going to lift you up. Hold on."

I pant my response and wrap my arms around his neck. His hands slide down my ass. He curls his fingers toward the inside of my thighs and they graze my pussy, making me shudder. He smiles into my neck and I bite his shoulder.

Finally his hands reach the back of my thighs, and in one fluid, strong motion he lifts me off the ground. My ankles hook behind his lower back, and he pushes me harder into the wall. He pulls back just a little so we're looking at each other and slowly lowers me onto his cock. He swears in French under his breath; I bite my lip and sigh heavily.

Why does he feel so good? Why do I want this, even though I know it's not right for me? What the hell is wrong with me? The questions filter through my head at rapid speed, but I don't attempt to figure out the answers. I don't care right now. All I care about is that he's here and we're doing this again. And it's perfect. *Again*.

Using the wall to hold me up and his hands under my ass to bounce me, he starts to fuck me.

"Oh God. This is always so good," he hisses as he lifts me and lowers me. "Shay, you're perfect."

"Perfect with you." Why the fuck would I say that?

He smiles at that, so I cover his mouth with my own to get rid of it. He keeps bouncing me, thrusting into me at the same time, and my back is sliding up and down on the tile. His eyes keep slipping to my chest as my tits bounce up and down, and I'm not self-conscious in the least. In fact, I cup them and push them up toward his mouth. He takes the hint, dips his head and traces my nipple with his tongue before sucking greedily on it. He bites down and I moan. I push my hands into his thick, wet hair and twist it between my fingers. God, I love doing that—and he likes the feel of it too, because he grunts and slams me harder against the tiles with his thrust.

He moves back to my mouth and kisses me hard. As the kiss starts to break, he uses his teeth to pull on my bottom lip and then lets go and moves to nip my earlobe.

"Touch yourself," he begs me, his accent thick, his breath tickling my ear, sending delightful shivers down my spine. "I want you to come with me. I'm close."

I move one hand from around his neck and slip it between us. His head dips to watch me as I my fingers find my clit and begin to move, creating glorious friction. The friction I'm creating for myself is almost unnecessary. I was already on the verge thanks to his solid, gifted dick and the look on his stunning face as he's overtaken by the pleasure. But the friction, along with watching him watching me touch myself, sends me catapulting toward the blissful abyss.

"Sebastian…I'm going to…"

"*Moi aussi, ma belle…*"

He yells and I whimper as we both come.

I'm dizzy and weak and I can't imagine how he's still holding me up. Then I realize his hands are barely doing the work. Instead he's crushed me into the wall using his body weight to pin me there as he struggles for breath. A few minutes later his arms flex back to life and he lifts me and carefully slides out of me. I unhook my feet and shakily find the tile floor beneath us.

We smile at each other, and I step back under the direct spray of the shower. He turns away from me to remove the condom. A second later he's beside me holding the shower gel.

"Time for that back scrubbing I promised," he says, turning me to face the wall. "I've got mad skills."

Yes. Yes, you do.

I want to fight him. To just tell him to get out, but that orgasm blew my brain, and my common sense, to oblivion. So I simply close my eyes and let him push my wet hair over my shoulder and slide a soapy washcloth across my bare back.

Chapter 20

Sebastian

Shay is quiet as we dress and as we leave the fitness center. I try to take her hand, but she pulls away and stuffs it in her pocket. She stops in the parking lot. "Where's your car?"

I point to the only car left in the parking lot, my Range Rover, and she looks confused so I elaborate. "The Aston Martin isn't meant for the rain. I drive this or my Beemer most of the season."

She makes a face, her adorable freckled nose crinkling up and her aqua eyes rolling upward. "Of course you do."

I frown and roll my wrist, which is a little achy because of the whole shower sex thing. She's dissing my cars? Or me because of my cars? It's not like I collect and drive monster trucks or something. All of my cars are tasteful and, although expensive, reliable modes of transportation. I'm about to tell her that but she quickens her pace as I hit the remote in my pocket and unlock the doors, and she walks ahead without me. I try to open her door, because that's what I do for women—all women, not just the ones I enjoy seeing naked—but she gets there first and is in the passenger seat pulling the door closed before I can reach it. I try not to frown, and I slide into the driver's seat. I look over at her as she buckles her seat belt.

"So you know I like cars, why don't you tell me something about you? Like your last name," I suggest with a smile.

Her head spins to face me. "You don't know my last name."

"You never told me."

She looks shocked but then shrugs defiantly. "It's the same as Trey's."

"I don't know Trey's."

"Ask your esteemed leader Avery Westwood," she replies instead of just telling me. Then she promptly changes the subject. "I live at…"

"I know where you live. I've been there, remember?"

She shrugs, eyes staring straight ahead as I back out of the stall and move toward the exit. "I wasn't sure you remembered. I mean, it was a while ago."

I'm confused by that statement. "It was a week and a half ago."

"Yeah, for someone like you, that could be a lifetime. You could have driven four or five other girls home since then," she says casually.

"I could have?" I question back. This woman, no matter how beautiful or how good she is to my cock, is starting to show me the downside to liking a woman with a smart mouth. "You're the one without a car. How many men have you invited in for impromptu sleepovers so you can catch a lift to work?"

The car gets deathly quiet. I know that was a borderline shitty thing to say, but so is what she said to me. Still, I shouldn't have said it. I open my mouth to apologize, but she starts talking first. Her voice is hard, and her tone is biting. "I didn't invite you to sleep over.

You kind of just invited yourself. And for the record, I don't have the opportunities you do. I'm just a lowly yoga instructor, not a hockey god with a collection of exotic cars so women know my dick is as big as my bank account."

Whoa. That was beyond harsh. I glance over to her. "So can you just tell me why you hate my guts, please? This is getting tedious."

"I don't hate your guts. I don't let guys I hate have sex with me," she blurts back suddenly and with way less attitude than everything she's said and done since we left the shower. She sighs, her eyes finally drifting to mine. "And I think this sex thing is...fun. And maybe we can keep doing it."

"The sex thing? Only?" I ask, looking for clarification because I think she's asking me to be her bed buddy.

"Yeah. I mean, it's fun, right?"

She is asking me to be a bed buddy. "Yeah. It's more than fun. It's great, but I think a relationship would be too. And that's what I want."

She frowns, shaking her head so adamantly it's almost offensive. "What makes you think I'm girlfriend material for you?"

I slow to a stop at a red light and turn to her. "You're smart and smart-mouthed. You're independent and strong-willed, which I love, even though most guys would think I'm nuts. There's just something about you that makes me...happy every time I see you. And I want to figure that out. Oh, and you're gorgeous as hell."

She runs a hand through her damp hair, pushing it back off her face except for one piece that sticks to her cheek. I reach out and gently brush it back. I literally see her quiver at my touch, but she pushes my hand away anyway. "Frenchie, I just don't want to be involved with a..."

She falters. I stare at her until the light turns green and I have to focus on the road again. "A French Canadian?" I ask trying to fill in the blank. "A guy with a dick as big as his bank account? A guy who makes you smile? Because that hot little mouth of yours turns up every time you see me. Like it or not."

"A hockey player."

"Why?"

I turn onto her street and slow down because I know when I get to her place she'll jump out and leave this whole conversation behind her. And I'm not ready to let her off the hook yet. "Your brother was a hockey player, right? He seems like a great guy."

"He is, because he doesn't play anymore."

"Come on, that's ridiculous."

"He used to fuck around all the time on his girlfriends in college. In fact, when he suffered the injury that ended his chances at going pro, three girls showed up at the hospital all claiming to be his girlfriend. Because the profession breeds arrogance and self-entitlement," she states flatly. "And that doesn't foster healthy relationships. I want a healthy relationship. I want a man I can trust."

I glance over at her, pausing at a stop sign much longer than I need to. "And so now, thanks to injury, he's not untrustworthy, arrogant, self-entitled anymore. He can suddenly have a healthy relationship? And that's because he stopped playing, not because he grew up and matured, like we *all* do?"

She frowns like she's annoyed, but something flickers in her eyes that's more melancholy than annoyance. I want her to tell me why but she's doesn't explain it. "Not everyone does, Sebastian. Not all hockey players do."

Okay. I see where this is coming from. I pull away from the stop sign, smiling softly at her. She looks at me like she doesn't want to like it, but she does. I can tell. "So just because your brother was a bit of a manwhore in college you're not going to give me a chance?"

For the briefest of seconds, I can see her register the stupidity of her own reasoning. But then her face grows dark and stalwart. "It's not just my brother," she says as she turns her face away from me to look out the window. Her hand reaches for the door handle. "I can walk from here. Just pull over."

"Shay," I start to protest but pull the car over anyway because, knowing her, she'll jump out of it whether I stop or not. "Shay...*ma belle.*"

"No. Don't," she snaps and glares at me while she undoes her seat belt. "I'm not falling for that French crap. I told you that. I'm not your usual puck bunny. I don't want your bank account or your fame, and I'm not about to get sucked into a world I'll get trapped in."

"What are you talking about?" I blink. I'm not asking this woman to marry me. Hell, I haven't even technically asked this woman on a date.

"There's too much temptation in your world, too many easy ways to hurt the person you claim to love," she babbles on. "It's just not what I want. Ever."

I stare at her. She's fucking insane. Of course she is. Because she's sexy and smart and quick-witted and mind-blowingly perfect around my cock, so of course she's insane. Thanks, Universe. "I've never fucked around on a girlfriend."

She doesn't even look the least bit contrite, even though it's clear from my tone that I'm offended. "When was your last relationship?"

Her smoky eyes are narrowed and her eyebrow is cocked, like

she's a cop on an episode of *Law & Order* or something. It makes me defensive. And angry.

"What difference does that make?" I demand because there is no way I'm telling her I broke up with Dawn the day before hooking up with her. She'll think that makes me a player. It doesn't. I don't control timing; fate does. I don't believe in a mandatory mourning time for relationships anyway. When it ends, it's over. I didn't expect to find someone else so soon, but I wasn't about to ignore a bona fide connection with someone because of some abstract rule about how long you should be single in between relationships. "If there's a connection, I am going to go after it. That's not because I'm a hockey player; it's because I want to find someone to share my big bank account and big dick with. One person. *Forever*. That's what women want men to want, isn't it? That makes me a fucking catch, *n'est pas?*"

She rolls her big, beautiful eyes. "Oh, enough with the French, Frenchie."

"I'm not doing it to impress you," I explain and sigh. "I think I'm done trying to do that at all."

She opens the car door but turns back to me before she gets out. "Look, you're a great lay. I won't lie about that, but that's all this was. It was fun and satisfying, but I won't date you."

"You're not telling me something. What is it?" I ask, but she just gives me a small, awkward wave and then gets out of the car. As she starts down the dark, damp street the half block to her apartment, I follow slowly in the car. She may have gone from the girl of my potential dreams to the biggest bag of crazy I've met in a while, but that doesn't mean I'm going to abandon her. I told Trey I would get her home safe and I will. She turns once and glares at me, but I just ignore her and idle outside her building until she's unlocked the door and is safely inside.

As I do a U-turn and begin back toward my townhouse I can't help but feel like I'm going to miss her. I barely knew her but I still can't help but feel that we had something that was more than just physical. I was going to miss getting to know her, as weird as that sounds.

Chapter 21

Shayne

I'm waiting at the bus stop, annoyed that the bus isn't on time and annoyed with myself because I should have gotten out here early. The sun is fighting to make its way out of the heavy cloud cover. Every now and then it wins the battle, and I get a ray of sunshine to warm me, but it doesn't last long. Where is the damn bus? I have a nutrition class to teach in forty minutes. I've been late twice this week already. Trey's ready to fire me, no joke.

I had called Audrey last night and told her about what happened—and the conversation on the car ride home. She ate it up like it was a recap of her favorite soap opera.

"Where is he now?"

"I don't know. On his way home, I guess," I said and sighed into the phone. "I am not an expert in the migratory patterns of hot-headed French defensemen."

"Key word in that was hot," Audrey had replied. "You think he's hot."

Yeah, so she was no help in my quest to stay hockey-free.

"He turned down my bed buddies suggestion."

She sighed into the phone. "That's because he's not a chicken shit like you. He knows this is more than sex. I was just trying to convince you to pretend it was all about sex so you'd at least keep seeing him until your brain caught up with your heart."

"Excuse me?"

"I was lying about the orgasms," Audrey confessed. "You're attracted to him as a human being, but you won't admit it because of your prior trauma."

"Please stop using your psych degree on me."

"Shaynie, he's good for you, not just your clit. Try to come to terms with that, will you?"

I hadn't answered her. I just told her I had to go and hung up. I had thought about Audrey's little psychoanalysis all night long. I did like Sebastian. But I had liked Dustin too, and all that got me in the end was a twelve-day cycle of antibiotics. And Dustin wasn't even a professional athlete. My dad was, and he probably slept with hundreds of women behind my mother's back.

Besides, even if I liked Sebastian, after my little cryptic tirade on the drive home, I'm sure he is done with my crazy ass. For all I know, he could easily forget about me. Maybe that connection I felt, and needed now to ignore, was one-sided this whole time. That would make sense because my father was the same way. I watched my mom struggle for a connection to him my whole life. Sure, they are married, but he didn't seem to really love her. He loves himself, for sure, and maybe Trey, but if he loved his wife, he rarely showed it. And although Trey has been slightly better with his emotions since rehab, I still thought I saw a glimmer of longing in his wife Sasha's eyes sometimes. Trey isn't one for outward signs of affection.

Sebastian may seem outwardly affectionate right now, but that's because this is new and we are drawn to each other like bunnies in heat. Last night, to try to cure myself of the lingering longing I have for him, I surfed the Tumblr account dedicated to wives and girlfriends of NHL players and found his thread. In the last year he's been photographed with three different women the blog called his girlfriend. I bet he was drawn to them too. And where are they now? I am not going to be girlfriend number four.

I sigh and crane my neck, looking down the street for any sign of the damn bus. I contemplate giving up and calling Uber or a cab, but I'm trying to save money. My car is toast. There was no saving the engine, so now I need to figure out how the hell to afford a new car. I am drowning in school loans and although Trey pays me well, Seattle is expensive and I just don't have a lot in my savings. Certainly not enough to buy a car. Not one that's worth owning, anyway.

A car horn honks and I look up. There in front of me is an all-too-familiar silver Audi. I contemplate turning and walking away, but she's staring right at me through the windshield and I'm staring back. I can't pretend I didn't see her. She pulls right up to the bus stop and rolls down her passenger window.

"I thought that was you, Shaynie!" my mother says brightly, leaning toward the open window. "Are you heading to work? I can give you a lift! I wanted to check in with Trey anyway."

I want to tell her I'd rather take the bus. I really would rather take it and if it had been on time, I would have, but the bus isn't here and I am late. Very late. And I know my mother won't take no for an answer anyway. So I pull open the passenger door and climb in.

She leans over the console between the chocolate leather seats and kisses my cheek. "So good to see you, sweetie." She pulls away from the bus stop and toward downtown. "I feel like you might as well live in Malaysia with the amount of times we see each other. I mean, you're literally less than twenty minutes from home, but you'd never know it."

And the guilt trip has started before we even manage to move a mile. Fabulous. I try not to frown, or sigh, or groan or do anything that she can latch on to and use to become more of a martyr. "My car died and I've been working a lot. A ton, actually. I barely see Audrey, and the only reason I see Trey is because he's at the gym."

She nods and reaches over to pat my hand, which is resting in my lap. "I know, honey. Not judging. Just saying I miss you, I guess."

Yeah, right.

"Is your cell phone working?" she asks, and here is layer two of the guilt trip. "Because I left you a couple of messages."

"You know I don't listen to messages," I reply because I've told her a million times I never check them and that it's a waste of time for her to leave one. I'll see her number on the missed call list and call her back, no need for voicemail. Only this week, I haven't called her back. "And again, I'm crazy busy. I was going to call you back tonight."

"Well, now you don't have to," she says, her tone light even though I know she's ticked she had to hunt me down. "I can tell you in person."

"Tell me what?"

"Daddy is being honored at the Winterhawks game Friday!"

When I don't say anything, she glances over at me and smiles expectantly. I stare back passively so she elaborates, her hands flailing wildly for emphasis. "They're retiring his number! You know what a big deal that is? The Winterhawks are yet to retire a jersey. This will be the first one. He's been doing interviews all week. I'm surprised you haven't heard one. He's very proud."

"I don't listen to sports shows, Mom," is all I say in a calm, flat voice even though I know what she's going to do next, and I'm already angry about it.

"So we need to be there on Friday night, obviously," she says, and my blood pressure spikes. "There's going to be a video tribute and they'll raise his banner and he'll drop the puck for the game."

"I'm not going, Mother."

I don't know why she bothers making a completely hurt and stunned face. She knew I was going to say that. Still, my mother is the queen of hurt and stunned faces. The world, it seems, has been wounding her and taking her by surprise her whole life. She's the person who would tie herself to some train tracks and then be startled by the locomotive's headlight when it barrels toward her. Her complete refusal to live in reality is the thing that makes me most crazy.

"Shayne, this is getting ridiculous and, quite frankly, embarrassing."

"Nobody cares if I attend Dad's stupid ceremony."

"Everyone knows he has two children," my mother replies in a clipped tone. "We were a very high-profile family in this city when your dad played, and you and your brother were media darlings."

She says that a lot. All I remember is being dragged to arenas to sit in the family box with a bunch of other glammed-up housewives and their bratty children. And my mother always made us go down to the locker room when the media was finishing their postgame interviews and basically shoved us at my dad. He'd bend down and swing us around or hug us and at first I used to love it, because I was young and starved for his affection, and this was the only time he gave it. Then I got older and realized that the only reason he gave it to us after games was to entertain the media and impress his fans. Then that's when I started hating it. I was eight.

"I hate hockey. I'm not going."

Here's the part where she tells me how I owe my life to hockey.

"You always forget, but your father's career gave you a very comfortable life," she lectures sternly; her thin lips, painted a pink that's way too light for her skin tone, are turned down in a hard frown.

"More comfortable than a history teacher's salary, right? I mean, that's why you never went back and finished your own degree," I mutter.

"Being a hockey player's wife is a career, Shayne," she retorts. "I've told you that."

"Because Dad told *you* that when you wanted to go back to college," I remind her, even though I know she hasn't forgotten.

She doesn't respond to that. Her lips are pressed tightly together and her grip on the steering wheel is making her knuckles turn white, so I take a deep breath and return to the original conversation, which is only slightly less unpleasant.

"I haven't attended one of his events in years. No one will make a big deal out of it if I miss this one too." She turns into the parking lot of Elevate. "And I'm not just being difficult. I teach flow yoga at seven on Fridays. Sorry. But thanks for the lift."

I expect her to pull over at the curb by the door, but she turns left and starts scanning the row for a free spot. "I'm coming in to check on your brother and make sure he's still going to be there for your father. Make sure we can count on one child."

I wait impatiently as she slowly noses into a vacant stall. I just want to get out of the car and away from the guilt trip. She turns off the car and opens her door. I do the same and as soon as my feet hit the pavement, I turn to her with a smile and a wave. "I have to run ahead. I'm late for a class I'm teaching. But thanks for the lift. Have fun Friday."

She mutters a good-bye, and I know she's still upset with me. I just don't care. I made it clear to my father five years ago that I would not be a part of his career again—and I would never take another dime from him. And I hadn't. That money was blood money and it was the blood of this family that it shed. I was not going to be a part of it.

I rush straight to the nutrition class, shoving my coat and bag in the corner of the room and lecturing in my street clothes, which I know Trey would hate. He wants us in his Elevate Fitness gear at all times. But hey, at least I got here in time. When the class is over, I head toward the changing room to get into the right clothes and start my shift at the juice bar. Trey calls my name across the foyer and stops me dead in my tracks. I turn and find him standing by his office door, a scowl on his face. He waves me over.

I walk over and squeeze past him into his office. He lets the door close behind me and says firmly, "You're going."

"Where?"

"To the Winterhawks game on Friday. To Dad's ceremony."

"Trey."

"Shayne. You are going." He crosses his giant arms across his huge chest. His chin juts out defiantly. "I canceled your yoga class and I'll drive your ass myself. You. Are. Going."

I glare at him. "You know how I feel about him. About his career. About that fucking sport."

"Yeah, I know. I just don't care," he returns harshly. "Shayne, I'm the one who had issues because of hockey. Dad is the one with concussion syndrome, not you. If we can go, you can go."

"My issues with what hockey has done to this family aren't just about your drug problem and Dad's health, and you know it," I reply hotly.

I turn to leave because I am done with this conversation, and he can cancel all the classes he wants, but I'm not going. I reach for the door and he says, "You know how I deal with it? I choose to believe that Mom and Dad's marriage would have been a joke even if Dad were a car salesman or a doctor. That they're just fucked-up people in general and would be no matter what he did for a living."

I stop and turn back to look at my brother. He runs a hand over his shorn head and rubs the back of his neck. He's trying to chill himself out. He's done that since he was a kid. "Look, Shaynie. I know you hate the things that have happened. I'm not a big fan either. But he's your fucking father. We're your family. Sebastian Deveau is going to eclipse Dad's scoring record and this is the Hawks giving him his last hurrah. Just suck it up and give him a few hours, okay?"

"Can we talk about how you clearly knew Sebastian played hockey and didn't tell me?" I change the subject and cross my arms angrily over my chest.

"That'll teach you for having one-night stands in my laundry room."

And shower room, I add silently.

"And let's talk about how hypocritical it is that you keep banging him."

"Let's not. And that's over. For good."

Trey unfolds his arms and sighs, his massive shoulders heaving up, then down. "It'll be easier for me at this ceremony thing if you're there."

I can't deny him now, and he knows it. I sobbed a promise to him when he woke up from his coma that I would help him through, and I meant it. I would help him through life without hockey. Life without drugs. So if he needs me, I have to be there. "You're serious? You mean that?"

He nods. I want to scream but instead I nod back. "Are you picking me up at my place or do you want to leave from here?"

"From here."

"Fine." I turn to leave, but he puts a hand on my shoulder and pulls me back into his wall of a chest for a hug.

"Thank you, Shayne."

"You're welcome."

Chapter 22

Sebastian

But it feels fine," I argue to the trainers and the team doctor. The doctor gives me a skeptical look. I shrug. "I mean, it doesn't hurt any more than it usually does. I've played with worse pain."

"The point is, it doesn't hurt less," the doctor points out. "We've been taping it and icing it and you've been doing therapy treatments and it's not getting better. So this is plan B."

"Benching me in the last regular season game of the year? With a tribute to the team's most iconic player?" I snarl like a petulant child. "That's plan B?"

"Yep. And a brace." I cringe. "I'm sorry, Sebastian."

I look past the trainers to Coach. He gives me a smile that I'm sure he thinks is encouraging, but it comes off as more of a grimace. "We warned you that you were a game-time decision."

"*Je sais*," I mutter in French. "I know."

"But take the skate. Be out there for the tribute since you're the reason he's losing his scoring record," Coach relents. "Then get your ass up to the box, okay?"

I nod sharply because I don't have any fucking choice. And really, he's letting me be out there for a big team moment so at least that's something. But fuck, I want to play. We're playing the Barons, and I love getting under Devin Garrison's skin out there on the ice. Jordan's brother has an unspoken grudge against me, which is stupid because he got the girl. But Devin can't forget that Callie once flirted with the idea of being with me. Well, I honestly don't think she ever seriously entertained the thought. By the end of the night I knew it and she knew it. But at the time he wasn't clued in to the fact that she was already his, so he hates me. I enjoy that extra rush I get by having to try harder because one of the best players in the league is out there to show me up. And now I'm not even playing.

I leave the training room and return to the locker room to grab my stick and put on my skates. I drop down between Westwood and Garrison and shove a foot into a skate. Jordan runs a hand through his hair and gives me a tentative smile. "In or out?"

"Out. But I'm lacing up anyway," I mutter.

"Great. Now I'm going to be Devin's only target out there." Jordan groans. "So are they doing surgery? How long are you out for?"

"They haven't used the S word yet," I reply and stand. "Just giving it some real time off first to see if it gets stronger."

Jordan gives me a real, sympathetic smile as he stands. "I'm sorry, Seb. I went through this bullshit too. I know how hard it is not to play."

Avery stands and starts for the door. We follow, grabbing our sticks from the equipment manager as we exit. As we wait in the tunnel, I see a group of people in street clothes at the end, near the door we use to hit the ice. Five people, two males in suits facing me and three females with their backs to me. They're all in shadows, but I still recognize Trey, and the man standing beside him is Glenn Beckford, the legend himself. Standing side by side I realize they look incredibly similar. And the pieces fall in place like cinder blocks crashing heavily, one by one, in my brain. Trey is Glenn Beckford's son, which obviously means...

I have that weird feeling, like the ground just shifted or I just lost a skate edge on the ice. My insides somersault. I push past Jordy and grab Avery by the shoulder just as the lights dim and one of the staff starts opening the panel that leads to the ice and do what she told me to do the other night in my car. "Is Trey's last name Beckford?"

Avery blinks at me, confused. "Yeah. I didn't mention that?"

I should have asked Avery sooner, but I was trying to push her from my mind and I was distracted by this damn wrist injury. I'm totally embarrassed and slightly horrified by the fact that I could tell you Shay has a beauty mark on the inside of her left thigh, but up until two seconds ago I hadn't even thought to ask her what her last name was. The revelation that Shayne and I are doing this whole relationship as screwed-up and backward as humanly possible feels like a slap to the face.

The announcer's voice booms over the loudspeaker. "Ladies and gentlemen..." Avery moves to the front, just behind Chooch, who always leads us onto the ice, and we all march along behind him. "Your Seattle Winterhawks!"

I'm in front of Garrison now, behind Dixon, as we file past Glenn Beckford, who is beaming at us. My teammates all reach out and tap their gloved hands on his shoulder or against his outreached hand as they pass. A spotlight from above comes down and aims it on Glenn to show the fans the moment. I know it must be on the Jumbotron because the roar is deafening. My eyes are on the back of the long-haired brunette who, as soon as the spotlight hits them, takes a step back and turns away from her father and comes face-to-face with me. Our eyes lock.

"Hello, Miss *Beckford*," I whisper as I pass. She just stands there and stares at me, looking almost sad.

I pass her and smile at Trey as I gently tap my glove on Mr. Beckford's shoulder. He smiles at me. My skates hit the ice and I glide across it to the other end. I find a loose puck, skate over to Chooch in the net, and release a light slapper. A sharp, quick bolt of pain sizzles up my wrist. Fuck.

Still I skate around, passing the puck to my teammates, gliding by the centerline and making eye contact with Devin Garrison, who levels me with a venomous scowl. My eyes keep drifting back to the corner glass, by the door we enter from, where the Beckford family is still standing, watching warmups. Glenn is talking animatedly. Trey is smiling almost forlornly. A pretty pregnant woman who must be his wife is holding his hand. The woman I can only assume is their mom, because she's got Shay's nose and wide mouth, is beaming as our PR manager talks to her. Shay is kind of off by herself, a few feet from her family. Her lips are a glossy peachy-pink and her eyelids shimmer. She looks fucking edible even with the unhappy look on her face.

I'm so confused. Why wouldn't she tell me she was the daughter of a hockey legend? And why would the daughter of a hockey great hate the sport that made her father an icon?

I can't help myself, and I skate along the boards behind Chooch's goal and glide right by the glass where she's standing. I'm flush with it and when our eyes connect, I wink. I look back over my shoulder after I've passed. She's staring after me; her cheeks are pink and she's got a faint smile playing on her lips.

Yeah… this isn't as over as I thought it was. Not yet.

Chapter 23

Shayne

The ceremony is shorter than I thought it would be, which is a blessing. But they show a video—a montage of the great Glenn Beckford on and off the ice. It's filled with a lot of fights and goals and the locker room after they won the Cup for the first time thanks to my dad's goal in overtime of game seven. All of that is painless to watch. But it's interspersed with images of our family, which my mom must have supplied. My dad trying to teach me to skate when I was four, my dad on the ice with Trey when he was seven. All of us gathered around the Stanley Cup at a party in our backyard. My dad's not looking at the camera. His arms are around me and my mom, but his eyes were looking left, at the wife of a teammate he was screwing. I know because later that night, I walked in on them half naked in the upstairs master bathroom.

When the picture flashes up on the screen, my mother reaches over and takes my dad's hand, and I want to burst out laughing. I told her, in tears, what I'd discovered and she told me, with no emotion at all except annoyance, to calm down and pull myself together.

Now was not the time or the place. I heard them screaming at each other later that night and fully expected my mom to tell Trey and me we were leaving him, but she never did. My father, for his part, apologized for what I saw and promised he would never do it again. He meant the fucking in our bathroom part, not the fucking other women who were not my mom part. My family is a joke. My dad is a joke, and this whole ceremony is a joke.

My expression must reflect my feelings because Trey takes a small step closer and leans into me. "Shaynie, rein it in. You look homicidal."

I blink and force my face to relax and look indifferent. It's all I can do. Happy or even serene are unreachable emotions right now. I really don't want to watch the rest of this, so I decide to look for something else to focus on. And that's when I find him—Frenchie—staring at me from his position lined up with his teammates in front of the team's bench. Those insanely blue eyes are focused on me, and when I meet them with my own he smirks his sexy smirk, and a wave of heat rolls through me and settles between my legs. But more than just sexual attraction, I feel calmer when I look at him.

Finally the video stops and they darken the lights and I can't see Sebastian anymore. Then a spotlight focuses on the jersey, the one with my dad's name and his old number, that they have strung up at the end of the ice, and they start to raise it with some ridiculously dramatic music. Trey is standing stoically beside me, his face passive. My dad has got his chest puffed out proudly and he's smiling. My mom is fucking beaming and wiping at her watery eyes. Of course she is. Riding the coattails, or skate blades, of her husband's success is all she's ever had. It's all she gets out of this marriage, and once again I feel a surge of willpower. I will not end up like her.

Now the speech part. My dad gets up there, and I focus back on Sebastian because the lights are on again. He's still staring back at me, same smirk, same intensity in his eyes. And the same two feelings wash over me. Lust and peace. Or maybe it's euphoria—some weird post-orgasmic flashback or something. Whatever it is, I'm just grateful it dissipates the anger and frustration that are clawing my insides and making me want to run from the arena screaming.

Chapter 24

Sebastian

I change into the light gray suit and purple tie I came to the arena in and make my way up in the elevator to the team-owned boxes. There are two, one for management and one for VIPs. Usually the players sit with the management and watch the game from their box, but there's no rule that we can't mingle with the VIPs, and so I pass the management box and head to the one next door. I would definitely prefer mingling with a certain VIP tonight.

The box is filled with people. Shay is in the corner leaning against the wall looking at her watch, not the game, with a white wine in her hand. Her father is at the buffet table set up near the back, and his face lights up when he sees me enter.

"Sebastian Deveau!" He booms my name, and everyone looks over. He marches right over to me but I keep my eyes glued to Shayne, who is staring right back. "The Winterhawks' best defenseman since me. Why aren't you on the ice?"

"Minor wrist injury," I admit quietly, and he looks at my brace while I shake his hand. "I'm sitting this one out, so I thought I'd come say congratulations."

"Thanks, kid," Glenn beams. Shayne rolls her eyes. I try not to smile at that. "Have a seat, stay a while. Let me introduce you to my family."

I nod and he walks me over to Trey with an arm around my shoulders. I smile at Trey. "We've met. I actually go to his fitness center, and Jordan Garrison's fiancée works there."

He looks shocked at that. "A hockey player's wife works? That's a first."

He laughs at his own joke, oblivious to the fact that no one else is laughing. Trey smiles at me, almost like an apology. "Hey, Seb. Good seeing you. This is my wife, Sasha."

The pretty blonde shakes my hand, and I notice her protruding belly. "Congrats."

"Thanks." She rubs her belly and Trey smiles.

Glenn grins and points toward his daughter-in-law's belly. "This sucker is our last hope of continuing my hockey dynasty."

Hockey dynasty? He won a Cup and had a decent slap shot. I'd hardly call that a dynasty. But I nod and smile and impatiently wait for him to introduce me to Shayne. Glenn turns me around and, his eyes a darker gray than Shayne's but similar, searches for her. I search too, but she's not in the corner where she'd been a minute ago. There's nothing but an abandoned wineglass.

"Where is Shayne?"

"She went out for some air. You know how she is." Mrs. Beckford steps forward. "I'm Elizabeth Beckford. Glenn's wife."

"Nice to meet you," I say and smile to hide my dismay. Something tells me Shay's not coming back, and I'm not okay with that. I cuff

Glenn on the shoulder. "I should get back to the other box, but again, congratulations. I can only hope they raise my jersey one day too."

"They just might, kid," he says and shakes my hand again. "If you can stay healthy. You know I was only injured once in my whole career. You've been out a couple times this year, haven't you? Guess they don't make 'em like they used to."

I force a chuckle at that, but it's not funny. The fact is, he probably had a few concussions in his time, judging by the number of hits to the head he took, but no one knew what to look for back then. I excuse myself again and head out into the circular hallway that loops the arena. Up here in the box section, it's carpeted black and the walls are a dark green with framed photos of Winterhawks in action every few feet. I glance down the hall in both directions. She's walking toward one of the staircases. I pause for a moment to admire the wiggle of her perfect butt and then stride after her.

I reach her just as her hand pushes the door to the stairwell open. I press my body into her back, place a hand over hers and follow her through the door, like we're one person. Once in the empty stairwell, she turns, stepping away from my touch, but I step into her and curl a hand around her hip.

"What are you doing?" She's so cute when she's trying to be indignant. It would work better, though, if her eyes didn't linger on my mouth.

"Why didn't you tell me your father was Glenn Beckford?"

"What difference does it make?"

I think about that a second and shrug before tilting my head and giving her a smirk. "Guess it doesn't. I'm still attracted to you, no matter who your parents are."

"Frenchie, I don't do hockey players," she says, crossing her arms as if to keep more space between us, which just makes me take another step closer. She steps back, her butt hitting the wall.

"Because of him?" I guess, and when she doesn't say anything, I continue. "Because he's a little arrogant and insensitive. An old-school hockey jock with ethics and morals that don't work nowadays."

"You don't know the half of it."

"You know what I do know? I know you *did* do a hockey player," I remind her, leaning my head so close I can smell the shampoo in her glossy hair. The rich vanilla smell reminds me of the last time I was that close to her, when we were naked in the shower at Elevate, and I start to get hard. "And you were good at it."

My lips skim her jaw, just below her ear, and she whispers, almost pants, "Oh my God."

And before she can say anything else, I kiss her. The press of my lips on hers is purposeful and determined. I am going to show her what she knows she wants but refuses to give herself. It takes exactly one pass of my tongue against her closed lips for her to give up her silly little fight, and she opens her mouth and kisses me back. The kiss isn't so focused and calculated now. Now it's deep, and urgent, and I really want to fuck her right here, right now.

The door clangs loudly as someone pushes it open behind us. I hear a gasp and a giggle. Shayne is about to push me away but I'm already moving. Frozen in shock, with the door slowly closing behind them, are Jessie and Callie Caplan. Jessie is clearly the one who gasped, her mouth is still open, and her eyes are as wide as hockey pucks. Callie, not surprisingly, is still giggling deviously. She's the first to speak, which is also not a shocker.

"Hey, Seb." She steps forward and gently punches my shoulder. "Good to see you're still getting a workout even though you're not on the ice."

"Callie!" Jessie chastises her younger sister. Her eyes move to Shayne and she smiles. "Please excuse my sister. We're pretty sure she's got some kind of disorder, like she was born without the tact gene."

Shayne doesn't respond to that; she just says swiftly, "I have to get back."

She moves past all of us and disappears back into the hallway. At least she didn't leave. I can always go back in there and finish what we started…or at least, I can try. Callie watches her go and turns back to me. "Sorry. We didn't mean to interrupt."

"It's fine. It wasn't going anywhere anyway," I reply and smile. "Came to watch your boyfriend try to kick my ass?"

"Yep, but I hear you're injured," she replies, her brown eyes twinkling. "Hope it's not serious. I'd like to see him kick your ass in the playoffs later this month."

I laugh. "I'm sure he'll get another chance."

"So you and Shayne? It's happening?" Jessie questions.

"Not really," I admit, and I know I look disappointed. "I mean, we were getting somewhere, but then she found out I play hockey, and now she's treating me like a serial killer."

"She plays tonsil hockey with serial killers?" Callie questions and winks at me. "She's even crazier than me. That's something."

"She won't date me," I clarify.

"But she'll fuck you?"

"Yeah, she's been swayed in that direction a few times…" I admit sheepishly. "But that's not what I want. I mean, not only what I want."

"Oh my God, what is wrong with men these days." Callie sighs and rolls her eyes. I realize Devin Garrison is much more of a man than me if he was able to tame this wild woman.

"I didn't know her dad was Glenn Beckford," Jessie laments as we all start down the stairs. "She never mentioned it. Not even after I told her I was engaged to a player. Of course, she's been avoiding me since the first day we met. I don't know what I did."

"You're engaged to a hockey player," Callie says simply and shrugs, like it's obvious. "This girl hates hockey players. That must have come from something her dad did, since he's the hockey player in her life. And you two are part of that profession."

"But why?" I can't help but ask. "What's the big fucking deal?"

"I can't tell you," Callie replies. "Our dad was a professional hockey player and we hate him, but not the sport."

I blink. I didn't know that. How did I not know that? Of course I was obsessed with hockey my whole life, watched every game I could growing up; my mind goes straight to Drew Caplan, who played for Sacramento. "Drew Caplan?"

They both nod, and their faces are wearing similar pained looks; it makes them look even more alike. The look passes from Callie's face first. "We don't talk about it. There's nothing to say. He bailed before our mom died and didn't come back after the fact. Anyway, hockey life isn't for everyone. Just ask Devin's ex-wife."

"Maybe Shayne had a crappy childhood growing up with her dad on the road all the time," Jessie suggests. "But either way, she shouldn't hold it against you. Or me."

"You're right. And I'm not going to let her." I nod and stop. We're on the landing with half a flight to go before we hit the ground level where the locker rooms and family lounge are located. I'm sure that's where they're headed. "I'm going back up there."

"Of course you are." Callie laughs. "Hockey players never take no for an answer."

I grin at her. "If Devin can wear you down, anything's possible."

Jessie bursts out laughing at that, and Callie swats her. I turn and take the stairs two at a time. Thank God for hockey conditioning. I'm not even out of breath when I swing open the door. I start striding down the hall toward the VIP box. The hall is empty except for one or two arena ushers wandering back and forth. That's why I notice them right away.

Glenn Beckford, in a dark corner of the curving hallway. Under a framed photo of him lifting the Stanley Cup, he's kissing a woman who's not his wife.

Chapter 25

Shayne

It's Sunday, late afternoon, the sun is high in the cloudless sky but it's freezing. I'm outside Hattie's Hat in Ballard, Audrey's favorite brunch place because it serves a billion different kinds of Bloody Marys, waiting for my always fashionably late best friend to grace me with her presence. Finally, after almost fifteen minutes, I see Audrey's car come down the block. She honks as she drives past and pulls to a stop at an empty meter half a block up.

"Hurry up, princess. I'm starving!" I call as she's paying the meter. I try not to sound too harsh, because it is her birthday, after all. She comes charging up the street looking fabulous, as always, and I'm glad I put a little extra time into my own appearance. Audrey is a good-looking girl with a flair for hair, makeup and fashion that make her downright stunning, in my opinion. Today she's wearing a long white clingy sundress with a pair of cork wedge sandals and black onyx jewelry. Her long, perfectly curled hair is spilling out over her shoulders. Her eye makeup is dark and smoldering and stunning. It's her day so I guess it is her right to have every eye in the place turn and look at her, which they do, when we finally get inside and the hostess seats us.

"How'd you get here?"

"Cab."

"Still no damn car?"

I shrug. "Working on it."

"Christ, I take less time deciding on a boyfriend," Audrey gripes.

Hattie's has got a seventies diner feel to it with wood-paneled walls and booths down one side and tables down the other. The hostess seats us at the last booth, because Audrey told her there were going to be four of us.

"Are you just angling for a better table, or did you invite Josh?" I ask, slipping into the booth across from her.

"I invited Jessie and Sasha."

I freeze and stare at her. "Really?"

Audrey nods, reaching up to pull off her hat and fluff her hair. "I ran into Jessie at the gym yesterday after your class, and I invited her. I really like her."

"Oh. Okay," I say quietly, and she kicks my leg lightly under the table.

"Shaynie, you seemed to love Jessie when you met her," Audrey reminds me. "What happened? She says you've been avoiding her since she started working there."

"She's fine. I'm not avoiding her; I just…" I sigh and open my menu so I don't have to look at Audrey's judgmental stare. "We just don't have a lot in common."

"Ha! Or too much in common," Audrey scoffs loudly and I give her a hard stare. Why is she doing this?

Sasha arrives first. I swear her belly is bigger than it was just a couple of days ago. She rubs her stomach as she wedges herself into the booth beside me. Audrey lets out an appreciative whistle. "When are you popping the kid out? He looks like he's ready to join us."

Sasha laughs. "Another two months to go. Although I'd be happy with an early appearance at this point."

I slide over and Sasha wedges herself into the booth beside me, leaning over quickly to give Audrey a happy birthday and a hug. The waitress comes over and Audrey tells her we're waiting for one more and orders two Bloody Marys—one for me and one for her. Sasha orders herbal tea. After the waitress walks away, Sasha announces, "Oh, and by the way, he's a she."

I jump and spin my head to face her. "You know?"

She nods. "We just found out but haven't told anyone yet."

I hug her. "I'm so happy for you!"

And then Jessie is walking toward us, smiling brightly. I give her a small wave. I don't hate her. I have no reason to hate her. I just don't want to get too close to her. I feel like I'll get sucked into a world—Seb's world—that I'm trying to avoid. When she gets to our booth, Audrey introduces her to Sasha and then starts discussing the day's plans. She wants to have a big brunch with lots of Bloody Marys and then go shopping and get pedicures. I want to pretend I have a stomach bug and ditch them at the mall.

The waitress comes over with our drinks. Jessie orders her own Bloody Mary and we all order various versions of eggs Benedict. Then Sasha starts making small talk with Jessie.

"So are you from Seattle?"

"No. I'm from Maine," she explains with a friendly smile. "A hole-in-the-wall town called Silver Bay."

"Huge hockey town," Audrey adds helpfully. "They've produced more NHL players than any other town in the United States."

"I see you've read the Wikipedia page," Jessie quips, and Audrey grins.

"My boyfriend is a huge hockey fan. When I told him I met your fiancé he started reciting facts and stats about him, his family, the town. I'm surprised I don't know his shoe size," Audrey says, taking a healthy sip of her drink.

I sip mine and pull out the wedge of celery and take a bite as Audrey continues talking. "Your sister is dating Jordan's brother, right? Is that how you met Jordan?"

Jessie smiles. "We've all known the Garrisons since we were kids. My mother was best friends with Mrs. Garrison when they were young."

I look at her, my eyes sliding to the sparkling multidiamond ring on her hand. She watched this guy grow up. She knew he was going to be a high-paid hockey star and she sunk her claws in early. So did her sister. It's typical in small towns. My dad and mom were from a small town near Minnesota. My mom, the daughter of a dairy farmer, did the same thing. I asked her once, after I knew about the cheating, why she didn't divorce him, and her answer was: "And go back to the farm?"

"My mom died when I was eight, and after that, Donna, Jordan's mom, really looked out for us." Jessie sips her own Bloody Mary. "That's delicious."

The icy wall that blocked Jessie off from my heart starts to melt.

Sasha sips her tea. "That must have been hard, losing your mom so young."

"It was no picnic," Jessie admits, and she stirs her drink with her

straw, her eyes on the table. She looks uncomfortable so I'm not surprised when she changes the subject. "So you're married to Trey and
expecting a little one? That's great!"

Sasha nods and smiles. "I was just telling everyone before you ar-
rived, it's going to be a girl."

Jessie grins. "Congrats! That's amazing."

Sasha sighs and runs a hand through her long blond hair. "Yeah.
Trey's father isn't going to think so. He's counting on Trey to add a
boy to the hockey legacy."

"Ouch." Jessie gives Sasha a sympathetic smile. "My father was the
same way. He was devastated he had three girls. I wonder if he'd have
stuck around to raise us if we were boys who could fulfill his second
chance at a hockey career."

"Your dad wanted to be a hockey player?" I hadn't meant to speak
but I had to.

"Jessie's father is Drew Caplan," Audrey announces, her eyes narrowed in on me like a teacher giving a child a life lesson. "He played
for Sacramento, was considered one of the best in the league, before
a car crash shattered his leg."

"A drunk driving accident," Jessie clarifies. "My father had
demons. Probably still does, wherever he is. But thankfully, that's
not my problem."

I stare at her. She sips her drink, and the waitress shows up with
our meals. As she places them all on the table, Jessie glances over at
me. "You looked miserable out there on the ice during the ceremony.
I'm guessing your hockey dad is no treat either?"

I nod. Wow. I did not in a million years see this coming. Jessie
Caplan's dad was a hockey nightmare like my own. I suddenly feel
like maybe Jessie is exactly who I want in my life. But I still don't

know why, if she saw the darker side of hockey, she is about to marry a player.

The conversation turns to talk about the rest of our day—what everyone is looking to buy, what color nail polish we'll get for our pedis. But every time Audrey looks at me it's with a knowing smirk. Then, as she looks up at me as the waitress clears our plates and Audrey and Sasha talk about a new store in the mall they want to check out, I turn to Jessie and say softly, "I'm sorry if I've been a bit of a bitch to you."

Jessie smiles easily. "You haven't been. You've just been kind of distant."

"I may have stereotyped you without knowing how much we have in common. I'm sorry."

"I get it. My sister even accused me of being a puck bunny when we were kids and I first hooked up with Jordan," Jessie says and reaches across the table to give my hand a squeeze. "You can make it up to me by including me in the next girls' day."

"For sure," I agree happily. Thank God she's willing to cut me some slack.

I glance up and notice Audrey's doe eyes glued to something over my shoulder. "Is that Sebastian?!"

I spin around and my eyes land on Frenchie, who is at a table across the restaurant with a couple of guys.

"Gonna go say hello to lover boy?"

I shake my head swiftly as Sasha asks, "Who?"

"Number eight for the Seattle Winterhawks. Leads the team in fights and penalty minutes. Currently the highest scoring defenseman in the NHL, about to crush Glenn Beckford's record, and a potential Trojan Magnum spokesman."

I reach across the table and smack Audrey's arm at that last comment while Jessie groans, "Too much information!"

Sasha's eyes shoot to Seb's table and then get wide. "Him? The injured player from the other night? You're *sleeping* with him?!"

"No!" I bark at my sister-in-law. "It was just a one-night stand."

"That happened twice," Audrey adds helpfully.

Three times, I correct inwardly. Now Jessie is staring at me in shock along with Sasha. "So that kiss I stumbled upon at the game wasn't a first-time thing?"

"They kissed at the game?" Audrey looks like someone just gave her a check for a million dollars. "Oh my God, you broke your own rules. Knowingly. You like him!"

"I have no idea why I am friends with you," I say to her and turn to Jessie and Sasha. "That was a mistake. Being around my father gave me temporary insanity. It was nothing. We're nothing. He's a hockey player."

Audrey looks past me at him again, and he must be looking back because she mouths the word "hello." Jessie waves. "Oh! He's with Chooch and Dix."

I can't help but look back over, and Seb winks at me. I turn away, trying to quell the ripple of heat that starts to flow through my veins.

He looks mouthwateringly good. His hair is styled, pushed back a little off his forehead and tousled. He's wearing a charcoal shirt. The color makes his eyes look even lighter somehow. His jeans are well worn and he has battered black boots on.

I have to admit, I had expected to see him before now. I thought he would follow me back into the private box at the hockey game, but I didn't see him again for the rest of the game. And he hadn't been by the gym yesterday. Whether I liked it or not, I found myself wondering where he was and what he was doing and why I hadn't seen or heard from him. My heart was the one asking the questions, while my brain screamed the obvious answers.

You haven't heard from him because he's done with you. You treated him like crap. He finally got sick of it, which is what you wanted. He's moved on to the billions of eager, hot girls that want him.

That's why, now that I see him sitting there laughing with his buddies, I have to ignore him. Because I finally got what I wanted. I can't screw that up. Sasha glances over her shoulder, at Frenchie and his friends, and back at me.

"He's got his very pretty eyes glued to you, Shayne."

"It like he's trying to remove your clothes with his eyeballs," Audrey comments.

"Well, that's not happening again," I vow, even though I do not sound at all convincing.

"Good-looking, great guy with a good income—why wouldn't you want to date him?" Jessie wants to know, her green eyes blinking innocently.

I sigh, loudly, and nervously play with my hair. I can feel his eyes on me. It's making me warm. "My dad and basically all his teammates were cheaters. I dated a hockey player in college and he was a cheater."

"Unfortunately, it's not uncommon," Jessie agrees, but she doesn't look concerned, which I would if I was engaged to one. "But for every player I know who cheats, I can name two who don't. I've never seen Seb in a long-term relationship, but I know him well, and I'm confident he would be in the *don't* column."

"And he gives her orgasms," Audrey adds, crunching on the celery in her now empty glass. I glare at her but she goes on, undaunted.

"Go Seb!" Jessie laughs. "He's also great at making cocktails. Seriously, Shayne, he's a catch."

"Can we talk about something else?" I beg, so embarrassed now I feel like running away. I take a long sip of my Bloody Mary. Audrey rolls her eyes at me but shows me some support and changes the subject, asking Sasha if they have baby names picked out yet. A few minutes later as Sasha is explaining how much Trey loves the name Brandy and how much she hates it, a fresh Bloody Mary is placed in front of me, and the hand holding it doesn't belong to the waiter. I look up and Sebastian is smirking down at me.

"Thank you," I say, because I don't know what else to say.

"You're welcome," he replies just as simply, and then he glances at Audrey, Jessie and Sasha with less smirk and more smile. "I ordered another round for all of you too."

Sasha grins, leans forward and extends her hand. "I'm Sasha, Shayne's sister-in-law. And thank you. Please join us."

Ugh!

Sasha slides out of the booth as Sebastian reaches over and grabs a chair from a nearby empty table. "I'll take that and you can slide into my place," she offers and pats her baby belly. "I'm running to the bathroom every ten minutes anyway."

As if to prove her point, she waddles off to the bathroom. He drops his sweet ass into the booth and then leans back and wraps his arm around the back. My stomach does a somersault. God, what a pathetic reaction. The waiter shows up a minute later with fresh drinks for Audrey and Jessie and a Pellegrino for Sasha. Audrey looks back at Sebastian's friends and points.

"Why don't you invite them over too?" Audrey asks with a smile.

"I can text Josh and Jessie can text Jordan and we can make this a real party."

"What about shopping and—"

Audrey cuts me off. "My birthday, my plans. And I'm changing them."

"*Bonne fête*, Audrey." Sebastian raises his drink at my best friend, and the biggest traitor in my life, and turns to wave his friends over. As he does, his arm presses more firmly against my shoulders and his fingers graze my upper arm. It makes me tingle—between my legs.

A moment later Michael Choochinsky and Chris Dixon are pulling up some extra chairs and we've formed a group. Everyone is chatting at once. Audrey starts talking with Chooch. Dix has two kids, so he starts talking to my sister about formula and baby toys and colic. Jordan shows up and we order another round and move to a bigger table across the restaurant. Sebastian still ends up beside me somehow. Then Josh is there. Everyone is laughing and chatting and another round is ordered. I try in vain to stare straight ahead and focus on what Sasha is saying to Dix, but I can feel the heat of Frenchie's stare beating into the side of my face, so finally I relent and glance at him.

"Miss me?" he asks, his light blue eyes dancing.

I roll my eyes but can't fight a bit of a grin myself, because he's just so ridiculous. "You haven't been around? Hadn't noticed."

Bald-faced lie.

He looks crushed. "Guess I'll have to work harder at giving you something to miss."

I wrap both hands around my Bloody Mary, put the straw between my lips and take a long, slow sip. He makes the smallest little noise in the back of his throat that I'm sure no one can hear but me.

"I missed you." He admits it so easily I'm floored. So floored I have no response. He seems to enjoy that and he leans closer—so close the stubble on his chin tickles my shoulder and I shiver a little. "Why are you so surprised by that? I'm not the one who is against this—us."

I turn to face him and pull back a little because he's leaning so close to me that if I don't our lips will touch. And that can't happen in public in front of everyone. Or ever. "Because you know exactly where to find me and you haven't found me."

His smile softens at that, becoming less cocky. "I thought you didn't want to be found. At least not by me."

"I don't," I reply softly, and for some reason my brain can't comprehend, my heart adds, "I shouldn't."

"You know what they say, Shay," he whispers, his stubble once again rubbing deliciously against my skin. "You won't miss me if I don't go away."

Wow. Seriously? He's been staying away from me because he wanted me to miss him? *So tell him you missed him, dumbass*, my heart wails at my brain, which completely ignores it. Instead I press my lips together and say nothing at all. Chooch says Sebastian's name, trying to pull him into the conversation about golf he's having with Josh and Jordan. I keep my hands around my glass to avoid resting one on his knee under the table. That's all I want to do. Touch him. God, I miss touching him.

Chapter 26

Sebastian

I'm smiling at the fact that this day turned out so very differently than I anticipated and I couldn't be happier.

When Dix and I originally joined our goalie for a liquid brunch, it was simply to help Chooch, who had called me from a hotel room this morning because he'd walked out on Ainsley the night before. He was contemplating going back to her, and this being the first step to really ridding him of her, I jumped at the chance to meet him and make sure he didn't weaken. Dix offered to join me. Dix was the most happily married guy I knew and the biggest advocate for coupledom, and even he knew Ainsley was a cancer Chooch need to cut out of his life.

A secondary reason, a selfish one, to meet Chooch was because it was a way to keep my mind off Shay. I was purposely avoiding her. I was giving her time to miss me—I hadn't been kidding about that. But I also didn't know what to say about what I'd seen her father do. Or if I should say anything. Not seeing her, though, was torture.

I had decided, right before Chooch called, that I was going to go to Elevate Fitness and talk to her. I wasn't sure what I was going to say, or if I would mention what I saw with her dad, but I needed to see her again. Whether she wanted to or not, she responded to that kiss in the stairwell. But Chooch needed me, and I never blew off a teammate. Especially because I know Chooch was toying with the idea of going back to Ainsley, and that would be the worst possible thing, for him and our team. He was still playing like shit and I was hoping—we all were—that if she stayed gone he would be able to focus. Still, I wanted to see Shayne again so much I ached.

And then fate intervened, and there she was. When I first noticed her across the restaurant, I wanted to walk right over and grab her pretty head and lay my lips on hers. But Chooch was in the middle of pouring his heart out. I waited as long as I could—about an hour—until I was literally twitching in my seat trying to fight the urge to go talk to her.

"Dude, what the fuck?!" Dix had said and waved a hand in front of my face to get my attention again. He had been telling us a story about how he knew it was right with his wife, Maxine. "You could do to listen to this too. Didn't your last relationship go all *Fatal Attraction*?"

"Sorry," I muttered.

Both Dix and Chooch turned around to see what was so distracting. "I've been…involved with the girl over there."

"The pregnant one?!" I give Dix a withering stare and he laughs. "What? With you anything is possible."

"The one next to the pregnant one," I explain, and both sets of eyes turn and stare at Shay. "Here name is Shay. She's the sister of Avery's old teammate, Trey. The guy who owns Elevate Fitness."

"Really? You're dating her?" Dix seemed shocked.

"Not technically." I sighed. I don't want to gossip about Shay so instead I just mutter, "It's complicated."

"She's hot," Dix says admiringly. "Nice eyes."

"Nice everything," I reply, and he smiles at that.

"She works at the gym, right? The girl in the green dress from the opening party?" Chooch says, his freckled face scrunching up a little as he strains to remember.

"Yoga teacher and nutritionist," I tell Chooch.

"So is she bendy?" Chooch wants to know. "I hear you can fuck yoga girls with their legs behind their heads."

I feel my skin turning pink. Dix chuckles, and Chooch raises his hand for a high-five. I reluctantly give it to him. "Shut up, okay," I demand. "It's not like that. I like her."

"What do you mean?" Dix acts like he's never, ever heard of the concept.

"I like her. I'm trying to date her," I explain.

"Then maybe you should go over there and, you know, *talk* to her." Dix's words drip with sarcasm and so does his smile.

"I want to," I admit. "It's just complicated."

"Well, then, I'm going to give you the same advice I'm giving Chooch," Dix says. "Give up and get out."

I shake my head and smile as I rise to my feet. "Nah. She's just worth it."

And that's when I gave in and ordered a round for them, delivering her drink in person.

Now here we are, three hours later, at a bar a few doors down from the restaurant, ordering more drinks, listening to the Bon Jovi cover band and having a blast. Sasha is the only one who bailed, heading home shortly after we joined the girls. Shay had tried to leave too, but Audrey had used to birthday-girl powers to veto that. Shay pouted a little bit at first, but now she is on the dance floor with Audrey and Josh rocking out to "You Give Love a Bad Name." She's moving her hips, her arms up by her head, her eyes almost closed as she sings along. She's looks fucking delicious. My mouth is watering.

So far two random guys have tried to dance with her, lumbering up behind and bumping against her. Every time she moved away from them, her sparkling gray eyes drifting to me. *She wants this as much as I do*, my brain screamed. Or maybe it was my dick. Sometimes, around her, it's hard to differentiate.

"He's going to do something he'll regret," I hear Dix say, and I tear my eyes off Shay. He's frowning, still looking over at Chooch, who is now standing even closer to the long, lean brunette.

"We want him over Ainsley, don't we?" Jordan counters, taking a swig from his beer bottle. "Sometimes the fastest route to that is fucking someone else."

"Chooch isn't technically broken up with Ainsley," I remind my teammates. "They haven't had a final talk. He just got mad at her and spent the night at a hotel. We need to get him home and make sure he ends this properly before he sleeps around."

Jessie must have walked up behind me in the middle of my little lecture because suddenly her slender arm is around my shoulder, and I glance sideways and see her face. "Seb is right. Ainsley might be a total bitch, but Chooch did love her. Let's make sure he doesn't disrespect that. Go over there and untangle him from the girl."

She gives her fiancé a little push; Jordan groans but wanders away from us and over to our goalie. She turns to me with a grin. "And now to fix your love life."

"I'd be forever grateful if you did," I reply honestly. "I have no idea how to do it myself."

Jessie looks over to where Shay is still dancing her ever-loving heart out. "She likes you. She likes me too, but she was blowing both of us off, and today I figured out why."

"Hockey."

"Her father, more specifically," Jessie adds and wraps another arm around my shoulder. "I think he's a total narcissistic dick."

"A cheating, narcissistic dick." I lower my voice a little, even though it's loud in here. "I saw him making out with a woman at the game the other night. Not his wife."

"Shut up," Jessie bursts out in shock and then she groans, dropping her head onto my shoulder. "Ugh. Did you tell her?"

"No. I didn't know what to say," I reply. "I mean, it's not my family or my business and…I think she knows anyway."

"I think you should tell her," Jessie says.

My eyes land on Shay again, and this time she's looking back. The song ends and the cover band goes right into "Living on a Prayer," one of the only Bon Jovi songs I like. I glance at Jessie, uneasy.

"I would want to know," she urges.

I don't answer her. I just take a deep breath and walk over to the edge of the dance floor. She's watching me the whole time, even though both she and Audrey are still bouncing around and singing along. I wiggle my finger at her, beckoning her to come to me. I don't expect her to do it. I almost expect her to flip me a middle finger or at the very least roll her pretty eyes and turn away. But to my utter amazement, she walks over to where I'm standing. Shay grabs my beer and takes a sip and then smiles as she hands it back. But it's a guarded smile. "You summoned?"

"You look great out there," I tell her as my eyes feast on her flushed cheeks and the dewy look of her skin.

"You should join me," she replies with a small seductive smile.

I shake my head reluctantly. "I don't dance."

She snorts at that. "No guy dances. They just rub themselves up against girls."

I raise an eyebrow. "Are you saying you want me to rub myself against you?"

She pauses and fights a smile. She loses the battle and grins as she reaches out, pinches the fabric of my sweater between her fingers and pulls. "That's exactly what I'm saying."

I wanted to talk to her about her dad, but she's flirty and happy and I'll be damned if I'm about to ruin that. It's such a rare moment, something I haven't seen since that first night.

I drop my half-empty beer on a nearby table and let her lead me onto the dance floor. I'm not graceful. I never have been. It's why I'm a defenseman. I just need to have speed and good aim—both for my shots and my hits. I'm about as good at moving to music as I would be at figure skating, which is not at all. But there is no way I am going to turn down the chance to touch her in public, like she's mine and only mine, for the world to see.

I might not be a dancer but I have a fairly decent voice and I know the words to this old eighties tune, so I lean close to her ear and sing. "Take my hand, we'll make it, I swear."

She looks up at me, our eyes latched on to each other. I reach up and move a hand through her hair, pushing it back off her shoulder, exposing her long, slender neck. I lean forward, take a deep breath of that scent that is all Shay—vanilla and lilacs or something—and let my lips ever so slightly touch the side of her neck.

She heaves a heavy breath and leans into the touch. I want to roar in victory. Instead I whisper, "Every man in this place wants you."

"Well, now they think I'm with you," she responds, and it makes my heart do a stutter step. I pull her closer and move my hips in rhythm with hers. I can feel her fingers curl into my hair. It sends a shiver down my spine.

"Every woman in this place wants you," she whispers.

"I only want you." The words leave my lips before I can filter them, and I instantly regret it. It's too honest. Too needy. Too much. But her eyes dart downward, as if suddenly shy, and then she steps a little closer. Our torsos are pressed against each other and she's just about riding my leg now. Since she hasn't run screaming yet, I decide to tell her everything I've been thinking. "Shay, hockey isn't who I am. It's what I do. You would like who I am if you let yourself. I'm good for you. And I know you're good for me."

When she looks up again, her kitten gray eyes seem dark. She's torn. Half of her wants to run, but half of her doesn't. I keep pushing, hoping that it gives the latter half more power to win the war. "I want to kiss you right now."

She licks her lips and we're not moving anymore. We're just standing there as everyone bounces and dances around us. "In public?" She acts mildly shocked. "So the world thinks I'm some puck bunny?"

She's still putting up her sarcastic, defiant walls, but she's not shutting me out or running away, so that's something. Still, I feel like I'm done with the games.

"So the world knows that I am fucking crazy about you." The smile on her lips fades and she looks suddenly deadly serious. I don't know what that means, but it makes me panic, so I do the only thing that I want to—I kiss her. Right there, on the dance floor in front of anyone and everyone, I cover her pretty little mouth with mine and my tongue sweeps over hers. She seems to melt, her body sinking into mine and her fingers tangling in the hair at my neck. The song is over and the next one is halfway done before we pull apart.

"My place?" I barely manage to get out between raspy breaths.

Without a word she leads me out of the club. *Victory!* my brain screams. Or maybe it's my dick. Once again, I can't differentiate.

Chapter 27

Shayne

I feel him before I see him. That's because I'm still in a deep, glorious sleep, and his lips are slowly tugging me back to reality. He's kissing my neck. Soft, feather-light kisses that graze over my throat and then my collarbone and then my breast as he pushes the duvet off me.

He stops and his tongue, all wet and warm, rolls circles around my right nipple. I press my shoulders into his deliciously comfortable mattress, arching my back to give him easier access. I can feel him smile against my skin at that.

"Morning, sunshine," he whispers before he moves onto my other nipple, shifting his body so he's half on top of me.

"We should talk," I say back as my brain fights off sleep and struggles to keep my hormones from drowning my common sense.

"*Je préfère les actions sur les mots.*"

Damn, the way his *R*s roll and his sleepy voice drops an octave, yeah, okay, maybe I get why women think French is sexy. I don't even care that I have no idea what he said. "Frenchie…"

His warm breath tickles my stomach as he moves lower and traces his tongue along my side, over my belly. He bites down my hip lightly and I can't help but arch my back a little. My hands reach out, find the back of his head, and I run my fingers over his soft hair made messy by sleep and last night's sex. He slips lower, under the duvet. My body tightens in anticipation.

"Before you can tell me why last night was a mistake, I'm going to remind you why you keep making it." His words make their way out from the blankets to my ears. He kisses the inside of my thigh. And then his head tilts in my hands and his tongue ever so softly slides across my most delicate parts, making sure to press more firmly as his tongue reaches my clit.

Oh my fucking God.

He does it again, and then I hear him chuckle. His hands slide gently over my thighs, moving inward. "You're arching your back so much, baby, I think it might break."

"Yoga instructor..." I pant as I feel his velvety tongue slip inside me. "Bendy."

He pushes farther inside me, wiggling his tongue and pressing his fingertips into my thighs, opening me farther. I am so close to coming—so very close—and I fight against it. I don't want it to end. I want him there forever. And ever. Oh God, it feels so good...

He moves his tongue upward, straight to my aching button, and circles it so slowly I want to squeal—and then I do as he pushes two fingers into me as far as they can go. I turn my head and moan into the pillow, the orgasm making my body quake.

"You're so fucking hot," he says into my pussy as his fingers keep moving me through the euphoric haze. "I've wanted to do this to you since the first time I saw you."

My body stills, but I'm still fighting for breath as he moves up, kissing another trail toward my face. He gently drops down on top of me, his hard, pulsing cock pressing into my belly. I feel a ripple of excitement that making me come with his tongue has turned him on so much. My face is turned, my cheek on the pillow. Sebastian leans forward and brushes my hair from my face and kisses my temple. I lift my arms and run my fingertips down his broad, muscled back.

"How you feeling?" he asks.

"Like I died and this is heaven." My orgasm has clearly obliterated my defenses.

"Are you sore from last night?"

Last night was crazy. We were both acting like animals in heat. We had basically thrown ourselves in a cab, hands and lips all over each other until we made it back to his place. Turns out he lives in Laurelhurst, which is one of the richest areas of Seattle. My brain somehow registered that as we fondled each other up the driveway.

I had my hands in his pants before he had his key in the door and was giving him a full-on blow job as soon as the door closed. I know the floors downstairs are marble because I was on my knees on them, but other than that, I don't remember much about his place. It was dark and all I cared about was quelling the insatiable urge I had for his touch, his skin, his tongue, his cock.

We'd fucked on the living room floor, with me on all fours and him taking me from behind. Before we'd even made it to the bedroom he had pushed me down on the stairs and fucked me there. Then we'd fucked in bed, good old missionary style, but he was pounding me so hard I had to put my hands on the cherrywood headboard to keep from getting a concussion.

I'd finally fallen asleep at three a.m., exhausted and, just as Sebastian suspected now, sore—but satisfied and able to ignore the shame I knew I was going to feel once I realized I'd broken my own rule—again. I fully intended to sneak out this morning before he woke up. Cab it home and take a cold shower and wash off the remnants of whatever spell he always casts on me. Then call him and explain to him, really explain, why we can never be a serious, actual thing. But he had to wake me up with his tongue between my legs and now…thanks to another mind-shattering orgasm, I can't even convince myself not to sleep with him one more…one *last* time.

I turn my face to his, our eyes locking. God, he is so beautiful. I've never seen anyone with eyes like his. It's more than just their color. It's how intuitive and expressive they seem. It's why I thought he was an accountant. He looks like he sees so much more—all the time—than what's on the surface.

I will never ever be able to get enough of this man. The thought is slightly terrifying as it runs through my head.

Sebastian starts to kiss me, but then his stomach gurgles loudly. I laugh. He joins me, self-consciously.

"I'm starving," he confesses and grins. "Wanna go to breakfast with me?"

I trace the outline of the scar in his eyebrow with my fingertip. Hockey players and their scars. They have them, they cause them. Those beautiful, intuitive eyes must see what I'm thinking because he reaches up and pulls my hand from his face and presses his lips to it. "Breakfast, *ma belle*. Just one meal. If you're so confident you're right about me—about all hockey players—then what are you scared of?"

"I'm not scared," I reply firmly, but my racing heart says otherwise.

"You're scared that the more time you spend with me, the more you'll realize I'm not the monster you think I am." He leans into the crook of my neck, his lips ghosting my skin. "Come on, baby, I dare you. Brunch with me."

"Dare?" I question, and he gives me the sexiest, cockiest grin. "Fine. But I'm paying—for both of us. I'm not looking for a free ride."

"I just gave you a ride." Seb wiggles his eyebrows. "Should I start charging for those?"

"Shut up." I can't help but laugh. "Let's just go to brunch."

Frenchie lights up like a kid on Christmas morning and jumps out of bed, naked and once again not afraid to show it. He pulls me out of bed too.

"First we shower," he insists and starts dragging me toward his bathroom.

"Together?" I question.

"Of course," he says smoothly. "That back of yours has to be scrubbed."

I feel a little flutter in my belly as I look at him. It's fear. Because Audrey is one hundred percent right—he is good for me and I like him. A lot. And it scares me but I think he might be worth the risk.

Chapter 28

Sebastian

Twenty minutes later, I'm freshly showered in a T-shirt and jeans drinking orange juice out of the container as I lean against the fridge door. I'm so incredibly happy. I really am. I'm not worried about my wrist issues anymore, even though it still aches almost constantly. I'm not stressed about the start of playoffs. Because once again, I'm with Shay. And when she's around I feel like everything else will be okay. She makes *me* okay.

I want to ask her out—on a real date. Something that shows her I'm not a typical hockey player and I'm serious about her and this relationship and she can trust me—trust *this*. But maybe I should wait until after the playoffs to tell her. I mean, playoff hockey is intense. There are curfews and stricter diets and training and practices and injury. There are always aches and pains and I'm always bitchy. Depending on how far we go, I'll be all gimpy and pathetic and probably cranky because I like to avoid taking pain meds. Not to mention the travel, which is every couple of days. No long home stands during playoffs. This is all part of the stuff that she hates about hockey. Is it smart to try and pull her into a commitment right now?

Shayne wanders into the living room trying to smooth the wrinkles out of her top with both hands. I can't help but laugh. "Wow. It totally looks like you've just been fucked."

She gives me a saucy glare. "Next time I'll make sure to fold them before getting on all fours for you."

I grin at the memory.

"You have a gorgeous grin, you know that?" she says and I flush. "It's disarmingly charming and beyond sexy."

"That's how I feel about your smile," I reply because it's the truth. "And everything else about you too."

She smiles shyly at me. *God, I think I'm falling in love with her.* How the fuck is that happening when I can't even grow a pair and ask her out? I put the now empty orange juice container on the counter and walk over to where she's leaning on the door frame to the kitchen.

"I used your toothbrush." She smiles evilly. "I owed you."

"Yes, you did." I laugh and lean forward and grab her hand, pulling her right into a kiss. She tastes of toothpaste, and it makes me smile again.

"Shay, listen," I swallow and try to gather my courage. "I want to ask you something—"

Knock! Knock! Knock!

Who the fuck is that? Shay looks up at me confused. They knock again.

"Just a second," I tell her and wander to the front door. I swing it open and find my sister standing on my stoop with her coworker, my ex-girlfriend Dawn.

"You forgot?" Stephanie rolls her eyes. "Golf. My work's charity golf tournament."

This is going to go badly.

"*Elle m'a dit que tu m'as promis,*" Stephanie tells me in French so Dawn doesn't understand.

Fuck me. I promised to attend the firm's charity golf game as a celebrity guest when I was dating Dawn. I'd completely forgotten about it.

"*Et vous ne pouvez pas annuler maintenant parce que notre patron vous attend.*"

"*Merde.*" It'll look bad for Stephanie if don't show up.

"Miss me, Sebastian?" Dawn asks, batting her eyelashes expectantly and reaching up to hug me.

"Guys, I kind of have other plans. I just didn't…"

"I'll see you later, Frenchie." Shayne's voice is airy and calm, which fills my stomach with dread. She's a blur as she whizzes past me, smiling serenely as she leaves.

"Wait! You don't have to go!" I say urgently because I want to spend the day with her. I want to spend *every* day with her.

"Seb, this is for charity," Dawn calls out as if reminding me I'm an asshole. "You promised me. Don't bail on this promise too."

What kind of bullshit is she trying to spew? I never promised her anything.

Without looking back, Shay gives a casual wave and keeps walking. "Bye. Have a good one!"

"That was *her,* wasn't it?" Stephanie gives me a sympathetic look. "The one?"

"I'll be back, guys," I say and dart outside, slamming my heavy oak door behind me.

I jump down the five stairs that lead up to my front door and do a quick sprint to catch Shayne two houses down, about to turn off my street toward a busy main road. She's only a foot in front of me; her long hair is over one shoulder, shielding her face from my view. She doesn't stop walking even though I know she knows I'm here.

"Shay." I step out in front of her and grab her arm just above the wrist. She glances at me and gently tugs her arm free. Her shoulders jut back and her head tips up a little.

"I totally forgot that I promised to play in a charity game at my sister's law firm," I mumble guiltily.

"Your sister?" Shayne questions with an arched eyebrow that screams "bullshit." But before I can swear up and down Stephanie and I share DNA, she shrugs. "No worries. Go. I'll Uber it."

Her tone is so distant it disturbs me. It's like we're strangers. Like I'm just an arbitrary client at the gym who forgot a training class.

"I'd rather spend the day with you," I say and place two fingers under her chin to draw her eyes up. "Seriously. I can cancel. My coach wouldn't want me swinging a golf club with my wrist issues anyway. Not before playoffs."

"Frenchie, really, it's fine," she insists and steps away. "We had random sex. You don't have to cancel your plans because of it."

She starts to walk away. And I grab her arm again. "Since we have sex every time we see each other, I don't think you can call it random anymore. Seriously, Stephanie is my sister. I swear. I know you want this moment to be a shining example of why you can't date a hockey player but it isn't."

"And the other one?"

Fuck.

"She's Stephanie's coworker." That's not a lie but it's a half truth and eventually it may bite me in the ass. And I know, I can feel it deep in my chest, that if I'm not brutally honest with this woman I will ruin everything. I run a hand through my hair and sigh. "And my ex-girlfriend."

She doesn't storm off at that. She doesn't blink. She doesn't frown. She simply says, "Oh."

She stares at me. I can't figure out if her silence is good or bad. I just know it's unnerving so I keep talking. "Everyone has exes. It doesn't make me a player."

"I know." She mumbles but she won't look me in the eye. I don't like that. Not one bit. "I have to go."

She tries to step around me, but I won't let her. She looks almost pained and I hold her shoulder with one hand and push her chin up gently with the other. She looks at me and I don't like the tight press of her lips or the way her gray eyes seem stormy. "Seb, I said I didn't want this."

"But you do want this."

"But this is why I shouldn't want this." She motions back toward my house.

"Dawn and I dated for a little over a month." I don't know if I'm saying the right thing. "She may have been more attached than I was, but as soon as I realized that we weren't on the same page, that she wasn't a fit for me, I ended it. I didn't lead her on. I didn't keep her around for sex. I ended it."

She sighs. "And yet here she is."

Before she can leave again, I kiss her. It's rough and dominant and demanding. She responds—*thank the hockey gods, she responds*—kissing me back with equal force and passion, just like the competitive, spirited, sexy woman I know she is.

"I won't let you use this as an excuse to ignore our connection," I murmur when we finally break apart. "So save your energy and stop trying."

She gives me the tiniest smile, but it's a smile. "You're not the boss of me."

"I'm not," I admit and glance down at my pants where my hard-on is making space limited. "But you're the boss of him, and he will not let you fire him."

She laughs. It's bright, bold and at the sound of it my heart feels like it scored an OT winner. "Don't make plans for tonight. As soon as I'm done with this charity thing, I'm taking you to dinner."

She opens her mouth but I kiss her words away. "Don't argue. Just be ready at seven. Later, Shay."

"You're arrogant, presumptuous and egotistical," she replies, but as she marches off down the street she says, "See you at seven."

I smile victoriously as I watch her ass swing as she walks away.

"Sebastian." I turn and see Stephanie on the stoop with Dawn, who has tears in her eyes.

Merde. Maudit. Calisse. Tabernac.

Chapter 29

Shayne

I'm still feeling conflicted when the Uber drops me off in front of my apartment. I like Sebastian Deveau. There's no denying that anymore. There's just not. To myself or anyone else if they ask—and Audrey will ask. But…I'm still grappling with the anxiety and fear that realization gave me this morning as he pressed his warm, wet body into mine in the shower and kissed me slow and deep as he washed my back. I'm on the brink of dating a hockey player. It's a complete impossibility. It's my worst nightmare and yet…I want it. I want to date Sebastian Deveau.

I have no reason not to believe that it was his sister and his ex who showed up on his doorstep this morning and that the whole thing was a weird, badly timed commitment he forgot about. In fact, he was brutally honest about it. He didn't sugarcoat it. He didn't lie. And he was right: everyone has exes. I had a few, but being that the last one was years ago in a different state, he is not about to show up on my doorstep.

As I open my front door and kick off my shoes, my stomach

grumbles and my cell phone rings. I see my sister-in-law's name on the call display as I wander into my kitchen. "Hey, Sash."

"Are you at the gym?"

"No. I'm not working today. Why?"

"Because Trey said he was going to work this morning but I called over there and Sara says it's his day off," she replies, and her voice is tight with worry.

"It is his day off," I reply and open my fridge, looking at the contents for something quick and easy I can consume. "You know that."

"Yeah, I do, but this morning he said he was going in anyway." Sasha sighed and I hear a slight quiver in her voice as she continues. "He's been stressed lately. The new business and the pregnancy and it's a lot of stress. He barely sleeps and he's been…on edge."

Sasha sounds so upset it rattles me, but I hope it's just the pregnancy that has her emotional. I grab a single-serve bottle of chocolate coconut milk out of the fridge and press the phone between my ear and shoulder as I twist it open. "Sara is a bit of a flake. Trey could be locked in his office and she didn't notice."

"He's not answering his cell either."

Okay. I have to admit that's weird. He's got a pregnant wife at home: he should always answer his cell. "Are you okay? Do you need something? I can swing by."

"No. I just…I just want to see my husband."

The angst in her voice is heartbreaking. I put down my coconut milk. "I'm going to head over there this afternoon and I'll send him home. He knows he has to keep his stress in check and it doesn't sound like he's doing that."

"I hope he takes your advice and comes home."

I smile into the phone. "Sasha, you forget I've had a lifetime of berating my brother and telling him what to do. He'll tell me I'm being my usual overbearing, bitchy self, but he'll do what I say."

She laughs a little at that. I tell her I'll call her later and hang up. I finish my milk, put the empty milk container in the recycling bin and head into my bedroom to change.

Twenty-five minutes later I walk into the gym slightly annoyed. I hate going to work on my day off. I'm pleased to see that the place is pretty busy. The gym's membership has been steadily climbing, but I know Trey is still concerned. The rent on this building is high and he's invested a ton in the renovations to make it as sleek and modern as it is. I worry still that he took on too much and I hate the added pressure he took on by borrowing money from our father. Dad is never one to let you forget when he helps you.

I know I spend more time than the average sister worrying about Trey. But I've been front row center to all the stress my father placed on him when it came to hockey. Trey's injury—no fault of his own—devastated our father more than it did Trey, and no matter how much he has denied it, I know in my heart that it was Dad's constant pressure to "get back at it" that caused Trey to down painkillers instead of giving up on hockey, which is what the doctors said he had to do.

I was the one who first noticed something was up, when I visited him at school after the injury and he vacillated between sluggish and agitated the entire weekend. And I was the one his roommate confided to, about thinking Trey was stealing money from him. And I was the one his college coach called when Trey vomited all over the ice in the middle of practice and then was found unconscious in the showers. I'm the one who got to the hospital first after draining my savings on a flight. I'm the one the doctor first told of his oxycodone addiction. I'm the one Trey cried to. When my father showed up he argued viciously with the doctor and even his own son, who was ready to admit he had a problem.

And even though that was years ago, I still feel like it was just yesterday. Almost losing my only brother, watching him hit bottom, all over a stupid sport and my father's ridiculous pressure, it left a scar on my soul. One that sometimes feels like it still hasn't healed. But I don't micromanage Trey. I don't. I just worry more than most.

Sara is at the juice bar; she's flushed and I'm guessing she just finished teaching one of her Pilates classes. She gives me a tight but professional smile. Sara and I used to get along great when she was first hired and we were prepping the gym for opening, but ever since the laundry room incident, she has been chilly, to say the least.

"Have you seen Trey?"

"It's his day off."

"And he hasn't come in?"

Sara shrugs. "Not that I know of."

Jessie walks out of the women's changing room dressed in jeans and a T-shirt. She must have just finished a shift. She grins at the sight of me, and I feel my face heat up as I return her grin with a sheepish one of my own. "Didn't think you'd be out and about so early after last night."

"What was last night?" Sara wants to know.

"We were out with a…friend…or dare I say boyfriend?" Jessie asks, her green eyes bright with hope. I feel a wave of panic ripple through me at that word.

"Not ready for that word," I reply swiftly, and I nervously tuck my hair behind my ear. "At least not yet."

"But maybe one day?" When I don't answer, her grin deepens.

"Is this about Sebastian Deveau?" Sara says, a bite to her voice. "Are you *dating* him?"

"We need to change the subject before I freak out, okay?" Jessie simply nods, but she's still grinning. "Have you seen Trey?"

"I told you he's not here," Sara huffs.

"He was here this morning when I started," Jessie replies, and I try not to give Sara a glare. "I talked to him briefly. He was in his office."

I glance over my shoulder down the hall to my brother's closed office door. "How did he seem? What time was it? Did you see him leave?"

"It was early. I got here at eight. He was upbeat. Way more upbeat than I was at that hour." She laughs a little.

I walk to his office. Jessie follows me as I dig my keys out from my purse. I have the only other full set that locks and unlocks every door in this place. I'm not officially the assistant manager, but unofficially I am. I just never asked for the title. I knock. No answer, so I try the handle. It's not locked. I push it open. Trey is slumped over his desk, eyes closed, mouth open, a puddle of drool next to his laptop.

I freeze and my stomach and heart seem to switch places. Is he…is he passed out or, oh my God, or…Jessie doesn't see what I think I see and she's smiling as she fights a laugh. "Sleeping on the job," she says and walks into the room. "Trey!"

At the sound of his name he startles and sits up. Thank freaking God. He blinks a few times and wipes his mouth on his sleeve as his eyes focus on us. He turns red—blushing easily is a family trait—and grabs a Kleenex to wipe up the drool. "Well, this is unprofessional."

Jessie smiles sympathetically. "Don't worry about it. You're the boss and it's your day off."

She turns to me and gives me a quick hug. "I'll leave you to talk, but Jordy and I are having people over tonight. Just an informal get-together. I'm cooking chili. You should come. It's the last real day for Jordan to do anything social before playoffs."

"I would love to! But I have plans tonight. A date."

"You do?" Trey interjects, so shocked it's kind of embarrassing.

Jessie grins because she knows exactly who my date is probably with. "Oh. Okay, well…the invite is for you and Seb, so maybe swing by beforehand and say hi. We'd love to see you."

I smile back and nod. "I'll tell him we should swing by."

She gives me another quick hug and waves good-bye to my brother. When I turn back to face him, I am more than ready for the look of disbelief on his face. He crosses his arms over his wide chest and quirks an eyebrow. "Just one time, huh?"

"I didn't come here to talk about my love life."

"It's a *love* life now?" he retorts. "I thought it was a one-time thing. A mistake. I thought you didn't associate with hockey players let alone have a love life with them."

"Why are you leaving your very pregnant wife at home on your day off to sleep at your desk?" I demand, ignoring his questioning completely. "Why are you so tired? Jessie said you were downright perky when you got here—and then you crash?"

He knows where I am going with this. He knows I know the signs and the symptoms of prescription drug abuse. Euphoric highs and uncontrollable drowsiness and mood swings and withdrawal from social activities and…

"Relax, Shayne," he spits out, annoyed. "I had a meeting with Avery this morning."

"Avery Westwood?"

"Yup." He's frowning.

"About the endorsement?" I ask, and I know the answer before he gives it, because I can see the disappointment and anger on his face.

"About how he won't be giving us one," Trey explains, when I could already deduce. He reaches up and rubs the back of his neck. "His management doesn't think it's a good fit for his image."

"Are you done now?" I ask, not even trying to hide the frustration in my voice. "Are you done trying to be friends with this asshole? Can you finally admit he's a jerk?"

"He's not in charge of his own life," Trey counters, and it angers the fuck out of me. "You don't know what it's like to be the number one hockey player in the world. He's not just an athlete; he's a brand."

"And he doesn't think we're good enough to be associated with his *brand*?" I question, and Trey kind of shrugs. "Then fuck him."

He rubs his neck again. "Yeah. I guess fuck him. But in the meantime, I paid for the radio spots and bought the online media and I don't have an endorsement to fill it."

"We'll find something," I say, but I'm not convinced. I know nothing about marketing and advertising and I'm pretty sure that there's nothing that can compete with what would have been an endorsement from the biggest athlete in town. "When do the ads start running?"

"Two weeks but creative is due next week."

"Okay. Let me think about it," I reply and walk over and give him a shove. "In the meantime go home and nap with your wife. Who misses you and is worried about you."

"She called you?"

"Yeah, and she was almost in tears."

"Pregnancy makes women weepy," he explains and sighs. "Seriously, she cried over a cell phone commercial last night."

"So suck it up and comfort her," I demand with a smile. "Your sperm did this to her."

"Please do not talk about my sperm," he replies and shivers in disgust.

"If you stay out of my love life," I counter and walk to the door, dragging him with me. I wait as he locks his office and we both start toward the exit.

"Shayne Augusta Beckford has a love life. With a hockey player." Trey shakes his head as step out into the warm spring day. He glances up, shielding his eyes as he looks up at the sky.

"What are you looking for?"

"Falling locusts," he jokes and turns to wink at me. "I mean clearly if you're dating an NHL player the apocalypse is on its way."

"Go home to your wife, butthead." I roll my eyes but I'm laughing.

"After I drive your ass home," he replies and grabs the back of my shirt like the annoying kid brother he is. "And will you please buy a damn car already."

Chapter 30

Sebastian

I throw my car keys in the general direction of the basket on the console table in my living room as I walk into the house and head straight to the kitchen for a beer. I'm not going to be able to drink once playoffs start and so I thank the hockey gods that this stupid charity golf thing happened this weekend and not next. Because I've never needed a drink more.

Stephanie wanders in after me and goes directly to the fridge, but instead of grabbing a beer, she takes one of those Starbucks drinks I keep here for her. She's moved her addictions to caffeine and chocolate over booze and drugs, and I'm completely okay with that. She jumps up on the island and twists the cap. It makes a loud pop.

"*Cauchemar*," I finally say.

"*Oui*," Stephanie agrees and reiterates when I say, "*Total* nightmare."

I had bowed out of playing in the tournament because I didn't want to aggravate my wrist, which pissed off an already pissed-off Dawn. She said it would make her look bad to her boss. Her boss, a tall, lanky older man with thick gray hair named Robert Voakes, didn't seem to mind in the least. He followed hockey and knew I'd sat a few games with an injury so he was sympathetic and just happy I showed up anyway. And even happier when I made a sizable donation. I spent the day in his cart going from hole to hole watching him and the others play and getting pouty death glares from Dawn. The day ended with a cocktail party at the clubhouse in which Dawn cornered me and asked me questions about Shay.

"So what? You're sleeping around now?" she had pouted. "God, Sebastian, we barely ended things."

"We very much terminated things," I replied calmly.

"So she's…what? Your new girlfriend?" Dawn's eyes had filled with tears and I wanted nothing more than to run out the door.

"It's heading that way, yes," I'd replied quietly. "Look, whether I met someone else or not, we were not going to work out. I'm sorry. You're a great girl, but it just wasn't working."

Thankfully, before Dawn could fully melt down, my sister interrupted. "Dawn, Mr. Voakes is asking for you. He wants to congratulate you on all your hard work putting this together. You should collect yourself and go see him."

Dawn blinked as if coming out of a trance and stepped away from me. She took a deep cleansing breath, wiped at her eyes and said, "I'll be back." Then she walked away.

"I'm getting the hell out of here," I had told Stephanie. She nodded and followed as we almost ran for the parking lot.

And now here we were after our successful escape. Stephanie's eyes, a darker blue than my own, narrowed in judgment. "Can you never do something like that again, okay?"

"What?" I question after a long swig from my beer bottle. "Date one of your coworkers? Forget to cancel obligations with an ex? Drag you into the middle of my drama?"

"All of the above."

I give her a sad, soft smile, like a lost puppy dog. She's never been able to stay angry when I give her that look. She rolls her eyes but smiles back. "I don't intend to have another ex-girlfriend, so don't worry."

She stares at me over the top of the bottle of her coffee drink. "You're that serious about the yoga instructor?"

"I am," I reply firmly, and my mind fills with images of Shay's face.

"She's that great?"

"She's stubborn, opinionated, sarcastic and competitive," I tell her with a smile.

Stephanie laughs. "Only you would find those qualities a turn-on."

I grin and sip my beer again. "I'm taking her on a real date tonight. To make up for that little disaster scene this morning."

My cell phone chimes from my pocket and I see Avery's number. I'd love to ignore it, but there are three calls you never ignore in hockey: the captain, the coach and the management. I answer it with a jovial hello.

"Hey," Avery says back, his voice all business as always. "So can you bring that cornbread you brought two years ago? Not the cornbread muffins you brought last year. The loaf from two years ago."

"What the fuck are you talking about?"

"To Jordan's. For the annual chili night." He replies like he's talking about something as ingrained into society as Christmas or Memorial Day. It takes me a minute of staring blankly at my refrigerator but then I remember. For the last couple of years a bunch of us have been going to Jordan's for our last meal before playoffs start. It started as a lark. We wanted one last night of beers and junk food before the crunch began. Jordan was single at the time and had just bought his big house so he hosted.

We won the Stanley Cup that year. Then we did it again last year but lost in the conference finals. A lot of athletes are superstitious, but Avery takes it to a ridiculous level. He follows the same strict routine every game day. He eats the same thing every game day. He listens to the same music. He won't even replace his jock, which is a totally disgusting thing he's had since he was nineteen. It's barely in one piece. And because we won the Stanley Cup the year we did the first chili night, he's insisted it's an annual event. And clearly he blames my missing cornbread for the loss last year.

I try not to smile at his craziness. "I'm not going tonight."

"Yeah, you are," he dismisses my statement. "And bring the bread, not the muffins, okay?"

"Seriously, Avery, I have a date. I can't make it."

"You have to make it," he argues back, and his voice is firm. "It's a tradition."

"Do it without me." I know this answer isn't acceptable to him, but there is no way I'm fucking up my date with Shayne because he believes in magic. "We have to do it without Larue since he got traded."

"I have no control over that," Avery replies tersely, his voice dripping in that hard, bullheaded quality it gets when he's frustrated because he's not getting what he wants. In his defense, no one has ever really said no to him, so it's not like he knows how to deal with it. "And that's fucking with the mojo enough, Deveau. I'm not going to let your dick ruin our odds completely."

"My dick is not going to cost us the Cup, Avs." Stephanie has no idea what we're talking about because she can only hear my side of the conversation, but when I say that, she bursts out laughing, covering her mouth to keep her chilled mocha from coming out all over my kitchen. "But thanks for giving it so much power."

"Sebastian. I need you to come." The tone of his voice is morphing from frustrated to desperate. "It'll set the course for us. I know you don't get it, but it will. Just fucking show up. Bring her if you want, but come. Don't fucking screw me."

"I won't screw you." I sigh because I know I have no choice. Avery has more power than any other captain in the league. When he butted heads with the coach the first year he started, they fired the coach. There have been rookies sent back down to the minors because he didn't like them, and he's had people traded who didn't get along with him. He runs the damn league, even though I'm not completely sure he knows that. But I do. So I'll go to the stupid chili night, at least for a few minutes, to quell his anxiety and keep him from blaming me for our playoff fate if it's disastrous.

"What time does it start?"

He heaves a loud sigh of relief, not even caring how fucking insane he comes across. "Seven. See you then, and bring your sister. She was there two years ago."

"Yeah." He hangs up and then I add, "See you then, Captain Crazy-pants."

Stephanie is still laughing but she's managed not to bring her drink through her nose, which I thought she might. "What the hell was that about?"

"I have to go to Jordan's to eat chili and so do you because my captain is certifiable." I scrub a hand over my face, which reminds me I have to shave for the last time tonight. Injuries, playoff beards, superstitious rituals: fuck, this is the absolute worst time to try and woo a woman who hates hockey.

Stephanie must see the worry on my face because she pats my shoulder. "Well, she'll either sink or swim."

"She can't sink," I murmur back. "I really like her, Steph."

"What can I do to help?"

"Make cornbread."

Stephanie looks confused but shrugs and immediately starts rummaging through my pantry for ingredients. I sigh. Damn it. This has disaster written all over it.

Chapter 31

Shayne

He knocks on my door early. It's only six thirty, and it makes me jump and smudge the attempt I'm making at eyeliner. Holy shit, why is he early? I quickly wipe the smudge and survey my face. I did an okay job, I guess. I mean I don't look nearly as glamorous as Audrey on any given day, but I look better than I normally do every day at the gym so...winning?

I realized after Trey dropped me off that I had nothing to do or think about but this impending "date." And by think, I mean obsess. Relentlessly. Where were we going? What should I wear? A dress? Jeans? Is this a real date or just food before we have sex again? And how do you go on a first date with someone you've already seen naked? Dates are for getting to know someone, figuring out what you have in common. It's going to be weird asking him what his favorite food is when I already know he's circumcised. And finding out about his childhood when I already know what his O face looks like. Fuck, we're doing this all backward, and I'm all about order.

I swing open my front door and he's standing there looking like something a bunch of horny female scientists cooked up in a laboratory. He's wearing a thin white Henley hugging his perfectly sculpted torso and shoulders. The buttons in the front are open, showing his smooth, tan skin and the edge of a bite mark I left on him last night. Oops. A pair of perfectly faded jeans hang off his delicious hips, his hair is tousled and brushed forward over his forehead, and his face is clean-shaven, not a hint of a shadow. Those piercing blue eyes are framed by those sexy dark glasses again.

"Glasses again?"

He smiles seductively. "I wanted to give off a porn vibe tonight, even if it's accountant porn."

I laugh and move so he can walk into my apartment. "I'll never live that down."

"No, you won't." He leans close and kisses my cheek, lingering for a long moment, and fuck, it makes my insides quiver. In my ear he whispers, "I'm hoping the glasses aren't the only porn-like thing that happens tonight."

As I turn pink, he reaches behind me and twists the dead bolt on my front door. I scowl. "Scared of my 'hood?"

"Hell, yes," he replies without hesitation. "Did you notice you didn't have to buzz me in? Because some sketchy-looking guy was walking out and just held the door for me. No questions asked. Just 'Hey, come on in, potential rapist or burglar or murderer.'"

I laugh and he frowns. "*Ma belle*, I'm serious. *C'est dangereux.*"

"English over here," I reply and roll my eyes at his amazingly hot French words. He finally notices I'm wearing a bathrobe. A big, fluffy, pink bathrobe. "I haven't decided on what to wear."

His eyes sweep over my robe and the corners of his irresistible mouth turn up. His left hand reaches between us and toys with the belt. "What're you wearing under that?"

"A snowsuit," I chirp back, and the irresistible mouth grows more irresistible as it slips into a smirk.

"Such a smart mouth…" he whispers as he tips his head down closer to my ear. "I have half a mind to pull that robe off and smack your beautiful ass. But unfortunately we have somewhere to be."

"Okay," I say, trying to hide my shock. Not shock at his words but shock that the idea of Sebastian smacking my ass created a ripple of desire that skittered up my spine. "Any clues on where we're going so I know what to put on?"

"Jeans are fine. I have something casual in mind."

"Okay, I'll be right back. Make yourself comfortable." I motion for him to head into the living room and then disappear into the bedroom.

"And bring a sweater for later. It might get cold and we'll be out-side."

I dig out my favorite jeans and my favorite non-athletic-wear top. It's a loose, flowy black shirt that falls off both shoulders. I decide to pair it with my over-the-knee black heeled boots. I grab some delicate dangling earrings with black tourmaline stones and a matching necklace and put them on as I glance around the room for my over-size red-and-gray poncho-style cardigan. I pull it off a pile of clothes on the chair in the corner. When I turn around he's leaning on the doorjamb, eyes glued to me.

I get flustered. "Were you watching me get dressed?"

He nods, and his tongue slips out of his mouth and wets his full lips. Like he's anticipating how I'll taste. *Because he wants to taste me.*

Oh my God, this man…"In my defense, I was going to just hang on your couch, but your feline hissed at me."

I laugh. "Roy doesn't like hockey players either."

He pretends to look miffed but that sexy mouth is quirked slightly in a smirk. I slide past him, and he steps into me so our bodies brush at every conceivable angle. It becomes so tight in the doorway that I can't move. My back is pressed to the frame and my front is pressed to Sebastian. "Aren't you going to ask me how my day was?"

"Did you get back together with your ex? Or fuck her on the ninth hole or something?" I blurt out completely crassly and totally inappropriately. It's been on my mind all day. I would be worried about any potential boyfriend spending the day with his ex, but a hockey player? Even worse. Because I honestly don't know Seb well enough to say one hundred percent that he's not anything like the hockey players I know and hate. I *feel* like he's different, but my feelings might be influenced by this insane carnal *need* I have for him.

He looks startled by my tactless questions but not guilty. "No, I definitely did not. But I did get a hard cock every time I thought of you. Which was often."

I feel my cheeks heat at that, and a delicious flutter happens in my stomach. His eyes, so freaking light behind the dark frame of the glasses that they are almost see-through today, sweep over my face, and it makes me feel like he's inspecting me, which makes me deeply uncomfortable. I'm about to squirm my way free of him when he lifts his hand and cups the side of my face, the rough pad of this thumb sweeping lightly over my nose to my cheekbone.

"Why do you hate your freckles?" he asks, and I'm once again amazed by his astuteness. He notices everything. That's not typical for any guy I've known let alone one that tends to take punches to the head for a living.

"Because they're freckles."

"They're adorable," he argues back, running his thumb along them again.

"Adorable is for cocker spaniel puppies and toddlers," I reply and try not to frown.

He ignores my snarky reply and leans down so our foreheads touch. "They're sexy. They give a softness to your otherwise hard edges," he tells me bluntly. "Stop trying so hard to cover them with makeup."

I instantly want to walk back into the bathroom and wipe off my already minimal makeup. But I won't. I can't. This man may have some kind of chemical in his body that I'm addicted to, but I'll be damned if he's going to run my life. My dad use to tell my mother how to dress and what she should look like, and I am not about to let him do that to me.

"Okay, when you stop taking punches to the face," I counter as I slide free from the wedge that is Frenchie and the doorjamb. "I'll stop covering the freckles on my face when you stop adding to the scars on yours."

I grab my purse off the arm of the couch, giving Roy a quick pet, and march toward the front door. I glance over my shoulder and try not to giggle as I watch Sebastian and Roy eyeball each other. Sebastian looks leery and Roy looks unimpressed. Seb follows me into the hall, and after I lock my door he takes my hand in his, and we start down the hall to the elevator. He bypasses it, though, and moves toward the stairs at the end of the hall. I hesitate. "Elevator is faster."

"It's also a piece of shit and I don't want to get stuck in it," he replies. "I took it up and I swear it barely made it."

"It's rickety but it never fails," I argue, because I know if we take the stairs we'll run into Wayne. Wayne is a harmless drunk who manages to scrounge up the rent every month on the studio apartment a few doors down from me, but he often ends up passing out in the stairwell, on his way to and from the laundry room or to get his mail or…just because.

He ignores me and tugs me past the elevator. "Listen, we need to make a quick stop before our date really begins."

I stare at the back of his head as we make out way down the stairs, him leading the way. "Okay…" My voice is cautious because his tone is contrite, like this place we need to go to is going to suck for both of us.

"Playoffs start tomorrow and our captain is batshit crazy so he's making a bunch of us go to—"

"Jordan and Jessie's for chili?" I finish for him as the conversation with Jessie filters back into my head.

We hit the first landing, on the floor below, and turn to continue down to the ground floor. No Wayne so far. Good. He stops suddenly and I stumble, almost banging into him. He catches me by the shoulders. "I ran into Jessie today and she mentioned it."

"I don't want to go and I definitely don't want to bring you." He freezes as soon as the words leave his mouth. "I don't mean that the way it sounds. I mean that I don't want to subject you to it. It's just a bunch of teammates, and it's not the way I wanted to start this date, but Avery is superstitious and we won the Cup the year we started this stupid chili night, so he thinks if we don't do it again we're doomed."

I frown. "Avery Westwood is going to be there?"

He nods, and as we turn to take the last seven steps that lead to the lobby, there's Wayne. His torso, wrapped in a dirty sweatshirt, is sprawled across three steps, his arms crossed on the landing with his head resting facedown on top of them. A spilled can of beer is on the step next to his ass, probably soaking his sweatpants. Sebastian's whole body tenses. I can feel his muscles tighten in his back and his arm as I bump against it after his abrupt stop.

"It's okay," I say and step around Seb. His fingers, intertwined with mine, clench protectively, but I ignore it and bend down next to Wayne. "Wayne. Wayne, wake up."

Wayne stirs, takes a sharp breath and promptly starts to cough. The stench of stale beer pollutes the air around us as he exhales, and when I look up, Sebastian is cringing. I turn back to Wayne and use my free hand to take his forearm and help him up. "Come on, you need to get to your apartment and sleep it off."

"Thanks, Susie, honey." He grins at me and uses the name he's been calling me since I met him, even though I told him it was Shayne. His smile is lopsided and one of his top front teeth is missing. The other ones are yellow. "I didn't mean to take a nap. Just, you know, couldn't help myself."

"Uh-huh." I nod and smile and yank on Sebastian's hand to try to get him to remove the scowl from his face. Wayne nods at Sebastian with a small, friendly, yet drunk, smile and stumbles down the hall toward his apartment.

I make sure he stumbles through the front door before I turn and lead Seb down the rest of the stairs. When we get to the bottom I speak before he has the chance—because I know he will and I know what he will say. "He's harmless."

"You need to move."

"No, I don't."

"Shay." His voice is stern and brimming with concern, but I don't like it.

Once we're seated inside his luxury SUV, which probably cost more than my entire year's pay, he glances over at me. "I'm going to worry about you living here."

"I'm going to worry about you getting your head smashed in on the ice," I retort. "Guess worry is what happens when two people…fornicate on a regular basis."

He doesn't even try to hold in his laughter at that. It's a loud, deep bark. His eyebrow, the one with the still-pink slice through it, rises. "Is that what we're doing? Fornicating on a regular basis?"

"That's what we've been doing so far," I say as he pulls out onto the busy street. "I mean it's regular for me. Probably not for you. You probably are used to it a few dozen times a week, but a couple times a month is pretty much a regular basis, considering before you I hadn't had sex for almost two years."

He hits the brake a little too hard at a stop sign, and I lurch forward. Thank God for seat belts. He turns to me with a look that's a medley of shock and awe, like he's just seen a ghost. "Two whole *years*? As in seven hundred and thirty days?"

"Longer, technically, because this was a leap year," I reply calmly and watch his face grow even more stunned. It makes me feel a little embarrassed, which then makes me feel a little annoyed. "That's a big deal to you?"

"It's not to you?" There's such shock in his deep voice that I start to feel awkward again. I hate being made to feel awkward.

"No," I mutter back and wrap my sweater more tightly around

me. "I've only had sex in relationships and I haven't had a relationship."

He seems to catch on that this is making me uncomfortable, because he reaches out and rests his right hand on my thigh, over my own hand. "So then I guess we're in a relationship."

"What?!"

"Well, if you only have sex in relationships, then that's what we're doing." Frenchie grins slyly and I have the urge to both slap and kiss it off his face. "I'm your boyfriend then. It's settled."

"Until you," I shoot back, flustered. "Now I'm all about the…the…" I'm trying to think of the right word.

"Bed buddy? Friend with benefits? Fuck toy?" Sebastian suggests helpfully. His smile slips from his full lips just a little as he adds, "We've been through this. I don't want to be any of those things. I'm campaigning for boyfriend."

"I can barely wrap my head around the fact that I willingly and repeatedly banged a hockey player," I confess, watching his rugged profile as he maneuvers in and out of freeway traffic. "I can't just jump right into a committed relationship with one. I need baby steps."

"What's his name?" Sebastian asks bluntly and glances at me with serious eyes. "Because this isn't just about what you've seen. It's about something you experienced."

"You're perceptive."

"I am. And a really good listener," he adds with a flash of his cocky grin. "So spit it out, Shay."

"His name was Dustin," I find myself admitting, even though it makes me uncomfortable. "I was already anti-hockey player in college, but I made an exception. And it bit me in the ass."

"You don't like your ass bitten. Noted," Seb quips, and I give him a tight smile. He sees this is really bothering me so he turns serious again. "He cheated?"

"Yep." I feel shame just thinking about how I found out, so I leave out the gory details.

He doesn't say anything for a few minutes, and then he puts his hand on my knee gently and gives it a small squeeze.

"You need me to prove you wrong," Sebastian announces in a soft but confident voice that I can't help but be soothed by. "Prove to you that all hockey players aren't two-timing, lying, hotheaded dirt bags. And I'll do that."

I don't respond because I don't know what to say. I mean, I know what I'm thinking—it's that I *really* want him to do just that and prove me wrong. I really, really do. But I don't dare admit that out loud.

Chapter 32

Sebastian

Jordan and Jessie's driveway is already full of cars so I park at the curb in front of his house. Shay is staring out the window at the large stone-and-wood home. Jordan didn't renovate like I did. He simply bought a new masterpiece. The house is stunning, I have to give him that. An impressive stone turret right through the middle of the house where the front door is, with a koi pod at the base and clean modern cedar siding on the rest of the structure. It's unique and eye-catching and clearly expensive. Shay hops out of the car before I have a chance to do the gentlemanly thing and help her.

She walks next to me as we climb the driveway and her eyes glance at every car. "Mercedes, BMW, Lexus, Range Rover. It looks like a luxury car lot."

"Speaking of cars, do you have one yet?" I ask casually.

"No, but I've found one online I'm going to make an offer on," she mutters back.

"What is it?"

She glances at me sheepishly. "Let's just say it would stick out like a sore thumb on this driveway."

I wrap an arm around her shoulder and lean down to whisper in her ear. "As long as it's reliable, it doesn't matter. I just need to know you'll be able to get to and from my place safely."

I punch the doorbell and wait. My plan is to spend fifteen minutes here, to appease Avery's ridiculous superstitions, and then take Shay to our real date—which I'd been fervently setting up via texts and emails from my phone all day while I endured that golf tournament. I've never, ever gone to this much trouble to impress a girl, and I'm nervous as hell.

The door swings open and Jordan is standing there. He's barefoot, wearing a bright red apron over his jeans and a T-shirt that says *Good Lookin' Is Cookin'* and he's holding a ladle in his left hand. "Hey! Come on in!"

We step into his massive entryway and as he closes the door he yells over his shoulder. "Seb's finally here, Avery. It's exactly like two years ago so call the league and tell them to just give us the Cup. That's how this superstition thing works, right?"

Shay smiles at that dig and I chuckle. "You're such a troublemaker."

"Someone has to point out his insanity," Jordan remarks and leans toward Shay. "Sorry you have to witness this. I swear not all hockey players are nutbars like Westwood. Seb will get you out of here as soon as possible."

She smiles at him, and so do I. Jordan isn't just the bumbling putz he likes to pretend he is. I put my hand on the small of her back and guide her toward the large kitchen at the back of the house. The smell hits us before anything else. It's delicious and my mouth starts to water. Shay says, "Smells amazing."

We enter the kitchen and it's brimming with people. Jessie is standing over the stove, in an apron that matches Jordan's, stirring a huge pot of chili. Avery is sitting at the island with a Pabst Blue Ribbon in his hand. My sister is leaning on the same island directly across from him. She must have just got here because she's pulling the Tupperware containers with the cornbread she made out of her tote bag. I glance into the attached family room and see Chooch slumped over on the couch looking miserable. The reason for his misery is sipping a glass of white wine beside him.

I turn to Jessie, and she knows exactly what has my face twisted up in horror. She steps away from the stove and hugs Shay hello and then meets my eye. "Avery invited *everyone* who was here two years ago. Because, you know…everything has to be exactly the same."

I turn and scowl at our captain and hiss, "They broke up."

Avery looks a little guilty, but not guilty enough, in my opinion, and he simply whispers back, "It's a couple of hours. It'll be fine."

Jordan and I exchange glances. Shay catches the exchange. "Everything okay?"

"Sure," I say and give her a quick smile. "I want you to meet my sister."

Stephanie puts the last of the cornbread on the island and comes over to us. She gives Shay a bright, friendly smile. "I'm Stephanie. I didn't get a chance to say hello earlier."

They shake hands and Shay looks a little embarrassed. Luckily, my sister picks up on it and adds, "I don't blame you for bolting. I would have hightailed it out there too if two random chicks showed up at my boyfriend's house at nine in the morning. I just would have run over him with my car first."

Shay laughs, and the ashamed look disappears from her face.

"Sadly, I don't have a car right now. But I'm glad to officially meet you."

Stephanie pulls her away from me. "Have you met everyone else?"

"Just Jordan and Jessie. Oh, and Chooch briefly."

At the sound of his name, Chooch looks over. His round eyes blink, like he's just remembered he's at a social function, and he stands up and walks into the kitchen. Ainsley watches him with a cold, hard glare. If he notices, he doesn't react. He smiles at Shay and waves. "Hi again."

Stephanie turns to Avery. "And this is Avery Westwood."

Avery gives her a friendly smile, and she gives him a cool one back that he doesn't seemed shock to receive, but I am. He clears his throat awkwardly. "Hi, Shayne. It's nice to finally meet you."

"Yeah," she replies coolly and pushes her long hair over her shoulder; she stands a little straighter. "I mean it's been forever. If you'd have visited my brother in the hospital, we'd have met years ago."

Uh-oh. I don't know the entire history between Avery and Trey Beckford, clearly. I know Trey broke two vertebrae in a hockey game when he played with Avery in college and that he tried to make a comeback from the injury but it didn't work out. At least that's Avery's side. I guess maybe Shay has a different side.

Stephanie glances between Avery and Shay, also noting the temperature drop in the room, and her eyes meet mine, confused. "So, anyone want a drink? Shayne, how about a Corona?"

"Sure. Thanks."

"And Seb will make margaritas," Avery announces, and I stare at him. He raises his can of beer toward the blender on the counter. "You and Chooch always make margaritas when we do chili night."

Right. Chooch and I had concocted some crazy coconut mint margarita drink the first year we did it. I glance at our goalie pleadingly, hoping he remembers what the hell ingredients we used because I sure as hell don't. Chooch points to a bag on the counter. "I brought the coconut and mint."

"I brought it," Ainsley corrects, and I turn and see her standing in the corner of the room. Her exotic features are somehow softer than they usually are. Less sharp…kind of sad. "You thought we used coconut milk, but it was actually coconut cream."

Chooch glances at her, his face void of any emotion, and simply nods. "Yeah."

Ainsley's eyes land on Shayne and I tense because she's not known to welcome any woman to the fold without taking a few swipes at her first. But today she just smiles—actually smiles.

"Hi. I'm Ainsley. Welcome to chili night," and then, because the girl can't do nice without screwing it up, she adds, "You must be Dawn."

Jordan actually drops his ladle. It smacks against the granite floor and the sound seems to echo because everyone else is completely silent. Stephanie is frozen, Shayne's Corona fisted in her hand. Jessie's eyes are as big as hockey pucks. Even Avery, who rarely shows emotion, is letting his mouth hang open in shock. Chooch, who was turned toward the bag of margarita supplies, tenses. His shoulders rise almost to his ears, and his head turns slowly toward Ainsley.

"Her name is Shayne," he tells her in a low, deep voice oozing venom. "What the fuck is wrong with you?"

Ainsley looks like she's just been wounded, and it's the first time I've seen an honest emotion, other than hate, cross her face. "What?

You told me he was dating a girl named Dawn. That was like two weeks ago."

Shayne shifts, moving a step away from me. Oh, fuck.

Chooch spins to face Ainsley full on now and steps toward her. His voice gets lower, more like a rumble. "That was over a month ago. Now shut up. Go home."

Tears tumble from Ainsley's dark brown eyes. She puts her wineglass on the counter and then wordlessly strides out of the room and down the hall.

Jessie sighs. "Fuck." She pulls off her apron and follows Ainsley down the hall.

"Sorry, Shayne," Chooch mumbles without looking at her.

"It's not your fault. I can see why she'd be confused," Shay replies, and I don't like that one bit.

"I need some air," Chooch mumbles and wanders out the door in the den that leads to the backyard.

"Ainsley can't leave before the chili," Avery says suddenly, and my fists clench.

I have to shove them into my pockets to keep from punching him. Instead I level him with a stare and am about to tell him to go fuck himself when Shay turns to him. Her gray eyes are clear and cool as she meets Avery's eye. "Aren't you worried that this superstition stuff is bad for your brand?"

"What?" Avery asks, his normally calm, collected tone dipping into something apprehensive.

Shay isn't backing down. "You know, if helping a friend restart his life in a positive way is bad for your brand, believing chili will win the Stanley Cup is probably going to make Reebok think twice before having you peddle their skates. But maybe Taco Bell will hire you as a spokesperson." She glances up at me and then at Jordy with false innocence all over her pretty face. "Is Taco Bell good for a hockey brand? Excuse me, I'm going to use the restroom."

Jordan points to his powder room, which is off the front hall. Without another word, Shay saunters out of the room. We all silently turn our gazes to Avery. He stares at us and then moves his eyes to the beer can in his hand. He looks guilty as shit. He knows exactly what Shay's scorn is about, even if the rest of us have no fucking clue. Finally Stephanie says, "I feel like we should applaud or at the very least snap."

My sister turns to Avery and swishes her arm out in front of her, snapping twice, once to the left and once to the right. Jordan laughs so hard he snorts. I grin, relieved for a break in the tension. Avery heaves a heavy breath. Stephanie drops forward on the island between her and Westwood and leans toward him, resting on her forearms. "So what did your brand do to her?"

He hesitates, his left index finger flicking at the tab on the can in his right hand. "Trey developed an addiction to painkillers when he tried to come back from his injury."

Oh. I didn't know this. How did I not know this? *Because you've been fucking not talking*, my brain reminds me. I glance at Stephanie. The smirk has left her lips and she looks suddenly serious. Avery doesn't know my sister's past. In fact, no one on the team does. It's not that I'm ashamed. It's just that it's in the past and that's where it's going to stay unless Stephanie decides otherwise. He looks up now, his face clearly awash in remorse. "I was leaving college to start my first year here and my dad...you know how he is."

Jordan and I make eye contact and both grimace. Yeah, we know how Avery's father is. The man is a fucking asshole, to put it mildly. He's a relentless, domineering, micromanaging dick.

"He told me it would be best if I distanced myself from Trey, so I never stopped by to see him in the hospital or rehab," Avery explains. "I mean he had a point. It was a big scandal that the college and the team didn't catch his drug use. A lot of people were saying the coaches knew and turned a blind eye and that he wasn't the only player to have substance issues. My dad thought if I was seen being sympathetic, it might be construed as approval or even, you know, like I was using too."

I'm so blown away by this new information—about Avery, but even more so about Shay's family—that I'm almost dizzy. I step back and lean against the counter as I try to absorb it. Jordan isn't so stunned, apparently. "Fuck, Avs, when my brother Cole got injured, he needed his friends and teammates around him more than ever. And he didn't have his family pressuring him the way I'm sure Glenn Beckford pushed Trey. You of all people should know the pressure his dad was probably putting on him."

Avery coughs, and his brown eyes are pleading as he says, "I know. I fucked up. That's why I wanted to bring all you guys to his opening. I wanted to show him I support him."

"Well, I guess that's something," I say, finally finding my voice. But I know that there must be more to it. I can tell by the look on Avery's face. "So…why is she still pissed? Is this about the endorsement?"

"Trey wanted me to do a commercial for him. I was going to, but…" He swallows hard and looks at his hands again.

"Your father thinks it's bad for your brand," I finish for him.

"Fuck, Westwood, come on. That's fucking brutal," Jordan

blurts out, running a hand through his blond hair and shaking his head.

Avery stands up suddenly, his voice raw and shaky. "I know, okay? But Trey's better off this way. The whole city is going to hate me in a few months anyway, so they won't want to go anywhere I recommend. I'm honestly doing him a favor."

"Why is the city going to hate you?" my sister asks, speaking for the first time since Avery's story began. I glance at her. She looks pained. I wonder how much of Trey's story is bringing up her own horrible memories.

Avery looks at me and then at Jordan. "My contract is up at the end of the season and…I'm probably not going to re-sign here."

"*What?*" Jordan and I bark it out at the exact same time. Honestly, if someone had just driven a Mack truck through the kitchen I would be less shocked. Avery Westwood *is* the Seattle Winterhawks. When they drafted him, the Winterhawks did something that has never been done before or since, they gave him a jersey with a C already on it. That's right; he had the captaincy handed to him the second he made the team.

Avery chose to go to college before he took it, though, which was unheard of, and I'm sure it was the one and only time he disobeyed his dad. Still, when he was done, he walked right onto the team and into the C. Winterhawks fans were instantly in love with him and the management gave him the biggest, longest starting contract in NHL history. And then he led us to the Cup, and after that I thought that he would be here till the day he hung up skates. And then he would coach here. That was the unspoken path that was effortlessly laid out in front of him. So why the hell wasn't he going to walk down it?

"It's not just about the hockey. I love you guys, you know that," Avery explains and scrubs a hand over his face.

Before he can explain exactly what the fuck it is making him abandon his golden ticket and the city and team that has had his back from the beginning, Ainsley marches back through the kitchen. She stops, looks around the room, clearly either oblivious to the tension in the room or too self-absorbed to care and says, "Where's Michael?"

Jordan points to the backyard and she heads outside.

Stephanie is the only one who doesn't watch her go. Her eyes never leave Avery and she jumps right back into the conversation like the interruption never happened.

"It's fine to look out for your brand. It's even the right thing to do from a business perspective," she says simply, her gaze holding Avery's with an intensity that only I know is about her own struggle with addiction. "But looking out for your friends...and standing up for what you actually know is right...that's the right thing to do as a human being."

Suddenly Jessie appears in the kitchen entry. "Seb. Umm... Shayne is leaving."

Chapter 33

Shayne

I honestly just intended to use the bathroom. I wanted a quiet place to take a few breaths and calm down. However, when I find their powder room, Jessie is standing outside the closed door and Ainsley is locked inside. Jessie gave me a sympathetic smile. "You can use one of our bathrooms upstairs."

"To be honest, I don't have to go." I sigh as I run a hand through my hair. "I just wanted to get away from Avery before I said something I regretted."

Jessie's sympathetic smile deepens. "He's definitely not that easy to understand. But I think deep down, if he would just think for himself, he's a good guy."

I glance at the bathroom door as I lean against the wall beside it. "So what's up with this?"

"Ainsley and Chooch are..." She seems to search for the right words. "Not together right now, but Avery invited her because she was here last time we did this and, you know..."

"Superstition," I finish for her and roll my eyes. "He's an idiot."

Jessie shrugs but nods. Then she changes the subject. "So how are things with Sebastian? I take it you're rethinking your ban on hockey players?"

I can't help but smile a little, but before I can answer, the bathroom door opens and the exotic beauty, who now has mascara slipping down her cheeks, is standing between us. "Do yourself a favor and don't fall into his trap."

Her dark eyes bore into me and I'm startled, to say the least. Jessie isn't as stunned and she says cautiously, "Ainsley...don't."

Ainsley glances at her with hard eyes. "What? You'd rather this girl get blindsided than know the truth?"

"What truth?" Jessie counters.

"You know why I called you Dawn? I wasn't trying to be a bitch, which I'm sure is what everyone assumes," Ainsley confesses. "It's because he was dating a girl named Dawn recently and he acted like it was incredibly serious. And a few weeks before Dawn showed up, he had Andie on his arm and acted like she was the one."

As I absorb this news I suddenly feel off-kilter. Like I've been lied to or I'm the butt of a joke. Jessie steps closer, her arms folded angrily over her chest, and her eyes are sharp with the same emotion. "Ainsley, if you weren't such a bitch, maybe you'd still have a relationship of your own. And FYI, trying to fuck up Sebastian's isn't going to win you any favors with Chooch or anyone else."

Jessie's vicious words don't seem to bother Ainsley. She lets a hard laugh escape her lips. "You think I was always a bitch? You don't think I became this way because of this life?" She turns her focus back to me and continues to enlighten me. "Sebastian used to be a manwhore like the rest of them. Just like her precious Jordan. Before

Jessie, Jordan fucked half of Seattle. Seb fucked the other half. Now he's serial dating his way through whatever is left."

Jessie rolls her eyes, but doesn't contest the part about her fiancé. Wow. If that's true, how is she okay with that? How does she trust that Jordan isn't still increasing his numbers behind her back? And oh my God, is Seb really doing that? Am I just another number in his experiment with monogamy?

Ainsley pauses and something flickers behind her dark eyes as she wipes at the mascara streaks on her cheeks. "Maybe that's the key…"

"Excuse me?" I can't help but ask.

Her eyes land on me again but they're bright with discovery. "Chooch and I have been together since we were fifteen. I've given up everything to be with him while he pursues his hockey career. And I've never been with anyone else, and he says he hasn't either. Maybe that's actually true…"

Jessie snorts in disbelief. "Maybe? It *is* true. Chooch was faithful to you, and you were a jealous bitch anyway."

Ainsley turns to Jessie. "Maybe he needs to have a few flings and then he'll come back to me. Like Jordan did with you."

"That's not what happened between Jordan and me," Jessie fires back.

"Or maybe he'll learn he doesn't have to settle down. What happens on the road stays on the road," I mutter, thinking of something I once heard one of my father's teammates snidely say as my father chuckled and winked in response. "Maybe he'll take you back, but he won't be faithful. Do you want to live like that?"

Jessie looks at me with concern. "They're not all like that."

I don't respond, but I know the look on my face says I don't believe it…because I don't think I do. Ainsley is clearly done with this fucked-up girl talk. She turns and walks back into the kitchen without a word to either of us.

Jessie and I watch her go, then look at each other. Jessie takes a deep breath and exhales slowly. "That isn't what happened between Jordan and me," she starts calmly. "He didn't dump me when we were kids so he could sow his wild oats."

I don't say anything, but I lift my eyebrows as if to say *oh, really?* Jessie smiles but it's sad and her eyes take on a forlorn look. "I was the one who walked away from him. Because I was young and scared and I didn't trust him. And my sister, Callie, had put it in my head that if I moved with Jordan instead of going to school in Arizona, I would be just like all those girls we hate."

I blink. Her smile grows sheepish and she adds, "Silver Bay is full of girls who want to ride potential NHLers right out of town. And I may have been young, but I watched my mom get screwed over by a hockey player and I let all that fear and anger cloud my reality. I left him the first chance I got, before I ever even gave us a chance, over something he didn't even do."

I am speechless. And confused. I don't know what to think. I mean…yeah, her story is easing the anger and panic Ainsley's words about Seb's past had started, but should they? She and Jordan aren't Sebastian and me. Just because they have a happy ending doesn't mean…

"I cost us a ton of time together and I try not to dwell on that because it would kill me if I did, but I never forget it either." She leans forward and hugs me. It's unexpected, and I bristle. Even though I know she's just being nice—and honest—I'm feeling more and more dread and panic grow inside me.

What the hell am I doing? I know better than this. I never

wanted to be part of this world. I worked my whole life to avoid this world. I suddenly want to be anywhere but here. I pull out of Jessie's embrace and turn away. "I want to go. Thank you for the invite and the talk, but I just...I need to go. I need to think."

"I'll go get Seb."

"No. I'll cab it. It's fine. Tell him I'll call him later."

"Shayne."

"Bye," I mumble as I open their front door.

I'm not even halfway down Jessie and Jordan's winding driveway when I hear his heavy footsteps behind me. His arm wraps around my bicep, warm and oddly comforting, and he turns me toward him. He steps right into me, so our hips are grazing and our chests are against each other. This man really has no sense of personal space, and as usual it's making me dizzy and hot.

"I'm not mad," I blurt out. "I just don't want to be here to help that asshole with his silly superstition and I need to think. I need to clear my head."

"Of what?"

"Of you," I reply honestly.

I bravely pull my gaze up to look into those unbelievable blue eyes. He's staring back at me through those dark glasses with such a heated gaze. I can't help but wonder if he's doing it on purpose, like it's some act, or if he really, truly wants me so much that it just emanates from him. I want it to be the latter so badly it scares me. He's a fucking hockey player with a past that exemplifies all my fears.

"I'm not just in your head," he replies in a rough whisper. "I'm deeper than that. I'm in your veins. I'm in your blood. You can fight against it all you want, but I know you know it's a losing battle."

I pull my lips into my mouth, mostly to keep them from connecting with his, which are precariously close to mine. "We have to see where this goes," he continues, his breath warm and inviting against my cheek. "*Tu sais ça.*"

"What?"

"You know that."

"How is it that something as simple as those three words sounds like you're asking me to take my clothes off?" I mutter back softly, trying to be my usual flippant self but feeling a little light-headed. "French is such a deceiving language."

He smirks at that. It's deep and playful and does even more to the space between my legs than his native tongue does. "I always want you to take your clothes off, no matter what language I'm speaking."

He makes me feel so sexy and desirable and…did Dawn feel this way too? Andie? "When did you break up with Dawn?"

He pauses and pulls back the slightest little bit. "Are you going to let me take you on that date I've planned or are you just going to go home alone?"

"You're not answering my question."

"I'll answer your question if you get in my car and let me drive us to the date I planned," he replies firmly.

I sigh. I can always jump out of the car at a stoplight or make him drive me home if I don't like where this conversation goes, I think. So I shrug and turn toward his SUV. He follows beside me, his wide hand pressed to my lower back, just a fraction of an inch above my ass, and I find myself wishing he'd let it slide lower.

He opens my door, then gets in on the other side. As he starts to pull away from the curb I can't help but ask. "What about chili night?"

"Fuck chili night and fuck Avery Westwood," he grumbles. I can tell there is more to this than just his captain's silly superstitions. I wonder what happened after I left the kitchen.

"So when did you break up with Dawn?"

"Before I met you," he replies casually, but his brow is knitted behind his glasses and his full lips are almost pulled down in a frown.

"Okay. How long before you met me?"

I watch him as he concentrates on the road. His Adam's apple bobs as he swallows, hard, but he doesn't respond. I'm thinking he's not going to reply at all and the silence between us is growing thick. Finally he answers. "You think the answer is going to change how you feel about me?"

"Maybe."

He lets out a hard huff of air through his nose at that and pushes his glasses up even though they weren't sliding down his nose to begin with. Must be a nervous habit. He shakes his head. "It doesn't change how I feel about you. Or what I feel for you."

He still doesn't answer the question and I glance out the windshield to assess where we are and how far I am from my neighborhood. Can I walk from here or do I need to call a cab? We're down by the waterfront, near Pike Place Market. He slows to a stop at a red light, and he must know I'm about to bolt because his right hand leaves the steering wheel and lands on my upper thigh, clutching it firmly.

"You already know the answer or you wouldn't be asking," he says quietly as his fingers spread over my jeans, his pinky finger moving up, very close to the center of my body. Very close. "And you're still here. Because it doesn't change how you feel. It's not making you any less drawn to me. Hearing me say it won't change anything either."

"I don't know when. Ainsley just said—"

"Of course Ainsley is to blame for this." Seb groans as he pulls forward as the light turns green, his hand still pressed to my inner thigh. "I'm so thankful that Chooch is finally ridding our lives of her."

"So you're all for just giving up and walking out on a serious relationship?"

"Don't twist this around, Shay," he warns as he pulls into a parking lot that borders the pier. He lets go of my thigh to pay the attendant and my leg suddenly feels cold. "I believe in long-term relationships. I want one. I just don't believe in staying with someone who is a vicious bitch and makes you miserable."

I say nothing as I watch him slip his wallet back into his jeans and maneuver the car into a parking spot. He jumps out and has my door open before I can even undo my seat belt. He wants to take my hand, like I'm some damsel who needs help getting out of the car. I swat his outstretched hand away and jump down of my own accord. Undaunted, he grabs my hand anyway and steers me to the back of the truck. Leaning down close to my ear, he whispers, "Always so feisty" before he opens the trunk and pulls out a canvas bag. I try to glimpse what's inside, but he yanks it from my view and gives me a wink.

An internal debate wars inside me. He was with Dawn probably within days of taking me on the dryer. Hockey player or not, any guy who jumped that quickly from one relationship to another would make me want to avoid him. Was I supposed to be rebound sex? I guess even if that was the first intention, it didn't exactly turn out that way, since I'm letting him lead me toward the pier, which is dark and looks abandoned. Even the big Ferris wheel at the end, a tourist trap, isn't lit up.

Just as the realization passes through my brain, the wheel comes to life, the neon lines outlining it, glowing a bright, dazzling blue like his eyes. A guy is standing at the base of the wheel, where tourists usually line up for rides. He smiles at Sebastian and suddenly my step falters.

"We're a little early, Mike," Sebastian says, stepping forward and letting go of my hand to shake his. "Hope that's not a problem."

"You paid for the whole night." The guy shrugs. "Not a problem at all."

"What's happening?" I ask in a rushed breath that I swear is nothing but adrenaline. Oh my God, did he reserve the Ferris wheel all night? For us?

"We're going on a little ride," he replies and puts the tote bag over his shoulder. "I want to excite you."

The guy opens the gate to allow us onto the wheel and Sebastian steps forward, but I don't move. I'm scared of heights. Not terrified or phobic, but scared enough that I avoid them as much as I can. He looks back at me, curious.

"Please do not let Ainsley's poisoned mind ruin this."

I swallow and shake my head. Before I can explain the truth, he blinks, and a challenging smile starts to part his lips. He gets it. "You're not scared, are you?"

"Heights are not my thing."

He chuckles; it's low and rough and tickles me deep in my gut. "You said one-night stands weren't your thing, and yet you enjoyed the hell out of it." He winks and, fuck, I want to slap him and kiss him again—at the exact same time. "You should give this a try too. I dare you."

He fucking dares me? What are we? Infants. "You're a little shit."

"A little shit you can trust," he counters and takes my hand, tugging my whole body with him as he walks through the gate and into one of the enclosed buckets. "I won't let anything happen to you."

For some insane reason, I let him pull me in with him. My knees are shaking and it feels like my blood is rushing much too quickly through my body. I *really* don't like heights. He pulls me down gently onto the seat beside him and lets his lips graze my cheek softly. I hear him breathe in heavily as he nuzzles my hair fleetingly and it makes me shudder. He positions his bag on the floor between his feet and gives Mike a one-minute sign with his hand.

The seat is hard and cold and I stare at Sebastian as he digs around in the tote bag, and I try not to panic. He pulls out a large, soft, gray cashmere throw blanket and begins to drape it over both of us. I smooth my half over my lap. It's as soft as a cloud. Seb digs back in his bag and comes out with a thermos and two metal camping mugs. He hands me one of the mugs as he unscrews the lid on the thermos. Steam curls up from it and he beckons for me to hold out my mug. As he pours the steaming liquid into my mug, the scent of chocolate fills my nostrils. And something else…something with a sharper scent.

He gives me a deep, almost dark smile and whispers. "Bailey's and hot chocolate. It'll keep you warm and calm your nerves."

With the thermos stored back in the bag and both our mugs filled, he turns to Mike and nods. Mike walks over to the controls. I feel a rush of fear. "Sebastian, I don't know about this…"

His eyes lock with mine and he smiles, but it's smug. "I think that's the first time you've ever used my full name."

Is it?

He leans closer; his lips brush my jaw. "You should say it next time you come."

The wheel lurches forward and I let out a squeak of panic. He slides closer so our bodies are pressed to each other and his arm is around my shoulders. I feel instantly warmer and instantly calmer. Not totally relaxed but much better than a second ago. We both take a sip of our hot chocolate. It's delicious. And the Bailey's leaves a soothing warm trail down my throat on its way to my belly.

I keep my eyes on him, refusing to look out at our surroundings, which I'm sure are inching farther and farther away as the wheel chugs upward. He notices my intense, focused stare and grins his sexy, panty-wetting grin. "You're honestly scared, aren't you?"

"I'm not," I argue, and his grin deepens because it's ridiculous. Fear is plastered all over my face, I know it. "I just am not a big fan of heights."

His grin is cocky and slightly arrogant. "I found something that throws you off balance. I like it."

"I'm not off balance, Frenchie," I retort to prove I'm just fine. Which I am so not. As I realize there is nothing in my peripheral vision but inky, black sky—the lights from the peer and the parking lot are gone—I press my hands harder against the warm mug to keep them from shaking.

"Look at the view," he demands quietly, turning his face to scan the horizon. "It's very pretty."

"So are you," I argue. "So I'll keep my eyes where they are."

His deep belly laugh fills the chilly air and causes the bucket we're in to shake. My heart lurches and tightens in fear. I reach out and grab his knee. "Stop!"

He laughs harder, and I grip his knee so tightly it hurts my fingers. He uses his arm around my shoulders to pull me closer and nuzzles his face against my neck. I know he's technically clean-shaven but it's rough and gives me a delicious tickle anyway. My fear dims ever so slightly. "You must be terrified if you're willing to hand me a compliment to keep from facing your fear."

His words are dripping with such smug egotism I'm surprised they aren't making a puddle at our feet. My competitive side roars to life, which also helps quell my fear. I am not going to let him feel like he's got something over me here. "It's got to be the lack of light. You look much better in the dark."

He didn't see that zinger coming and it shows as his cocky little grin slips, but then he laughs again and the bucket we're in—now a million feet above the ground—rocks again. I make a weird little sound—like a gurgle of fear—and clutch his leg again, this time much higher than his knee. His laughter stops instantly. "*Ma belle*, if your hand gets any higher you're going to death grip something that will ruin the night for both of us."

Our eyes meet again. "Then stop shaking this death trap."

His eyes soften. "Drink, *mon amour*."

Despite the fact that I hate being told what to do, I raise my mug to my lips and take a big sip. The warm, alcoholic liquid does help calm me down. He sips his own and leans close again. "Look out. I promise it's worth it."

"I don't like to be scared," I reply firmly. "I appreciate the gesture and the trouble you went through. And I'm enjoying being with you and the boozy hot chocolate, but there's no need for me to terrify myself."

He reaches up and pushes my hair back over my shoulder. His hand stays tangled in it, loosely cupping the back of my neck. His rough fingertips gently rub back and forth over the nape of my neck.

It's making me horny, which at least is helping me ignore the fear. "I think you need to live a little. Take some risks."

"You're a risk," I mutter back. He smiles and tilts his head. My stomach flutters as I think he's going to kiss me but his lips simply glide by mine. I almost groan with disappointment.

"Nah..." he argues softly. He finishes the hot chocolate in his mug and places it on the seat next to him. Then he raises his hand and puts it under my chin and tries to gently nudge my face toward the skyline stretching out in front of us. I let him but promptly close my eyes. I feel his lips against the crook of my neck and it makes me shiver. He sucks lightly on the skin there for just a moment before pulling back to whisper, "I dare you."

"You're lucky I don't throw you out of this thing," I spit back as his hand drops from my chin and lands in my lap on top of the blanket.

"You'd have to open your pretty little eyes to do it, so something tells me I'm safe."

I feel his hand move under the blanket and come to rest in the crease in my leg where my thigh meets my hip and my... His fingers fan out. *Oh my God.*

My eyes open, and before I can turn my face to look at him, the man with his fingers spread across my inner thigh, pressing against my core through my jeans, presses his forehead to my cheek, keeping my face straight forward. I have no choice but to look out at the skyline stretched before me.

We are so freaking high! The entire city is spread out below us, glimmering and shimmering, and it's breathtaking, but so is my fear. Even though I know it's the worst possible decision, I inch forward in my seat and look down through the glass of our bucket. The water below looks like a giant black hole and I am overwhelmed by the panic for a second until I feel his fingers move. They brush purposefully against the center of my jeans and the spike of fear is equally matched by a spike of pleasure.

"Frenchie…"

He either doesn't hear the caution in my voice or he just doesn't give a fuck, because his fingers press harder and begin to move against my middle. He's pressing the seam of my jeans into me; I only wore a thin, very lacy thong and the friction is… It's fucking incredible. I bite my top lip.

"See…it's not so bad, is it?" he murmurs in my ear, his breath warm against my cheek, and his fingers pressing and rubbing in just the right place. "It's pretty, isn't it?"

I nod and put my hot chocolate mug down beside me. His lips press firmly to my cheek, a fraction of an inch from my mouth. "What are you doing?"

"Distracting you from your fear."

He kisses me again. I turn my head, as our bucket crests the top of the wheel and…stops.

My body jolts, and I sit up perfectly straight and clutch him again exactly where he was worried I would clutch him, but I'm not nearly as forceful as I want to be. His hand between my legs lifts as he startles.

"Why are we stopped?" I ask, my eyes wild and my head turning from side to side, looking for something trapping us up here. The pod looks fine, but then again it's dark. "We're stuck? Oh my God, we're stuck!"

He's…laughing? He's fucking laughing! I twist to face him on the tiny bench. He tries not to laugh, pressing his lips together tightly, but it's impossible and he laughs even harder. I hate him.

"Frenchie! I don't want to sit up here swinging in the abyss!" I wail and yeah, I am totally wailing.

He stops laughing, but he's still smiling, so I still want to punch him. He lifts his hands like I'm holding a gun. "Okay! Okay! Relax, I just thought, if he gave us a moment at the top, you would enjoy the gorgeous view and I would enjoy you."

The bucket continues to rock ever so slightly and my heart lurches with every tiny swing. I place my palm flat on my chest and try to sound calm and serious as I say, "Sebastian, I want to get down. Please."

"Okay. Okay," he coos and slides close to me again. "All I have to do is text him when I want it started up again."

"Text him."

"Kiss me first."

"Are you kidding me?" I would seriously punch him except I'm sure his phone has a password and I won't be able to text Mike to start this death trap.

He shrugs, smirking. "You might not be able to enjoy the view, but I still want to enjoy you. That way the night isn't a total loss."

"You're a crazy, insane egomaniac, you know that?"

He nods and leans closer. "Yeah. So?"

I take a deep breath and close my eyes. "Text him."

"Kiss me." His hand slides back between my thighs but this time lies still. I open my eyes and he's taken off his glasses. Even in the darkness, his eyes are light and mischievous and so damn sexy under those dark, thick eyebrows. He squeezes my thigh. "Just. One. Kiss."

"Enjoy it because it's the only time you're going to touch me tonight." Then I reach up, grab the back of his head and kiss him for all he's worth.

Chapter 34

Sebastian

Shay is not fucking around. The kiss is aggressive. Her lips are strong and they part mine instantly, her tongue sweeping into my mouth like she owns it. She twists her fingers in my hair, tugging, and her body leans into it, her legs parting slightly and giving me better access. She most likely didn't mean to do it, but I'm taking advantage anyway. I press my fingers into her jeans and then slowly slide them upward.

Without a second's hesitation I unbutton them. If she notices, she doesn't react; she's too busy with the kiss, which is so hot I swear it's causing every ounce of blood I have to rush to my dick. She pulls my lower lip between her teeth but her gentle tug turns into a warning bite as I slide her zipper down.

"Frenchie."

"Sebastian," I correct her. "Remember I like the way it sounds when you say it. Now I want to hear you pant it."

"And I want to be on solid ground again," she replies, but there's much less conviction in her voice since the kiss. So I move my fingers into the space created by her open zipper. Lace greets my touch and I smile as I press my lips to her jaw and kiss my way up to her ear-lobe.

"Look at that view, *ma belle*," I whisper and skirt the edge of her underwear. "Just look for a second. Take it in. This city…that brought you and me together."

Her lips part and I know she's going to tell me no, or tell me to text Mike again, so I kiss her and slip my fingers under her lacy underwear. She surprises me because she doesn't scoot away from my hand or grab it and move it away. She pushes into me, parting her legs and lifting her ass a little to give me even more access. My fingers slide over that neat little triangle of hair and down lower where I find her wet and wanting.

I force myself not to smile into the kiss but damn, I'm fucking happy. I love her response to me because I have the exact same response to her, as the hard bulge pressing against my jeans proves. She reaches for my hair again as I slide two fingers into her.

She moans into my mouth and bites my bottom lip. I burrow my face against her neck, my lips tracing every inch of skin I can. "You're so beautiful, Shay," I whisper against her skin. "You may be scared but you're turned on too. You like being pushed out of your comfort zone. You enjoy the way I challenge you."

I start to pump my fingers in and out of her; she bucks up to meet me as her mouth turns away from mine and her head starts to tip back, her mouth falling open and a sexy little pant slipping out. Her hips push into my hand, and I tease her clit with my thumb. "Frenchie…oh my God."

"Say my name, baby," I demand, rubbing her clit and pushing my fingers deeper. "I love the feel of you hot, wet around my fingers. I want you to look at the view and I want you to come on my hand. And I want you to say my name when you do it."

She's close. Her hips are moving hard against me. Her skin is pink, and her eyes half closed and fluttering, a taut moan escaping her parted lips. I'm so absorbed in watching her chase her release that I don't even realize she put her hand on top of the bulge in my jeans.

"Say *my* name," she challenges in return and begins to rub her palm over my length. Holy fuck, this girl just never lets me win—and it's so fucking perfect.

I push deeper, palming her and rubbing every part of her. "Oh…yes…"

She's managed to get my zipper down and she doesn't even flinch when she touches my hot, hard flesh instead of underwear, which I don't wear all the time and am not wearing tonight. Her fingers play over my tip, playing with my precum, and I'm already so turned on it sends spikes of heat barreling up my spine. I am so close to coming it's insane. I haven't gotten off with a woman on anything less that a wet mouth or a wet pussy since I was a teenager. The woman is going to make me come with just the tips of her fingers.

"Oh…Oh…"

"Say my name." I gently bite down on her earlobe and curl my fingers, deeper, and find her sweet spot.

Her eyes open, she's looking out at the world below us and she gasps. "Sebastian…"

Her fingers wrap around my length as best they can in the confined space and as I watch her come, I push up into her hand.

She tightens her grip and I punch up my hips again and come. I fucking come from watching her come and a few feeble pumps into her hand. And when I do her name tumbles from my lips. "Shayne…"

The words I bite back are *I think I'm falling in love with you.*

Chapter 35

Shayne

The next morning I wake up early. The sun is barely cresting. Sebastian is dead asleep, snoring lightly, his head turned away from me and pressed into the pillow. He has one arm under his pillow and the other one stretched out kind of hanging off the bed. He's kicked the duvet off and he's only got the sheet twisted around his naked body. I have the ridiculous urge to dig my phone out of my purse and take a picture of him because I want to remember this—his beautiful, naked, sleeping body—forever. Or at least it would give me something to look at while he is in the playoffs.

I don't expect to see him much until they're over. When my father made the playoffs, which was almost every year of his professional career, the coach often sequestered them in hotel rooms, even for the home games. It was a tactic he used to keep the players focused. My mother hated it. My brother and I hated it at first too, until we were older, and not having Dad around actually felt like a relief. As soon as we were teens and I caught him cheating and he started really pressuring Trey about hockey, Glenn Beckford's presence was no longer a blessing. I used to fantasize about my mom leaving him. What kid's "dream" is a broken family?

I wonder about Sebastian's family life. What was he like growing up? Is he close to both his parents? I met Stephanie, but does he have other siblings? I'm overwhelmed once again by how little I know about him. It's overwhelming because it's at such odds with how much I feel for him. And my feelings for him are beyond physical at this point, which makes this whole thing even crazier. How do I care for someone whom I barely know?

I lift the covers and slip out. The early morning air has a chill, so I make sure to cover him with the duvet he kicked off, and then I grab my underwear off the floor and pull them back on. I don't feel like getting totally dressed so I glance around the room, which is more immaculate than any guy's room I know. Sebastian isn't messy. But I do see a blue hoodie hanging on a hook inside his open walk-in closet door, so I snag it and pull it on. It's warm and fuzzy and smells like him, and luckily it hangs to my midthigh so I'm not going to be prancing around his house with my ass hanging out.

I pad out of his bedroom and downstairs. This is my second night in his house—in his bed—and both experiences have been wildly different. The first night when we came home from the bar, everything was a blur. I didn't look around. I didn't see anything but him. I concentrated solely on his naked body and giving it pleasure—and getting pleasure from it. I was high on the rush of breaking my own rules—my biggest, longest, strongest rule—and I had tunnel vision. And then I'd bolted the next day.

Last night, after our adventure on the Great Seattle Wheel, was completely different. After the ride we were both famished so we stopped at a fast-food place and indulged in burgers, fries and milk shakes. It was sinfully delicious. Being terrified and turned on at the same time, and then orgasming while hanging above the world, burns a ton of calories, I guess. When we got back to his place he opened some wine and we curled up on his upstairs balcony on the outdoor bed he has up there. We watched the water and talked. Well, mostly kissed. When we landed in his bed we didn't have the wild, urgent sex we'd had the night before. This time it was slow and calculated and there was no denying—to him or to myself—that I knew exactly what I was doing. I was willingly sleeping with Sebastian Deveau, the all-star defenseman for the Seattle Winterhawks, and I was enjoying it. *Loving* it.

Now I let my eyes take in everything I glanced at last night. Sebastian's house is an amazing tribute to the midcentury modern style. Purposeful clean lines of wood and glass, and the furniture is all low and lean and yet inviting without being cold. I stand at the bottom of the stairs and scan the open-concept first floor. I can't help but notice that there isn't a lot of hockey memorabilia. My father turned our house into a shrine to the sport—and himself. We had framed photos of him playing in every room, his Cup rings were on display on the mantel; pucks he'd collected for his first hat trick, his Cup-winning goal, his hundredth point, were all in Plexiglas cases placed in rooms like the den, the living room, even the kitchen, for crying out loud.

I hadn't really done the research, but I was sure that Sebastian had accolades and mementos he could be displaying. In the corner of the living room, on a teak bookcase that looked more like a piece of art than a storage unit, he had a few framed photos. Curious, I walked over to them. There was one of him and Stephanie as preteens. Holy crap, he was a cute kid. Goofy hair, chubby cheeks and those same ice blue eyes with the same mischievous twinkle, although without the sexually charged flicker behind it. Stephanie looks less happy, but she is still smiling. She also appears painfully thin, but I guess she was probably in that awkward stage all kids hit during or right before puberty.

Next to that is a framed photo of a couple. I assume it is his parents because they are the right age. The woman has his same eyes and mouth. The man doesn't look like him at all. There are also two young teenage girls crowded into the photo who also don't resemble him. A third frame houses a picture of him skating across the ice at the Winterhawks arena with the Stanley Cup hoisted above his head.

I find myself smiling at that because he looks so happy in it. And even if I don't like the sport, I understand the effort that goes into getting to the end of the season, of winning it all. The sacrifices are emotional and physical. I have to admire the commitment of any athlete who becomes the best. And Sebastian Deveau had done that. I hear a creak behind me and turn to find him standing on the stairs, a few steps from the bottom. He's wearing underwear and nothing else as his sleepy eyes focus on me and he scratches the back of his head, running his fingers through his bed head.

"Hi."

"*Bonjour.*" He winks. I roll my eyes. He lets out a sleepy chuckle. "Are you done snooping or should I go back to bed and give you some more time?"

I give him a wide, innocent stare. "I'm not snooping. These things are on display, begging for attention."

He chuckles again and descends the rest of the stairs. "Just so you know, you're welcome to snoop around. Open drawers, closets, whatever. I have nothing to hide."

"Nothing?" I question, because that seems impossible.

"Baby, I have nothing I'm ashamed of. Nothing I can't share." He smiles and turns and starts toward the kitchen. I follow.

"You know, for a hockey player, you sure don't have a lot of hockey stuff," I can't help but comment.

He walks over to a kettle on the stove and fills it with water from the wall-mounted pot filler above the six-burner stainless-steel stove. He places it on a burner and turns it on. I lean my elbows on the giant wood island with the amazing turquoise countertop as he turns back to me.

"I know what I do for a living. I don't need to turn my house into a reminder," he replies with a shrug. "My home is a tribute to my other passion. Architecture."

My eyebrows fly up before I can contain my surprise and he grins at that, proud of my reaction. "Yeah, you didn't see that coming, did you?" He is smug as he crosses his arms over his broad, bare chest. "I'm studying architecture and interior design online. I'm in my second year. It'll take me longer than most, but I'm hoping to get a degree in five or six years."

"Seriously?"

He walks to the other side of the island and mimics my pose. Our hands bump in the middle of the turquoise surface and he puts his hands on top of mine. "I don't know if you know this, but hockey isn't a career you can ride to the grave. It'll be done by the time I'm thirty-five and that's if I'm lucky."

Of course I know this. "Yeah, but that's what the money is for," and now it's my turn to school him. "You're getting millions a year so you can coast once this career eats you up and spits you and your battered body out."

He nods in agreement, and then I half-jokingly add, "Are you not saving your money? Is it being blown on hookers, blow and gambling debts?"

"Hardly." He rolls his eyes and squeezes my hands under his. "But I am not going to be the guy who sits around waiting for guest spots on sport shows to talk about what once was. I'm going to reinvent myself."

"As an architect?"

He shrugs. "Maybe. All I know is I loved renovating this place so I followed that interest. Maybe another thing will interest me in the next few years and I'll go after that."

I stare at him and flashes of him in his uniform on the ice at my dad's jersey retirement fill my head and then a montage on YouTube that I watched of him fighting joins it. They clash so hard with this person standing in front of me. I find myself whispering, "Who are you?"

His full lips pull up slightly and he whispers back, "I'm many things, but the one thing that should matter to you is that I'm the man who is crazy about you."

He lifts my hands and kisses my knuckles softly. The kettle starts to whistle, and it snaps the thick rope of emotions that seems to be wrapping itself around me with his words and pulling me down a path I'm still not entirely sure I should take.

"I didn't take you for a tea guy," I say when I can finally find my voice again. He turns off the flame under the kettle and turns to grab something in one of the cupboards under the island.

He pulls out a French press and shows it to me before putting it down on the island and reaching for the kettle. "I like my coffee the way you like your men. Dark and rich and—"

"Cuban?" I add, and he stops what he's doing and pins me with his eyes. I wait a couple heartbeats before I clarify. "I like my coffee Cuban."

"Well, you're stuck with French," he returns and scoops some grounds from a fancy French roast coffee bag into the press. "In more ways than one."

When the coffee is ready, he fills two cups, adds the amount of half and half and sugar I request and gives me one of the mugs before taking my hand and leading me toward the wall of windows on the front of the house that gives an unobstructed view of the water. There's an incredibly long, low, tufted couch in front of it. He sits at one end, his wide bare back positioned against the arm, and I move toward the other end, but he still has me by the hand and he pulls me down so that his chest is my backrest.

"By the way," he murmurs against the shell of my ear, "you look fucktastic in my team sweatshirt."

I almost snort coffee through my nose at that comment. Fighting off a coughing fit and struggling to swallow, I glance down at the sweatshirt I grabbed and realize it's got a giant white Winterhawks logo in the center of it. I manage to swallow and choke out, "I look like a puck bunny."

"Puck bunnies wish they looked like you." He laughs and I'm debating pulling the thing off my body, but I'm so comfortable against him, and he's got his arm wrapped around my waist holding me in place, so I decide to just ignore it and sip my coffee again.

"I have a flight at one thirty this afternoon," he says after a few minutes of comfortable silence. That news comes as a surprise.

"Where are you going?"

I swear orgasms kill brain cells because as soon as he says, "Playoffs," I realize I'm an idiot. Round one starts tomorrow. If the Winterhawks are starting the series somewhere else, it means they're playing a team that is seeded higher than them.

"Who are you playing?"

"The fucking Thunder," he replies, and I feel him heave a heavy breath. "I fucking hate those douchebags. They knocked us out last year."

I nod and sip my coffee. "So you'll be gone for four or five days?"

"Yeah, but I'll call and text…I just need your number." I smile at the stupidity of this. He doesn't even have my phone number. This is nuts. Seriously, the way this whole thing happened between us—it's *nuts*. If there's a path to true love, we've thrown away the directions and are careening down it in reverse, blindfolded. He squeezes me tighter around the waist. "So can I have your number, Shay?"

"Do you have any other siblings?" I ask. "Besides Stephanie?"

"Umm…two stepsisters," he explains. "My mom remarried a couple years ago and he has two daughters."

"When did your parents divorce?"

"When I was ten."

"And you grew up in Quebec?"

I feel him shake his head behind me. "Mostly. But I was born in New Brunswick. I'm technically Acadian French. My great-grandparents actually settled in Maine from France and then my grandparents moved to New Brunswick. Then my mom and dad moved to Quebec for my father's job when I was three. We stayed there after the divorce, until I was sixteen, and then I moved back to New Brunswick because I made a junior team there. I lived with my grandparents until I was eighteen and entered the draft."

I stare out the window at the calm water as he speaks. When he's done with his story he leans close to my ear again. "So? Do I pass whatever weird background check you're putting me through? Do I get your number now?"

I laugh. Man, he must think I'm a nutjob. He slips out from behind me and walks over to the console table where he dropped his wallet, keys and phone last night. As I scoot back to nestle in the corner of the couch he vacated, he tosses me his wallet before picking up his phone.

"You can verify my name, age and date of birth, write down my DL and do an official background check if you want, but I'll take those digits now." He's grinning again, holding his phone up ready for the numbers.

I give him my phone number and glance down at his wallet where it landed open on my left thigh. His driver's license is glaring up at me. He's a Leo. He's almost two years older than I am. And… "Holy shit!"

He smirks and puts down his phone, finished entering my information. He knows exactly what I'm gawking at. "I know. It's a lot of names."

"Sebastian Gabriel Maxim Louis Deveau."

"I think my parents knew they weren't having any more kids so they just dumped all the potential names on me." He shrugs. "What's your middle name?"

I shake my head. "Nope."

"Nope? That's worse than Shayne," he teases and I flip him my middle finger. He pretends to be offended. "Come on, I just vomited my life story."

"I'll tell you anything. Just not my middle name."

"Why not?"

"Because it is, in fact, worse than Shayne."

"It's okay, Shay. It won't turn me off. Nothing could turn me off."

I ignore him. "What else did you want to know?"

"Trey your only sibling?"

I nod.

His blue eyes dim and he looks thoughtful, like he's contemplating what to say next. "How come Trey doesn't play hockey?"

"He did." I pause. I don't know if I want to tell him everything. "It didn't work out."

"How come?"

I pause and then shrug, not wanting to share my brother's past with him because it's not mine to share, so I decide to give a nonanswer. "I'm glad he quit because he would always be under my father's shadow if he made the NHL anyway."

Sebastian seems to think about it for a minute, and then that smirky, devious grin covers his sexy features again. "Or he could've just eclipsed the crap out of Glenn Beckford and his records. Like I'm doing."

"There's the Frenchie I know. The one with the giant ego."

I get up off the couch and walk over to him. He smiles down at me. "What can I say? I'm confident in my abilities."

I put the mug down, glad the conversation took a turn, and not ready to go back to fifty questions about my life. So I do what I've wanted to do since he walked down the stairs looking all sleepy and sexy as fuck. I drop to my knees, taking his underwear with me, and say, "So am I."

Chapter 36

Sebastian

The flight to San Francisco was painless. I text Shay as soon as we land. Nothing special, just a "thinking of you" type of text. I knew she had yoga and nutrition classes all afternoon so I didn't expect to hear back from her right away. The charter bus dropped us off at the hotel and after I settled into my room, I got a text from Jordan asking if I wanted to go grab food.

As I leave my room to meet him and Chooch in the lobby, Westwood steps out of his room and into the hall. I'm dressed in jeans and an untucked button-down shirt. Avery is still in his travel suit. He glances up at me and a guilty look passes over his features, and I'm wondering if he still feels like shit for what he told us at Jordan's last night. I hadn't thought about it much, thanks to Shay, but now it comes rushing back to me. The fucker is considering leaving the team.

"Hey," he says tentatively as I pass, and he falls in step next to me. "You going for food?"

I nod. He rubs the back of his neck and then loosens his tie a little, thinks better of it and tightens it again. "I have to do press in conference room C, wherever the fuck that is."

Avery swearing is a rarity, so I know he's rattled. It weakens my resolve and I suddenly don't want to give him the cold shoulder anymore. "Any new developments from last night?"

"Los Angeles, Brooklyn, and Manhattan are interested," he tells me, and I'm startled by how honest he's being. Avery never talks about his business affairs with anyone, ever. "Winterhawks are willing to throw everything they have at me to get me to stay."

I swallow. I know what that means. That means they'll tie up all the money they can in him and others will be traded to keep the club under the monetary cap enforced by the league. Jordan, Chooch, and I all make almost as much money as Avery currently makes. If they want to give him more, they'll most likely trade one of us or combine two other players. He's staring at me waiting for a reaction. I just nod again.

We reach the elevator bank and I punch the down button as he keeps talking. "It's not about the money. I mean, it's not about my salary. It's about a higher profile."

"You're the face of the entire league," I remind him. "The only one of us that I'm betting ninety percent of North Americans could name. How much higher a profile can you get?"

"I mean for business opportunities and endorsements," he mutters, and it sounds rehearsed and robotic, and I know he's just regurgitating his father's words.

I try so hard not to roll my eyes that it makes me grimace. I may think he's being a fucking asshole right now, but he's still my friend. And more than anything, he's still my captain, and I can't start an argument with him the day before we start our Cup run.

The elevator arrives and we both step in. I punch G and he scans the panel and then hits three, muttering, "I think they said three," as he runs a hand over his dark hair, smoothing it.

Then he turns his dark eyes back to me. "Look, I know you probably hate me over all this shit. But I want you to know that no matter what's going to happen in the future, I'm going to give this team one hundred percent right now."

"I know that," I reply and meet his eye. "But honestly, Avs, I keep wondering when you're going to give yourself one hundred percent."

"What does that mean?"

"It means when are you going to stop doing what your management advises, what the team needs, what looks good? Just do whatever the fuck makes you happy. Do you even know what makes you happy, Avery? Do you know what happy is?"

My words are harsh, but I mean them as a friend. I am honestly worried about this guy. He's always walked around like he has the weight of the world on his shoulders—I noticed that long before the NHL—but lately it's like his shoulders are literally sagging from the pressure. He just isn't handling it well anymore.

I clap a hand on his shoulder as if to prove I'm saying this from a place of love. His eyes are clouded, his brows drawn, his mouth set in a tight line, but I can see he isn't angry with me. "Yeah. I know what happy is," he replies, his voice deep as always but not steady. "It's something other people feel."

The elevator dings and the doors open on the third floor. He gets off with nothing more than a wave at me as he disappears down the hall. Wow. I actually feel bad for the bastard. Jordan is sprawled across a couch in the lobby staring at his phone when I get there. Chooch is standing next to him. When they see me, they both walk over and we head out the front floors. There are a few fans standing on the sidewalk; we pause long enough to take some photos and sign a few autographs but duck away quickly.

San Francisco feels colder than Seattle, and I zip up the front of my jacket as I tell the guys about my conversation with Avery. They both look grim. Jordan swears under his breath. "I can't believe he's really going to leave."

"Well, if you think about it, he's not happy anywhere, so what difference does it make?" Chooch says as we wait for a light to change. "I mean, at least if he does what his manager asshole father wants, he'll have one less thing making him miserable. If he stays, it's one more thing keeping him from being happy."

"The only thing keeping him from being happy is himself," I add.

Jordan gives me a crooked, smartass grin. "Look at you all wise and shit."

I can't help but laugh. "Yeah, well, I've never been one to deny pleasure or happiness."

We cross the street and Chooch asks, "Speaking of…how'd things go with Bendy McTwisty yoga girl? You never came back last night."

"Shay. Her name is Shay." I smile. "Things are good. I think."

I pull out my phone. Still no response to my text. But that doesn't mean anything other than that she's busy. I think.

"So are you two official?" Jordan inquires as we pull open the door to one of our favorite Italian places in the city. "Jessie asked me to ask you if you had 'the talk' yet."

He puts the words "the talk" in air quotes and rolls his eyes. "You tell that nosy woman of yours that I'm so smooth I don't need a talk."

"Yeah, she'll love that." Jordan smirks. "She'll call you a dumbass."

We settle in, pulling off our jackets and taking seats around a round table with a red tablecloth. "We haven't really had a talk, but she's in this. It scares the shit out of her, but she's in it."

"I'm out of it," Chooch suddenly mutters, and we both turn back to him. "I broke up with Ainsley. Officially. Completely."

Jordan and I exchange looks. Chooch runs a hand over his shaggy hair and sighs. "She actually offered to have an open relationship. She thought it was random sex that I was missing, not, you know, a caring, loving partner who doesn't act like a vicious bitch to everyone I know."

Jordan's face darkens. "So is she moving back to Alberta? Back to her family?"

Chooch shrugs. "Eventually. Probably. But until she figures it out, I'm letting her live in the house and I'm at the Four Seasons."

Jordan and I exchange glances again. Having our goalie's life in upheaval and living in a hotel during playoffs is a recipe for disaster. Especially when you combine it with the bullshit already happening with Avery. I'm opening my mouth and making the offer without even thinking about it. "When we get back to Seattle, you are moving in with me."

Chooch looks genuinely surprised. "You don't have to…" he starts.

"I have a huge three-bedroom house that is pretty fucking spectacular." I grin immodestly. "It's better than the Four Seasons and I'll enjoy the company."

"What about Yoga Shay?"

"She doesn't come with the offer," I joke and he laughs. It's the first real laugh I've heard from him in a while. "We'll be in lockdown mode anyway and I probably won't see her all that much. When I do, I promise to try and keep the screaming to a minimum. But it'll be hard because my mad skills make her vocal."

Jordan and Chooch both groan; I smile and open my menu. But I can't help but notice that my phone isn't buzzing. Why isn't she getting back to me?

Chapter 37

Shayne

As soon as he walks into the police station my heart clenches. He looks absolutely frightened. The kind of pure, deep-rooted fear that grips every part of you. His shoulders are tense, his eyes are wild, and his jaw is clenched so tightly I'm scared he'll break his teeth. I stand up from the uncomfortable chair I'm in across from a detective, and when his eyes land on me I can see a wave of relief flood him, relaxing every part of his body from his toes to his face.

He crosses the room in a blur and has me by the shoulders, shoving my face into his chest and crushing me to him. "Are you okay? You look okay, but are you?"

I try to nod but there's no room against his torso. I place my hands on his chest and push. He gets the hint and stops hugging me, but his hands stay clamped on my shoulders. "I'm fine, Trey. I swear it was no big deal."

"You were fucking mugged at knifepoint. That's a big fucking deal," he barks, and the detective arches an eyebrow at him. He shoots him an apologetic glance. "Sorry. I just...I told her she shouldn't live there."

"It's not a big deal," I argue calmly, even though I'm rattled to my core and I have to work really hard to keep my voice steady. "He cornered me, showed me the knife and demanded my wallet."

"Your sister was smart. She handed it over and didn't cause a scene," the detective pipes in.

Trey looks down at me with approval in his eyes and he rubs my shoulder. "Well, if you're finally going to listen to instructions and not talk back, this is the right time to do it. Thank God you figured that out."

"I did, however, hurl my wallet at him and run like a bat out of hell," I confess. "Because I'm brave like that."

I know it's stupid to be embarrassed that I didn't put up a fight, but I am anyway. Trey hugs me again, slightly less forcefully. "You're fucking moving."

"No. I'm not," I argue, even though I'm probably going to start to look at rental listings. Just in case there's something else out there I can afford.

Trey lets me go and turns back to the police officer. "Does she need to go to the doctor? The hospital? Should we have her checked out?"

He points to me. "That's up to her. She did take a bit of a tumble."

I flex my left hand and feel the burn from where I turned the corner at the end of the block and tripped on the uneven sidewalk. My palm is scraped and my left knee and my yoga pants are torn, and I probably had a mild cardiac event thinking the mugger would catch me, but it turns out he wasn't even chasing me. When I ran, he must have just grabbed my wallet and taken off.

"I'm okay. Just scrapes. I just really want to go home."

"You're not going back there!"

"Trey, it didn't happen in my house or anything. It was a block away. I was taking a shortcut home," I explain. At least being annoyed at him is helping me calm down. "When I get a new car this won't happen again."

I just don't have the cash for a decent car right now. I'd been trying to decide if I should use what little savings I do have to move into an apartment in a better area instead of buying another car. This incident, which was terrifying, made me realize I have to act soon. But if I admitted that to Trey, he'd feel guilty and try to pay me more, which I know he can't afford.

"And when, exactly, are you getting a new car?"

"Umm…shortly."

He swears under his breath but before he can lecture me, I hear my name from an all too familiar, overdramatic voice. I turn and see my mother and father marching toward us. My mom is already crying. My dad's face is set in a weird scowl or grimace or something.

"Shaynie. Oh my God!" She literally throws herself at me and I glare up at my brother.

"You were mugged," Trey replies to my unspoken anger at the fact he called our parents.

I untangle myself from my mother, and my father stalks over and shocks me by grabbing my face in his big hands. He looks right into my eyes, and I swear I see anguish. "Are you okay?"

I nod because I can't seem to find my voice. His hands press more firmly and he repeats the question. This time I manage to croak out an answer. "He didn't hurt me."

My father releases me and turns to the police officer, who clearly recognizes him, because he's got that awed look on his face I know too well. "Can we take our daughter home now? Do you need anything else?"

"Yes, sir. I have her mugger's description and a record of the incident. We'll be in touch tomorrow or the next day with more information," he says and pauses before adding, "I'm a huge fan, Mr. Beckford."

My father's face morphs into one of his trademark confident smiles. "Thanks, Officer…Seabrook. Very nice to hear. I'm hoping you can make a point of working hard to catch this bastard since it'd mean a great deal to me."

Yeah, because if you weren't such a sports icon, they wouldn't even bother looking for a man with a weapon who steals from women. Leave it to my dad to make my mugging about him. I give Trey another *thanks a lot* glare and start to untangle myself from our mother, who is hugging me again.

"I just want to go home and forget this happened, okay?"

My father and I both shake hands with the police officer who was helping me, and as Trey, my mom and I all make our way out of the station, my father stops for several selfies with officers along the way. Of course.

Outside it's dark and warm, but I still feel a chill. I rub my arms. Trey unzips and shrugs out of his hoodie and drapes it over my shoulders. It feels as big as a blanket and I'm reminded of Sebastian's hoodie that I wore this morning. God, I loved that thing, Winterhawks logo and all. I should have stolen it.

Sebastian. I dig my phone out of my coat pocket and check. Yep. He's texted twice and called once, but there's no voicemail. He must think I'm ignoring him. And as I take a deep breath of night air I'm thinking maybe I should ignore him. I know telling him about this will screw up his concentration. And being a hockey kid, I know the sport is equal parts mental game and physical game.

I shove my phone back in my pocket, and my mother clutches my arm. "I'll make up your old bedroom."

"What?"

"As soon as we get home, I'll make up your bedroom."

"I'm not going to your home," I tell her firmly. "I'm going to mine."

"You shouldn't be alone after this, Shayne," Trey says, and I want to punch him. "Especially not your home."

"I'm a grown woman and I am going home. My home." My father walks up just as I finish speaking and he stares down at me with a condemning stare.

"You're moving out of that shit box," he barks and runs a hand over his graying hair. "You can move in with your mother or you can live in the pool house. We renovated it a few years ago, you know that. It's self-contained, got its own kitchen and bathroom."

My mother had acted devastated when I moved back to Seattle after college and refused to live in the renovated pool house. She proclaimed she did it just for me and that it was my father's idea. I would never live with them again; I don't know how they didn't catch on to that fact when I refused any of their money for school and when I didn't even tell them I was moving back. Trey was the one who let it slip.

"Look, I appreciate that you two are trying to be parental and everything. I understand that being mugged is scary for everyone, not just me." I was truly being serious here, but with every word I could see the flicker of anger behind my dad's gray eyes grow brighter. "I'm grateful for the offer, but I am not, under any circumstances, moving back home."

"Shayne, I've had enough with your bullshit," my father spits out, so frustrated his face is turning red. "You're holding a grudge at your own expense and it's just dumb at this point. Grow up."

He yanks his wallet out of his back pocket and shoves a wad of bills in my hand and leans in close to my face, his expression softening for a moment. "I love you, Shaynie. I don't know what I would do if something happened to you."

He kisses my forehead quickly and then stalks across the parking lot, back to his car. My mother, her lip quivering, shakes her head at me and whispers, "You're punishing me too. Not just him, you know."

And then she stumbles away after him. I hear Trey sigh next to me and I look up. He watches them until my dad pulls out of the parking lot. "I'll drive you to that crack den you call an apartment."

I roll my eyes but follow him to his car. I look down at the cash in my hand. It's four hundred dollars in fifty-dollar bills. I try to hand it to Trey, but he shakes his head. "Use it to put a down payment on a new car or a deposit on a decent apartment."

"No."

"Well, you'll have to try and give it back to him yourself, because I'm not helping you this time," he says.

As we're buckling up, my phone rings and I dig it out. It's Sebastian. Again. I hesitate. Trey leans over and glances at the screen. I decide to answer the call rather than deal with the fifty invasive questions I'm sure he's about to pepper me with. "Hey."

"Shay, baby, I was beginning to think you were blowing me off." His voice is soothing. It's like the warm hug I've been craving.

"No. I wasn't," I promise and when I take a breath it's shaky. "I had a really bad day."

Trey snorts beside me at the way I underplayed that, and I raise my middle finger in his general direction. "I've been thinking about you nonstop, *ma belle*," Seb confesses in a husky voice. "I hope you know as soon as this plane lands in four days I'm coming to see you."

"Good," I say, and I know I have to get off the phone. It's not just that it's awkward talking to him with my brother right beside me; it's also that the way his voice is making me feel so warm and comforted is making the reality of what happened to me sink in, and I feel like I might cry. "Trey is driving me home right now. Can I call you back later?"

There's a pause. "We have a curfew. I'm supposed to be lights out in ten minutes."

"Oh. Okay." Fucking hockey.

"Call me back anyway."

"No. It's fine. We'll talk tomorrow. It's no big deal," I tell him, and Trey chuffs sarcastically beside me. "Have a good night and a good game tomorrow. Bye."

As soon as I hit the end button Trey starts in. "Are you sure you know what you're doing?"

"With Sebastian?" I counter, and I decide to be my usual flippant self. "Well, I got an A in sex ed in high school and I got a little hands-on training in college."

"Oh my God, shut up!" Trey demands and shakes his head in disgust. "I mean with your life in general, Shayne."

"My life is fine."

His eyebrow quirks and the look on his face is sheer disbelief. "You don't have enough money to buy a car, you live in a crap area of town where you get mugged because you won't take help from our father due to your morals against his profession and life choices, but yet you're involved with someone who does the exact same thing for a living and probably lives the same lifestyle."

"Sebastian is nothing like Dad," I spit out hotly, and the suggestion has me furious. "You're not cheating on Sasha, are you?"

"Of course not," he says as he turns onto my street.

"Well, you were a hockey player," I remind him. "And you aren't like Dad."

He gives me a quick, bitter smile. "Yeah, but I was. And I'll be honest with you, Shayne, it's hard not to be that way when you're playing. Women are everywhere and your adrenaline is always high. After a win you want to celebrate and after a loss you want to commiserate and there are always more than a few pieces of tail willing to help you do it."

"Never ever say 'tail' to me again. Never," I tell him as he slows and pulls to the curb in front of my building. "So are you saying Jordan is cheating on Jessie?"

"No. I'm not. I'm just saying that the option is ever present." He turns off the engine and crosses his arms over the steering wheel as he turns and levels me with a stare. "Deveau seems like a good guy. Hothead on the ice but smart and genuine off. Maybe he's one of the good ones. But are you really going to be able to get past your own baggage to see it? I know you, Shayne, and that's not going to be easy. You're likely to fuck this whole thing up trying."

"Thanks for your vote of confidence," I snap, and those tears from earlier are threatening to fill my eyes again. "Remind me not to call you the next time I need help, because if this is your idea of it, I'd be better off on my own."

I unclip my seat belt and jump out. By the time I reach the door, my brother is right behind me. "I'm walking you in because I'm worried about you. Deal with it."

I ignore him and unlock the front door. He follows me in and I storm to the elevator and punch the button. Trey puts his hands on my shoulders, but I shrug out of them.

"Shaynie, I love you, and I'm just worried that this isn't going to end well for you." I can hear the sincerity in his voice, but it doesn't make it sting any less.

"You don't know him, and maybe you don't know me as well as you think you do."

The elevator arrives, and we step in as one of my sketchy neighbors steps out. It's a dude who lives on the floor below me who I am pretty sure sells drugs. He glances at us as he steps off and I ignore him. Trey eyeballs him skeptically and then shoots me a horrified glare, but I ignore it.

As we chug up to my floor, Trey says, "Why didn't you tell him about the mugging?"

"He's starting playoffs tomorrow." I step off the elevator and march to my door. After unlocking it, I swing it open and flip on the light in the front hall. "Hello! Burglars, rapists, murderers! I'm home!"

When no one responds, I turn to Trey. "Happy now? Go home."

He ignores me and pushes into my apartment. I stand by the kitchen door with my arms crossed as I watch him wander from room to room. Finally he stands in front of me. "So what if he's in playoffs?"

"So he's got to concentrate. You know that." How is he so stupid suddenly? "Remember when Dad was in playoffs he barely even spoke to us? Remember when I broke my arm in gymnastics and

Mom called him to let him know and he was furious? They lost the series and he blamed family issues pulling his head out of the game. I'm not going to do that to Seb over a stolen wallet."

Trey stares at me expectantly, like he's waiting for me to clue in. When I stare back blankly he starts to shake his head slowly. He leans down and kisses the top of my head. "And there's the baggage I was talking about."

He starts to my door but stops at the threshold and examines the dead bolts on my door—I am suddenly very happy there are two and two chains. He seems satisfied with that. "Keep this locked up tight and call me for anything at anytime. Got it?"

He leaves, and I poke my head out the door and watch him walk to the elevator. As he gets into it, he calls out without turning around. "If he's different and you don't think he's like Dad, then tell him about tonight, Shayne."

I don't have time to think of a snotty response before the elevator doors slide shut.

Chapter 38

Sebastian

The first person I see when we walk through the door is Sara. She's about to give me bitchface, which is her go-to since she caught me with Shayne, but then she sees my face. "Oh my God!" she squeaks. "It didn't look that bad on TV."

"It's not that bad," I promise. "It's just swollen."

I knew I shouldn't come here like this. Damn it. But I really wanted to see Shay. It's been a rough few days. We won the first game clean and easy, but the second game the Comets came out with a chip on their shoulder. It was rough; there was almost as much going on after the whistles as there was during the game. I caught a high stick in front of the net. That douchebag Braddock nailed me and actually had the nerve to lip off to the ref that it was an accident. I had a nice slice through my chin, but because he drew blood, we got a four-minute power play and scored what ended up being the game winner. Now my chin is swollen and bruised, along with being stitched, and judging by the way Sara is looking at me, I look like Frankenstein's monster. At least my wrist healed before my face got mutilated. There's only so much pain I can take at once. Maybe I should wait to see Shay until I look better.

I don't think Sara even heard my response, because she's spotted Avery, who came with me. Her eyes grow wide and her smile grows even wider. "Avery Westwood! Great game this afternoon! That goal was a beauty!"

"Thanks. Two down, two more to go." Avery gives her his typical milk-'n'-cookies smile, the one that's launched a thousand products.

"You'll sweep them. I know it!"

"Shh!" He tries to make it sound casual, but I know Avery, and the "sweep" word is on his superstitious "never say out loud" list of playoff words. He thinks it's a jinx, like when a goalie hasn't let in a goal and someone says "shutout" before the end of the game. And as if on cue...

"I just know you'll do it. I bet Choochinsky even gets a shutout next game! He's playing great! You're going to win the Cup this year!"

I interrupt because if I don't, Avery might have to sacrifice a goat or something to make up for all the jinxes he thinks she's putting out there.

"Is Shay...Shayne here?" I ask, but I think I already know the answer. She has an eight o'clock yoga class. So I'm a little shocked when Sara shakes her head.

"She isn't. Had to cancel her class so she could go to the police station."

"What? Why?"

"The mugging. They think they got the guy, and she had to go identify him." Sara says this casually as she starts putting the fruit in the fridge for the night.

"She was mugged?!"

"Holy shit," Avery adds under his breath, but loud enough that I can hear him.

Sara freezes and blinks, then frowns. "Yeah. How do you not know that?"

Yeah, how the fuck do I not know that?

"Is Trey here?"

Sara motions with her head toward his office. I turn and Avery follows. "She didn't tell you she was mugged?"

I shake my head, but I don't respond because I can't think of a good reason why I shouldn't know this. Two seconds later I'm standing in Trey's open door with Avery right behind me. Trey's sitting behind his desk. I clear my throat. He jerks his head up and his posture straightens at the sight of me.

"Hey, Trey."

"Sebastian." He walks around the desk and shakes my hand as his eyes land on my chin. "Tough win."

Clearly he watched the game. I nod, and he notices Avery over my shoulder. "Avery."

He doesn't extend his hand this time, just nods. Avery deserves that, and he knows it, which is why he tagged along when I said I was heading to Elevate to see Shayne.

"Sara just told me Shayne was mugged," I say to him.

Trey almost grimaces at that. "Yeah. She's fine. He didn't touch her, but he got her wallet. It's been a pain in the ass for her to run all over town without a car trying to get her ATM card and driver's license replaced. But it could have been a lot worse. He had a knife, for fuck's sake."

"A knife?" Avery sounds as horrified as I feel.

"But she's okay?" I ask, even though he just said she was.

His face softens a little. "Yeah. Honestly, she was a little shaken up, I could tell, but she wouldn't admit it."

"Of course not." I almost smile at that.

"But she's okay. She really needs to get a car or move. Or both."

I nod. "That neighborhood is fucking horrible."

"Totally!" he agrees with a grateful smile, because clearly she hasn't been agreeing with him.

"I thought she was looking into a new car?"

He sighs and sits on the edge of his desk. "She was, but she honestly can't afford anything decent. She's got student loans and she won't take money from our parents. I'd give her a raise, but I can't. Business is steady but slow. And the commercials I had planned won't be as effective as I thought they would be."

"About that," Avery says and he looks as awkward as he sounds. Avery isn't great at taking responsibility for his actions, mostly because he's never had to. People let him get away with shit because he's Avery Westwood. "Can I talk to you about that?"

Trey shrugs. I don't want to stick around for this. As fun as it would be to watch Avery apologize for probably the first time in his life, all I want to do is see Shay for myself and make sure she's okay. "Is she still at the police station?"

"Not sure. Want me to text her?"

"Nah. I'll do it. Thanks, Trey." I start to leave but his words stop me.

"So, like, this thing with Shayne…" I turn back to look at him. "I hear you're dating or something?"

"I'd like to think so," I answer, because I *would* like to think so. But I would also like to think the woman I'm dating would tell me about any life-threatening situations she was in, so at this point…I'm not sure what the fuck we're doing.

He gives me a half smile as if to show he's only half joking when he warns, "She's a smart-mouthed, obstinate pain in the ass, but I love her dearly, so I will fucking end you if you hurt her."

"Fair enough," I reply and nod solemnly like I'm accepting his terms—and I am. If I hurt her I will let him kill me.

I text her as I walk across the parking lot. *Hey, babe. Where are you?*

She responds right away. *Are you back?*

I am. And I want to see you. Do I head to the police station or your house?

There's an expected pause after that text. But as I climb into my car she responds.

I'm in a cab on the way home. Meet me there?

On my way, I respond.

I buzz her when I get to her door because no one is walking out and leaving the door wide open like last time. She doesn't ask who it is; she just opens the front door. I take the stairs two at a time until I'm on her floor. No passed-out smelly drunk guy this time. She has the door open before I can knock. Her pretty gray eyes land on my face and flare. "Holy shit! Your face!"

She reaches up and gently cups the side of my face next to the cut and rocks up on her tiptoes to examine it. She's barefoot, wearing a pair of very tight, very short workout shorts and a vintage T-shirt with the Eagles's band logo on the front. "Does it hurt?"

"Not as much as finding out from your brother that you were mugged," I tell her and reach up and remove her hand from my throbbing face, lacing my fingers with hers, and stare down at her intently.

She looks genuinely perplexed, which perplexes me. "You're in playoffs."

"Yeah. So?"

She looks even more confused by that and tries to pull her hand from mine, but I'm not having it. She stares right in my eye and explains. "You can't focus if people are yammering at you about crap. I was fine. And there was nothing you could do from San Francisco anyway."

"I could have listened," I tell her, and I'm really amazed I have to. "Trey said you were upset. Even if it was just over the phone, I could have been there for you."

She looks even more confused than before, and I have no idea why. What the hell does she think, that I would be annoyed by finding out she was attacked? What the hell is wrong with...

"Is this about your dad?"

"What?" She bites her bottom lip and her eyes shift to the scuffed hardwood, and I know it *is* about Glenn Beckford. Fuck, how did I ever idolize this guy? I take a deep breath and pull her into the apartment. I walk her through the room, past her sketchy cat, who's giving me the hairy eyeball again, and into the bedroom. The light beside her bed is on and the sheets are rumpled like she was in it recently.

"Sit," I command, and just like I knew she would, she hesitates. I fucking love the way she challenges me, but I add the word please.

She lowers her cute little ass to the edge of the mattress at the foot of the bed, but she keeps her eyes cast downward. "Eyes up."

She looks up only to glare at me. I grin and my dick starts to get hard. "So your dad used to zone out during playoffs?"

"He was never all that zoned in when it came to family," she mutters and sighs. "But I know that this is why you guys play the sport. To get to the playoffs."

"Yep." I nod and start to unbutton my shirt, toeing off my shoes at the same time. "But there are two kinds of players. The ones who use it as an excuse to mistreat and ignore the people who love them, and the ones who find balance."

"Haven't met one of those balanced ones yet," she mutters.

"Yes, you have," I say flatly and unbutton my cuffs. I came straight from the airport and the team plane so I'm wearing a charcoal dress shirt and black dress pants.

She looks up at me wordlessly, but there's skepticism on her pretty face. Man, her dad did a number on her. She bites her bottom lip as I shrug out of my shirt. I try not to flash her a cocky grin but man, I love the way she looks at me. It's wild: she always looks like she's struggling to control herself. It's a battle she knows she's going to lose, and I know she sees that as weakness but I see it as a sign we're meant to be. Even though I haven't known her long, I know her well and I know that she hates when things get under her skin, but she doesn't hate me and I've rattled her in a delicious way since the second we met.

I reach for my belt. "You're wearing too much clothing."

She smirks as she looks down at her T-shirt and tiny workout shorts. "Just because you tend to put on stripteases in my apartment doesn't mean I have to join in."

I shrug and my pants drop to my ankles. "Too mesmerized by my fantastic body to move? Oh well, I'll have to help you."

She's still got a sexy little smirk on her face as she returns my shrug. "Meh. You're body is okay, but mesmerizing is a stretch, Frenchie."

"I dare you to say you're not so turned on right now your skin is tingling."

"I'm not."

I step out of my pants and walk toward her. I bend and capture her mouth with mine while my hand goes straight for the small space between her legs and I cup her sex. My fingers slip into the leg of her shorts and press up. I grin against her lips. "Liar."

I push her down on the bed with the weight of my body and lie on top of her. I don't want to remove my hand from between her legs, but I do because there's something I need to know. I pull back from the kiss and stare down at her. "Are you okay? Honestly? Tell me."

"Yeah," she says softly. "It was scary, but I'm okay."

I feel my shoulders relax as she runs her fingertips over my back. I drop my full weight onto her and nuzzle her neck, inhaling that intoxicating scent that is all Shay. Her hands run up my neck and into my hair and she whispers, "I'm better now that you're here."

For her, I know that's a huge thing to admit. She doesn't want to need anyone to feel anything and I am the last person she wants to need. I almost tell her I'm falling in love with her, but I want to do it when I don't have a hard-on pressed against her. So instead I kiss her, pushing all my emotions into the way I move my lips over hers and the way my tongue moves in her mouth. Her fingers tangle in my hair and I start to push her T-shirt up.

I wanted this to be slow and deliberate, but the kiss and the emotions passing through it are like kindling on a fire, and everything starts sparking at once, and the next thing I know all our clothes are gone and my uncovered dick is precariously close to heaven. And I feel every muscle in my body strain as I fight against just sliding into her.

"Condom," she reminds me softly against the shell of my ear before she bites down on the lobe.

I groan and drop my head into the crook of her neck. "I forgot to bring one."

"I bought some," she whispers, and pulls her hand off my back and reaches toward to night table.

She hands me a box of Magnums and I grin. "You're the best girlfriend in the world."

She looks almost fearful when the words leave my mouth, and it makes me worried. Are we not on the same page here? After all this? Before I can ask, and before the uncertainty I'm feeling starts to deflate my dick, she kisses my lips and rolls us over so she's on top, kneeling between my legs. "Put it on."

She almost growls the words and my dick gets harder. "Bossy."

I do what she demands and she leans over me, her hair dropping down around her, creating curtains on either side of our faces. Her gray eyes look dark, almost like charcoal, and her pink lips are pulled up a little in a devious smile. "I'm in charge tonight."

She reaches down and grabs my dick, firm and hard, and I fight the desire to buck up into her grip. Because she wants that. She wants to know I fucking love it when she's bossy and that it turns me on when she tells me what to do. But my competitive nature won't let me give her that satisfaction. So I make sure my ass stays flat against the mattress, even when she starts to stroke me.

Her lips move back to my ear, her long hair blanketing my face. "I'm going to ride you until your eyes roll back in your pretty little head."

This girl. Fuck.

Before I can unscramble my brain enough to give her a snarky answer, she's sliding over my shaft and I am lost. Lost in the feel of her and the way she makes me feel. She's got her head tipped back and her spine is slightly arched and her naked body is on display and I have never seen anything more spectacular in my whole life. This woman, her spirit, her body, her smart fucking mouth is it for me. I know this. And I suddenly need her to know it. I reach for her arm and I push up into her and try to tug her down. She resists. Her eyes flutter down to mine. "I'm in charge."

She lifts up, then rolls her hips, grinding down onto me, causing ripples of pleasure to shoot down my spine. Her hand, the one I tried to grab, slips over her taut stomach and then lower. She touches herself, fingers exploring and rubbing as she rides me, her breasts bouncing. I am so close to coming I see stars.

I sit up and grab the back of her neck before she can stop me. I crush my mouth to hers. When we break apart her pace picks up. Her hand slides back to her clit and she lets out the most fantastic little moan as she starts to come and *oh fuck...*

Panting, I drop back down on the mattress and watch the show. She's coming. I can feel it, and I push up hard and let my own release take over, reaching up to pull her down on top of me. I run my hand through her silky hair and whisper, "You're borrowing my car."

"What?" she murmurs back sleepily.

"You're going to use one of my cars until you get your own."

"No, thanks," she replies, her voice less groggy.

"I'm not offering. I'm telling."

"Excuse me?" There is zero sleepiness in her voice now.

I may be ruining a moment, but oh well. I press my lips to her neck for a chaste kiss before giving her a snarky response. "You got to be bossy and now I do."

"I'm not taking your car."

"Then you're moving."

"Are you kidding me right now?"

The moment is definitely lost. I gently pull out of her and try not to groan my protest. As soon as we are no longer attached, she gets off the bed and starts to put her clothes back on. But I'm not having it. As she reaches for her underwear, I take them out of her hand and toss them across the room.

"I didn't sign on for this," she rants and walks over to where her underwear landed by the bathroom door. "I don't need another dad or anyone who thinks they can tell me what to do."

"And I don't need a girlfriend who is too stubborn to be safe," I reply and again take her underwear from her as she tries to pick them up. This time I toss them toward the living room, and when she glares at me I grin and wink.

"Fuck off," she hisses and storms past me. Giving up on the underwear, she tries to pull her T-shirt over her head. I hold onto the hem, making it impossible for her to lift her arms and pull it over her head. She tries to pull away. I step into her and push her against the wall next to her dresser. My naked body is pinning her now and the spark of rage in those gray eyes is like the flash of a lighthouse light—a bright, undeniable warning.

"I am not some fucking puck bunny you need to support," she protests in a low voice. "I don't need you to take care of me."

"And I'm not some asshole who doesn't give a shit about your well-being."

I yank the T-shirt from her arms and throw it over my shoulder and close the space left between us. My lips are a fraction of an inch from her smart mouth and I want to close that space too, but she would probably slap me. It's not even that threat that stops me, though. It's that I have too much that still needs to be said. "I care about you. More than I have about anyone in a long time. Maybe ever. And I'm not going to let you do risky stupid shit to prove some kind of point you don't need to make."

Now I kiss her, because I'm more scared to see her reaction to that than I am of getting slapped. She responds to the kiss, which gives me courage. "You'll borrow a fucking car or I'll buy you a new one." I swallow and give her the one last option that I can't deny is a possibility. "Or you can end this thing between us. Those are your only options, Shay."

Now I pull back so I can see her reaction. Her jaw clenches. Her eyes narrow. And then she kisses me. It's angry and hot and I know she hates herself for it, but she's not picking that last option. I try not to smile against her lips but it's so damn hard.

Chapter 39

Shayne

"Oh my God, this thing is insane," Audrey says, the whole sentence coming out like a gasp. Josh lets out a low whistle from the backseat, confirming he agrees with his girlfriend.

I frown and Audrey openly laughs at me. "You are the only person in the universe who would be pissed at being given a luxury car."

"He didn't *give* it to me," I argue as I carefully turn into the gated VIP parking lot for the arena. "I'm borrowing it until I get a new one of my own. Which will be this weekend. I found a great deal on a used Sportage in Everett."

"You're going to go from a BMW to a Kia? Willingly?" In the rearview mirror I watch Josh shake his head in disdain. "Shayne, you're certifiable."

I ease into a spot at the far end of the parking lot, away from where most of the other cars are parked near the entrance. It's safer that way, so that no one dings Sebastian's car. When I begrudgingly agreed to his terms to borrow a car, I assumed it would be his SUV because there was no way he'd offer me the Aston Martin.

But the next morning he'd driven me over to his place and opened the four-car garage that was a freestanding structure in an alley behind his house and offered me any car in there. Including the Aston Martin. I swear to God he is insane. I picked the BMW after a quick Google search that told me it was the least expensive of the four.

I was a wreck driving it because I was constantly worried about scratches or dents. But I had to admit, it was an amazing vehicle. I'd never driven anything as state-of-the-art or as decadent. The leather seats felt like butter. They were heated and air-conditioned. It handled amazingly. I was in love. And I was beginning to think I wasn't just in love with the car, which made me even more nervous than the thought of scratches on the Beemer.

We all get out of the car and I hit the lock on the key fob. As we walk toward the entrance, Audrey and Josh chatter to each other excitedly. It's their first VIP game. I used to do this all the time as a kid, but this is the first one in a long time. And I definitely never thought I'd be doing it again. Audrey links her arm through mine. "I'm proud of you, Shaynie."

I glance up at her because she's in some killer heels. "For…?"

She smiles mischievously. "For finally doing something wrong."

"What are you talking about?" I pause a few feet from the door to dig the passes Sebastian gave me out of my purse.

"Your one-night stand," she explains and laughs. "It's probably the only thing I've seen you, little miss perfectionist, screw up since we met. And I'm so glad you did."

Josh chuckles, and I can't help but laugh a little at that too. Then I hear my name called from behind us in the lot and I turn and see my father striding toward us. He's in a suit, and I suddenly have flashbacks to my youth. Only if he was playing, he certainly wouldn't be talking to me before a game.

"Dad. What are you doing here?"

"I was asked to do an interview at intermission," he explains. "Seems no one can get enough of my stories about the glory days."

Oh, you would be wrong about that, Dad.

Of course I don't argue out loud. Instead Audrey steps forward and reacquaints herself with my dad before introducing Josh, who fawns all over my father, telling him what a big fan he is. When their love fest is over, he turns back to me. "What are *you* doing here would be a better question."

"I...I got tickets from..."

I'm not sure I want to finish my sentence, but before I can even try, my dad, as usual, doesn't wait to hear what I have to say. "And why are you driving a BMW? I know you didn't buy it, so who owns it?"

He glances at Audrey and Josh, who both turn to me. Well, here goes nothing. "It's my boyfriend's."

Audrey grins wildly at my admission. My father looks flabbergasted. "You're dating someone?"

"Yeah." I shrug. "I'm borrowing his car until I buy a new one, which should be this weekend."

"Who?"

I take a deep breath. "Sebastian Deveau."

My father's reaction is priceless—at first. He blinks his big gray eyes. His mouth twitches, then falls open, and then slams shut. He looks confused, startled and quite frankly flummoxed. But then it becomes exactly what I dreaded—smug. "My little Shaynie is dating a hockey player?"

I feel the anger make my body rigid. So rigid I don't even respond with a nod. He laughs a big, deep belly laugh. Audrey must understand how this is making me feel, so she hooks her arm through mine again and says, "He's a really great guy."

"Yeah, despite his profession," I add bitingly.

My dad stops laughing at that, but the smug smile doesn't die with the laughter. "Oh, we're all great guys when we want to be." Then he steps forward and pats my shoulder as he pushes open the door to the arena. "See you later, honey. I don't want to be late."

His words were condescending and flippant. And as we enter the arena behind him, flashing our passes at the security guard there, I watch him trot away, and I fight the urge to flip him off behind his back, in front of all the people milling about the concourse. Most of whom are recognizing him and pointing with excited smiles on their faces.

"What the hell does that mean, that we all are when we want to be?" Josh asks to no one in particular.

"It means he thinks Seb is acting like he's not a womanizer but really is," I mutter back. "Just like dear old Dad was."

Josh and Audrey don't respond because, really, what do you say? *Sorry your dad was a womanizing manwhore and just acted like a complete douche.* I glance at the passes and the section marked on them and start heading down the concrete corridor in that direction, even though the last thing I want is to watch a hockey game right now.

Two hours later and I'm regretting being here even more. The Winterhawks are about four minutes away from losing the second of two

here at home, which would put the series at 2–2. The energy in the
building is tense, and it's even worse on the ice.

The Winterhawks were up 2–0 early in the first and added a goal
to that in the opening minute of the second period, but the Thunder captain, Levi Casco, scored two goals. And a defenseman named
Duncan Darby stole the puck from Sebastian and scored at the beginning of the third to tie the game. Then the Thunder's assistant
captain, Jude Braddock, scored, giving the Thunder the lead. If they
win this game, it's going to be a nightmare going back to San Francisco. The Winterhawks will have lost the momentum and probably
some confidence.

There's a faceoff just left of the Thunder goalie and Jordan wins it,
shooting the puck back to Sebastian, who spins to get free of Darby
and manages to get a shot off on net. The Thunder's goalie blocks
the shot, but the puck bounces off him and Seb clambers for the
rebound shot as the Thunder team converges on him. He gets the
shot off, but, unfortunately, the goalie gloves the puck. The whistle
blows, but the shoving and swearing with the pile of Thunder and
Winterhawks players in front of the net doesn't stop.

I can see, even from here, the frustration all over Sebastian's face.
The linesmen both get in there and start to tug on jerseys, breaking
up the scrum.

As the ref gathers the puck for another faceoff, I watch Sebastian
glide toward Jordan. Braddock's jaw keeps flapping, and he must
say something that gets to Jordan, because he spins back to Braddock. They both drop their sticks but not their gloves and start
shoving each other. Sebastian skates over, I think to break it up, and
Braddock's mouth starts moving again, and then suddenly Sebastian's glove is flying over Jordan's shoulder and Braddock is tumbling

backward onto the ice after getting a solid punch to the side of his helmet.

Whistles blow. Seb is hauled off to the penalty box and a second later so is Jordan because, even though the whistle had blown, he dropped his glove and skates at Braddock.

"You've got a feisty one," Audrey murmurs, and I can't tell if she's impressed or horrified. I don't look over to find out. I'm too busy glaring at Sebastian in the penalty box.

"He just cost them the game," I whisper, more to myself than anyone else, but Josh hears me.

"Yeah, you can't pull the goalie and go hard to the net when you've got two guys in the box. This one is over." He sounds like a kid who just found out Santa Claus isn't real.

And three minutes later it's confirmed. The Thunder win 4–3, tying the series and ending this one with a massive brawl on the ice. Every single player on the ice is shoving or punching someone and the players on the bench are yelling at the other bench, sticks up and curses hurling.

"We should go," I say quietly.

"I thought Seb said we should go downstairs after the game and meet him in the family lounge," Josh reminds me.

"I don't know about that now..." I caution, my instincts from childhood kicking in. After losses like this, my mother learned to stay away. Just head straight home and don't expect my father to join until the wee hours of the morning, if at all.

But then our conversation from the other night, the one he started while taking off his clothes in my bedroom, comes back to me.

"But there are two kinds of players. The ones that use it as an excuse

to mistreat and ignore the people who love them, and the ones who find balance."

"*Haven't met one of those balanced ones yet.*"

"*Yes, you have.*"

"Yeah, okay," I say to Josh. "Let's go down and meet him."

Chapter 40

Sebastian

Glenn Beckford waltzes into the room like he owns it as I'm tightening the knot on my tie. Most of the guys are in their suits now, but no one is really leaving the locker room yet. Everyone is still trying to come to terms with the way that game imploded on us before facing our families and loved ones. I know I'm not looking forward to seeing Shay. I know she won't like what she saw. I don't regret going after Jude Braddock and I won't pretend I do, and I know she'll like my lack of remorse even less.

I grew up watching her dad lose his temper on the ice. He was a real pest: his nasty, personal attacks on the other team's players often landed him in the penalty box without him even throwing a punch. By the time he retired, Glenn Beckford held the record for the most unsportsmanlike penalty minutes in the league. At least my penalty minutes are usually for my actions and not my words. I defend teammates and don't take low blows with my fists or my mouth.

He stands there and surveys the room.

"Undisciplined loss out there, boys," he lectures loudly, like he's our coach or something. "You just made this whole series harder for yourselves, but you can rein it in and get it back next time. I know you can. Westwood, I don't have to tell you it's up to you to make sure of it."

Avery frowns at him but, ever the Boy Scout, he doesn't tell him to shut up. Avery, being the captain, has already given us a lecture, as has our actual coach. Neither of those lectures did anything to improve my mood, so this third one isn't helping either. I glance over at Jordan, who is shrugging into his navy blue suit jacket. I grab my own from the hook in my locker and turn to find Glenn's eyes pinning me. He grins, but it's not friendly. It's dark and cool.

"Deveau," he addresses me. "You had some good chances out there. You probably would have had more if you didn't have your ass in the box at the end."

"Yeah, well, next time," I reply tersely and give him a smile I know looks as fake as it feels. Jordan walks up beside me and mutters something about finding Jessie, but he doesn't walk away because Glenn is standing directly in front of both of us now.

"What'd that little runt Braddock say to you two to make you so angry it cost you the game?"

That's fucking harsh. What Jude Braddock did was ask Jordan if his fiancée was as easy as her sister. Turns out Braddock and Callie had fooled around a few years ago. There's a code on the ice: you can knock a guy about almost anything—their skill, their intelligence, their looks—but children, wives or girlfriends are supposed to be off limits. So, yeah, Jordan wanted to kill him—and I went after him too, because I heard it and I will always back up my boys.

Jordan bristles beside me now as he faces this over-the-hill blowhard. "He made a personal attack. Directed at my fiancée and her family."

Glenn's expression doesn't change. He looks as unimpressed as he did a second ago. "What? Did he claim to bang her before you or something?"

I can feel the anger radiating off Jordan, but Glenn doesn't seem to feel it. In fact he seems completely oblivious to the crassness of his words. "Guys will say anything to get under your skin on the ice. Even if it's true, you have to blow it off. You can't cost your whole team a game over some chick."

I put a hand on Jordy's shoulder and squeeze. "Go find Jessie," I urge, because I don't want him to start something with Shay's dad. Oh God, this man is going to be in my life for a while. That realization fills me with dread.

Jordan storms out of the room. I glance at Avery, who is eyeing the situation cautiously as he buttons his dress shirt. Our eyes meet and I see the plea in them to stay calm. I have to, he's right, but I want to tell this jerk to get bent. I inhale deeply and try to excuse myself like Jordan did. "I have to go. I have friends waiting in the lounge."

"You mean my daughter?" Our eyes connect. "I saw her arrive in the car you gave her. Thanks for that, by the way. She won't let me help her. Now if you could get her an apartment in a better area of town, I wouldn't have to worry so much."

"I didn't give her a car," I reply, because I feel like it would matter to Shay that her dad knows she's not accepting handouts from me either. "She's borrowing it until this weekend when she gets her own."

He scratches the back of his neck while he absorbs that information. "Pity. I thought maybe she'd come to her senses and realize she can't do this on her own. Not as a silly yoga instructor anyway."

"She's also a nutritionist," I remind him, and I can't believe I have to defend her to her own father. "And an amazing human being, for the record."

His gray eyes land on mine again, and he breaks into a soft, friendly grin. "Deveau, you don't have to prove your feelings for my daughter to me. I know she's a wonderful person, albeit a bit too opinionated and stubborn most of the time." He reaches out and cups my shoulder in a fatherly gesture. "I'm happy you want to take that on. I hope it works out for the long haul. But I'm warning you: she's never going to be easy. She doesn't play by the hockey wives code. Consider that carefully, my friend. You'll be giving up a lot of your extracurricular activity."

"Glenn, why don't you come to the friends and family lounge with me. I'm sure everyone would love to see you there," I say smoothly, and without waiting for an answer, I escort Beckford out of the locker room.

My girlfriend's father has no clue how close I was to punching him. I'm not even sure I realize how close I was until Chooch, who was sitting across the locker room watching the whole thing, says, "Unclench those fists, Seb."

I relax my hands and shake them out before shoving them into my pockets. "Did that guy just honestly warn you that if you date his daughter she might not let you fuck other people?"

"Yeah. Not because he cares if I cheat on her, but because she might."

"He made it seem like that fact was a fault in her character." Chooch is also blown away, judging by the awed pitch to his voice. "Who the fuck thinks not being able to cheat is a bad thing?"

"A man who thinks it's okay to make out with his former teammate's wife at his own jersey retirement ceremony," I reply and watch Chooch's jaw drop. But it's weird because even though he looks fittingly shocked, Chooch's eyes don't seem to be focused on me. They're looking past me.

I turn and see Shay standing in the open locker room door.

"What did you just say?" Her voice is low and serious and it settles over the entire room, covering it in an ominous silence as the few remaining players glance up.

"You're not supposed to be in here."

It's the truth. Family and friends aren't allowed in the locker room. But it's the worst possible thing I could say. She's staring at me with such intensity, such hurt and anger and pain that I just…panic. After the words leave my mouth she lifts the lanyard with her VIP pass from around her neck and says, "You couldn't be more right. I knew I was never supposed to be here."

And then she drops the pass on the locker room floor and disappears.

Chapter 41

Shayne

I make it all the way to the parking lot before I realize that I don't want to drive his car home. If I drive his car home, I'll have to see him again when he comes to pick it up. And I don't want to see him again. Not now. Maybe never.

I can hear him behind me so I turn, ready to give him the key, but he starts talking before I can. "What was I supposed to do, Shay? How was I supposed to tell you?"

"You know how you tell me? You just do. You tell me. It doesn't matter when or how, just say it," I explain angrily. "Or do you condone his behavior? Are you following the old boys' code? Covering it up because that's what hockey brothers do."

He looks like I just stabbed him. "Of course I fucking don't. Jesus, Shay, can't you figure that out by now?"

"The only thing I've figured out is we jumped into this ass backwards and way too fast," I blurt out, and the scary part is I kind of mean it. Ever since I met Sebastian, everything I've done has been completely out of character. And the exhilaration of that has suddenly and completely melted into regret. I jumped out of the plane and now I'm realizing my chute might not open.

He says something in French under his breath. I think it's a swear word. "Shay, I saw him kissing a woman once."

"At the jersey retirement."

He nods. "Right after you had rejected me *again*. And then when you stopped rejecting me, I was scared that telling you would change that."

I press the palm of my hand into my forehead and close my eyes. "Not telling me changes that. Protecting his cheating does that."

When I open my eyes, he's taken a step closer to me. "Shayne. You're making this a bigger deal than it is. I don't condone what he's doing, and I would never do this to you. Or anyone. Ever. So don't try and make this about us."

We're right in front of each other now. Other people are in the parking lot too. Chris Dixon and his wife and kids are walking to their car. Jordan and Jessie are walking hand in hand toward their car. Sebastian watches them go and the turns to me. "Jordan and Jessie are in love."

"I know."

"It's real, and it started with an undeniable connection, that they just couldn't break no matter how hard they tried. And, trust me, they tried," Sebastian tells me, and his baby blue eyes turn pleading. "Tell me you don't feel that kind of connection between us?"

I struggle to pull air into my lungs because suddenly breathing is impossible. I don't answer him, exactly. "I need to be able to trust the person I am with, and after tonight..."

"This is bullshit," he says harshly. "You've been looking for a way to talk yourself out of this since I talked you into it. And you know what? I'm going to let you this time."

He lifts his eyes and gives me a look I've never seen on his face before—defeat.

"I didn't tell you what I saw your dad doing. I should have. I wanted to, but that isn't enough for you." He shakes his head and shoves his hands into the pockets of his suit pants. "So that's it. This was always some sort of competition, I guess. I just never expected to lose."

My emotions are doing a one eighty. All that anger and regret I felt minutes ago is now confusion and fear—and loss. I've lost him. Oh God, is that what I really wanted? Because suddenly, now that it's real, it's not. It's not at all.

"Sebastian…"

"Look, take the car home." He takes my hand and drops the key back into it. For the first time ever his touch is abrupt. "I drove the Aston here anyway. I'll pick it up from you in a few days or send Chooch to get it or something."

He turns and heads back toward the arena doors. I see Chooch standing there awkwardly, waiting for him. I want to stop him but I can't. I know that it's over. I can feel it in my bones, and the pain is literally immobilizing. So I stand there, his car key dangling from my hand, and watch him drive away.

Chapter 42

Shayne

I'm blurry eyed with exhaustion as I ease off the freeway and into the upscale residential neighborhood I grew up in. It's early, so there's not a lot of traffic. My mom hardly sleeps, so I know she'll be up, even though it's not even seven yet. My dad will still be asleep. He's always been a late sleeper. I lay awake half the night last night, which is why I'm heading to their house so early. I want to tell my mom what's happening. She has a right to know. And I want to confront my father and tell him I know and that I don't approve. It won't make a difference to him, but I want to do it anyway. Fighting with him is still better than sitting at home thinking about Sebastian.

My mind and my heart are stuck on Sebastian. I feel like I had a right to be upset with him for hiding my father's infidelity from me. And in a way, when he said he was going to let me go, and I realized there would be no chase this time, it felt like a relief. A horrible relief. It's the only way I can describe it. I no longer have to take risks with my heart. I don't have to go against my safe, simple nature and trust this wild, complex hockey player. But at the same time, deep down where it counts, in the dark recesses of my jaded little heart, I don't want to go back to safe and simple. I don't even know if I can anymore.

I turn onto the street I grew up on. Nothing's changed here in years except maybe the trees have gotten taller. The oak in the front yard of our place used to be shorter than our second level. Now it eclipses the second floor, fully shadowing what had been my bedroom window. I pull into the driveway behind my mom's car and put Seb's car in park.

I ring the bell and look up toward the security camera I know is hidden in the bottom of the porch light. My dad installed it when he was still playing and would be away for long periods of time. My mom swings open the door, still in a set of gray silk pajamas and slippers with a dark lavender bathrobe over them. "Shayne! Are you okay?"

I don't know how to answer that. So I don't. "Can I come in?"

She nods and holds the door wider. "Of course."

I step into the house I've been avoiding for years. It looks different. She's redecorated since the last time I was here. The dark carpet that was in the entryway when I was growing up is now espresso wood. The walls, which were cream, are now a pure white with dark wood crown molding.

"Dad still sleeping?" I ask and try not to sound so hopeful, but I don't want to see him.

"I was just having coffee. Can I get you some? We have an amazing coffee machine," she gushes and puts a hand on my back, guiding me toward the kitchen at the back of the house, as if I won't remember where it is. "I don't ever go to Starbucks anymore. I can be my own barista."

The kitchen has been redone too. It's now all white—cabinets, floors, walls, with a gorgeous blue glass tile backsplash and stainless-steel appliances. "This is gorgeous, Mom."

She beams. "Thanks! I picked out everything myself. Your dad wanted a designer, but I have an eye for these things. I think it's perfect."

"It is," I agree and sit at the breakfast bar.

"Let me make you a latte. Caramel or vanilla?" She smiles so brightly I can't say no. And her grin deepens when I tell her caramel because she remembers that's my favorite flavor of anything.

My heart starts to ache again, but this time not for the loss of Sebastian. For my mom. She loves me, and I've been punishing her for her choices that really have nothing to do with me. And I know I'll want to do it again if she reacts the way I think she'll react when I tell her what I know. I watch her quietly as she putters about the pristine kitchen, hitting switches and moving dials on the large built-in coffee machine on the counter next to the stove.

She puts the steamy mug with perfect foam down on the counter in front of me and picks up her own half-empty one from before I got here and leans on the counter in front of me. I sip the drink and smile at her because it's delicious. She smiles back, victorious.

"Mom, you didn't answer me. Is Dad still asleep?"

She shakes her head. "He stayed in the city last night."

I stare at her and she stares at her coffee mug. This conversation isn't going to be painful for her. She already knows. I can tell. I can feel it in my bones. "How long has it been going on?"

She finally looks up from her coffee. She looks tired, emotionally. "I realized he was seeing Lacey again last week. I think it started when they saw each other at the jersey ceremony."

"I thought it was because he was playing. He was on the road and the lifestyle was too hard and athletes had too much tension and energy to exude," I say and place my mug a little too roughly on the counter, so it clanks loudly. "Well, he's not a fucking athlete anymore."

My mom takes a deep breath. "No he's fucking not an athlete anymore," she agrees, and her voice has an edge to it I've never heard before, not to mention the fact that she swore—and let me swear. "Now I have no excuses for him. He's just a plain old cheater."

I feel like she should cry. But she doesn't. She looks, scarily, like she doesn't give a shit. She levels me with a stare. "Shayne, I know you don't approve and I don't expect you to. I don't expect anyone to. The fact is, I loved your father, but I loved what he could give me even more. And I'm paying the price for that."

"Mom, it's never too late to fix things," I tell her softly. "Leave him. Find someone who will love you. You deserve it."

She smiles at me, but it's rueful, and then she lifts herself off the counter and smooths her mussed hair. "Your dad loves me. He's just not in love with me. I don't know if he ever was. But like I said, I was in love with the fact that he got me out of my small town and off my parents' farm more than I was in love with him, so I guess we're even. And I got what I wanted." She runs her hand along the smooth marble countertop, giant diamond wedding ring glinting in the sun coming through the window. "Everything money could buy, and most important, he gave me you and Trey. Believe it or not, that's what I am most grateful for."

She picks up her mug again and takes a sip of her coffee before turning to look out the window and over her massive backyard with the pool and spa. "Besides, it won't last with Lacey. Or the next one he finds. I'm what lasts. I'm the glue that keeps him together and he knows that. This isn't everyone's version of love, but it's ours."

I stare at her in awe and horror. Growing up, my mother told us she loved us almost every day. She told us to love each other too, but I realize now there is a very distinct difference between being told to do something and seeing something happen. I didn't see or feel love actually happening in my house. I saw jealousy and lies and denial and anger. Their version of love was the only thing I experienced, and it's left me without the ability to trust or love someone completely.

"What if I can never trust anyone?" I feel the hot tears slip down my cheeks.

She walks around the island and hugs me, and I don't fight it for the first time since I was young. "Don't let our mistakes be your downfall, Shaynie. Please."

"I think it's too late."

She pulls back and looks at me with a small smile. "You just told me it's never too late to fix things. Take your own advice."

Can I fix this? Will he let me?

Chapter 43

Sebastian

I hold the door to the recording studio open for Stephanie and she steps inside. I follow and Chooch walks in after me. I tell the woman at the front desk that we're here for the Elevate Fitness recording and she ushers us back to a tiny, dimly lit room with mixing boards and leather couches. A glass wall looks into a room with microphones and headphones everywhere. I drop down onto a couch and shake my head when the receptionist asks if I'd like anything to drink. Steph orders a peppermint tea and Chooch asks for a bottle of water.

When she's gone Chooch leans toward me from the couch to my left. "You barely looked at her."

"Yeah? So?"

"So she's worth looking at," Chooch explains. "And that's not like you."

"You're the single one. Go for it," I mutter and rub a hand over my ever-growing facial hair because it's itchy as hell. Thank God this isn't a TV commercial. I look like a homeless guy and Chooch, who grows facial hair in weird patches, looks like a teen caught in his awkward phase. As much as the playoff beard annoys me, I'll be devastated if I get to shave after our game tomorrow night.

"I thought you said you and Shayne were over?" Chooch questions.

"We are, but it's only been six days. Give me a break."

"You've never needed one before," he comments.

I glare at him. His thin lips snap together and he leans back on the couch.

The receptionist walks back in with their drinks and I glance up at her. She's tall, lithe, with pretty blue eyes, nice brown hair and a warm, friendly smile. And I might as well be looking at a toaster oven. That's how much I care.

She asks me one more time if I need anything, and when I politely decline again, she informs us that Trey and the recording engineer will be here in five minutes.

I can feel Stephanie's eyes on me so I turn. She pats my knee and smiles. "So when are you going to talk to her?"

"I'm not. It's done," I reply and pick at the cuff of my Henley. "We handled the whole thing wrong from the beginning. And for a while there I thought it might work anyway. But she was looking for a reason to run, and I couldn't stop her from finding one. I realize now it's impossible to force someone to give you a chance, so I'm moving on."

"I've seen you moving on and this"—she waves her hand up and down in front of me like a model showing off a prize on *The Price Is Right*—"this is not moving on. This is wallowing and suffering and longing. This is what you've wanted. Love."

"Then love sucks," I bite back.

Chooch chuckles. "Yeah, it does. But when it doesn't. Man, oh man…"

I want to glare at him, but he's got such a far-off look in his eye and a whimsical smile on his face that I don't think he'd notice. Trey and some dude with two sleeve tattoos walks in.

"Hey! Thanks so much for taking the time to do this," Trey says as he shakes my hand and then Chooch's. "I can't tell you how much it means to me."

"No problem," Chooch replies with an easy shrug. "It'll be fun."

"I know Avery wanted to do it himself, but…well, you know," my sister says and I give her an incredulous look. Since when does Stephanie Deveau defend Avery Westwood? What? Is she his publicist now?

Trey nods. "Yeah, once he explained his situation it made perfect sense. I'm thrilled to have you guys."

The guy with the tats introduces himself as Owen, the sound engineer. He asks who wants to go first. Chooch volunteers, so Owen takes him into the other room, the one through the glass, and sets him up.

Trey hands me a script and sits down on the couch Chooch vacated as Stephanie picks up her tea and heads to the door. "I'm going to go get chatty with the receptionist. See if she's single and if she has any interest in Chooch."

I can't help but laugh at that despite my mood. "Look at you, wingman."

She grins. "Why the hell not? Get him back on the horse. Unlike you, he's ready for another horse. You still have miles to go on yours, whether you admit it or not."

She leaves the room and Trey follows her with his eyes before turning back to me. "I feel like she just called my sister a horse."

"She did," I reply and then clear my throat awkwardly. "We broke up."

Trey sighs. "I thought maybe something like that was going on. She's been showing up at work every morning with her eyes all red and her skin blotchy. When I asked her if she wanted to come to the recording today, she acted like I asked her if she wanted to drink a salmonella milk shake."

I smile, but it's mirthless. We don't say anything for a long time. I glance at the script, which he assures me is a guideline and not something I need to repeat verbatim. I can tell he's just so thrilled we've agreed to endorse his place. It was Avery's idea. After that night at Jordan's, he seemed really broken up about not helping Trey out, so he did the second best thing, he asked us to. It made me realize that Avery never wants to hurt anyone and that maybe I was giving him a harder time than I had to about not re-signing with the team.

Owen comes back in, and we sit quietly and listen as Chooch records a few versions of his endorsement. He sounds articulate and believable, but Owen complains about the mic quality and disappears back into the other room.

Trey leans back and rests his ankle on his knee. He's looking at me but his expression is unreadable. Our brief conversation from a few weeks ago when he found out I was dating his sister surfaces in my cloudy head. I sit a little straighter. "So is this the part where you kill me? Because I would recommend you do it after I record so you can use my endorsement posthumously."

"You use big words for a French kid. No wonder my sister likes you. She's always loved vocabulary and wordy people. It's why my quietness makes her insane," Trey jokes. I'm kind of kidding also, about him killing me, but I wonder if he will make good on that threat eventually. He smiles. "I know you didn't hurt her. If you hurt her she'd be furious, but she's crying, so that means she did this to herself. And she knows it."

I feel like I need to tell him the whole story. "I saw something I should have told her about but I didn't. So I kind of annihilated what little trust she'd let herself build in me."

Trey looks confused by that, and I realize I'm probably going to have to tell him I watched his dad cheat on his mother. Dear God, when did my life become a telenovela?

"Your dad…" I begin awkwardly. "I saw him at his jersey retirement…he was getting close to…"

"Lacey Millbury?" Trey finishes for me, and I nod. "Yeah, that's been on and off since I was a kid."

"Your dad and his teammate's wife?" I have to reconfirm because it seems insane to me. Not only are you fucking with your marriage, but you're fucking with the second most important relationship you've got when you're a hockey player: the bond with your team.

"Shayne caught them when she was fourteen," he elaborates. "We were having a Cup party and dear old Dad and Lacey disappeared to bang in the upstairs bathroom. Shayne walked in on them. Doggie style."

I grimace and so does Trey. Because really, no one wants to see their dad like that. Ever. With anyone. Trey swallows down the visual and continues. "She was devastated and angry and would have made a huge scene, but my mother grabbed her and took her to her room. Mom was more angry at Shayne for wanting to announce her discovery than she was at her own husband. Looking back, I realize my mother knew it had been going on, but she was all about public image. Still is. She'd rather look like a happy home than be one."

"That's horrible," I can't help but say, and I have a new respect for my own mom, who got out of a loveless marriage, even though it wasn't easy on her financially or emotionally.

Trey shrugs. "Yeah, well, it's not my marriage. And I promised myself it never would be. Sure, I had my fun in college, but I always knew if I ever did settle down, I would do it with someone I wanted to be faithful to."

"I know." I nod because he's describing my philosophy.

"Shayne took it a lot more personally, though. Not only did she blame the hockey lifestyle, but she also developed trust issues. And she became...closed off. Until you."

Owen walks back in and sits down at the console, hits a button, and leans into a mic and tells Chooch to go again. We listen to a take or two and then Trey leans toward me. "The one thing I have to say about my sister is that when she makes a mistake, it guts her. And if you give her another chance, she'll never make it again."

I turn my eyes from him to the carpet beneath my shoes because I don't want him to see the conflicted look I'm sure is all over my face. Is he saying Shay thinks ending things with me was a mistake?

If so, then I guess it's a game of who's willing to risk the next move...

Chapter 44

Shayne

As soon as class is over, Audrey marches to the front of the room and pulls me to her sweaty body. Normally I would fuss and push her away. I'm not one for PDA with men or women, but I'm on the verge of tears for the hundredth time in a week, which makes her embrace comforting. I hug her back, and she kisses the top of my head like a mom or big sister.

"Shaynie, call him," she urges softly.

"I don't even know what to say," I admit, my voice wobbling. "I don't think there's anything I can say to make him change his mind. You didn't see the look on his face, Audrey. He just totally shut down."

"You were being a bit of a lunatic." Audrey pats my head as she lets me go. "Men never know how to react to that, even if it's justi-fied. And in this case, it kind of was, Shayne. Don't forget that. He should have told you about your dad."

"Yes. He should have. It just triggered every negative experience and every stereotype I'd developed about hockey players and I just…" I pause and take a deep breath and wipe at my eyes because I think tears might fall again.

"You used it as an excuse to screw up something that terrifies the shit out of you anyway," Audrey finishes for me as she bends to roll up my yoga mat for me.

"Yeah. That's exactly what I did." I sniff. "Maybe it was for the best. I mean the whole thing started off so crazy. He was a one-night stand, and then he wasn't. He knew I hated hockey players so he didn't tell me he was one. That's lying. This whole thing started with lies."

Audrey finishes rolling the mat and stands up but she doesn't speak, so I continue. "I mean how many relationships become life-long love stories when the people have seen each other naked on multiple occasions before they even know each other's last names?"

"No idea," Audrey replies as we walk over to the corner to drop off the mat. "But I'm sure not very many."

She smiles at me, and it's not sympathetic. It's kind of supercilious, which I don't get. But I don't want to ask her about it because I've not finished my rant. I was up all night last night thinking of all the reasons why Sebastian and I had to crash and burn, why this wasn't just me messing up something that was destined to be amazing. I even wrote it down. Just one giant cons column in a notebook while I sat at my kitchen table at four a.m. It didn't make me feel a whole hell of a lot better but I figured if I expressed the facts to someone else, and they agreed, that would make me feel better.

"I let him and his ability to give orgasms cloud my better judgment," I announce.

"Evil, evil orgasms." Audrey is not even pretending not to mock me now.

"Audrey!"

We exit the yoga room and she wraps an arm around my shoulders as we head toward the juice bar. Jessie is behind it finishing off a super green smoothie for Mrs. Waters. "Let me finish this for you, because I know you too well."

We sit next to each other. Jessie smiles at us and we twist our stools to face each other. "After you let the possibility of reoccurring orgasms override your ridiculous hatred of all things and people that have anything to do with pucks and ice, you then didn't let yourself freak out over the fact that Sebastian was a serial monogamist."

"Right! I mean with anyone, hockey player or not, the fact that his last serious relationship ended basically at the same time he met me should have had me bailing," I agree and reach over the bar to grab two coconut waters from the cooler built into the bar.

"Yeah. It's got to mean that you two couldn't possibly have legit feelings for each other because there are rules to true love." Audrey nods her head emphatically as if agreeing, but she's actually being a sarcastic little brat. "A mandatory waiting period of three months between romantic encounters and a full oral history of your pasts as well as full names and family trees and debt history must be exchanged before tongues enter each other's mouths…or other orifices. If all those boxes aren't checked, your feelings can't be real."

She's spewing so much sarcasm right now I'm surprised it doesn't knock me off my bar stool.

"Hey, best friend, you need to read the manual again. You're doing it wrong," I quip, trying to make light of it, but I'm actually getting kind of pissed off. Jessie giggles at that so I know, even though she has her back to us as she chops fruit on the back bar, she's been listening the whole time.

Audrey's pretty face breaks into another smile but this one is sympathetic. "I'm sorry, Shayne. I really am, but I am not going to help you talk yourself out of trying to win him back. Because I think you should."

I swallow a mouthful of coconut water and admit to her what I haven't even dared to admit to myself. "I don't know how to do that."

She drops her hand on top of mine on the bar and squeezes. "You can start by talking to him."

Jessie reaches under the bar and dangles the key to his BMW in front of me. "He still hasn't picked up his car."

She doesn't have to tell me this, because I see it in the parking lot every morning.

"But he told me he wanted to pick it up while I was in a class," I remind her, because I explained all this to her on the phone the day after it happened. Of course, maybe it wasn't clear through my sobbing. "He doesn't want to see me."

"Yeah, and you didn't want to fall in love with a hockey player." Audrey winks and pats my hand again. "In the words of the Stones, you can't always get what you want."

Jessie leans closer and adds, "But if you try sometimes…" She and Audrey start to sing. "You just might get what you need."

I can't help but laugh at them, but it comes out as a nervous squawk because all the sadness in my body is being replaced with terror as a plan forms in my brain. The Winterhawks are in San Francisco for the next four days. They would leave tonight. They had to win tomorrow night or be eliminated.

If this were my dad, the last thing he would want would be my mom, or any woman, distracting him. It wouldn't matter what was going on, or how serious, he would be furious if his focus was pulled off of hockey for even a second. Dustin had been the same way. The one playoff run while we were together in college he barely even spoke to me. He told me he needed to be alone to focus, but he was actually off getting chlamydia between playoff games. But Sebastian isn't Glenn Beckford or Dustin. He kept trying to prove that to me, and now I have to prove to him I am not going to hold other people's mistakes against him.

As if she can hear my thoughts, Jessie leans on the counter and smiles at me encouragingly. "Go see him before they leave tonight. Do it for me. If you two get back together, then Seb will have a date for my wedding this summer!"

I laugh at that and her grin deepens. I pull myself off the bar stool and hand her my empty coconut water. "I need to take a shower and try to make myself decent. I have a plan, but I'll need your help."

"Tell me what you need and I'll do it," Jessie promises and glances behind her at the clock on the wall.

"Can you get me a Deveau jersey?" I ask, embarrassed.

She grins and nods emphatically. "Piece of cake!" Jessie glances at the clock on the wall. "They have practice for another twenty minutes, and then they're heading to the airport. You get ready; I'll get the jersey."

Here goes nothing.

Chapter 45

Sebastian

Jordan and Avery are pulling into the VIP lot at the airport at the same time I am. I park in the spot next to Jordan, get out of my SUV and head to the trunk to get my luggage. His playoff beard is in full, unruly mountain-man mode, just like mine. I know our crazy facial hair contrasts ridiculously with the suits we wear to and from games. We get weird looks from some travelers at the airport, but hockey fans get it.

"How's the wrist?" Jordan asks me, and I look at my left hand with the splint on it.

"It's better. It'll be fine by game time." I'd strained it again in the last game, but the doctors were confident it wasn't serious. The splint was just a precaution.

He smiles at me and we start toward Avery, who is also yanking his travel bag out of the back of his car. "You wanna go through the main concourse?"

We fly private and so we're at a smaller airport a few miles from Sea-Tac. The fans in recent years have figured this out and a dedicated bunch often show up to greet us when we land or see us off, especially during playoffs. We have the option of going through a different gate, one that avoids the main concourse where the fans congregate, if we're not in the mood for autographs and pictures. I usually don't mind it, but this afternoon, I'm not in the mood.

I shake my head no. Jordan's smile deepens and he shrugs. "Tough luck, we're doing it anyway."

"What?" I blink. Avery falls in step beside us as Jordan puts a hand on my shoulder and steers me to the main entrance.

"He's doing the fan thing, right, Avery?" Jordan says.

"Yeah. Captain's orders," Avery replies, and I glare at him. Something is going on; I just don't know what.

I'm about to ask when I realize there's no point. These two shit-heads won't tell me anyway. Jordan and Avery make small talk as we make our way toward the concourse. I keep my eyes on the tile floor in front of me and listen halfheartedly. Every airport staff member we pass wishes us a good game and I smile and nod at all of them. Then I hesitate, because once we pass through another set of glass doors we'll be in an open hallway with fans lined up on either side of the rope the staff put out. I could walk to the right, out another door takes you to security but avoids the open concourse, and get on the plane without anyone noticing. Jordan must know I'm about to bolt, because I feel his hand between my shoulders and he gives me a small push toward the other door.

"Come on, Deveau. There's some fans who want to see you." He gives me his best lopsided grin. "And one I think you'll want to see."

"What the fuck are you talking about?" I ask, but I find myself following along anyway without getting an answer. Jordan is first through the doors and I hear the fans cheer. I walk out behind him

to more clapping and yelling. There are about forty people all hud-
dled together behind the rope stanchions the airport has set up.
Everyone is wearing something with a Winterhawks logo. There are
baseball hats, T-shirts, tank tops and a ton of jerseys. I see a lot of
Westwood jerseys and some Garrison and some Choochinsky and a
few of mine. I stop at the first cluster, take a pen from a girl who is
squealing, and sign the back of her Deveau jersey.

As I continue down the line, a forced smile that I hope looks
natural on my face, I scan the homemade signs some people have
brought. Most of them are wishing us luck; some are putting
down the Thunder. I particularly like the one that says *Thunder
Are Vomit*. One being held up at the end of the line catches my
eye. It's white cardboard with glittery blue letters and it says *Forgive Me, Frenchie.*

I freeze midsignature on someone's jersey. The guy glances over
his shoulder. "Are you done?"

"No. Sorry. Hold on." I finish the signature and pose for a photo
with his girlfriend and then march down the line, ignoring everyone
in between me and that sign bobbing about the crowd.

Someone calls out my name, wanting me to stop, and I do, begrudgingly, and sign a T-shirt with my number on it. Then Avery,
who has been hovering just inside the doors, steps out and the crowd
sees him and goes wild. I'm invisible and I'm thrilled. I march toward the sign.

She's standing there, at the end of the line, all by herself with soft
gray eyes and a nervous look on her pretty features. Our eyes lock,
and she gives me a soft smile before biting her lower lip as her cheeks
turn pink. I let my eyes sweep over her—she's wearing jeans and
a Winterhawks jersey with my name and number. Her hair is in a

long, low braid over her shoulder and I see her freckles are not covered up. Fuck, she's perfect.

"Hi," she says, barely above a whisper.

"Nice jersey," I say, and she turns a deeper shade of pink.

She laughs and it makes me feel incredible, so I grin back. "What can I say, I'm a fan."

I feign my best exaggerated and shocked expression. "Shayne Middle Name Unknown Beckford is a hockey fan! Everyone hunker down with canned goods. The apocalypse is coming."

She laughs again. "I'm not a hockey fan. I'm a Sebastian Gabriel Maxim Louis Deveau fan. Big difference."

I like that. A lot.

Her expression grows serious, the smile slipping from her face as she tilts her head up and looks at me with worried eyes. "I don't want to bother you before a game, but I had to tell you before you left," she explains.

"Tell me what?" I ask, feeling my usual playful attitude start to stir for the first time since our fight. "That sign is a demand, not an explanation."

She grins at that. "Yeah, well, you know me."

"I do?"

"Yes, you do," she confirms with a nod, and I notice the guy beside her has stopped looking at Avery down the line and is looking at us, so I take a couple steps away from the crowd and she follows me, the rope still between us. She takes a deep breath and then says, "You know me better than I thought. And I know you too. I know you're loyal and supportive and caring and that you're not like any other hockey player I've had the displeasure of knowing."

She pauses and I fight a smile, because I don't want to give in to her yet—even though I know it's inevitable. The minute I saw that sign something in me that had broken felt whole again and I'm pretty sure it was my heart. "You're finally using your brain, Shay. I'm impressed."

"I'm not using my brain at all, actually. I'm trusting my heart." She laughs. "My brain is an evil pessimist but my heart is a hopeful romantic. And my heart says you're the one for me. And I'm the only one for you."

I can't resist touching her, so I reach over the rope and pull her into me. It's supposed to be a friendly hug, but it triggers hormones that race through my body that are much more than friendship. She pulls her hands from her pockets and wraps them around my back briefly before letting go.

"I miss you," she whispers.

The words are like a warm blanket wrapped around me. "I've missed you too."

I let her go, because I'm about to kiss her, and that would create a scene. Then she reaches into her pocket and hands me the key to my car. I don't move to take it from her. "What did you buy?"

"A bus pass," she tells me, but before I can argue she adds, "And I used the extra money to rent an apartment in a better area of town. I move next week."

She dangles the key in front of me again. This time I reach out to take it, and she notices the splint on my left hand. She grasps it softly and our eyes meet. "It's not a big deal. Just a little sore. Most guys would pop some pain pills and not even notice it."

"But you won't?"

"I don't take pain medication, or any medication if I can avoid it," I admit to her. "My sister had a drug problem as a teenager and

I just…I'm aware it's a slippery slope." She looks stunned. I smile. "We have a lot in common, Shay. We just never bothered to find out."

"You know about Trey."

I nod. "Avery mentioned it when you were in the bathroom at Jordan's," I explain. "I was really hoping you would open up to me about it. You can trust me."

"I realize that now." She slowly lifts the sign and shakes it at me with a small smile. "Forgive me, Frenchie?"

I pretend to think about it for a long moment. Avery is almost at the end of the line now, and once he's gone to the plane I have to as well or else I'll become the center of attention again. "I think I can give you a chance to win me back."

She blinks at that, shocked, as her mouth drops a little. When I wink at her she seems to recover. "So there's another inning left in us?"

I scoff at her use of baseball terminology. "No innings in this game. But I think we may have a third period left to play."

She smiles, but bites her bottom lip and then warns, "I'm not great at this, as I've proven. So I can't guarantee I won't end up in the penalty box a few more times."

I reach up and smooth back a lock of her hair that slipped loose from her braid and tuck it behind her ear. "I might end up in the box too."

"Yeah, but I like you in the box," she murmurs with a wicked grin. "As long as it's mine."

Our eyes meet. My hand, still by her ear, slides to her neck. "I want to kiss you so badly right now, but…"

"You can't," she finishes for me, and then her eyes glance at the other fans, who are mostly still distracted by Avery. When she looks back at me, she's grinning mischievously. "But I can kiss you."

She pushes up on her tiptoes, wraps a hand around the back of my neck and presses her lips to mine. She's not playing either; this is a real kiss. Her lips open and her tongue sweeps over mine, and just when I'm ready to skip the flight and drag her back to my house, she pulls away.

Someone whistles loudly at us, but when I look over, there are only a couple of people who noticed, thankfully. I give them a small smile and turn back to her. "Something to think about when you're alone in your hotel room." She winks at me and takes a step back. "Go. Win some hockey."

I nod and force myself to step away. Avery is beside me now, and he waves at Shayne before saying, "Come on, Romeo."

I walk away, backward, my eyes still on her until we're through the doors and she's out of sight. I swear there are actual sparks in the air between our stares. My feelings for her haven't smoldered at all. She still lights every possible fire inside me, mentally and physically.

Chapter 46

Shayne

No!" The scream is unanimous and so loud I hope my new neighbors don't file a complaint, but I wouldn't be surprised if they do.

The captain of the San Francisco Thunder, Levi Casco, glides toward his bench, away from Chooch, who is on his knees, his helmeted head hanging down in defeat, and Casco raises his arms in victory. His teammates swarm him, spilling onto the ice from the bench and jumping on top of him.

As the camera pulls back, I scan the dejected Winterhawks players as they skate away from the celebration, toward their bench. I see Sebastian, head hung low, resting his forehead against his stick as he sits on the bench.

I move my eyes from the screen to my guests. Jessie is sitting at the other end of my couch, leaning forward. Her green eyes are glued to the screen and her elbows rest on her knees with her hands covering her mouth. Stephanie is sitting in my Papasan chair in the corner, not looking at the Winterhawks' defeat. She's got her head tipped back and her eyes closed with a frown on her face.

"Fuck," Stephanie whispers to the universe.

"Yeah." Jessie groans the word more than says it.

I watch the Winterhawks skate off the bench and start a haphazard line for the obligatory sportsman handshake. The Thunder are still peeling themselves off the ice where they jumped on top of Casco.

The Winterhawks' season is over. They lost in the first round of the playoffs, which, according to my father, is worse than not making them at all. His team lost twice in the first round that I remember, the last time being when I was sixteen. Even though it was a home game and we lived twenty minutes from the arena, he didn't come home until four in the morning. He was drunk. I remember being woken up by his angry, slurred words. I guess Trey had either waited up for him or woken up and gone downstairs to share his sympathies, but my father didn't think that was endearing. I woke up to him tearing a piece out of my poor fourteen-year-old brother who idolized him. According to dear old Dad, Trey was a loser for saying "you'll get 'em next year," because all that mattered was this year. Winning next time doesn't change the fact that they failed this time. Failure is not acceptable—ever—and if Trey would get that through his skull, maybe he'd try harder on his own team, which had lost a few nights prior.

I had gotten out of bed and gone downstairs to grab Trey and drag him back to his room before he cried in front of Dad and made the whole thing worse. I remember smelling whiskey and perfume—not my mother's—emanating from Dad.

But Sebastian is not my father. He's his own type of hockey player. He's his own type of man, as he's proven to me over and over.

Deep breaths, Shayne. Don't start letting past trauma ruin your life.

"Steph, what's he like after something like this?" I ask softly. "Should I stay away tonight or text him or…?"

Stephanie opens her eyes and turns her head to look at me. She gives me a small, warm smile. "He's depressed, but he's not usually bitchy or anything. He's quiet, though. He doesn't like to talk about it—or really talk at all—for a day or two. But he doesn't like to be alone either, so if you had plans to meet him when the plane lands tonight, keep 'em."

I nod and give her a thankful smile. Jessie sags back into the couch. "Jordan is going to be bitchy. And Devin is going to call and rub it in, because he and Luc are still in it. Ridiculous brotherly love."

She laughs at her own words and shakes her head. "Honestly, they show they love each other by pushing each other's buttons. With a sledgehammer."

I smile at that. I have a feeling it would have been awesome to grow up in Jessie's small town with Jordan and his brothers. Wild and crazy but amazing. And I'm dying to meet her sisters too. Seb's already mentioned he wants me to go to Jordan and Jessie's wedding with him this summer so I'll get the chance. I realize that taking a chance on Sebastian has brought more than just him into my life, and I'm grateful. So grateful.

Stephanie's phone beeps and she grabs it off the coffee table. After glancing at the screen and typing back a message she says, "The plane is supposed to land at midnight."

"Seb text you?"

Stephanie shakes her head. "No, it was…Chooch. I guess because I'm staying at Seb's while they're on the road. He doesn't want to startle me if I'm sleeping."

She stands up and stretches. "I'm going to get going and vacate their guest room before they get back. Seb and Chooch will need their space. But not from you. He doesn't need space from you. Remember that!"

She's pointing at me like a lecturing schoolteacher. It makes me smile guiltily and raise my hands. "Okay! Okay!"

Jessie stands too, and when I do, she reaches over and hugs me. "Good luck with your sad panda."

"Good luck with yours too."

"Thanks for having us over. I love your new place," Steph says as we stand. I glance around the space, which is slightly smaller than my previous one but it has its own balcony and a dishwasher, and I can walk outside with much less chance of being mugged.

I hug them both and then close the door behind them. Damn, I wish the Winterhawks had won the game. I walk over to my phone on the coffee table and pull up his number and send him a simple text with my new address and the words *I'm here if you need me.*

Slightly after midnight my front door buzzes. I was dozing on the couch so it startles me. I walk over to the intercom, press the button and say, "Hello?"

"It's me."

The sound of his voice sends butterflies fluttering around my abdomen, and without a word I buzz him in. When he opens my apartment door he's wearing his Winterhawks workout gear—track pants, a kangaroo hoodie and sneakers—and dragging his travel bags with him. The hood is up over his head, and as he glances at me while he toes out of his shoes, I'm struck by how tired he looks and how piercing his blue eyes are against the dark shelter of the hoodie.

I'm standing in the archway that divides the front entry from the living-dining room wearing nothing but a T-shirt and a pair of underwear. He walks to me, leaving his bags in the front hall, and I try not to freak out. I don't know what to expect and I can't draw on previous experience, but honestly, I wouldn't blame him if he was angry right now.

He stops directly in front of me and puts his hands on my hips. Then he drops his head onto my shoulder. It's like an act of defeat. Of surrender. And it's heavy with sadness and cloaked in the weight of his now broken dreams of another Cup. I cradle the back of his hooded head and whisper against the fabric next to my cheek, "I'm sorry."

"*Moi aussi*," he whispers back hoarsely. I don't know much French but I know that means "me too." He lifts his head and those crystal blue eyes land on mine again.

I want to make this better for him, but I can't. So instead of taking away the pain of the loss I decide to try to give him a new emotion. I push up on my toes and kiss him. He responds immediately and with a passion I wasn't expecting in his current mood. As our tongues meet I reach up and push the hood off his head so I can run my hands through his thick hair.

Without hesitation I grab the bottom of his hoodie and start to pull it up over his body. He lifts his arm and helps me remove it, and then his big, warm hands are under my T-shirt and seconds later, it's gone too. He's needy and I am suddenly too and it's creating a frenetic urgency to everything. We can't get naked fast enough.

When all our clothes are lying on the wood floor, he cups my ass and lifts me up, carrying me to my bedroom, which is still full of boxes. The only thing I have really set up in there is the bed. He turns and sits on the edge of it. My knees are on either side of him and he's holding my ass, so I'm hovering above his dick, which is rock hard and pointing up at me. His eyes fly around the room for a second and then he asks, "Condom?"

"I'm on birth control," I admit. "Have been the entire time."

He tips his head up to look at me. I nod as if he needs more confirmation. But that's not what he wants to know. "Are you my girlfriend?"

I run a hand over his head, through his hair and down to cup his cheek before I say with one hundred percent certainty, "I'm your girlfriend."

His hands on my ass move to my hips and he pushes me down onto his dick. We stay perfectly still except for our lips and tongues as we absorb the moment.

His hands are warm and solid against my skin, one splayed across my lower back and the other around the nape of my neck. I wrap my arms tightly around his neck, arch my back and moan. I can feel his dick twitch with need inside me. This will be our only gentle moment, I can tell. He wants to work out all his frustration and loss on me—and I want to let him, desperately. With his hands on my hips he lifts me slightly and he pushes his cock deep inside me with one strong, hard thrust.

Chapter 47

Sebastian

It's too much and not enough at the very same time. Being with her, no barriers for the first time, feeling her wet warmth wrapped around me is amazing, and I want this feeling—the love I feel, the trust I can see in her eyes and the pleasure of it, to last forever. But the undeniable delicious friction as she rides me, setting a teasing rhythm, controlling every wave of pleasure—it's too much. I want the control tonight. I *need* it.

Holding her against my body, I stand and turn and place her back against the mattress, her legs hanging over the side as I bend my knees to be lower and stay inside her. I need to control her—control *this*—tonight. I lost control of the series, the game, had no control over how our season ended, but her pleasure and mine, I still own that and I am not giving that over. Not tonight. I put my hands behind her knees and watch our joined bodies as I push into her.

My rhythm is fast and unyielding. I grab one of her legs and hike it up so her ankle rests against my shoulder. A few more hard, steady, pleasurable thrusts and just as many gratifying moans from her beautiful mouth and I kiss her ankle and lean over her. My torso is almost flat on top of her and her calf is basically against her head, which means my dick is so deep inside her I'm seeing stars. God, I love her flexibility. Long live yoga.

"Sebastian…oh God…so close…" Her eyelashes are fluttering wildly and her head is thrashing from side to side and her hands are reaching above her head, grasping at some kind of imaginary anchor to keep her on the edge where pleasure and euphoria dance. But there is no anchor and I'm intent on throwing her into the abyss.

I grab her hands together and pull them toward me. She loops them around my neck and lets them wind a path down to my ass where she grabs it so hard I know there'll be marks.

"Seb…" She whispers my name before she begs, "Harder. Fuck me harder."

I drive my dick as deep as it can go. Oh God, I want to come.

"I'm going to…" Her sentence morphs into a moan.

"Look at me, baby. Look at me when you come," I insist and her eyes, barely open, focus on mine.

"Seb." I feel her walls clench and her back arches violently and she whimpers loudly.

I can't hold on. I explode inside her. I swear I almost lose consciousness, and when I float back to reality, I'm still on top of her. She's stroking my back with her fingertips, and the heavy feeling of the loss comes back to me as well. I sigh.

"There'll be more chances," she says intuitively. "You've got a young, strong team."

"Yeah, but I wanted it so bad this year," I confess and slowly, gently pull out of her. We both move to the top of the bed and pull the covers down. "The minute we make the playoffs I just want it so bad. I have to lift the Cup again. I don't want to have won it just once."

"You'll win it all again," she promises, and even though I know it's her wish and not any kind of promise, it still comforts me. "You're the best defenseman in the league. You'll make it happen."

I pull the sheets up around us and she curls into my side. This feels right. This feels good. She yawns against my chest and I kiss the top of her head. "Tired?"

"Not really," she replies. "You?"

"No," I reply and try not to frown. "I have all the time in the world for sleeping now."

We just lie there tangled up together in peaceful silence for a few moments. She finally says, "Tell me about your life. How did you find hockey? When did you fall in love with it?"

"The minute I put on skates," I tell her easily. I remember it like it was yesterday. "It was love at first sight. Have you ever felt that before?"

She tilts her head and looks up at me with the softest, most beautiful smile I've ever seen in my entire life. "I think I have." She kisses me softly and says, "Tell me more."

We spend the night doing what we've avoided or forgotten to do since the moment we met: talk. I tell her about my childhood, my parents' divorce, Stephanie's slip into addiction and her climb back out. She tells me about her childhood and Trey's problems. She talks about college, and this asshole Dustin who I thank God didn't make the NHL, because if he had I would try to kill him every game I played against him. I tell her about making the league and my mom marrying my old coach.

The sun is rising when we finally drift off, and the pain of the loss, the end of our playoff run, is dulled, replaced by amazing new feelings filling every part of me—contentment, hope and most of all love. I love this woman and I think she loves me too. So I might not have another Cup, but I've definitely won.

Epilogue

Shayne

The phone feels like it's louder than a fire alarm as it cuts through the dark room at four in the morning. Sebastian jumps beside me and almost falls off the bed. I bolt to a sitting position and grab it off the night table without even looking at the number on the call display.

"What the fuck?!" I spew out angrily.

"I'm at the hospital!"

All my annoyance evaporates, and I jump out of bed and flip on the light. Seb groans and covers his eyes with his forearm. "I'll be right there!"

"Okay, hurry! Her contraction are coming fast and furious," Trey says, and he sounds like a nervous wreck.

"Well, get off the phone and go be with her," I reply and hang up on him.

I run around his bedroom, hunting down my clothes. He watches me curiously. "Baby time?"

I nod. "Oh my God! I can't believe it! I'm going to be an aunt!"

He laughs at my excitement as I find my underwear and pull it on, almost toppling over, because although my mind is wide awake, my body feels like it's still asleep. He sits up, the sheets dropping to reveal his perfect naked torso. My God, he's delicious. I grab the maxi dress I wore to his house, but before I tug it over my head I reach down and grab the T-shirt he had on yesterday and toss it at him. He looks at me curiously and I nervously ask, "Will you come with me? Even though it probably means spending time with my parents?"

He grins. "Of course, baby. I would follow you into hell."

We get to the hospital twenty minutes later and run up to Labor and Delivery. Trey is in the waiting room talking to my mom. I can tell by the way his whole face is glowing brighter than a spotlight that he's a dad.

He sees us over her shoulder and his grin gets bigger, prouder. "Six pounds, eleven ounces."

"Yay!" I walk over to him and high-five him before hugging him. "How's Sasha?"

"Amazing," he confesses. "Well, I mean she was amazing. I can't believe what you women go through. Holy shit. But she's fine. She's resting. If you want to see her, baby Beckford will be in the nursery in a few minutes."

I hug him again. Sebastian reaches out and shakes Trey's hand. "Congratulations. Do we have a name?"

Trey pauses and glances at me. "Daisy."

I burst out laughing and hug him again. "It's perfect!"

"Of course you think so." My mom smiles. "But it is lovely. I can't wait to meet her."

My brother excuses himself to go back to Sasha, and as we

walk with my mom to the nursery, I lace my fingers with Seb. My mom looks over and gives him a small smile. "Nice to see you again. Sebastian, isn't it? I remember you from the ceremony last year."

Sebastian nods and gives her a friendly smile. "Congrats on being a grandmother, Mrs. Beckford."

"Thank you." She pauses before adding, "You must be the reason my daughter is so happy."

"He is," I respond before he can, and he squeezes my hand. "Do I need to ask why Dad isn't here with you?"

"He told me he was going on a fishing weekend with the boys," my mother explains and sighs. "Which means he's in Cabo with a woman."

Seb looks at me tentatively. I lean down and kiss my mom's cheek but don't say anything because there is nothing to say. She's choosing this life, and I will support her because the alternative, I've learned, is punishing her, and even if I don't agree with her choices, she doesn't deserve to be punished.

When we reach the nursery, Sebastian is the first to notice her. She's in the front row at the end wrapped in all pink. Her face is red but she's not crying. She's sleeping peacefully.

"She looks exactly like Trey did," my mom whispers, and she wipes a tear. I hug her before letting go and walking closer to the glass. Sebastian comes up behind me as I stare at my sleeping niece and he circles my waist.

"Your family makes cute babies," he whispers against the shell of my ear. "That's good to know."

My stomach and my heart seem to switch places at that—in a good way. And I know I need to tell him what I've been feeling for a while now. I've been feeling it since probably almost the minute we met, but I let myself ignore it. Since we officially put a label on this after his playoff loss six weeks ago, there's been no denying the feeling.

So after taking a hundred pictures of Daisy through the glass and visiting Sasha and Trey in her room one more time, I decide as we walk back to the car in the parking lot I need to tell him how I feel. Before I can he asks, "So what's with the name Daisy? You guys all acted like there was something to it? Is it a family name?"

I shake my head as we approach the Aston Martin and reach for his hand again. "Not really. But when I was a kid I wanted to change my name to Daisy. And I bullied Trey into calling me that for about a week, until my dad came home from a road trip and told me I was being stupid. I asked him if I could use it as a new middle name instead, and he said no, even though my middle name is worse than my first."

"Ah, the mysterious middle name." Sebastian laughs. "I keep forgetting to steal your driver's license."

I ignore that. "Glenn said no, of course. My name was my name and there was no changing it."

He grins at me. "I guess he would hate me calling you Shay, then."

"Probably," I reply and wink. "So please make sure to do it in front of him a lot."

He laughs, and as we reach the car I stop and pull him toward me. I kiss him hard on the mouth and he likes it, grabbing my waist and pulling me closer. "Let's get home so I can peel you out of these clothes and fuck you into next week."

I flush at his bluntness, which is so fucking hot. Then I look around the parking lot, which is filled with cars but devoid of people. "Or we could just do it in the Aston Martin. Doesn't James Bond drive this? I bet he would approve."

He steps backward, pushing me into the side of the car. "Don't tempt me."

"I dare you," I whisper against his mouth, knowing full well he won't do it, but he'll want to because he's the most competitive person I know besides myself, and he hates passing up challenges.

He groans and attacks my mouth with a blazing hot kiss. When he pulls away, I struggle to catch my breath as he whispers, "Shay, baby. God, I love you."

He beat me to it. That's what I was going to tell him. I open my eyes and stare into his. He looks so sure and confident about what he just said—about his feelings for me—and it makes me happier than I have ever been in my entire life.

"Augusta," I whisper.

His heavy eyebrows pinch and he stares at me with a curious blink. "Augusta?"

"My middle name," I confess sheepishly. "He named me after his favorite golf course."

"Oh my God, you're right. It's worse than Shayne." He starts to smile and then laugh.

"And I would never admit that unless I loved you too." I kiss him and laugh into it. "Now take me home and make good on that fucking me into next week promise."

"Anything you say, Shayne Augusta Beckford." He opens my door and I climb in. He leans into the open door and whispers, "I love you and your ridiculous name."

"I love you and your ridiculously long-winded name," I call back as he closes my door and walks around the car. I close my eyes, rest my head against the leather headrest and smile to myself.

I am so lucky I got out of my own way and let myself fall in love with this man. He is everything I never knew I wanted and then some.

Check out the next book in Victoria Denault's Hometown Players series,
featuring Stephanie and Avery

ON THE LINE

Available December 2016!

About the Author

Victoria Denault loves long walks on the beach, cinnamon dolce lattes and writing angst-filled romance. She lives in L.A. but grew up in Montreal, which is why she is fluent in English, French and hockey.

Learn more at:

VictoriaDenault.com

Facebook.com/AuthorVictoriaDenault

Twitter: @BooksbyVictoria

9 781455 541256